TASHA'S CAULDRON OF EVERYTHING

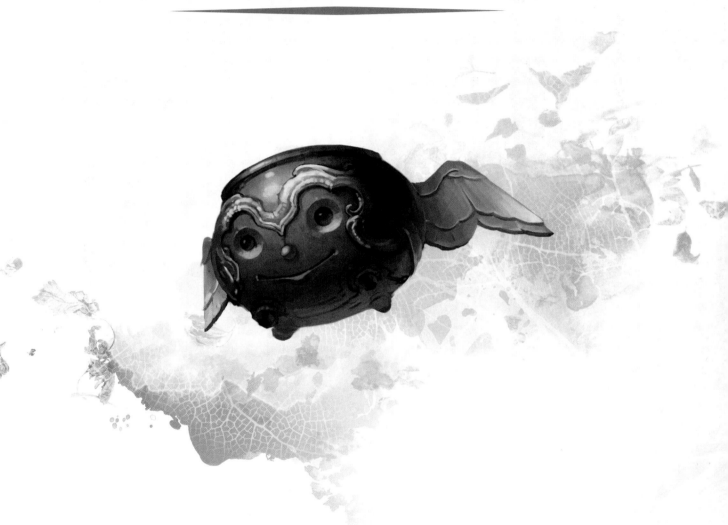

CREDITS

Lead Designer: Jeremy Crawford
Art Director: Kate Irwin

Design: Dan Dillon, Ben Petrisor, F. Wesley Schneider,
Elisa Teague
Additional Design: Bill Benham, Adam Lee, Ari Levitch,
Christopher Perkins, Taymoor Rehman, Kate Welch,
Ray Winninger
Rules Development: Jeremy Crawford, Dan Dillon,
Ben Petrisor, Taymoor Rehman
Editing: Michele Carter, Christopher Perkins, Jessica Ross,
F. Wesley Schneider, James Wyatt

Lead Graphic Designer: Trish Yochum
Graphic Designers: Trystan Falcone, Emi Tanji
Cover Illustrators: Wylie Beckert, Magali Villeneuve
Interior Illustrators: Mark Behm, Eric Belisle, Zoltan Boros,
Christopher Burdett, Sidharth Chaturvedi, David René
Christensen, Nikki Dawes, Olga Drebas, Caroline Gariba,
Sam Keiser, Julian Kok, Titus Lunter, Andrew Mar, Marcela
Medeiros, Brynn Metheney, Robson Michel, Scott Murphy,
Irina Nordsol, Robin Olausson, Claudio Pozas, Livia
Prima, April Prime, David Sladek, Crystal Sully, Brian
Valeza, Svetlin Velinov, Anna Veltkamp, Shawn Wood,
Zuzanna Wuzyk, Kieran Yanner
Concept Illustrator: Shawn Wood

Project Engineer: Cynda Callaway
Imaging Technicians: Kevin Yee
Prepress Specialist: Jefferson Dunlap

D&D GAME STUDIO

Executive Producer: Ray Winninger
Principal Designers: Jeremy Crawford, Christopher Perkins
Design Manager: Steve Scott
Design Department: F. Wesley Schneider, Dan Dillon,
Adam Lee, Ari Levitch, Ben Petrisor
Senior Art Director: Richard Whitters
Art Department: Kate Irwin, Emi Tanji, Trish Yochum,
Shawn Wood
Senior Producer: Dan Tovar
Producers: Bill Benham, Lea Heliotis
Director of Product Management: Liz Schuh
Licensing Manager: Hilary Ross
Product Managers: Natalie Egan, Chris Lindsay, Hilary Ross
Brand Manager: Shelly Mazzanoble
Publicity: Greg Tito
Community Management: Brandy Camel

This book contains some content that originally appeared in
Sword Coast Adventurer's Guide (2015), *Guildmasters' Guide
to Ravnica* (2018), *Eberron: Rising from the Last War* (2019),
and *Mythic Odysseys of Theros* (2020).

ON THE COVER

Spellbook in hand, the wizard Tasha casts a spell on a brew
bubbling in her magic cauldron, in this painting by Magali
Villeneuve.

ON THE ALT-COVER

Artist Wylie Beckert shows Tasha conjuring images of her
past and future, wielding an incantation taught by her
mother, Baba Yaga, while the abyssal lord Graz'zt looks on.

620C7878000001 EN
ISBN: 978-0-7869-6702-5
First Printing: November 2020

9 8 7 6 5 4 3 2 1

UK CA CE

*Disclaimer: Contained herein are the observations of the archmage Tasha. Later known as
the Witch Queen and then Iggwilv, she is one of the greatest wizards in the history of the
multiverse. We fear there is an incantation hidden within these notes and have therefore
bound this tome with powerful wards. If you are reading this, the first ward has already
been broken! If you dare read any further, we cannot guarantee the safety of your soul or
that you won't open a portal to another plane of existence. If a portal does appear, pray
that nothing worse than Tasha's mother Baba Yaga appears. And if the mother of hags arrives, be sure to offer only praises of her daughter. Or offer muffins. She loves muffins.*

CONTENTS

USING THIS BOOK

Tasha's Cauldron of Everything offers a host of new options for DUNGEONS & DRAGONS, and our journey through those options is accompanied by the notes of the wizard Tasha. Creator of the spell *Tasha's hideous laughter*, Tasha's life is one of the most storied in the D&D multiverse. Raised by Baba Yaga, the Mother of Witches herself, Tasha adventured across the world of Greyhawk and became the friend and sometimes enemy of other famous adventurers, like Mordenkainen. In time, she ruled as the Witch Queen and later changed her name to Iggwilv—a figure of legend who is whispered about, feared, and admired.

Written for players and Dungeon Masters alike, this book offers options to enhance characters and campaigns in any D&D world, whether you're adventuring in Greyhawk, another official D&D setting, or a world of your own creation.

WHAT YOU'LL FIND WITHIN

Chapter 1 brims with new features and subclasses for the classes in the *Player's Handbook*, and it presents the artificer class, a master of magical invention. The chapter also offers feats for groups that use them.

Chapter 2 contains patrons who can become one of the driving forces behind your group's adventures.

Chapter 3 sparkles with new magical options, including spells, magical spellbooks, artifacts, and magic-infused tattoos—available for both player characters and monsters to use.

Chapter 4 holds various rules that a DM may incorporate into a campaign, including rules on sidekicks who level up with the player characters and on supernatural environments. The chapter ends with a collection of puzzles ready to be deployed in any adventure that the DM would like to spice up with some puzzling.

IT'S ALL OPTIONAL

Everything in this book is optional. Each group, guided by the DM, decides which of these options, if any, to incorporate into a campaign. You can use some, all, or none of them. We encourage you to choose the ones that fit best with your campaign's story and with your group's style of play.

Whatever options you choose to use, this book relies on the rules in the *Player's Handbook*, *Monster Manual*, and *Dungeon Master's Guide*, and it can be paired with the options in *Xanathar's Guide to Everything* and other D&D books.

> ### UNEARTHED ARCANA
> Much of the material in this book originally appeared in Unearthed Arcana, a series of online articles we publish to explore rules that might officially become part of the game. Some Unearthed Arcana offerings don't end up resonating with fans and are set aside. The Unearthed Arcana material that inspired the options in the following chapters was well received and, thanks to feedback from thousands of D&D fans, has been refined into the official forms presented here.

TEN RULES TO REMEMBER

1. THE DM ADJUDICATES THE RULES

The rules of D&D cover many of the twists and turns that come up in play, but the possibilities are so vast that the rules can't cover everything. When you encounter something that the rules don't cover or if you're unsure how to interpret a rule, the DM decides how to proceed, aiming for a course that brings the most enjoyment to your whole group.

2. EXCEPTIONS SUPERSEDE GENERAL RULES

General rules govern each part of the game. For example, the combat rules tell you that melee weapon attacks use Strength and ranged weapon attacks use Dexterity. That's a general rule, and a general rule is in effect as long as something in the game doesn't explicitly say otherwise.

The game also includes elements—class features, spells, magic items, monster abilities, and the like—that sometimes contradict a general rule. When an exception and a general rule disagree, the exception wins. For example, if a feature says you can make melee weapon attacks using your Charisma, you can do so, even though that statement disagrees with the general rule.

3. ADVANTAGE AND DISADVANTAGE

Even if more than one factor gives you advantage or disadvantage on a roll, you have it only once, and if you have advantage and disadvantage on the same roll, they cancel each other.

4. REACTION TIMING

Certain game features let you take a special action, called a reaction, in response to an event. Making opportunity attacks and casting the *shield* spell are two typical uses of reactions. If you're unsure when a reaction occurs in relation to its trigger, here's the rule: the reaction happens after its trigger, unless the description of the reaction explicitly says otherwise. Once you take a reaction, you can't take another one until the start of your next turn.

My dear, sweet, lucky reader,

You know me. You've heard of my exploits. You've spread my titles: Natasha the Dark, Hura of Ket, Baba Yaga's daughter, witch par excellence, and, if you're not trying to impress, just plain Tasha.

For longer than I care to confess, I've sought out mysteries and wonders that beggar description. (Well, wonders that beggar the descriptions of those not raised in an immortal's dancing hut, as I was.) Within this tome, you'll find a sampling of the curiosities I've documented during my travels, including my exploits with the infamous Company of Seven; my studies with the original Mad Archmage, Zagig Yragerne; and my correspondences with world-hopping (and sanctimonious) luminaries like Mordenkainen. Unfortunately, at Mordenkainen's request, a panel of experts from the Greyhawk Guild of Wizardry—which I'm assured is an esteemed center of learning and not at all an elaborate scam to swindle highborn rubes—has been granted editorial oversight of this work. As a result, I understand that some of my "less traditional" findings have been saddled with various rules, for the supposed "safe continuance of the mystical arts and, indeed, all life in the multiverse."

No matter. Through a combination of irrefutable arguments and spells, I've convinced the editorial board to furnish me with this advance copy of their work.

In reviewing it, I've added a variety of helpful marginalia. I expect that—with the inclusion of my insights, guidance, threats, and critiques—clever minds will have all they need to advance their accounting of the multiverse's infinite audacities. And even if not, read on and maybe you'll learn something my archmage semi-peers are terrified of you learning.

I'm drawing back the curtain of reality for you, reader dearest. Summon your courage, and take a peek.

TASHA

5. PROFICIENCY BONUS

If your proficiency bonus applies to a roll, you can add the bonus only once to the roll, even if multiple things in the game say your bonus applies. Moreover, if more than one thing tells you to double or halve your bonus, you double it only once or halve it only once before applying it. Whether multiplied, divided, or left at its normal value, the bonus can be used only once per roll.

6. BONUS ACTION SPELLS

If you want to cast a spell that has a casting time of 1 bonus action, remember that you can't cast any other spells before or after it on the same turn, except for cantrips with a casting time of 1 action.

7. CONCENTRATION

As soon as you start casting a spell or using a special ability that requires concentration, your concentration on another effect ends instantly.

8. TEMPORARY HIT POINTS

Temporary hit points aren't cumulative. If you have temporary hit points and receive more of them, you don't add them together, unless a game feature says you can. Instead, you decide which temporary hit points to keep.

9. ROUND DOWN

Whenever you divide or multiply a number in the game, round down if you end up with a fraction, even if the fraction is one-half or greater.

10. HAVE FUN

You don't need to know every rule to enjoy D&D, and each group has its own style—different ways it likes to tell stories and to use the rules. Embrace what your group enjoys most. In short, follow your bliss!

THE WIZARD TASHA STUDIES
MAGIC OUTSIDE THE HUT OF HER
ADOPTIVE MOTHER, BABA YAGA.

CHAPTER 1
CHARACTER OPTIONS

WHEN YOU MAKE YOUR D&D CHARACTER, you have an array of options in the *Player's Handbook* to create the sort of adventurer you want. This chapter adds to those options, making it possible to realize even more character concepts. If you combine these options with those in *Xanathar's Guide to Everything*, the possibilities for your characters become vast.

Here are the options featured in this chapter:

- A way to customize your character's origin by changing some of your racial traits
- Guidance on changing your subclass
- The artificer class, a master of magical invention
- Class features and subclasses for every class in the *Player's Handbook*
- Feats for anyone who uses that optional rule

CUSTOMIZING YOUR ORIGIN

At 1st level, you choose various aspects of your character, including ability scores, race, class, and background. Together these elements help paint a picture of your character's origin and give you the ability to create many different types of characters. Despite that versatility, a typical character race in D&D includes little or no choice—a lack that can make it difficult to realize certain character concepts. The following subsections address that lack by adding choice to your character's race, allowing you to customize your ability scores, languages, and certain proficiencies to fit the origin you have in mind for your character. Character race in the game represents your character's fantasy species, combined with certain cultural assumptions. The following options step outside those assumptions to pave the way for truly unique characters.

ABILITY SCORE INCREASES

Whatever D&D race you choose for your character, you get a trait called Ability Score Increase. This increase reflects an archetypal bit of excellence in the adventurers of this kind in D&D's past. For example, if you're a dwarf, your Constitution increases by 2, because dwarf heroes in D&D are often exceptionally tough. This increase doesn't apply to every dwarf, just to dwarf adventurers, and it exists to reinforce an archetype. That reinforcement is appropriate if you want to lean into the archetype, but it's unhelpful if your character doesn't conform to the archetype.

If you'd like your character to follow their own path, you may ignore your Ability Score Increase trait and assign ability score increases tailored to your character. Here's how to do it: take any ability score increase you gain in your race or subrace and apply it to an ability score of your choice. If you gain more than one increase, you can't apply those increases to the same ability score, and you can't increase a score above 20.

For example, if the Ability Score Increase trait of your race or subrace increases your Constitution by 2 and your Wisdom by 1, you could instead increase your Intelligence by 2 and your Charisma by 1.

LANGUAGES

Your character's race includes languages that your character is assumed to know, usually Common and the language of your ancestors. For example, a halfling adventurer is assumed to know Common and Halfling. Here's the thing: D&D adventurers are extraordinary, and your character might have grown up speaking languages different from the ones in your Languages trait.

To customize the languages you know, you may replace each language in your Languages trait with a language from the following list: Abyssal, Celestial, Common, Deep Speech, Draconic, Dwarvish, Elvish, Giant, Gnomish, Goblin, Halfling, Infernal, Orc, Primordial, Sylvan, or Undercommon.

Your DM may add or remove languages from that list, depending on what languages are appropriate for your campaign.

PROFICIENCIES

Some races and subraces grant proficiencies. These proficiencies are usually cultural, and your character might not have any connection with the culture in question or might have pursued different training. You can replace each of those proficiencies with a different one of your choice, following the restrictions on the Proficiency Swaps table.

PROFICIENCY SWAPS

Proficiency	Replacement Proficiency
Skill	Skill
Armor	Simple/martial weapon or tool
Simple weapon	Simple weapon or tool
Martial weapon	Simple/martial weapon or tool
Tool	Tool or simple weapon

For example, high elf adventurers have proficiency with longswords, which are martial weapons. Consulting the Proficiency Swaps table, we see that your high elf can swap that proficiency for proficiency with another weapon or a tool. Your elf might be a musician, who chooses proficiency with a musical instrument—a type of tool—instead of with longswords. Similarly, elves start with proficiency in the Perception skill. Your elf might not have the keen senses associated with your kin and could take proficiency in a different skill, such as Performance.

The "Equipment" chapter of the *Player's Handbook* includes weapons and tools suitable for these swaps, and your DM might allow additional options.

PERSONALITY

The description of a race might suggest various things about the behavior and personality of that people's archetypal adventurers. You may ignore those suggestions, whether they're about alignment, moods, interests, or any other personality trait. Your character's personality and behavior are entirely yours to determine.

CHANGING A SKILL

Sometimes you pick a skill proficiency that ends up not being very useful in the campaign or that no longer fits your character's story. In those cases, talk to your DM about replacing that skill proficiency with another skill proficiency offered by your class at 1st level. A convenient time for such a change is when you reach a level that grants you the Ability Score Increase feature, representing that your character has spent a level or two studying the new skill and letting the old one atrophy.

CHANGING YOUR SUBCLASS

Each character class involves the choice of a subclass at 1st, 2nd, or 3rd level. A subclass represents an area of specialization and offers different class features as you level up. With your DM's approval, you can change your subclass when you would normally gain a new subclass feature. If you decide to make this change, choose another subclass that belongs to your class and replace all your old subclass features with the features of the new subclass that are for your new level and lower.

TRAINING TIME

To change your subclass, your DM might require you to spend time devoted to the transition, as you study the ways of the new specialization. This transition requires a number of days equal to twice your new level in the class; a higher level represents more to learn.

The DM might also require an expenditure of money to pay for training, magical reagents, or other goods needed for the transition. The cost is typically 100 gp times your new level. This cost might be accompanied by a quest of some sort. For example, a sorcerer who wants to adopt a Draconic Bloodline could be required to receive blood, a blessing, or both from an ancient dragon.

If you return to a subclass that you previously held, you forgo the gold cost, and the time required for the transition is halved.

SUDDEN CHANGE

Sometimes a character undergoes a dramatic transformation in their beliefs and abilities. When a character experiences a profound self-realization or faces an entity or a place of overwhelming power, beauty, or terror, the DM might allow an immediate subclass change. Here are a few examples:

- An Oath of Devotion paladin failed to stop a demonic horde from ravaging her homeland. After spending a night in sorrowful prayer, she rises the next morning with the features of the Oath of Vengeance, ready to hunt down the horde.
- A wizard lies down for a nap beneath an oak tree whose roots reach into the Feywild. In his dreams, he faces visions of multiple possible futures. When he awakens, his subclass features have been replaced by those of the School of Divination.
- A cleric of the War Domain has spent years in conflict with the enemies of her temple. But one day, she wanders into a sun-dappled glade, where her god once shed a tear of mercy over the world's suffering. Drinking from the glade's brook, the cleric is filled with such compassion for all people that she now bears the powers of the Life Domain, ready to heal rather than make war.

CAROLINE GARIBA

ARTIFICER

Masters of invention, artificers use ingenuity and magic to unlock extraordinary capabilities in objects. They see magic as a complex system waiting to be decoded and then harnessed in their spells and inventions. You can find everything you need to play one of these inventors in the next few sections.

Artificers use a variety of tools to channel their arcane power. To cast a spell, an artificer might use alchemist's supplies to create a potent elixir, calligrapher's supplies to inscribe a sigil of power, or tinker's tools to craft a temporary charm. The magic of artificers is tied to their tools and their talents, and few other characters can produce the right tool for a job as well as an artificer.

ARTIFICERS IN MANY WORLDS

Throughout the D&D multiverse, artificers create inventions and magic items of peace and war. Many lives have been brightened or saved because of the work of kind artificers, but countless lives have also been lost because of the mass destruction unleashed by certain artificers' creations.

In the Forgotten Realms, the island of Lantan is home to many artificers, and in the world of Dragonlance, tinker gnomes are often members of this class. The strange technologies in the Barrier Peaks of the world of Greyhawk have inspired some folk to walk the path of the artificer, and in Mystara, various nations employ artificers to keep airships and other wondrous devices operational.

Artificers in the City of Sigil share discoveries from throughout the multiverse, and from there, the gnome artificer Vi runs a cosmos-spanning business that hires adventurers to fix problems that others deem unfixable. In Vi's home world, Eberron, magic is harnessed as a form of science and deployed throughout society, largely as a result of the wondrous ingenuity of artificers.

CREATING AN ARTIFICER

> Artificers invent cutting-edge problems, then try to solve them—loudly and often with collateral damage.
> TASHA

To create an artificer, consult the following subsections, which give you hit points, proficiencies, and starting equipment. Then look at the Artificer table to see which features you get at each level. The descriptions of those features appear in the "Artificer Features" section.

THE GNOME ARTIFICER VI AND HER COCKATRICE-LIKE ELDRITCH CANNON BATTLE FOES ATOP A LIGHTNING TRAIN.

The Artificer

Level	Proficiency Bonus	Class Features	Infusions Known	Infused Items	Cantrips Known	1st	2nd	3rd	4th	5th
						—Spell Slots per Spell Level—				
1st	+2	Magical Tinkering, Spellcasting	—	—	2	2	—	—	—	—
2nd	+2	Infuse Item	4	2	2	2	—	—	—	—
3rd	+2	Artificer Specialist, The Right Tool for the Job	4	2	2	3	—	—	—	—
4th	+2	Ability Score Improvement	4	2	2	3	—	—	—	—
5th	+3	Artificer Specialist feature	4	2	2	4	2	—	—	—
6th	+3	Tool Expertise	6	3	2	4	2	—	—	—
7th	+3	Flash of Genius	6	3	2	4	3	—	—	—
8th	+3	Ability Score Improvement	6	3	2	4	3	—	—	—
9th	+4	Artificer Specialist feature	6	3	2	4	3	2	—	—
10th	+4	Magic Item Adept	8	4	3	4	3	2	—	—
11th	+4	Spell-Storing Item	8	4	3	4	3	3	—	—
12th	+4	Ability Score Improvement	8	4	3	4	3	3	—	—
13th	+5	—	8	4	3	4	3	3	1	—
14th	+5	Magic Item Savant	10	5	4	4	3	3	1	—
15th	+5	Artificer Specialist feature	10	5	4	4	3	3	2	—
16th	+5	Ability Score Improvement	10	5	4	4	3	3	2	—
17th	+6	—	10	5	4	4	3	3	3	1
18th	+6	Magic Item Master	12	6	4	4	3	3	3	1
19th	+6	Ability Score Improvement	12	6	4	4	3	3	3	2
20th	+6	Soul of Artifice	12	6	4	4	3	3	3	2

Quick Build

You can make an artificer quickly by following these suggestions. First, put your highest ability score in Intelligence, followed by Constitution or Dexterity. Second, choose the guild artisan background.

Hit Points

Hit Dice: 1d8 per artificer level

Hit Points at 1st Level: 8 + your Constitution modifier

Hit Points at Higher Levels: 1d8 (or 5) + your Constitution modifier per artificer level after 1st

Proficiencies

Armor: Light armor, medium armor, shields

Weapons: Simple weapons

Tools: Thieves' tools, tinker's tools, one type of artisan's tools of your choice

Saving Throws: Constitution, Intelligence

Skills: Choose two from Arcana, History, Investigation, Medicine, Nature, Perception, Sleight of Hand

The secrets of gunpowder weapons have been discovered in various corners of the D&D multiverse. If your Dungeon Master uses the rules on firearms in the *Dungeon Master's Guide* and your artificer has been exposed to the operation of such weapons, your artificer is proficient with them.

Starting Equipment

You start with the following equipment, in addition to the equipment granted by your background:

- any two simple weapons of your choice
- a light crossbow and 20 bolts
- your choice of studded leather armor or scale mail
- thieves' tools and a dungeoneer's pack

If you forgo this starting equipment, as well as the items offered by your background, you start with 5d4 × 10 gp to buy your equipment.

> ### Multiclassing and the Artificer
>
> If your group uses the optional rule on multiclassing in the *Player's Handbook*, here's what you need to know if you choose artificer as one of your classes.
>
> **Ability Score Minimum.** As a multiclass character, you must have at least an Intelligence score of 13 to take a level in this class, or to take a level in another class if you are already an artificer.
>
> **Proficiencies Gained.** If artificer isn't your initial class, here are the proficiencies you gain when you take your first level as an artificer: light armor, medium armor, shields, thieves' tools, tinker's tools.
>
> **Spell Slots.** Add half your levels (rounded up) in the artificer class to the appropriate levels from other classes to determine your available spell slots.

Class Features

As an artificer, you gain the following class features, which are summarized in the Artificer table.

Magical Tinkering

1st-level artificer feature

You've learned how to invest a spark of magic into mundane objects. To use this ability, you must have thieves' tools or artisan's tools in hand. You then touch a Tiny nonmagical object as an action and give it one of the following magical properties of your choice:

- The object sheds bright light in a 5-foot radius and dim light for an additional 5 feet.
- Whenever tapped by a creature, the object emits a recorded message that can be heard up to 10 feet away. You utter the message when you bestow this property on the object, and the recording can be no more than 6 seconds long.
- The object continuously emits your choice of an odor or a nonverbal sound (wind, waves, chirping, or the like). The chosen phenomenon is perceivable up to 10 feet away.
- A static visual effect appears on one of the object's surfaces. This effect can be a picture, up to 25 words of text, lines and shapes, or a mixture of these elements, as you like.

The chosen property lasts indefinitely. As an action, you can touch the object and end the property early.

You can bestow magic on multiple objects, touching one object each time you use this feature, though a single object can only bear one property at a time. The maximum number of objects you can affect with this feature at one time is equal to your Intelligence modifier (minimum of one object). If you try to exceed your maximum, the oldest property immediately ends, and then the new property applies.

Spellcasting

1st-level artificer feature

You've studied the workings of magic and how to cast spells, channeling the magic through objects. To observers, you don't appear to be casting spells in a conventional way; you appear to produce wonders from mundane items and outlandish inventions.

Tools Required

You produce your artificer spell effects through your tools. You must have a spellcasting focus—specifically thieves' tools or some kind of artisan's tool—in hand when you cast any spell with this Spellcasting feature (meaning the spell has an "M" component

---

> **The Magic of Artifice**
>
> As an artificer, you use tools when you cast your spells. When describing your spellcasting, think about how you're using a tool. For example, if you cast *cure wounds* using alchemist's supplies, you could be quickly producing a salve. If you cast it using tinker's tools, you might have a miniature mechanical spider that binds wounds. The effect of the spell is the same either way.
>
> Such details don't limit you in any way or provide you with any benefit beyond the spell's effects. You don't have to justify how you're using tools to cast a spell. But describing your spellcasting creatively is a fun way to distinguish yourself from other spellcasters.

when you cast it). You must be proficient with the tool to use it in this way. See the equipment chapter in the *Player's Handbook* for descriptions of these tools.

After you gain the Infuse Item feature at 2nd level, you can also use any item bearing one of your infusions as a spellcasting focus.

Cantrips (0-Level Spells)

You know two cantrips of your choice from the artificer spell list. At higher levels, you learn additional artificer cantrips of your choice, as shown in the Cantrips Known column of the Artificer table.

When you gain a level in this class, you can replace one of the artificer cantrips you know with another cantrip from the artificer spell list.

Preparing and Casting Spells

The Artificer table shows how many spell slots you have to cast your artificer spells. To cast one of your artificer spells of 1st level or higher, you must expend a slot of the spell's level or higher. You regain all expended spell slots when you finish a long rest.

You prepare the list of artificer spells that are available for you to cast, choosing from the artificer spell list. When you do so, choose a number of artificer spells equal to your Intelligence modifier + half your artificer level, rounded down (minimum of one spell). The spells must be of a level for which you have spell slots.

For example, if you are a 5th-level artificer, you have four 1st-level and two 2nd-level spell slots. With an Intelligence of 14, your list of prepared spells can include four spells of 1st or 2nd level, in any combination. If you prepare the 1st-level spell *cure wounds*, you can cast it using a 1st-level or a 2nd-level slot. Casting the spell doesn't remove it from your list of prepared spells.

You can change your list of prepared spells when you finish a long rest. Preparing a new list of artificer spells requires time spent tinkering with your spellcasting focuses: at least 1 minute per spell level for each spell on your list.

Spellcasting Ability

Intelligence is your spellcasting ability for your artificer spells; your understanding of the theory behind magic allows you to wield these spells with superior skill. You use your Intelligence whenever an artificer spell refers to your spellcasting ability. In addition, you use your Intelligence modifier when setting the saving throw DC for an artificer spell you cast and when making an attack roll with one.

> **Spell save DC** = 8 + your proficiency bonus + your Intelligence modifier
>
> **Spell attack modifier** = your proficiency bonus + your Intelligence modifier

Ritual Casting

You can cast an artificer spell as a ritual if that spell has the ritual tag and you have the spell prepared.

Artificer Spell List

Here's the list of spells you consult when you learn an artificer spell. The list is organized by spell level, not character level. If a spell can be cast as a ritual, the ritual tag appears after the spell's name.

Each spell is in the *Player's Handbook*, unless it has one asterisk (a spell in chapter 3) or two asterisks (a spell in *Xanathar's Guide to Everything*).

Cantrips (0 Level)

Acid splash
Booming blade*
Create bonfire**
Dancing lights
Fire bolt
Frostbite**
Green-flame blade*
Guidance
Light
Lightning lure*
Mage hand
Magic stone**
Mending
Message
Poison spray
Prestidigitation
Ray of frost
Resistance
Shocking grasp
Spare the dying
Sword burst*
Thorn whip
Thunderclap**

1st Level

Absorb elements**
Alarm (ritual)

Catapult**
Cure wounds
Detect magic (ritual)
Disguise self
Expeditious retreat
Faerie fire
False life
Feather fall
Grease
Identify (ritual)
Jump
Longstrider
Purify food and drink
Sanctuary
Snare**
Tasha's caustic brew*

2nd Level

Aid
Alter self
Arcane lock
Blur
Continual flame
Darkvision
Enhance ability
Enlarge/reduce
Heat metal
Invisibility

Lesser restoration
Levitate
Magic mouth (ritual)
Magic weapon
Protection from poison
Pyrotechnics**
Rope trick
See invisibility
Skywrite** (ritual)
Spider climb
Web

3rd Level

Blink
Catnap**
Create food and water
Dispel magic
Elemental weapon
Flame arrows**
Fly
Glyph of warding
Haste
Intellect fortress*
Protection from energy
Revivify
Tiny servant**

Water breathing (ritual)
Water walk (ritual)

4th Level

Arcane eye
Elemental bane**
Fabricate
Freedom of movement
Leomund's secret chest
Mordenkainen's faithful hound
Mordenkainen's private sanctum
Otiluke's resilient sphere
Stone shape
Stoneskin
Summon construct*

5th Level

Animate objects
Bigby's hand
Creation
Greater restoration
Skill empowerment**
Transmute rock**
Wall of stone

Infuse Item

2nd-level artificer feature

You've gained the ability to imbue mundane items with certain magical infusions, turning those objects into magic items.

Infusions Known

When you gain this feature, pick four artificer infusions to learn, choosing from the "Artificer Infusions" section at the end of the class's description. You learn additional infusions of your choice when you reach certain levels in this class, as shown in the Infusions Known column of the Artificer table.

Whenever you gain a level in this class, you can replace one of the artificer infusions you learned with a new one.

Infusing an Item

Whenever you finish a long rest, you can touch a nonmagical object and imbue it with one of your artificer infusions, turning it into a magic item. An infusion works on only certain kinds of objects, as specified in the infusion's description. If the item requires attunement, you can attune yourself to it the instant you infuse the item. If you decide to attune to the item later, you must do so using the normal process for attunement (see the attunement rules in the *Dungeon Master's Guide*).

Your infusion remains in an item indefinitely, but when you die, the infusion vanishes after a number of days equal to your Intelligence modifier (minimum of 1 day). The infusion also vanishes if you replace your knowledge of the infusion.

You can infuse more than one nonmagical object at the end of a long rest; the maximum number of objects appears in the Infused Items column of the Artificer table. You must touch each of the objects, and each of your infusions can be in only one object at a time. Moreover, no object can bear more than one of your infusions at a time. If you try to exceed your maximum number of infusions, the oldest infusion ends, and then the new infusion applies.

If an infusion ends on an item that contains other things, like a *bag of holding*, its contents harmlessly appear in and around its space.

ARTIFICER SPECIALIST

3rd-level artificer feature

Choose the type of specialist you are: Alchemist, Armorer, Artillerist, or Battle Smith, each of which is detailed after the class's description. Your choice grants you features at 5th level and again at 9th and 15th level.

THE RIGHT TOOL FOR THE JOB

3rd-level artificer feature

You've learned how to produce exactly the tool you need: with thieves' tools or artisan's tools in hand, you can magically create one set of artisan's tools in an unoccupied space within 5 feet of you. This creation requires 1 hour of uninterrupted work, which can coincide with a short or long rest. Though the product of magic, the tools are nonmagical, and they vanish when you use this feature again.

ABILITY SCORE IMPROVEMENT

4th-level artificer feature

When you reach 4th level and again at 8th, 12th, 16th, and 19th level, you can increase one ability score of your choice by 2, or you can increase two ability scores of your choice by 1. As normal, you can't increase an ability score above 20 using this feature.

TOOL EXPERTISE

6th-level artificer feature

Your proficiency bonus is now doubled for any ability check you make that uses your proficiency with a tool.

FLASH OF GENIUS

7th-level artificer feature

You've gained the ability to come up with solutions under pressure. When you or another creature you can see within 30 feet of you makes an ability check or a saving throw, you can use your reaction to add your Intelligence modifier to the roll.

You can use this feature a number of times equal to your Intelligence modifier (minimum of once). You regain all expended uses when you finish a long rest.

MAGIC ITEM ADEPT

10th-level artificer feature

You've achieved a profound understanding of how to use and make magic items:

- You can attune to up to four magic items at once.
- If you craft a magic item with a rarity of common or uncommon, it takes you a quarter of the normal time, and it costs you half as much of the usual gold.

SPELL-STORING ITEM

11th-level artificer feature

You can now store a spell in an object. Whenever you finish a long rest, you can touch one simple or martial weapon or one item that you can use as a spellcasting focus, and you store a spell in it, choosing a 1st- or 2nd-level spell from the artificer spell list that requires 1 action to cast (you needn't have it prepared).

DWARF ALCHEMIST WITH
HOMUNCULUS SERVANT

While holding the object, a creature can take an action to produce the spell's effect from it, using your spellcasting ability modifier. If the spell requires concentration, the creature must concentrate. The spell stays in the object until it's been used a number of times equal to twice your Intelligence modifier (minimum of twice) or until you use this feature again to store a spell in an object.

MAGIC ITEM SAVANT

14th-level artificer feature

Your skill with magic items deepens:

- You can attune to up to five magic items at once.
- You ignore all class, race, spell, and level requirements on attuning to or using a magic item.

MAGIC ITEM MASTER

18th-level artificer feature

You can now attune to up to six magic items at once.

SOUL OF ARTIFICE

20th-level artificer feature

You have developed a mystical connection to your magic items, which you can draw on for protection:

- You gain a +1 bonus to all saving throws per magic item you are currently attuned to.
- If you're reduced to 0 hit points but not killed outright, you can use your reaction to end one of your artificer infusions, causing you to drop to 1 hit point instead of 0.

ARTIFICER SPECIALISTS

Artificers pursue many disciplines. Here are specialist options you can choose from at 3rd level.

ALCHEMIST

> The magic of both alchemists and witches relies on a powerful multiversal truth: mortals can't resist anything with bubbles.
>
> TASHA

An Alchemist is an expert at combining reagents to produce mystical effects. Alchemists use their creations to give life and to leech it away. Alchemy is the oldest of artificer traditions, and its versatility has long been valued during times of war and peace.

TOOL PROFICIENCY

3rd-level Alchemist feature

You gain proficiency with alchemist's supplies. If you already have this proficiency, you gain proficiency with one other type of artisan's tools of your choice.

ALCHEMIST SPELLS

3rd-level Alchemist feature

You always have certain spells prepared after you reach particular levels in this class, as shown in the Alchemist Spells table. These spells count as artificer spells for you, but they don't count against the number of artificer spells you prepare.

ALCHEMIST SPELLS

Artificer Level	Spell
3rd	*healing word, ray of sickness*
5th	*flaming sphere, Melf's acid arrow*
9th	*gaseous form, mass healing word*
13th	*blight, death ward*
17th	*cloudkill, raise dead*

EXPERIMENTAL ELIXIR

3rd-level Alchemist feature

Whenever you finish a long rest, you can magically produce an *experimental elixir* in an empty flask you touch. Roll on the Experimental Elixir table for the elixir's effect, which is triggered when someone drinks the elixir. As an action, a creature can drink the elixir or administer it to an incapacitated creature.

You can create additional *experimental elixirs* by expending a spell slot of 1st level or higher for each one. When you do so, you use your action to create the elixir in an empty flask you touch, and you choose the elixir's effect from the Experimental Elixir table.

Creating an *experimental elixir* requires you to have alchemist supplies on your person, and any elixir you create with this feature lasts until it is drunk or until the end of your next long rest.

When you reach certain levels in this class, you can make more elixirs at the end of a long rest: two at 6th level and three at 15th level. Roll for each elixir's effect separately. Each elixir requires its own flask.

EXPERIMENTAL ELIXIR

d6	Effect
1	**Healing.** The drinker regains a number of hit points equal to 2d4 + your Intelligence modifier.
2	**Swiftness.** The drinker's walking speed increases by 10 feet for 1 hour.
3	**Resilience.** The drinker gains a +1 bonus to AC for 10 minutes.
4	**Boldness.** The drinker can roll a d4 and add the number rolled to every attack roll and saving throw they make for the next minute.

d6	Effect
5	**Flight.** The drinker gains a flying speed of 10 feet for 10 minutes.
6	**Transformation.** The drinker's body is transformed as if by the *alter self* spell. The drinker determines the transformation caused by the spell, the effects of which last for 10 minutes.

ALCHEMICAL SAVANT
5th-level Alchemist feature

You've developed masterful command of magical chemicals, enhancing the healing and damage you create through them. Whenever you cast a spell using your alchemist's supplies as the spellcasting focus, you gain a bonus to one roll of the spell. That roll must restore hit points or be a damage roll that deals acid, fire, necrotic, or poison damage, and the bonus equals your Intelligence modifier (minimum of +1).

RESTORATIVE REAGENTS
9th-level Alchemist feature

You can incorporate restorative reagents into some of your works:

- Whenever a creature drinks an *experimental elixir* you created, the creature gains temporary hit points equal to 2d6 + your Intelligence modifier (minimum of 1 temporary hit point).
- You can cast *lesser restoration* without expending a spell slot and without preparing the spell, provided you use alchemist's supplies as the spellcasting focus. You can do so a number of times equal to your Intelligence modifier (minimum of once), and you regain all expended uses when you finish a long rest.

CHEMICAL MASTERY
15th-level Alchemist feature

You have been exposed to so many chemicals that they pose little risk to you, and you can use them to quickly end certain ailments:

- You gain resistance to acid damage and poison damage, and you are immune to the poisoned condition.
- You can cast *greater restoration* and *heal* without expending a spell slot, without preparing the spell, and without material components, provided you use alchemist's supplies as the spellcasting focus. Once you cast either spell with this feature, you can't cast that spell with it again until you finish a long rest.

ARMORER

> Classic artificer logic right here: "What if, when our invention goes explosively wrong, we're inside it?"
> TASHA

An artificer who specializes as an Armorer modifies armor to function almost like a second skin. The armor is enhanced to hone the artificer's magic, unleash potent attacks, and generate a formidable defense. The artificer bonds with this armor, becoming one with it even as they experiment with it and refine its magical capabilities.

TOOLS OF THE TRADE
3rd-level Armorer feature

You gain proficiency with heavy armor. You also gain proficiency with smith's tools. If you already have this tool proficiency, you gain proficiency with one other type of artisan's tools of your choice.

ARMORER SPELLS
3rd-level Armorer feature

You always have certain spells prepared after you reach particular levels in this class, as shown in the Armorer Spells table. These spells count as artificer spells for you, but they don't count against the number of artificer spells you prepare.

ARMORER SPELLS

Artificer Level	Spell
3rd	*magic missile, thunderwave*
5th	*mirror image, shatter*
9th	*hypnotic pattern, lightning bolt*
13th	*fire shield, greater invisibility*
17th	*passwall, wall of force*

ARCANE ARMOR
3rd-level Armorer feature

Your metallurgical pursuits have led to you making armor a conduit for your magic. As an action, you can turn a suit of armor you are wearing into Arcane Armor, provided you have smith's tools in hand.

You gain the following benefits while wearing this armor:

- If the armor normally has a Strength requirement, the arcane armor lacks this requirement for you.
- You can use the arcane armor as a spellcasting focus for your artificer spells.
- The armor attaches to you and can't be removed against your will. It also expands to cover your entire body, although you can retract or deploy the helmet as a bonus action. The armor replaces any

ARMORERS, A DROW INFILTRATOR
AND A TIEFLING GUARDIAN

missing limbs, functioning identically to a limb it replaces.

- You can doff or don the armor as an action.

The armor continues to be Arcane Armor until you don another suit of armor or you die.

ARMOR MODEL
3rd-level Armorer feature

You can customize your Arcane Armor. When you do so, choose one of the following armor models: Guardian or Infiltrator. The model you choose gives you special benefits while you wear it.

Each model includes a special weapon. When you attack with that weapon, you can add your Intelligence modifier, instead of Strength or Dexterity, to the attack and damage rolls.

You can change the armor's model whenever you finish a short or long rest, provided you have smith's tools in hand.

Guardian. You design your armor to be in the front line of conflict. It has the following features:

Thunder Gauntlets. Each of the armor's gauntlets counts as a simple melee weapon while you aren't holding anything in it, and it deals 1d8 thunder damage on a hit. A creature hit by the gauntlet has disadvantage on attack rolls against targets other than you until the start of your next turn, as the armor magically emits a distracting pulse when the creature attacks someone else.

Defensive Field. As a bonus action, you can gain temporary hit points equal to your level in this class, replacing any temporary hit points you already have. You lose these temporary hit points if you doff the armor. You can use this bonus action a number of times equal to your proficiency bonus, and you regain all expended uses when you finish a long rest.

Infiltrator. You customize your armor for subtle undertakings. It has the following features:

Lightning Launcher. A gemlike node appears on one of your armored fists or on the chest (your choice). It counts as a simple ranged weapon, with a normal range of 90 feet and a long range of 300 feet, and it deals 1d6 lightning damage on a hit. Once on each of your turns when you hit a creature with it, you can deal an extra 1d6 lightning damage to that target.

Powered Steps. Your walking speed increases by 5 feet.

Dampening Field. You have advantage on Dexterity (Stealth) checks. If the armor normally imposes disadvantage on such checks, the advantage and disadvantage cancel each other, as normal.

EXTRA ATTACK
5th-level Armorer feature

You can attack twice, rather than once, whenever you take the Attack action on your turn.

BRIAN VALEZA

ARMOR MODIFICATIONS
9th-level Armorer feature

You learn how to use your artificer infusions to specially modify your Arcane Armor. That armor now counts as separate items for the purposes of your Infuse Items feature: armor (the chest piece), boots, helmet, and the armor's special weapon. Each of those items can bear one of your infusions, and the infusions transfer over if you change your armor's model with the Armor Model feature. In addition, the maximum number of items you can infuse at once increases by 2, but those extra items must be part of your Arcane Armor.

PERFECTED ARMOR
15th-level Armorer feature

Your Arcane Armor gains additional benefits based on its model, as shown below.

Guardian. When a Huge or smaller creature you can see ends its turn within 30 feet of you, you can use your reaction to magically force the creature to make a Strength saving throw against your spell save DC, pulling the creature up to 30 feet toward you to an unoccupied space. If you pull the target to a space within 5 feet of you, you can make a melee weapon attack against it as part of this reaction.

You can use this reaction a number of times equal to your proficiency bonus, and you regain all expended uses of it when you finish a long rest.

Infiltrator. Any creature that takes lightning damage from your Lightning Launcher glimmers with magical light until the start of your next turn. The glimmering creature sheds dim light in a 5-foot radius, and it has disadvantage on attack rolls against you, as the light jolts it if it attacks you. In addition, the next attack roll against it has advantage, and if that attack hits, the target takes an extra 1d6 lightning damage.

ARTILLERIST

> Some artificers ask the hard questions: "Couldn't there be even more collateral damage?"
>
> TASHA

An Artillerist specializes in using magic to hurl energy, projectiles, and explosions on a battlefield. This destructive power is valued by armies in the wars on many different worlds. And when war passes, some members of this specialization seek to build a more peaceful world by using their powers to fight the resurgence of strife. The world-hopping gnome artificer Vi has been especially vocal about making things right: "It's about time we fixed things instead of blowing them all to hell."

TOOL PROFICIENCY
3rd-level Artillerist feature

You gain proficiency with woodcarver's tools. If you already have this proficiency, you gain proficiency with one other type of artisan's tools of your choice.

ARTILLERIST SPELLS
3rd-level Artillerist feature

You always have certain spells prepared after you reach particular levels in this class, as shown in the Artillerist Spells table. These spells count as artificer spells for you, but they don't count against the number of artificer spells you prepare.

ARTILLERIST SPELLS

Artificer Level	Spell
3rd	*shield, thunderwave*
5th	*scorching ray, shatter*
9th	*fireball, wind wall*
13th	*ice storm, wall of fire*
17th	*cone of cold, wall of force*

ELDRITCH CANNON
3rd-level Artillerist feature

You've learned how to create a magical cannon. Using woodcarver's tools or smith's tools, you can take an action to magically create a Small or Tiny eldritch cannon in an unoccupied space on a horizontal surface within 5 feet of you. A Small eldritch cannon occupies its space, and a Tiny one can be held in one hand.

Once you create a cannon, you can't do so again until you finish a long rest or until you expend a spell slot to create one. You can have only one cannon at a time and can't create one while your cannon is present.

The cannon is a magical object. Regardless of size, the cannon has an AC of 18 and a number of hit points equal to five times your artificer level. It is immune to poison damage and psychic damage. If it is forced to make an ability check or a saving throw, treat all its ability scores as 10 (+0). If the *mending* spell is cast on it, it regains 2d6 hit points. It disappears if it is reduced to 0 hit points or after 1 hour. You can dismiss it early as an action.

When you create the cannon, you determine its appearance and whether it has legs. You also decide which type it is, choosing from the options on the Eldritch Cannons table. On each of your turns, you can take a bonus action to cause the cannon to activate if you are within 60 feet of it. As part of the same bonus action, you can direct the cannon to walk or climb up to 15 feet to an unoccupied space, provided it has legs.

HUMAN ARTILLERIST
WITH ELDRITCH CANNON

ELDRITCH CANNONS

Cannon	Activation
Flamethrower	The cannon exhales fire in an adjacent 15-foot cone that you designate. Each creature in that area must make a Dexterity saving throw against your spell save DC, taking 2d8 fire damage on a failed save or half as much damage on a successful one. The fire ignites any flammable objects in the area that aren't being worn or carried.
Force Ballista	Make a ranged spell attack, originating from the cannon, at one creature or object within 120 feet of it. On a hit, the target takes 2d8 force damage, and if the target is a creature, it is pushed up to 5 feet away from the cannon.
Protector	The cannon emits a burst of positive energy that grants itself and each creature of your choice within 10 feet of it a number of temporary hit points equal to 1d8 + your Intelligence modifier (minimum of +1).

ARCANE FIREARM
5th-level Artillerist feature

You know how to turn a wand, staff, or rod into an arcane firearm, a conduit for your destructive spells. When you finish a long rest, you can use woodcarver's tools to carve special sigils into a wand, staff, or rod and thereby turn it into your arcane firearm. The sigils disappear from the object if you later carve them on a different item. The sigils otherwise last indefinitely.

You can use your arcane firearm as a spellcasting focus for your artificer spells. When you cast an artificer spell through the firearm, roll a d8, and you gain a bonus to one of the spell's damage rolls equal to the number rolled.

EXPLOSIVE CANNON
9th-level Artillerist feature

Every eldritch cannon you create is now more destructive:

- The cannon's damage rolls all increase by 1d8.
- As an action, you can command the cannon to detonate if you are within 60 feet of it. Doing so destroys the cannon and forces each creature within 20 feet of it to make a Dexterity saving throw against your spell save DC, taking 3d8 force damage on a failed save or half as much damage on a successful one.

FORTIFIED POSITION
15th-level Artillerist feature

You're a master at forming well-defended emplacements using your Eldritch Cannon:

- You and your allies have half cover while within 10 feet of a cannon you create with Eldritch Cannon, as a result of a shimmering field of magical protection that the cannon emits.
- You can now have two cannons at the same time. You can create two with the same action (but not the same spell slot), and you can activate both of them with the same bonus action. You determine whether the cannons are identical to each other or different. You can't create a third cannon while you have two.

BATTLE SMITH

Commanding nothing less than the power to create life, many battle smiths turn their genius toward forging technologically remarkable puppies and kitties.
Maybe I've underestimated them.

TASHA

Armies require protection, and someone has to put things back together if defenses fail. A combination of protector and medic, a Battle Smith is an expert at defending others and repairing both materiel and personnel. To aid in their work, Battle Smiths are accompanied by a steel defender, a protective companion of their own creation. Many soldiers tell stories of nearly dying before being saved by a Battle Smith and a steel defender.

In the world of Eberron, Battle Smiths played a key role in House Cannith's work on battle constructs and the original warforged, and after the Last War, these artificers led efforts to aid those who were injured in the war's horrific battles.

Tool Proficiency
3rd-level Battle Smith feature

You gain proficiency with smith's tools. If you already have this proficiency, you gain proficiency with one other type of artisan's tools of your choice.

Battle Smith Spells
3rd-level Battle Smith feature

You always have certain spells prepared after you reach particular levels in this class, as shown in the Battle Smith Spells table. These spells count as artificer spells for you, but they don't count against the number of artificer spells you prepare.

Battle Smith Spells

Artificer Level	Spell
3rd	*heroism, shield*
5th	*branding smite, warding bond*
9th	*aura of vitality, conjure barrage*
13th	*aura of purity, fire shield*
17th	*banishing smite, mass cure wounds*

Battle Ready
3rd-level Battle Smith feature

Your combat training and your experiments with magic have paid off in two ways:

- You gain proficiency with martial weapons.
- When you attack with a magic weapon, you can use your Intelligence modifier, instead of Strength or Dexterity modifier, for the attack and damage rolls.

Steel Defender
3rd-level Battle Smith feature

Your tinkering has borne you a companion, a steel defender. It's friendly to you and your companions, and it obeys your commands. See its game statistics in the Steel Defender stat block, which uses your proficiency bonus (PB) in several places. You determine the creature's appearance and whether it

has two legs or four; your choice has no effect on its game statistics.

In combat, the defender shares your initiative count, but it takes its turn immediately after yours. It can move and use its reaction on its own, but the only action it takes on its turn is the Dodge action, unless you take a bonus action on your turn to command it to take another action. That action can be one in its stat block or some other action. If you are incapacitated, the defender can take any action of its choice, not just Dodge.

If the *mending* spell is cast on the defender, it regains 2d6 hit points. If it has died within the last hour, you can use your smith's tools as an action to revive it, provided you are within 5 feet of it and you expend a spell slot of 1st level or higher. The defender returns to life after 1 minute with all its hit points restored.

At the end of a long rest, you can create a new steel defender if you have smith's tools with you. If you already have a defender from this feature, the first one immediately perishes. The defender also perishes if you die.

STEEL DEFENDER
Medium construct

Armor Class 15 (natural armor)
Hit Points 2 + your Intelligence modifier + five times your artificer level (the defender has a number of Hit Dice [d8s] equal to your artificer level)
Speed 40 ft.

STR	DEX	CON	INT	WIS	CHA
14 (+2)	12 (+1)	14 (+2)	4 (−3)	10 (+0)	6 (−2)

Saving Throws Dex +1 plus PB, Con +2 plus PB
Skills Athletics +2 plus PB, Perception +0 plus PB × 2
Damage Immunities poison
Condition Immunities charmed, exhaustion, poisoned
Senses darkvision 60 ft., passive Perception 10 + (PB × 2)
Languages understands the languages you speak
Challenge —   **Proficiency Bonus (PB)** equals your bonus

Vigilant. The defender can't be surprised.

Actions

Force-Empowered Rend. *Melee Weapon Attack:* your spell attack modifier to hit, reach 5 ft., one target you can see. *Hit:* 1d8 + PB force damage.

Repair (3/Day). The magical mechanisms inside the defender restore 2d8 + PB hit points to itself or to one construct or object within 5 feet of it.

Reaction

Deflect Attack. The defender imposes disadvantage on the attack roll of one creature it can see that is within 5 feet of it, provided the attack roll is against a creature other than the defender.

Extra Attack
5th-level Battle Smith feature

You can attack twice, rather than once, whenever you take the Attack action on your turn.

Arcane Jolt
9th-level Battle Smith feature

You've learned new ways to channel arcane energy to harm or heal. When either you hit a target with a magic weapon attack or your steel defender hits a target, you can channel magical energy through the strike to create one of the following effects:

- The target takes an extra 2d6 force damage.
- Choose one creature or object you can see within 30 feet of the target. Healing energy flows into the chosen recipient, restoring 2d6 hit points to it.

You can use this energy a number of times equal to your Intelligence modifier (minimum of once), but you can do so no more than once on a turn. You regain all expended uses when you finish a long rest.

Improved Defender
15th-level Battle Smith feature

Your Arcane Jolt and steel defender have become more powerful:

- The extra damage and the healing of your Arcane Jolt both increase to 4d6.
- Your steel defender gains a +2 bonus to Armor Class.
- Whenever your steel defender uses its Deflect Attack, the attacker takes force damage equal to 1d4 + your Intelligence modifier.

Artificer Infusions

Artificer infusions are extraordinary processes that rapidly turn a nonmagical object into a magic item. The description of each of the following infusions details the type of object that can receive it, along with whether the resulting magic item requires attunement.

Some infusions specify a minimum artificer level. You can't learn such an infusion until you are at least that level.

Unless an infusion's description says otherwise, you can't learn an infusion more than once.

Arcane Propulsion Armor
Prerequisite: 14th-level artificer
Item: A suit of armor (requires attunement)

The wearer of this armor gains these benefits:

- The wearer's walking speed increases by 5 feet.
- The armor includes gauntlets, each of which is a magic melee weapon that can be wielded only when the hand is holding nothing. The wearer is proficient with the gauntlets, and each one deals 1d8 force damage on a hit and has the thrown property, with a normal range of 20 feet and a long range of 60 feet. When thrown, the gauntlet detaches and flies at the attack's target, then immediately returns to the wearer and reattaches.
- The armor can't be removed against the wearer's will.
- If the wearer is missing any limbs, the armor replaces those limbs—hands, arms, feet, legs, or similar appendages. The replacements function identically to the body parts they replace.

Armor of Magical Strength
Item: A suit of armor (requires attunement)

This armor has 6 charges. The wearer can expend the armor's charges in the following ways:

- When the wearer makes a Strength check or a Strength saving throw, it can expend 1 charge to add a bonus to the roll equal to its Intelligence modifier.
- If the creature would be knocked prone, it can use its reaction to expend 1 charge to avoid being knocked prone.

The armor regains 1d6 expended charges daily at dawn.

GNOME BATTLE SMITH
WITH STEEL DEFENDER

BRIAN VALEZA

Boots of the Winding Path

Prerequisite: 6th-level artificer
Item: A pair of boots (requires attunement)

While wearing these boots, a creature can teleport up to 15 feet as a bonus action to an unoccupied space the creature can see. The creature must have occupied that space at some point during the current turn.

Enhanced Arcane Focus

Item: A rod, staff, or wand (requires attunement)

While holding this item, a creature gains a +1 bonus to spell attack rolls. In addition, the creature ignores half cover when making a spell attack.

The bonus increases to +2 when you reach 10th level in this class.

Enhanced Defense

Item: A suit of armor or a shield

A creature gains a +1 bonus to Armor Class while wearing (armor) or wielding (shield) the infused item.

The bonus increases to +2 when you reach 10th level in this class.

Enhanced Weapon

Item: A simple or martial weapon

This magic weapon grants a +1 bonus to attack and damage rolls made with it.

The bonus increases to +2 when you reach 10th level in this class.

Helm of Awareness

Prerequisite: 10th-level artificer
Item: A helmet (requires attunement)

While wearing this helmet, a creature has advantage on initiative rolls. In addition, the wearer can't be surprised, provided it isn't incapacitated.

Homunculus Servant

Item: A gem or crystal worth at least 100 gp

You learn intricate methods for magically creating a special homunculus that serves you. The item you infuse serves as the creature's heart, around which the creature's body instantly forms.

You determine the homunculus's appearance. Some artificers prefer mechanical-looking birds, whereas some like winged vials or miniature, animate cauldrons.

Homunculus Servant
Tiny construct

Armor Class 13 (natural armor)
Hit Points 1 + your Intelligence modifier + your artificer level (the homunculus has a number of Hit Dice [d4s] equal to your artificer level)
Speed 20 ft., fly 30 ft.

STR	DEX	CON	INT	WIS	CHA
4 (−3)	15 (+2)	12 (+1)	10 (+0)	10 (+0)	7 (−2)

Saving Throws Dex +2 plus PB
Skills Perception +0 plus PB × 2, Stealth +2 plus PB
Damage Immunities poison
Condition Immunities exhaustion, poisoned
Senses darkvision 60 ft., passive Perception 10 + (PB × 2)
Languages understands the languages you speak
Challenge —   **Proficiency Bonus (PB)** equals your bonus

Evasion. If the homunculus is subjected to an effect that allows it to make a Dexterity saving throw to take only half damage, it instead takes no damage if it succeeds on the saving throw, and only half damage if it fails. It can't use this trait if it's incapacitated.

Actions

Force Strike. *Ranged Weapon Attack:* your spell attack modifier to hit, range 30 ft., one target you can see. *Hit:* 1d4 + PB force damage.

Reactions

Channel Magic. The homunculus delivers a spell you cast that has a range of touch. The homunculus must be within 120 feet of you.

The homunculus is friendly to you and your companions, and it obeys your commands. See this creature's game statistics in the Homunculus Servant stat block, which uses your proficiency bonus (PB) in several places.

In combat, the homunculus shares your initiative count, but it takes its turn immediately after yours. It can move and use its reaction on its own, but the only action it takes on its turn is the Dodge action, unless you take a bonus action on your turn to command it to take another action. That action can be one in its stat block or some other action. If you are incapacitated, the homunculus can take any action of its choice, not just Dodge.

The homunculus regains 2d6 hit points if the *mending* spell is cast on it. If you or the homunculus dies, it vanishes, leaving its heart in its space.

Mind Sharpener
Item: A suit of armor or robes

The infused item can send a jolt to the wearer to refocus their mind. The item has 4 charges. When the wearer fails a Constitution saving throw to maintain concentration on a spell, the wearer can use its reaction to expend 1 of the item's charges to succeed instead. The item regains 1d4 expended charges daily at dawn.

Radiant Weapon
Prerequisite: 6th-level artificer
Item: A simple or martial weapon (requires attunement)

This magic weapon grants a +1 bonus to attack and damage rolls made with it. While holding it, the wielder can take a bonus action to cause it to shed bright light in a 30-foot radius and dim light for an additional 30 feet. The wielder can extinguish the light as a bonus action.

The weapon has 4 charges. As a reaction immediately after being hit by an attack, the wielder can expend 1 charge and cause the attacker to be blinded until the end of the attacker's next turn, unless the attacker succeeds on a Constitution saving throw against your spell save DC. The weapon regains 1d4 expended charges daily at dawn.

Repeating Shot
Item: A simple or martial weapon with the ammunition property (requires attunement)

This magic weapon grants a +1 bonus to attack and damage rolls made with it when it's used to make a ranged attack, and it ignores the loading property if it has it.

If you load no ammunition in the weapon, it produces its own, automatically creating one piece of magic ammunition when you make a ranged attack with it. The ammunition created by the weapon vanishes the instant after it hits or misses a target.

Replicate Magic Item
Using this infusion, you replicate a particular magic item. You can learn this infusion multiple times; each time you do so, choose a magic item that you can make with it, picking from the Replicable Items tables. A table's title tells you the level you must be in the class to choose an item from the table. Alternatively, you can choose the magic item from among the common magic items in the game, not including potions or scrolls.

In the tables, an item's entry tells you whether the item requires attunement. See the item's description in the *Dungeon Master's Guide* for more information about it, including the type of object required for its making.

Replicable Items (2nd-Level Artificer)

Magic Item	Attunement
Alchemy jug	No
Bag of holding	No
Cap of water breathing	No
Goggles of night	No
Rope of climbing	No
Sending stones	No
Wand of magic detection	No
Wand of secrets	No

Replicable Items (6th-Level Artificer)

Magic Item	Attunement
Boots of elvenkind	No
Cloak of elvenkind	Yes
Cloak of the manta ray	No
Eyes of charming	Yes
Gloves of thievery	No
Lantern of revealing	No
Pipes of haunting	No
Ring of water walking	No

Replicable Items (10th-Level Artificer)

Magic Item	Attunement
Boots of striding and springing	Yes
Boots of the winterlands	Yes
Bracers of archery	Yes
Brooch of shielding	Yes
Cloak of protection	Yes
Eyes of the eagle	Yes
Gauntlets of ogre power	Yes
Gloves of missile snaring	Yes
Gloves of swimming and climbing	Yes
Hat of disguise	Yes
Headband of intellect	Yes
Helm of telepathy	Yes
Medallion of thoughts	Yes
Necklace of adaptation	Yes
Periapt of wound closure	Yes
Pipes of the sewers	Yes
Quiver of Ehlonna	No
Ring of jumping	Yes
Ring of mind shielding	Yes
Slippers of spider climbing	Yes
Winged boots	Yes

Replicable Items (14th-Level Artificer)

Magic Item	Attunement
Amulet of health	Yes
Belt of hill giant strength	Yes
Boots of levitation	Yes
Boots of speed	Yes
Bracers of defense	Yes
Cloak of the bat	Yes
Dimensional shackles	No
Gem of seeing	Yes
Horn of blasting	No
Ring of free action	Yes
Ring of protection	Yes
Ring of the ram	Yes

Repulsion Shield

Prerequisite: 6th-level artificer
Item: A shield (requires attunement)

A creature gains a +1 bonus to Armor Class while wielding this shield.

The shield has 4 charges. While holding it, the wielder can use a reaction immediately after being hit by a melee attack to expend 1 of the shield's charges and push the attacker up to 15 feet away. The shield regains 1d4 expended charges daily at dawn.

Resistant Armor

Prerequisite: 6th-level artificer
Item: A suit of armor (requires attunement)

While wearing this armor, a creature has resistance to one of the following damage types, which you choose when you infuse the item: acid, cold, fire, force, lightning, necrotic, poison, psychic, radiant, or thunder.

Returning Weapon

Item: A simple or martial weapon with the thrown property

This magic weapon grants a +1 bonus to attack and damage rolls made with it, and it returns to the wielder's hand immediately after it is used to make a ranged attack.

Spell-Refueling Ring

Prerequisite: 6th-level artificer
Item: A ring (requires attunement)

While wearing this ring, the creature can recover one expended spell slot as an action. The recovered slot can be of 3rd level or lower. Once used, the ring can't be used again until the next dawn.

BARBARIAN

The barbarian class receives new features and subclasses in this section.

OPTIONAL CLASS FEATURES

You gain class features in the *Player's Handbook* when you reach certain levels in your class. This section offers additional features that you can gain as a barbarian.

Unlike the features in the *Player's Handbook*, you don't gain the features here automatically. Consulting with your DM, you decide whether to gain a feature in this section if you meet the level requirement noted in the feature's description. These features can be selected separately from one another; you can use one, both, or none of them.

PRIMAL KNOWLEDGE

3rd-level barbarian feature

When you reach 3rd level and again at 10th level, you gain proficiency in one skill of your choice from the list of skills available to barbarians at 1st level.

INSTINCTIVE POUNCE

7th-level barbarian feature

As part of the bonus action you take to enter your rage, you can move up to half your speed.

HUMAN BARBARIAN OF THE BEAST

PRIMAL PATHS

At 3rd level, a barbarian gains the Primal Path feature, which offers you the choice of a subclass. The following options are available to you when making that choice: Path of the Beast and Path of Wild Magic.

PATH OF THE BEAST

> You have to respect anyone who lets their inner beast out for a brisk jog and healthy throat-ripping.
> TASHA

Barbarians who walk the Path of the Beast draw their rage from a bestial spark burning within their souls. That beast bursts forth in the throes of rage, physically transforming the barbarian.

Such a barbarian might be inhabited by a primal spirit or be descended from shape-shifters. You can choose the origin of your feral might or determine it by rolling on the Origin of the Beast table.

ORIGIN OF THE BEAST

d4	Origin
1	One of your parents is a lycanthrope, and you've inherited some of their curse.
2	You are descended from an archdruid and inherited the ability to partially change shape.
3	A fey spirit gifted you with the ability to adopt different bestial aspects.
4	An ancient animal spirit dwells within you, allowing you to walk this path.

FORM OF THE BEAST
3rd-level Path of the Beast feature

When you enter your rage, you can transform, revealing the bestial power within you. Until the rage ends, you manifest a natural weapon. It counts as a simple melee weapon for you, and you add your Strength modifier to the attack and damage rolls when you attack with it, as normal.

You choose the weapon's form each time you rage:

Bite. Your mouth transforms into a bestial muzzle or great mandibles (your choice). It deals 1d8 piercing damage on a hit. Once on each of your turns when you damage a creature with this bite, you regain a number of hit points equal to your proficiency bonus, provided you have less than half your hit points when you hit.

Claws. Each of your hands transforms into a claw, which you can use as a weapon if it's empty. It deals 1d6 slashing damage on a hit. Once on each of your turns when you attack with a claw using

SHAWN WOOD

the Attack action, you can make one additional claw attack as part of the same action.

Tail. You grow a lashing, spiny tail, which deals 1d8 piercing damage on a hit and has the reach property. If a creature you can see within 10 feet of you hits you with an attack roll, you can use your reaction to swipe your tail and roll a d8, applying a bonus to your AC equal to the number rolled, potentially causing the attack to miss you.

BESTIAL SOUL
6th-level Path of the Beast feature

The feral power within you increases, causing the natural weapons of your Form of the Beast to count as magical for the purpose of overcoming resistance and immunity to nonmagical attacks and damage.

You can also alter your form to help you adapt to your surroundings. When you finish a short or long rest, choose one of the following benefits, which lasts until you finish your next short or long rest:

- You gain a swimming speed equal to your walking speed, and you can breathe underwater.
- You gain a climbing speed equal to your walking speed, and you can climb difficult surfaces, including upside down on ceilings, without needing to make an ability check.
- When you jump, you can make a Strength (Athletics) check and extend your jump by a number of feet equal to the check's total. You can make this special check only once per turn.

INFECTIOUS FURY
10th-level Path of the Beast feature

When you hit a creature with your natural weapons while you are raging, the beast within you can curse your target with rabid fury. The target must succeed on a Wisdom saving throw (DC equal to 8 + your Constitution modifier + your proficiency bonus) or suffer one of the following effects (your choice):

- The target must use its reaction to make a melee attack against another creature of your choice that you can see.
- The target takes 2d12 psychic damage.

You can use this feature a number of times equal to your proficiency bonus, and you regain all expended uses when you finish a long rest.

CALL THE HUNT
14th-level Path of the Beast feature

The beast within you grows so powerful that you can spread its ferocity to others and gain resilience from them joining your hunt. When you enter your rage, you can choose a number of other willing creatures you can see within 30 feet of you equal to your Constitution modifier (minimum of one creature).

You gain 5 temporary hit points for each creature that accepts this feature. Until the rage ends, the chosen creatures can each use the following benefit once on each of their turns: when the creature hits a target with an attack roll and deals damage to it, the creature can roll a d6 and gain a bonus to the damage equal to the number rolled.

You can use this feature a number of times equal to your proficiency bonus, and you regain all expended uses when you finish a long rest.

PATH OF WILD MAGIC

> I don't recommend letting magic take the reins, but I'm not your mom. Live deliciously.
> TASHA

Many places in the multiverse abound with beauty, intense emotion, and rampant magic; the Feywild, the Upper Planes, and other realms of supernatural power radiate with such forces and can profoundly influence people. As folk of deep feeling, barbarians are especially susceptible to these wild influences, with some barbarians being transformed by the magic. These magic-suffused barbarians walk the Path of Wild Magic. Elf, tiefling, aasimar, and genasi barbarians often seek this path, eager to manifest the otherworldly magic of their ancestors.

MAGIC AWARENESS
3rd-level Path of Wild Magic feature

As an action, you can open your awareness to the presence of concentrated magic. Until the end of your next turn, you know the location of any spell or magic item within 60 feet of you that isn't behind total cover. When you sense a spell, you learn which school of magic it belongs to.

You can use this feature a number of times equal to your proficiency bonus, and you regain all expended uses when you finish a long rest.

WILD SURGE
3rd-level Path of Wild Magic feature

The magical energy roiling inside you sometimes erupts from you. When you enter your rage, roll on the Wild Magic table to determine the magical effect produced.

If the effect requires a saving throw, the DC equals 8 + your proficiency bonus + your Constitution modifier.

Wild Magic

d8	Magical Effect
1	Shadowy tendrils lash around you. Each creature of your choice that you can see within 30 feet of you must succeed on a Constitution saving throw or take 1d12 necrotic damage. You also gain 1d12 temporary hit points.
2	You teleport up to 30 feet to an unoccupied space you can see. Until your rage ends, you can use this effect again on each of your turns as a bonus action.
3	An intangible spirit, which looks like a flumph or a pixie (your choice), appears within 5 feet of one creature of your choice that you can see within 30 feet of you. At the end of the current turn, the spirit explodes, and each creature within 5 feet of it must succeed on a Dexterity saving throw or take 1d6 force damage. Until your rage ends, you can use this effect again, summoning another spirit, on each of your turns as a bonus action.
4	Magic infuses one weapon of your choice that you are holding. Until your rage ends, the weapon's damage type changes to force, and it gains the light and thrown properties, with a normal range of 20 feet and a long range of 60 feet. If the weapon leaves your hand, the weapon reappears in your hand at the end of the current turn.
5	Whenever a creature hits you with an attack roll before your rage ends, that creature takes 1d6 force damage, as magic lashes out in retribution.
6	Until your rage ends, you are surrounded by multicolored, protective lights; you gain a +1 bonus to AC, and while within 10 feet of you, your allies gain the same bonus.
7	Flowers and vines temporarily grow around you; until your rage ends, the ground within 15 feet of you is difficult terrain for your enemies.
8	A bolt of light shoots from your chest. Another creature of your choice that you can see within 30 feet of you must succeed on a Constitution saving throw or take 1d6 radiant damage and be blinded until the start of your next turn. Until your rage ends, you can use this effect again on each of your turns as a bonus action.

WOOD ELF BARBARIAN
OF WILD MAGIC

Bolstering Magic
6th-level Path of Wild Magic feature

You can harness your wild magic to bolster yourself or a companion. As an action, you can touch one creature (which can be yourself) and confer one of the following benefits of your choice to that creature:

- For 10 minutes, the creature can roll a d3 whenever making an attack roll or an ability check and add the number rolled to the d20 roll.
- Roll a d3. The creature regains one expended spell slot, the level of which equals the number rolled or lower (the creature's choice). Once a creature receives this benefit, that creature can't receive it again until after a long rest.

You can take this action a number of times equal to your proficiency bonus, and you regain all expended uses when you finish a long rest.

Unstable Backlash
10th-level Path of Wild Magic feature

When you are imperiled during your rage, the magic within you can lash out; immediately after you take damage or fail a saving throw while raging, you can use your reaction to roll on the Wild Magic table and immediately produce the effect rolled. This effect replaces your current Wild Magic effect.

Controlled Surge
14th-level Path of Wild Magic feature

Whenever you roll on the Wild Magic table, you can roll the die twice and choose which of the two effects to unleash. If you roll the same number on both dice, you can ignore the number and choose any effect on the table.

SHAWN WOOD (L), ZOLTAN BOROS (R)

BARD

The bard class receives new features and sub-classes in this section.

OPTIONAL CLASS FEATURES

You gain class features in the *Player's Handbook* when you reach certain levels in your class. This section offers additional features that you can gain as a bard. Unlike the features in the *Player's Handbook*, you don't gain the features here automatically. Consulting with your DM, you decide whether to gain a feature in this section if you meet the level requirement noted in the feature's description. These features can be selected separately from one another; you can use some, all, or none of them.

ADDITIONAL BARD SPELLS

1st-level bard feature

The spells in the following list expand the bard spell list in the *Player's Handbook*. The list is organized by spell level, not character level. If a spell can be cast as a ritual, the ritual tag appears after the spell's name. Each spell is in the *Player's Handbook*, unless it has an asterisk (a spell in chapter 3). *Xanathar's Guide to Everything* also offers more spells.

1ST LEVEL
Color spray
Command

2ND LEVEL
Aid
Enlarge/reduce
Mirror image

3RD LEVEL
Intellect fortress*
Mass healing word
Slow

4TH LEVEL
Phantasmal killer

5TH LEVEL
Rary's telepathic bond (ritual)

6TH LEVEL
Heroes' feast

7TH LEVEL
Dream of the blue veil*
Prismatic spray

8TH LEVEL
Antipathy/sympathy

9TH LEVEL
Prismatic wall

MAGICAL INSPIRATION

2nd-level bard feature

If a creature has a Bardic Inspiration die from you and casts a spell that restores hit points or deals damage, the creature can roll that die and choose a target affected by the spell. Add the number rolled as a bonus to the hit points regained or the damage dealt. The Bardic Inspiration die is then lost.

A DRAGONBORN BARD OF THE COLLEGE OF CREATION ANIMATES A STATUE TO DANCE.

Bardic Versatility

4th-level bard feature

Whenever you reach a level in this class that grants the Ability Score Improvement feature, you can do one of the following, representing a change in focus as you use your skills and magic:

- Replace one of the skills you chose for the Expertise feature with one of your other skill proficiencies that isn't benefiting from Expertise.
- Replace one cantrip you learned from this class's Spellcasting feature with another cantrip from the bard spell list.

Bard Colleges

At 3rd level, a bard gains the Bard College feature, which offers you the choice of a subclass. The following options are available to you when making that choice: College of Creation and College of Eloquence.

College of Creation

> One bard's song of creation is the score to another person's nightmares.
>
> TASHA

Bards believe the cosmos is a work of art—the creation of the first dragons and gods. That creative work included harmonies that continue to resound through existence today, a power known as the Song of Creation. The bards of the College of Creation draw on that primeval song through dance, music, and poetry, and their teachers share this lesson: "Before the sun and the moon, there was the Song, and its music awoke the first dawn. Its melodies so delighted the stones and trees that some of them gained a voice of their own. And now they sing too. Learn the Song, students, and you too can teach the mountains to sing and dance."

Dwarves and gnomes often encourage their bards to become students of the Song of Creation. And among dragonborn, the Song of Creation is revered, for legends portray Bahamut and Tiamat—the greatest of dragons—as two of the song's first singers.

Mote of Potential

3rd-level College of Creation feature

Whenever you give a creature a Bardic Inspiration die, you can utter a note from the Song of Creation to create a Tiny mote of potential, which orbits within 5 feet of that creature. The mote is intangible and invulnerable, and it lasts until the Bardic

Inspiration die is lost. The mote looks like a musical note, a star, a flower, or another symbol of art or life that you choose.

When the creature uses the Bardic Inspiration die, the mote provides an additional effect based on whether the die benefits an ability check, an attack roll, or a saving throw, as detailed below:

Ability Check. When the creature rolls the Bardic Inspiration die to add it to an ability check, the creature can roll the Bardic Inspiration die again and choose which roll to use, as the mote pops and emits colorful, harmless sparks for a moment.

Attack Roll. Immediately after the creature rolls the Bardic Inspiration die to add it to an attack roll against a target, the mote thunderously shatters. The target and each creature of your choice that you can see within 5 feet of it must succeed on a Constitution saving throw against your spell save DC or take thunder damage equal to the number rolled on the Bardic Inspiration die.

Saving Throw. Immediately after the creature rolls the Bardic Inspiration die and adds it to a saving throw, the mote vanishes with the sound of soft music, causing the creature to gain temporary hit points equal to the number rolled on the Bardic Inspiration die plus your Charisma modifier (minimum of 1 temporary hit point).

Performance of Creation

3rd-level College of Creation feature

As an action, you can channel the magic of the Song of Creation to create one nonmagical item of your choice in an unoccupied space within 10 feet of you. The item must appear on a surface or in a liquid that can support it. The gp value of the item can't be more than 20 times your bard level, and the item must be Medium or smaller. The item glimmers softly, and a creature can faintly hear music when touching it. The created item disappears after a number of hours equal to your proficiency bonus. For examples of items you can create, see the equipment chapter of the *Player's Handbook*.

Once you create an item with this feature, you can't do so again until you finish a long rest, unless you expend a spell slot of 2nd level or higher to use this feature again. You can have only one item created by this feature at a time; if you use this action and already have an item from this feature, the first one immediately vanishes.

The size of the item you can create with this feature increases by one size category when you reach 6th level (Large) and 14th level (Huge).

DANCING ITEM
Large or smaller construct

Armor Class 16 (natural armor)
Hit Points 10 + five times your bard level
Speed 30 ft., fly 30 ft. (hover)

STR	DEX	CON	INT	WIS	CHA
18 (+4)	14 (+2)	16 (+3)	4 (−3)	10 (+0)	6 (−2)

Damage Immunities poison, psychic
Condition Immunities charmed, exhaustion, poisoned, frightened
Senses darkvision 60 ft., passive Perception 10
Languages understands the languages you speak
Challenge —   **Proficiency Bonus (PB)** equals your bonus

Immutable Form. The item is immune to any spell or effect that would alter its form.

Irrepressible Dance. When any creature starts its turn within 10 feet of the item, the item can increase or decrease (your choice) the walking speed of that creature by 10 feet until the end of the turn, provided the item isn't incapacitated.

ACTIONS

Force-Empowered Slam. *Melee Weapon Attack:* your spell attack modifier to hit, reach 5 ft., one target you can see. *Hit:* 1d10 + PB force damage.

ANIMATING PERFORMANCE
6th-level College of Creation feature

As an action, you can target a Large or smaller non-magical item you can see within 30 feet of you and animate it. The animate item uses the Dancing Item stat block, which uses your proficiency bonus (PB). The item is friendly to you and your companions and obeys your commands. It lives for 1 hour, until it is reduced to 0 hit points, or until you die.

In combat, the item shares your initiative count, but it takes its turn immediately after yours. It can move and use its reaction on its own, but the only action it takes on its turn is the Dodge action, unless you take a bonus action on your turn to command it to take another action. That action can be one in its stat block or some other action. If you are incapacitated, the item can take any action of its choice, not just Dodge.

When you use your Bardic Inspiration feature, you can command the item as part of the same bonus action you use for Bardic Inspiration.

Once you animate an item with this feature, you can't do so again until you finish a long rest, unless you expend a spell slot of 3rd level or higher to use this feature again. You can have only one item animated by this feature at a time; if you use this action and already have a dancing item from this feature, the first one immediately becomes inanimate.

DROW BARD
OF ELOQUENCE

CREATIVE CRESCENDO
14th-level College of Creation feature

When you use your Performance of Creation feature, you can create more than one item at once. The number of items equals your Charisma modifier (minimum of two items). If you create an item that would exceed that number, you choose which of the previously created items disappears. Only one of these items can be of the maximum size you can create; the rest must be Small or Tiny.

You are no longer limited by gp value when creating items with Performance of Creation.

COLLEGE OF ELOQUENCE

Note to self: revisit work on a speech-negating spell. Necessity level: ear-bleeding.

TASHA

Adherents of the College of Eloquence master the art of oratory. These bards wield a blend of logic and theatrical wordplay, winning over skeptics and detractors with logical arguments and plucking at heartstrings to appeal to the emotions of audiences.

Silver Tongue
3rd-level College of Eloquence feature

You are a master at saying the right thing at the right time. When you make a Charisma (Persuasion) or Charisma (Deception) check, you can treat a d20 roll of 9 or lower as a 10.

Unsettling Words
3rd-level College of Eloquence feature

You can spin words laced with magic that unsettle a creature and cause it to doubt itself. As a bonus action, you can expend one use of your Bardic Inspiration and choose one creature you can see within 60 feet of you. Roll the Bardic Inspiration die. The creature must subtract the number rolled from the next saving throw it makes before the start of your next turn.

Unfailing Inspiration
6th-level College of Eloquence feature

Your inspiring words are so persuasive that others feel driven to succeed. When a creature adds one of your Bardic Inspiration dice to its ability check, attack roll, or saving throw and the roll fails, the creature can keep the Bardic Inspiration die.

Universal Speech
6th-level College of Eloquence feature

You gain the ability to make your speech intelligible to any creature. As an action, choose one or more creatures within 60 feet of you, up to a number equal to your Charisma modifier (minimum of one creature). The chosen creatures can magically understand you, regardless of the language you speak, for 1 hour.

Once you use this feature, you can't use it again until you finish a long rest, unless you expend a spell slot of any level to use it again.

Infectious Inspiration
14th-level College of Eloquence feature

When you successfully inspire someone, the power of your eloquence can now spread to someone else. When a creature within 60 feet of you adds one of your Bardic Inspiration dice to its ability check, attack roll, or saving throw and the roll succeeds, you can use your reaction to encourage a different creature (other than yourself) that can hear you within 60 feet of you, giving it a Bardic Inspiration die without expending any of your Bardic Inspiration uses.

You can use this reaction a number of times equal to your Charisma modifier (minimum of once), and you regain all expended uses when you finish a long rest.

Cleric

The cleric class receives new features and subclasses in this section.

Optional Class Features

You gain class features in the *Player's Handbook* when you reach certain levels in your class. This section offers additional features that you can gain as a cleric. Unlike the features in the *Player's Handbook*, you don't gain the features here automatically. Consulting with your DM, you decide whether to gain a feature in this section if you meet the level requirement noted in the feature's description. These features can be selected separately from one another; you can use some, all, or none of them.

If you take a feature that replaces another feature, you gain no benefit from the replaced one and don't qualify for anything in the game that requires it.

Additional Cleric Spells

1st-level cleric feature

The spells in the following list expand the cleric spell list in the *Player's Handbook*. The list is organized by spell level, not character level. If a spell can be cast as a ritual, the ritual tag appears after the spell's name. Each spell is in the *Player's Handbook*, unless it has an asterisk (a spell in chapter 3). *Xanathar's Guide to Everything* also offers more spells.

3rd Level
Aura of vitality
Spirit shroud*

4th Level
Aura of life
Aura of purity

5th Level
Summon celestial*

6th Level
Sunbeam

8th Level
Sunburst

9th Level
Power word heal

Harness Divine Power

2nd-level cleric feature

You can expend a use of your Channel Divinity to fuel your spells. As a bonus action, you touch your holy symbol, utter a prayer, and regain one expended spell slot, the level of which can be no higher than half your proficiency bonus (rounded up). The number of times you can use this feature is based on the level you've reached in this class: 2nd level, once; 6th level, twice; and 18th level, thrice. You regain all expended uses when you finish a long rest.

CANTRIP VERSATILITY

4th-level cleric feature

Whenever you reach a level in this class that grants the Ability Score Improvement feature, you can replace one cantrip you learned from this class's Spellcasting feature with another cantrip from the cleric spell list.

BLESSED STRIKES

8th-level cleric feature, which replaces the Divine Strike or Potent Spellcasting feature

You are blessed with divine might in battle. When a creature takes damage from one of your cantrips or weapon attacks, you can also deal 1d8 radiant damage to that creature. Once you deal this damage, you can't use this feature again until the start of your next turn.

DIVINE DOMAINS

At 1st level, a cleric gains the Divine Domain feature, which offers you the choice of a subclass. The following options are available to you when making that choice: Order Domain, Peace Domain, and Twilight Domain.

ORDER DOMAIN

> Finally, a whole faith about coloring inside the lines.
> TASHA

The Order Domain represents discipline, as well as devotion to the laws that govern a society, an institution, or a philosophy. Clerics of Order meditate on logic and justice as they serve their gods, examples of which appear in the Order Deities table.

Clerics of Order believe that well-crafted laws establish legitimate hierarchies, and those selected by law to lead must be obeyed. Those who obey must do so to the best of their ability, and if those who lead fail to protect the law, they must be replaced. In this manner, law weaves a web of obligations that create order and security in a chaotic multiverse.

A CLERIC HARNESSES DIVINE POWER.

ORDER DEITIES

Example Deity	Pantheon
Aureon	Eberron
Bane	Forgotten Realms
Majere	Dragonlance
Pholtus	Greyhawk
Tyr	Forgotten Realms
Wee Jas	Greyhawk

DOMAIN SPELLS

1st-level Order Domain feature

You gain domain spells at the cleric levels listed in the Order Domain Spells table. See the Divine Domain class feature in the *Player's Handbook* for how domain spells work.

ORDER DOMAIN SPELLS

Cleric Level	Spells
1st	*command, heroism*
3rd	*hold person, zone of truth*
5th	*mass healing word, slow*
7th	*compulsion, locate creature*
9th	*commune, dominate person*

NIKKI DAWES

DRAGONBORN
CLERIC OF ORDER

BONUS PROFICIENCIES
1st-level Order Domain feature

You gain proficiency with heavy armor. You also gain proficiency in the Intimidation or Persuasion skill (your choice).

VOICE OF AUTHORITY
1st-level Order Domain feature

You can invoke the power of law to embolden an ally to attack. If you cast a spell with a spell slot of 1st level or higher and target an ally with the spell, that ally can use their reaction immediately after the spell to make one weapon attack against a creature of your choice that you can see.

If the spell targets more than one ally, you choose the ally who can make the attack.

CHANNEL DIVINITY: ORDER'S DEMAND
2nd-level Order Domain feature

You can use your Channel Divinity to exert an intimidating presence over others.

As an action, you present your holy symbol, and each creature of your choice that can see or hear you within 30 feet of you must succeed on a Wisdom saving throw or be charmed by you until the end of your next turn or until the charmed creature takes any damage. You can also cause any of the charmed creatures to drop what they are holding when they fail the saving throw.

EMBODIMENT OF THE LAW
6th-level Order Domain feature

You have become remarkably adept at channeling magical energy to compel others.

If you cast a spell of the enchantment school using a spell slot of 1st level or higher, you can change the spell's casting time to 1 bonus action for this casting, provided the spell's casting time is normally 1 action.

You can use this feature a number of times equal to your Wisdom modifier (minimum of once), and you regain all expended uses of it when you finish a long rest.

DIVINE STRIKE
8th-level Order Domain feature

You gain the ability to infuse your weapon strikes with divine energy. Once on each of your turns when you hit a creature with a weapon attack, you can cause the attack to deal an extra 1d8 psychic damage to the target. When you reach 14th level, the extra damage increases to 2d8.

ORDER'S WRATH
17th-level Order Domain feature

Enemies you designate for destruction wilt under the combined efforts of you and your allies. If you deal your Divine Strike damage to a creature on your turn, you can curse that creature until the start of your next turn. The next time one of your allies hits the cursed creature with an attack, the target also takes 2d8 psychic damage, and the curse ends. You can curse a creature in this way only once per turn.

PEACE DOMAIN

> Have these peaceful clerics even considered that they're subverting a most holy system, one where bad decisions coincide with the teaching power of pain?
>
> TASHA

The balm of peace thrives at the heart of healthy communities, between friendly nations, and in the souls of the kindhearted. The gods of peace inspire people of all sorts to resolve conflict and to stand up against those forces that try to prevent peace from flourishing. See the Peace Deities table for a list of some of the gods associated with this domain.

Clerics of the Peace Domain preside over the signing of treaties, and they are often asked to arbitrate in disputes. These clerics' blessings draw people together and help them shoulder one another's burdens, and the clerics' magic aids those who are driven to fight for the way of peace.

NIKKI DAWES

Peace Deities

Example Deity	Pantheon
Angharradh	Elven
Berronar Truesilver	Dwarven
Boldrei	Eberron
Cyrrollalee	Halfling
Eldath	Forgotten Realms
Gaerdal Ironhand	Gnomish
Paladine	Dragonlance
Rao	Greyhawk

Domain Spells
1st-level Peace Domain feature

You gain domain spells at the cleric levels listed in the Peace Domain Spells table. See the Divine Domain class feature for how domain spells work.

Peace Domain Spells

Cleric Level	Spells
1st	heroism, sanctuary
3rd	aid, warding bond
5th	beacon of hope, sending
7th	aura of purity, Otiluke's resilient sphere
9th	greater restoration, Rary's telepathic bond

Implement of Peace
1st-leve Peace Domain feature

You gain proficiency in the Insight, Performance, or Persuasion skill (your choice).

Emboldening Bond
1st-level Peace Domain feature

You can forge an empowering bond among people who are at peace with one another. As an action, you choose a number of willing creatures within 30 feet of you (this can include yourself) equal to your proficiency bonus. You create a magical bond among them for 10 minutes or until you use this feature again. While any bonded creature is within 30 feet of another, the creature can roll a d4 and add the number rolled to an attack roll, an ability check, or a saving throw it makes. Each creature can add the d4 no more than once per turn.

You can use this feature a number of times equal to your proficiency bonus, and you regain all expended uses when you finish a long rest.

Channel Divinity: Balm of Peace
2nd-level Peace Domain feature

You can use your Channel Divinity to make your very presence a soothing balm. As an action, you can move up to your speed, without provoking opportunity attacks, and when you move within 5 feet

HUMAN CLERIC
OF PEACE

of any other creature during this action, you can restore a number of hit points to that creature equal to 2d6 + your Wisdom modifier (minimum of 1 hit point). A creature can receive this healing only once whenever you take this action.

Protective Bond
6th-level Peace Domain feature

The bond you forge between people helps them protect each other. When a creature affected by your Emboldening Bond feature is about to take damage, a second bonded creature within 30 feet of the first can use its reaction to teleport to an unoccupied space within 5 feet of the first creature. The second creature then takes all the damage instead.

Potent Spellcasting
8th-level Peace Domain feature

You add your Wisdom modifier to the damage you deal with any cleric cantrip.

Expansive Bond
17th-level Peace Domain feature

The benefits of your Emboldening Bond and Protective Bond features now work when the creatures are within 60 feet of each other. Moreover, when a creature uses Protective Bond to take someone else's damage, the creature has resistance to that damage.

NIKKI DAWES

TWILIGHT DOMAIN

> I can't believe I'm writing this, but I think I could get behind a faith focused on mood lighting and evening wear.
>
> TASHA

The twilit transition from light into darkness often brings calm and even joy, as the day's labors end and the hours of rest begin. The darkness can also bring terrors, but the gods of twilight guard against the horrors of the night.

Clerics who serve these deities—examples of which appear on the Twilight Deities table—bring comfort to those who seek rest and protect them by venturing into the encroaching darkness to ensure that the dark is a comfort, not a terror.

TWILIGHT DEITIES

Example Deity	Pantheon
Boldrei	Eberron
Celestian	Greyhawk
Dol Arrah	Eberron
Helm	Forgotten Realms
Ilmater	Forgotten Realms
Mishakal	Dragonlance
Selûne	Forgotten Realms
Yondalla	Halfling

DOMAIN SPELLS
1st-level Twilight Domain feature

You gain domain spells at the cleric levels listed in the Twilight Domain Spells table. See the Divine Domain class feature for how domain spells work.

TWILIGHT DOMAIN SPELLS

Cleric Level	Spells
1st	*faerie fire, sleep*
3rd	*moonbeam, see invisibility*
5th	*aura of vitality, Leomund's tiny hut*
7th	*aura of life, greater invisibility*
9th	*circle of power, mislead*

BONUS PROFICIENCIES
1st-level Twilight Domain feature

You gain proficiency with martial weapons and heavy armor.

HUMAN CLERIC OF TWILIGHT

EYES OF NIGHT
1st-level Twilight Domain feature

You can see through the deepest gloom. You have darkvision out to a range of 300 feet. In that radius, you can see in dim light as if it were bright light and in darkness as if it were dim light.

As an action, you can magically share the darkvision of this feature with willing creatures you can see within 10 feet of you, up to a number of creatures equal to your Wisdom modifier (minimum of one creature). The shared darkvision lasts for 1 hour. Once you share it, you can't do so again until you finish a long rest, unless you expend a spell slot of any level to share it again.

Vigilant Blessing

1st-level Twilight Domain feature

The night has taught you to be vigilant. As an action, you give one creature you touch (including possibly yourself) advantage on the next initiative roll the creature makes. This benefit ends immediately after the roll or if you use this feature again.

Channel Divinity: Twilight Sanctuary

2nd-level Twilight Domain feature

You can use your Channel Divinity to refresh your allies with soothing twilight.

As an action, you present your holy symbol, and a sphere of twilight emanates from you. The sphere is centered on you, has a 30-foot radius, and is filled with dim light. The sphere moves with you, and it lasts for 1 minute or until you are incapacitated or die. Whenever a creature (including you) ends its turn in the sphere, you can grant that creature one of these benefits:

- You grant it temporary hit points equal to 1d6 plus your cleric level.
- You end one effect on it causing it to be charmed or frightened.

Steps of Night

6th-level Twilight Domain feature

You can draw on the mystical power of night to rise into the air. As a bonus action when you are in dim light or darkness, you can magically give yourself a flying speed equal to your walking speed for 1 minute. You can use this bonus action a number of times equal to your proficiency bonus, and you regain all expended uses when you finish a long rest.

Divine Strike

8th-level Twilight Domain feature

You gain the ability to infuse your weapon strikes with divine energy. Once on each of your turns when you hit a creature with a weapon attack, you can cause the attack to deal an extra 1d8 radiant damage. When you reach 14th level, the extra damage increases to 2d8.

Twilight Shroud

17th-level Twilight Domain feature

The twilight that you summon offers a protective embrace: you and your allies have half cover while in the sphere created by your Twilight Sanctuary.

DRUID

The druid class receives new features and subclasses in this section.

OPTIONAL CLASS FEATURES

You gain class features in the *Player's Handbook* when you reach certain levels in your class. This section offers additional features that you can gain as a druid. Unlike the features in the *Player's Handbook*, you don't gain the features here automatically. Consulting with your DM, you decide whether to gain a feature in this section if you meet the level requirement noted in the feature's description. These features can be selected separately from one another; you can use some, all, or none of them.

ADDITIONAL DRUID SPELLS

1st-level druid feature

The spells in the following list expand the druid spell list in the *Player's Handbook*. The list is organized by spell level, not character level. If a spell can be cast as a ritual, the ritual tag appears after the spell's name. Each spell is in the *Player's Handbook*, unless it has an asterisk (a spell in chapter 3). *Xanathar's Guide to Everything* also offers more spells.

1ST LEVEL
Protection from evil and good

2ND LEVEL
Augury (ritual)
Continual flame
Enlarge/reduce
Summon beast*

3RD LEVEL
Aura of vitality
Elemental weapon
Revivify
Summon fey*

4TH LEVEL
Divination (ritual)
Fire shield
Summon elemental*

5TH LEVEL
Cone of cold

6TH LEVEL
Flesh to stone

7TH LEVEL
Symbol

8TH LEVEL
Incendiary cloud

WILD COMPANION

2nd-level druid feature

You gain the ability to summon a spirit that assumes an animal form: as an action, you can expend a use of your Wild Shape feature to cast the *find familiar* spell, without material components.

DRUID WITH WILD COMPANION

When you cast the spell in this way, the familiar is a fey instead of a beast, and the familiar disappears after a number of hours equal to half your druid level.

CANTRIP VERSATILITY

4th-level druid feature

Whenever you reach a level in this class that grants the Ability Score Improvement feature, you can replace one cantrip you learned from this class's Spellcasting feature with another cantrip from the druid spell list.

DRUID CIRCLES

At 2nd level, a druid gains the Druid Circle feature, which offers you the choice of a subclass. The following options are available to you when making that choice: Circle of Spores, Circle of Stars, and Circle of Wildfire.

CIRCLE OF SPORES

> I'm an avid collector of spores, molds, and fungi—my most prized find being a sapiens zuggtmata from the depths of Mount Zogon. I wouldn't want it steering a corpse around and touching my stuff, though.
>
> TASHA

Druids of the Circle of Spores find beauty in decay. They see within mold and other fungi the ability to transform lifeless material into abundant, albeit somewhat strange, life. These druids believe that life and death are parts of a grand cycle, with one leading to the other and then back again. Death isn't the end of life, but instead a change of state that sees life shift into a new form.

Druids of this circle have a complex relationship with the undead. They see nothing inherently wrong with undeath, which they consider to be a companion to life and death. But these druids believe that the natural cycle is healthiest when each segment of it is vibrant and changing. Undead that seek to replace all life with undeath, or that try to avoid passing to a final rest, violate the cycle and must be thwarted.

CIRCLE SPELLS

2nd-level Circle of Spores feature

Your symbiotic link to fungi and your ability to tap into the cycle of life and death grants you access to certain spells. At 2nd level, you learn the *chill touch* cantrip.

At 3rd, 5th, 7th, and 9th level you gain access to the spells listed for that level in the Circle of Spores Spells table. Once you gain access to one of these spells, you always have it prepared, and it doesn't count against the number of spells you can prepare each day. If you gain access to a spell that doesn't appear on the druid spell list, the spell is nonetheless a druid spell for you.

CIRCLE OF SPORES SPELLS

Druid Level	Spells
2nd	*chill touch*
3rd	*blindness/deafness, gentle repose*
5th	*animate dead, gaseous form*
7th	*blight, confusion*
9th	*cloudkill, contagion*

HALO OF SPORES

2nd-level Circle of Spores feature

You are surrounded by invisible, necrotic spores that are harmless until you unleash them on a creature nearby. When a creature you can see moves into a space within 10 feet of you or starts its turn there, you can use your reaction to deal 1d4 necrotic damage to that creature unless it succeeds on a Constitution saving throw against your spell save DC. The necrotic damage increases to 1d6 at 6th level, 1d8 at 10th level, and 1d10 at 14th level.

KIERAN YANNER

A GNOME DRUID OF SPORES PICKS MUSHROOMS
WITH HIS BULLYWUG ZOMBIE COMPANION.

SYMBIOTIC ENTITY
2nd-level Circle of Spores feature

You gain the ability to channel magic into your spores. As an action, you can expend a use of your Wild Shape feature to awaken those spores, rather than transforming into a beast form, and you gain 4 temporary hit points for each level you have in this class. While this feature is active, you gain the following benefits:

- When you deal your Halo of Spores damage, roll the damage die a second time and add it to the total.
- Your melee weapon attacks deal an extra 1d6 necrotic damage to any target they hit.

These benefits last for 10 minutes, until you lose all these temporary hit points, or until you use your Wild Shape again.

FUNGAL INFESTATION
6th-level Circle of Spores feature

Your spores gain the ability to infest a corpse and animate it. If a beast or a humanoid that is Small or Medium dies within 10 feet of you, you can use your reaction to animate it, causing it to stand up immediately with 1 hit point. The creature uses the Zombie stat block in the *Monster Manual*. It remains animate for 1 hour, after which time it collapses and dies.

In combat, the zombie's turn comes immediately after yours. It obeys your mental commands, and the only action it can take is the Attack action, making one melee attack.

You can use this feature a number of times equal to your Wisdom modifier (minimum of once), and you regain all expended uses of it when you finish a long rest.

SPREADING SPORES
10th-level Circle of Spores feature

You gain the ability to seed an area with deadly spores. As a bonus action while your Symbiotic Entity feature is active, you can hurl spores up to 30 feet away, where they swirl in a 10-foot cube for 1 minute. The spores disappear early if you use this feature again, if you dismiss them as a bonus action, or if your Symbiotic Entity feature is no longer active.

Whenever a creature moves into the cube or starts its turn there, that creature takes your Halo of Spores damage, unless the creature succeeds on a Constitution saving throw against your spell save DC. A creature can take this damage no more than once per turn.

While the cube of spores persists, you can't use your Halo of Spores reaction.

TIEFLING DRUID
OF STARS

FUNGAL BODY

14th-level Circle of Spores feature

The fungal spores in your body alter you: you can't be blinded, deafened, frightened, or poisoned, and any critical hit against you counts as a normal hit instead, unless you're incapacitated.

CIRCLE OF STARS

> What about the dark places between the stars? Don't you realize that's where the good stuff is?
>
> TASHA

The Circle of Stars allows druids to draw on the power of starlight. These druids have tracked heavenly patterns since time immemorial, discovering secrets hidden amid the constellations. By revealing and understanding these secrets, the Circle of the Stars seeks to harness the powers of the cosmos.

Many druids of this circle keep records of the constellations and the stars' effects on the world. Some groups document these observations at megalithic sites, which serve as enigmatic libraries of lore. These repositories might take the form of stone circles, pyramids, petroglyphs, and underground temples—any construction durable enough to protect the circle's sacred knowledge even against a great cataclysm.

STAR MAP

2nd-level Circle of the Stars feature

You've created a star chart as part of your heavenly studies. It is a Tiny object and can serve as a spell-casting focus for your druid spells. You determine its form by rolling on the Star Map table or by choosing one.

While holding this map, you have these benefits:

- You know the *guidance* cantrip.
- You have the *guiding bolt* spell prepared. It counts as a druid spell for you, and it doesn't count against the number of spells you can have prepared.
- You can cast *guiding bolt* without expending a spell slot. You can do so a number of times equal to your proficiency bonus, and you regain all expended uses when you finish a long rest.

If you lose the map, you can perform a 1-hour ceremony to magically create a replacement. This ceremony can be performed during a short or long rest, and it destroys the previous map.

STAR MAP

d6	Map Form
1	A scroll covered with depictions of constellations
2	A stone tablet with fine holes drilled through it
3	A speckled owlbear hide, tooled with raised marks
4	A collection of maps bound in an ebony cover
5	A crystal that projects starry patterns when placed before a light
6	Glass disks that depict constellations

STARRY FORM

2nd-level Circle of the Stars feature

As a bonus action, you can expend a use of your Wild Shape feature to take on a starry form, rather than transforming into a beast.

While in your starry form, you retain your game statistics, but your body becomes luminous; your joints glimmer like stars, and glowing lines connect them as on a star chart. This form sheds bright light in a 10-foot radius and dim light for an additional 10 feet. The form lasts for 10 minutes. It ends early if you dismiss it (no action required), are incapacitated, die, or use this feature again.

Whenever you assume your starry form, choose which of the following constellations glimmers on your body; your choice gives you certain benefits while in the form:

Archer. A constellation of an archer appears on you. When you activate this form, and as a bonus action on your subsequent turns while it lasts, you can make a ranged spell attack, hurling a luminous arrow that targets one creature within 60 feet of you. On a hit, the attack deals radiant damage equal to 1d8 + your Wisdom modifier.

Chalice. A constellation of a life-giving goblet appears on you. Whenever you cast a spell using a spell slot that restores hit points to a creature, you or another creature within 30 feet of you can regain hit points equal to 1d8 + your Wisdom modifier.

Dragon. A constellation of a wise dragon appears on you. When you make an Intelligence or a Wisdom check or a Constitution saving throw to maintain concentration on a spell, you can treat a roll of 9 or lower on the d20 as a 10.

COSMIC OMEN
6th-level Circle of the Stars feature

Whenever you finish a long rest, you can consult your Star Map for omens. When you do so, roll a die. Until you finish your next long rest, you gain access to a special reaction based on whether you rolled an even or an odd number on the die:

Weal (even). Whenever a creature you can see within 30 feet of you is about to make an attack roll, a saving throw, or an ability check, you can use your reaction to roll a d6 and add the number rolled to the total.

Woe (odd). Whenever a creature you can see within 30 feet of you is about to make an attack roll, a saving throw, or an ability check, you can use your reaction to roll a d6 and subtract the number rolled from the total.

You can use this reaction a number of times equal to your proficiency bonus, and you regain all expended uses when you finish a long rest.

TWINKLING CONSTELLATIONS
10th-level Circle of the Stars feature

The constellations of your Starry Form improve. The 1d8 of the Archer and the Chalice becomes 2d8, and while the Dragon is active, you have a flying speed of 20 feet and can hover.

Moreover, at the start of each of your turns while in your Starry Form, you can change which constellation glimmers on your body.

FULL OF STARS
14th-level Circle of the Stars feature

While in your Starry Form, you become partially incorporeal, giving you resistance to bludgeoning, piercing, and slashing damage.

CIRCLE OF WILDFIRE

> *I can't tell you how many times I've burned everything to the ground and started over.*
>
> TASHA

Druids within the Circle of Wildfire understand that destruction is sometimes the precursor of creation, such as when a forest fire promotes later growth. These druids bond with a primal spirit that harbors both destructive and creative power, allowing the druids to create controlled flames that burn away one thing but give life to another.

CIRCLE SPELLS
2nd-level Circle of Wildfire feature

You have formed a bond with a wildfire spirit, a primal being of creation and destruction. Your link with this spirit grants you access to some spells when you reach certain levels in this class, as shown on the Circle of Wildfire Spells table.

Once you gain access to one of these spells, you always have it prepared, and it doesn't count against the number of spells you can prepare each day. If you gain access to a spell that doesn't appear on the druid spell list, the spell is nonetheless a druid spell for you.

DWARF DRUID
OF WILDFIRE

CIRCLE OF WILDFIRE SPELLS

Druid Level	Spells
2nd	*burning hands, cure wounds*
3rd	*flaming sphere, scorching ray*
5th	*plant growth, revivify*
7th	*aura of life, fire shield*
9th	*flame strike, mass cure wounds*

SUMMON WILDFIRE SPIRIT
2nd-level Circle of Wildfire feature

You can summon the primal spirit bound to your soul. As an action, you can expend one use of your Wild Shape feature to summon your wildfire spirit, rather than assuming a beast form.

The spirit appears in an unoccupied space of your choice that you can see within 30 feet of you. Each creature within 10 feet of the spirit (other than you) when it appears must succeed on a Dexterity saving throw against your spell save DC or take 2d6 fire damage.

The spirit is friendly to you and your companions and obeys your commands. See this creature's game statistics in the Wildfire Spirit stat block, which uses your proficiency bonus (PB) in several places. You determine the spirit's appearance. Some spirits take the form of a humanoid figure made of gnarled branches covered in flame, while others look like beasts wreathed in fire.

WILDFIRE SPIRIT
Small elemental

Armor Class 13 (natural armor)
Hit Points 5 + five times your druid level
Speed 30 ft., fly 30 ft. (hover)

STR	DEX	CON	INT	WIS	CHA
10 (+0)	14 (+2)	14 (+2)	13 (+1)	15 (+2)	11 (+0)

Damage Immunities fire
Condition Immunities charmed, frightened, grappled, prone, restrained
Senses darkvision 60 ft., passive Perception 12
Languages understands the languages you speak
Challenge —   **Proficiency Bonus (PB)** equals your bonus

ACTIONS

Flame Seed. *Ranged Weapon Attack:* your spell attack modifier to hit, range 60 ft., one target you can see. *Hit:* 1d6 + PB fire damage.

Fiery Teleportation. The spirit and each willing creature of your choice within 5 feet of it teleport up to 15 feet to unoccupied spaces you can see. Then each creature within 5 feet of the space that the spirit left must succeed on a Dexterity saving throw against your spell save DC or take 1d6 + PB fire damage.

In combat, the spirit shares your initiative count, but it takes its turn immediately after yours. The only action it takes on its turn is the Dodge action, unless you take a bonus action on your turn to command it to take another action. That action can be one in its stat block or some other action. If you are incapacitated, the spirit can take any action of its choice, not just Dodge.

The spirit manifests for 1 hour, until it is reduced to 0 hit points, until you use this feature to summon the spirit again, or until you die.

ENHANCED BOND
6th-level Circle of Wildfire feature

The bond with your wildfire spirit enhances your destructive and restorative spells. Whenever you cast a spell that deals fire damage or restores hit points while your wildfire spirit is summoned, roll a d8, and you gain a bonus equal to the number rolled to one damage or healing roll of the spell.

In addition, when you cast a spell with a range other than self, the spell can originate from you or your wildfire spirit.

CAUTERIZING FLAMES
10th-level Circle of Wildfire feature

You gain the ability to turn death into magical flames that can heal or incinerate. When a Small or larger creature dies within 30 feet of you or your wildfire spirit, a harmless spectral flame springs forth in the dead creature's space and flickers there for 1 minute. When a creature you can see enters that space, you can use your reaction to extinguish the spectral flame there and either heal the creature or deal fire damage to it. The healing or damage equals 2d10 + your Wisdom modifier.

You can use this reaction a number of times equal to your proficiency bonus, and you regain all expended uses when you finish a long rest.

BLAZING REVIVAL
14th-level Circle of Wildfire feature

The bond with your wildfire spirit can save you from death. If the spirit is within 120 feet of you when you are reduced to 0 hit points and thereby fall unconscious, you can cause the spirit to drop to 0 hit points. You then regain half your hit points and immediately rise to your feet.

Once you use this feature, you can't use it again until you finish a long rest.

ROBSON MICHEL

FIGHTER

The fighter class receives new features and subclasses in this section.

OPTIONAL CLASS FEATURES

You gain class features in the *Player's Handbook* when you reach certain levels in your class. This section offers additional features that you can gain as a fighter. Unlike the features in the *Player's Handbook*, you don't gain the features here automatically. Consulting with your DM, you decide whether to gain a feature in this section if you meet the level requirement noted in the feature's description. These features can be selected separately from one another; you can use some, all, or none of them.

FIGHTING STYLE OPTIONS

1st-level fighter feature

When you choose a fighting style, the following styles are added to your list of options.

BLIND FIGHTING

You have blindsight with a range of 10 feet. Within that range, you can effectively see anything that isn't behind total cover, even if you're blinded or in darkness. Moreover, you can see an invisible creature within that range, unless the creature successfully hides from you.

INTERCEPTION

When a creature you can see hits a target, other than you, within 5 feet of you with an attack, you can use your reaction to reduce the damage the target takes by 1d10 + your proficiency bonus (to a minimum of 0 damage). You must be wielding a shield or a simple or martial weapon to use this reaction.

SUPERIOR TECHNIQUE

You learn one maneuver of your choice from among those available to the Battle Master archetype. If a maneuver you use requires your target to make a saving throw to resist the maneuver's effects, the saving throw DC equals 8 + your proficiency bonus + your Strength or Dexterity modifier (your choice).

You gain one superiority die, which is a d6 (this die is added to any superiority dice you have from another source). This die is used to fuel your maneuvers. A superiority die is expended when you use it. You regain your expended superiority dice when you finish a short or long rest.

A YOUNG FIGHTER SPARS WITH AN INSTRUCTOR.

Thrown Weapon Fighting

You can draw a weapon that has the thrown property as part of the attack you make with the weapon.

In addition, when you hit with a ranged attack using a thrown weapon, you gain a +2 bonus to the damage roll.

Unarmed Fighting

Your unarmed strikes can deal bludgeoning damage equal to 1d6 + your Strength modifier on a hit. If you aren't wielding any weapons or a shield when you make the attack roll, the d6 becomes a d8.

At the start of each of your turns, you can deal 1d4 bludgeoning damage to one creature grappled by you.

Martial Versatility

4th-level fighter feature

Whenever you reach a level in this class that grants the Ability Score Improvement feature, you can do one of the following, as you shift the focus of your martial practice:

- Replace a fighting style you know with another fighting style available to fighters.
- If you know any maneuvers from the Battle Master archetype, you can replace one maneuver you know with a different maneuver.

Maneuver Options

If you have access to maneuvers, the following maneuvers are added to the list of options available to you. Maneuvers are available to Battle Masters but also to characters who have a special feature like the Superior Technique fighting style or the Martial Adept feat.

Ambush

When you make a Dexterity (Stealth) check or an initiative roll, you can expend one superiority die and add the die to the roll, provided you aren't incapacitated.

Bait and Switch

When you're within 5 feet of a creature on your turn, you can expend one superiority die and switch places with that creature, provided you spend at least 5 feet of movement and the creature is willing and isn't incapacitated. This movement doesn't provoke opportunity attacks.

Roll the superiority die. Until the start of your next turn, you or the other creature (your choice) gains a bonus to AC equal to the number rolled.

Brace

When a creature you can see moves into the reach you have with the melee weapon you're wielding, you can use your reaction to expend one superiority die and make one attack against the creature, using that weapon. If the attack hits, add the superiority die to the weapon's damage roll.

Commanding Presence

When you make a Charisma (Intimidation), a Charisma (Performance), or a Charisma (Persuasion) check, you can expend one superiority die and add the superiority die to the ability check.

Grappling Strike

Immediately after you hit a creature with a melee attack on your turn, you can expend one superiority die and then try to grapple the target as a bonus action (see the *Player's Handbook* for rules on grappling). Add the superiority die to your Strength (Athletics) check.

Quick Toss

As a bonus action, you can expend one superiority die and make a ranged attack with a weapon that has the thrown property. You can draw the weapon as part of making this attack. If you hit, add the superiority die to the weapon's damage roll.

Tactical Assessment

When you make an Intelligence (Investigation), an Intelligence (History), or a Wisdom (Insight) check, you can expend one superiority die and add the superiority die to the ability check.

Martial Archetypes

At 3rd level, a fighter gains the Martial Archetype feature, which offers you the choice of a subclass. The following options are available to you when making that choice: Psi Warrior and Rune Knight.

Psi Warrior

> Brains over brawn? Mind over matter? These canny warriors rightly answer, "Why not both?"
>
> TASHA

Awake to the psionic power within, a Psi Warrior is a fighter who augments their physical might with psi-infused weapon strikes, telekinetic lashes, and barriers of mental force. Many githyanki train to become such warriors, as do some of the most disciplined high elves. In the world of Eberron, many young kalashtar dream of becoming Psi Warriors.

As a Psi Warrior, you might have honed your psionic abilities through solo discipline, unlocked it under the tutelage of a master, or refined it at an academy dedicated to wielding the mind's power as both weapon and shield.

PSIONIC POWER
3rd-level Psi Warrior feature

You harbor a wellspring of psionic energy within yourself. This energy is represented by your Psionic Energy dice, which are each a d6. You have a number of these dice equal to twice your proficiency bonus, and they fuel various psionic powers you have, which are detailed below.

Some of your powers expend the Psionic Energy die they use, as specified in a power's description, and you can't use a power if it requires you to use a die when your dice are all expended. You regain all your expended Psionic Energy dice when you finish a long rest. In addition, as a bonus action, you can regain one expended Psionic Energy die, but you can't do so again until you finish a short or long rest.

When you reach certain levels in this class, the size of your Psionic Energy dice increases: at 5th level (d8), 11th level (d10), and 17th level (d12).

The powers below use your Psionic Energy dice.

Protective Field. When you or another creature you can see within 30 feet of you takes damage, you can use your reaction to expend one Psionic Energy die, roll the die, and reduce the damage taken by the number rolled plus your Intelligence modifier (minimum reduction of 1), as you create a momentary shield of telekinetic force.

Psionic Strike. You can propel your weapons with psionic force. Once on each of your turns, immediately after you hit a target within 30 feet of you with an attack and deal damage to it with a weapon, you can expend one Psionic Energy die, rolling it and dealing force damage to the target equal to the number rolled plus your Intelligence modifier.

Telekinetic Movement. You can move an object or a creature with your mind. As an action, you target one loose object that is Large or smaller or one willing creature, other than yourself. If you can see the target and it is within 30 feet of you, you can move it up to 30 feet to an unoccupied space you can see. Alternatively, if it is a Tiny object, you can move it to or from your hand. Either way, you can move the target horizontally, vertically, or both. Once you take this action, you can't do so again until you finish a short or long rest, unless you expend a Psionic Energy die to take it again.

HIGH ELF
PSI WARRIOR

TELEKINETIC ADEPT
7th-level Psi Warrior feature

You have mastered new ways to use your telekinetic abilities, detailed below.

Psi-Powered Leap. As a bonus action, you can propel your body with your mind. You gain a flying speed equal to twice your walking speed until the end of the current turn. Once you take this bonus action, you can't do so again until you finish a short or long rest, unless you expend a Psionic Energy die to take it again.

Telekinetic Thrust. When you deal damage to a target with your Psionic Strike, you can force the target to make a Strength saving throw against a DC equal to 8 + your proficiency bonus + your Intelligence modifier. If the save fails, you can knock the target prone or move it up to 10 feet in any direction horizontally.

GUARDED MIND
10th-level Psi Warrior feature

The psionic energy flowing through you has bolstered your mind. You have resistance to psychic damage. Moreover, if you start your turn charmed or frightened, you can expend a Psionic Energy die and end every effect on yourself subjecting you to those conditions.

BULWARK OF FORCE
15th-level Psi Warrior feature

You can shield yourself and others with telekinetic force. As a bonus action, you can choose creatures, which can include you, that you can see within 30 feet of you, up to a number of creatures equal to your Intelligence modifier (minimum of one creature). Each of the chosen creatures is protected by half cover for 1 minute or until you're incapacitated.

Once you take this bonus action, you can't do so again until you finish a long rest, unless you expend a Psionic Energy die to take it again.

TELEKINETIC MASTER
18th-level Psi Warrior feature

Your ability to move creatures and objects with your mind is matched by few. You can cast the *telekinesis* spell, requiring no components, and your spellcasting ability for the spell is Intelligence. On each of your turns while you concentrate on the spell, including the turn when you cast it, you can make one attack with a weapon as a bonus action.

Once you cast the spell with this feature, you can't do so again until you finish a long rest, unless you expend a Psionic Energy die to cast it again.

RUNE KNIGHT

> You're researching ancient arts and drawing runes. It's okay to just say you want to be a witch!
>
> TASHA

Rune Knights enhance their martial prowess using the supernatural power of runes, an ancient practice that originated with giants. Rune cutters can be found among any family of giants, and you likely learned your methods first or second hand from such a mystical artisan. Whether you found the giant's work carved into a hill or cave, learned of the runes from a sage, or met the giant in person, you studied the giant's craft and learned how to apply magic runes to empower your equipment.

BONUS PROFICIENCIES
3rd-level Rune Knight feature

You gain proficiency with smith's tools, and you learn to speak, read, and write Giant.

RUNE CARVER
3rd-level Rune Knight feature

You can use magic runes to enhance your gear. You learn two runes of your choice, from among the runes described below, and each time you gain a level in this class, you can replace one rune you know with a different one from this feature. When you reach certain levels in this class, you learn additional runes, as shown in the Runes Known table.

RUNES KNOWN

Fighter Level	Number of Runes
3rd	2
7th	3
10th	4
15th	5

Whenever you finish a long rest, you can touch a number of objects equal to the number of runes you know, and you inscribe a different rune onto each of the objects. To be eligible, an object must be a weapon, a suit of armor, a shield, a piece of jewelry, or something else you can wear or hold in a hand. Your rune remains on an object until you finish a long rest, and an object can bear only one of your runes at a time.

The following runes are available to you when you learn a rune. If a rune has a level requirement, you must be at least that level in this class to learn the rune. If a rune requires a saving throw, your Rune Magic save DC equals 8 + your proficiency bonus + your Constitution modifier.

Cloud Rune. This rune emulates the deceptive magic used by some cloud giants. While wearing or carrying an object inscribed with this rune, you have advantage on Dexterity (Sleight of Hand) checks and Charisma (Deception) checks.

In addition, when you or a creature you can see within 30 feet of you is hit by an attack roll, you can use your reaction to invoke the rune and choose a different creature within 30 feet of you, other than the attacker. The chosen creature becomes the target of the attack, using the same roll. This magic can transfer the attack's effects regardless of the attack's range. Once you invoke this rune, you can't do so again until you finish a short or long rest.

Fire Rune. This rune's magic channels the masterful craftsmanship of great smiths. While wearing or carrying an object inscribed with this rune, your proficiency bonus is doubled for any ability check you make that uses your proficiency with a tool.

In addition, when you hit a creature with an attack using a weapon, you can invoke the rune to summon fiery shackles: the target takes an extra 2d6 fire damage, and it must succeed on a Strength saving throw or be restrained for 1 minute. While restrained by the shackles, the target takes 2d6 fire damage at the start of each of its turns. The target can repeat the saving throw at the end of each of its turns, banishing the shackles on a success. Once you invoke this rune, you can't do so again until you finish a short or long rest.

Frost Rune. This rune's magic evokes the might of those who survive in the wintry wilderness, such as frost giants. While wearing or carrying an object inscribed with this rune, you have advantage on Wisdom (Animal Handling) checks and Charisma (Intimidation) checks.

In addition, you can invoke the rune as a bonus action to increase your sturdiness. For 10 minutes, you gain a +2 bonus to all ability checks and saving throws that use Strength or Constitution. Once you invoke this rune, you can't do so again until you finish a short or long rest.

Stone Rune. This rune's magic channels the judiciousness associated with stone giants. While wearing or carrying an object inscribed with this rune, you have advantage on Wisdom (Insight) checks, and you have darkvision out to a range of 120 feet.

In addition, when a creature you can see ends its turn within 30 feet of you, you can use your reaction to invoke the rune and force the creature to make a Wisdom saving throw. Unless the save succeeds, the creature is charmed by you for 1 minute. While charmed in this way, the creature has a speed of 0 and is incapacitated, descending into a dreamy stupor. The creature repeats the saving throw at the end of each of its turns, ending the effect on a success. Once you invoke this rune, you can't do so again until you finish a short or long rest.

Hill Rune (7th Level or Higher). This rune's magic bestows a resilience reminiscent of a hill giant. While wearing or carrying an object that bears this rune, you have advantage on saving throws against being poisoned, and you have resistance against poison damage.

In addition, you can invoke the rune as a bonus action, gaining resistance to bludgeoning, piercing, and slashing damage for 1 minute. Once you invoke this rune, you can't do so again until you finish a short or long rest.

Storm Rune (7th Level or Higher). Using this rune, you can glimpse the future like a storm giant seer. While wearing or carrying an object inscribed with this rune, you have advantage on Intelligence (Arcana) checks, and you can't be surprised as long as you aren't incapacitated.

In addition, you can invoke the rune as a bonus action to enter a prophetic state for 1 minute or until you're incapacitated. Until the state ends, when you or another creature you can see within 60 feet of you makes an attack roll, a saving throw, or an ability check, you can use your reaction to cause the roll to have advantage or disadvantage. Once you invoke this rune, you can't do so again until you finish a short or long rest.

ORC RUNE KNIGHT

GIANT'S MIGHT
3rd-level Rune Knight feature

You have learned how to imbue yourself with the might of giants. As a bonus action, you magically gain the following benefits, which last for 1 minute:

- If you are smaller than Large, you become Large, along with anything you are wearing. If you lack the room to become Large, your size doesn't change.
- You have advantage on Strength checks and Strength saving throws.
- Once on each of your turns, one of your attacks with a weapon or an unarmed strike can deal an extra 1d6 damage to a target on a hit.

You can use this feature a number of times equal to your proficiency bonus, and you regain all expended uses of it when you finish a long rest.

RUNIC SHIELD
7th-level Rune Knight feature

You learn to invoke your rune magic to protect your allies. When another creature you can see within 60 feet of you is hit by an attack roll, you can use your reaction to force the attacker to reroll the d20 and use the new roll.

You can use this feature a number of times equal to your proficiency bonus, and you regain all expended uses when you finish a long rest.

GREAT STATURE
10th-level Rune Knight feature

The magic of your runes permanently alters you. When you gain this feature, roll 3d4. You grow a number of inches in height equal to the roll.

Moreover, the extra damage you deal with your Giant's Might feature increases to 1d8.

MASTER OF RUNES
15th-level Rune Knight feature

You can invoke each rune you know from your Rune Carver feature twice, rather than once, and you regain all expended uses when you finish a short or long rest.

RUNIC JUGGERNAUT
18th-level Rune Knight feature

You learn how to amplify your rune-powered transformation. As a result, the extra damage you deal with the Giant's Might feature increases to 1d10. Moreover, when you use that feature, your size can increase to Huge, and while you are that size, your reach increases by 5 feet.

BATTLE MASTER BUILDS

A Martial Archetype option in the *Player's Handbook*, the Battle Master showcases just how versatile a fighter can be. The suite of maneuvers you choose, when combined with a fighting style and feats, allows you to create a broad range of fighters, each with its own flavor and play style. Below are recommendations for how you might build a Battle Master to reflect various types of warriors.

Each of these builds contains suggested fighting styles, maneuvers, and feats. Those suggestions are from the *Player's Handbook*, except for the ones followed by an asterisk, which indicates an option introduced in this book.

ARCHER

Fighting Style: Archery
Maneuvers: Disarming Strike, Distracting Strike, Precision Attack
Feats: Sharpshooter

You prefer to deal with your enemies from afar, trusting in a well-placed arrow, javelin, or sling bullet to end a fight without a response. You rely on accuracy and probably subscribe to the axiom that "those who live by the sword die by the bow."

BODYGUARD

Fighting Style: Interception,* Protection
Maneuvers: Bait and Switch,* Disarming Attack, Goading Attack, Grappling Strike*
Feats: Alert, Observant, Sentinel, Tough

Love, money, or some other obligation motivates you to place your own body between harm and the one you're sworn to protect. You have honed the ability to sniff out potential threats and see your charge through dangerous situations.

BRAWLER

Fighting Style: Blind Fighting,* Two-Weapon Fighting, Unarmed Fighting*
Maneuvers: Ambush,* Disarming Attack, Feinting Attack, Pushing Attack, Trip Attack
Feats: Athlete, Durable, Grappler, Resilient, Shield Master, Tavern Brawler, Tough

When bottles start breaking and chairs start flying, you're in your element. You love a good scrap, and you've likely seen your share of them. You may or may not have formal training, and while others might call you a dirty fighter, you're still alive.

DUELIST

Fighting Style: Dueling, Two-Weapon Fighting
Maneuvers: Evasive Footwork, Feinting Attack, Lunging Attack, Parry, Precision Attack, Riposte
Feats: Defensive Duelist, Dual Wielder, Observant, Savage Attacker, Weapon Master

You regard the duel as a proud tradition, a test of skill and wits that brings honor to those who can defeat an enemy while respecting the art. Your search for improvement is a consuming passion, and you draw on the expertise of the masters who've come before you as you work to perfect your form.

GLADIATOR

Fighting Style: Defense, Two-Weapon Fighting
Maneuvers: Goading Attack, Menacing Attack, Sweeping Attack, Trip Attack
Feats: Athlete, Charger, Dual Wielder, Durable, Grappler, Savage Attacker, Tough, Weapon Master

You've fought to entertain crowds, whether for sport or as punishment. Along the way, you learned to use all manner of weapons to battle all kinds of adversaries. You're practical yet theatrical, and you know how to employ fear as an effective tool in a fight.

HOPLITE

Fighting Style: Defense, Thrown Weapon Fighting*
Maneuvers: Brace,* Lunging Attack, Parry, Precision Attack
Feats: Athlete, Grappler, Polearm Master, Sentinel, Shield Master

With spear and shield, you follow in the footsteps of the heroes of ages past. You rely on discipline and athleticism to overcome improbable odds. Whether fighting in ranks alongside your comrades or squaring off as a lone warrior, you're equal to the task.

LANCER

Fighting Style: Dueling
Maneuvers: Lunging Attack, Menacing Attack, Precision Attack, Pushing Attack
Feats: Heavy Armor Master, Mounted Combatant, Savage Attacker

When the cavalry is called in, that means you. You ride out to greet your enemy with the point of your weapon. As you charge, the ground trembles, and only the heaviest blows can deter you.

OUTRIDER

Fighting Style: Archery
Maneuvers: Ambush,* Distracting Strike, Goading Attack, Precision Attack, Quick Toss*
Feats: Alert, Crossbow Expert, Mounted Combatant, Observant, Sharpshooter

You find freedom in the saddle and a companion in your mount. A headlong charge into combat is a blunt instrument for oafs. You prefer mobility and range, opting to find advantageous positions that allow you to deal with foes at full gallop while evading the most dangerous threats.

PUGILIST

Fighting Style: Unarmed Fighting*
Maneuvers: Disarming Attack, Evasive Footwork, Grappling Strike,* Menacing Attack, Pushing Attack, Riposte, Trip Attack
Feats: Athlete, Durable, Grappler, Savage Attacker, Tavern Brawler

Where others rely on steel, you've got your fists. Whether through training or experience, you've developed a superior technique that can help you overcome an enemy in an up-close fight.

SHOCK TROOPER

Fighting Style: Great Weapon Fighting
Maneuvers: Menacing Attack, Pushing Attack, Sweeping Attack
Feats: Charger, Great Weapon Master, Heavy Armor Master

SHOCK TROOPER

Subtlety is not your style. You're trained to get straight into the fighting, busting through enemy lines and applying tremendous pressure quickly. Those who ignore you in combat do so at their peril.

SKIRMISHER

Fighting Style: Archery, Thrown Weapon Fighting*
Maneuvers: Ambush,* Bait and Switch,* Distracting Strike, Quick Toss*
Feats: Alert, Dual Wielder, Mobile, Skulker

You thrive amid the chaos of battle. You use your mobility and versatility in combat to soften your adversaries and disrupt their formations. An enemy's plan rarely survives contact with you.

STRATEGIST

Fighting Style: Defense
Maneuvers: Commander's Strike, Commanding Presence,* Maneuvering Attack, Rally, Tactical Assessment*
Feats: Inspiring Leader, Keen Mind, Linguist

To you, battles unfold like a game of chess. You understand that strength and speed are important in a fight, but it takes intellect and experience to know how best to apply them. That's where you come in.

MONK

The monk class receives new features and sub-classes in this section.

OPTIONAL CLASS FEATURES

You gain class features in the *Player's Handbook* when you reach certain levels in your class. This section offers additional features that you can gain as a monk. Unlike the features in the *Player's Handbook*, you don't gain the features here automatically. Consulting with your DM, you decide whether to gain a feature in this section if you meet the level requirement noted in the feature's description. These features can be selected separately from one another; you can use some, all, or none of them.

DEDICATED WEAPON

2nd-level monk feature

You train yourself to use a variety of weapons as monk weapons, not just simple melee weapons and shortswords. Whenever you finish a short or long rest, you can touch one weapon, focus your ki on it, and then count that weapon as a monk weapon until you use this feature again.

The chosen weapon must meet these criteria:

- The weapon must be a simple or martial weapon.
- You must be proficient with it.
- It must lack the heavy and special properties.

KI-FUELED ATTACK

3rd-level monk feature

If you spend 1 ki point or more as part of your action on your turn, you can make one attack with an unarmed strike or a monk weapon as a bonus action before the end of the turn.

AN ORC MONK OF THE FOUR ELEMENTS
UNLEASHES A KI-FUELED ATTACK.

Quickened Healing

4th-level monk feature

As an action, you can spend 2 ki points and roll a Martial Arts die. You regain a number of hit points equal to the number rolled plus your proficiency bonus.

Focused Aim

5th-level monk feature

When you miss with an attack roll, you can spend 1 to 3 ki points to increase your attack roll by 2 for each of these ki points you spend, potentially turning the miss into a hit.

Monastic Traditions

At 3rd level, a monk gains the Monastic Tradition feature, which offers you the choice of a subclass. The following options are available to you when making that choice: Way of Mercy or Way of the Astral Self.

Way of Mercy

> Plague doctor—some looks never go out of style.
> TASHA

Monks of the Way of Mercy learn to manipulate the life force of others to bring aid to those in need. They are wandering physicians to the poor and hurt. However, to those beyond their help, they bring a swift end as an act of mercy.

Those who follow the Way of Mercy might be members of a religious order, administering to the needy and making grim choices rooted in reality rather than idealism. Some might be gentle-voiced healers, beloved by their communities, while others might be masked bringers of macabre mercies.

The walkers of this way usually don robes with deep cowls, and they often conceal their faces with masks, presenting themselves as the faceless bringers of life and death.

Implements of Mercy

3rd-level Way of Mercy feature

You gain proficiency in the Insight and Medicine skills, and you gain proficiency with the herbalism kit.

You also gain a special mask, which you often wear when using the features of this subclass. You determine its appearance, or generate it randomly by rolling on the Merciful Mask table.

WOOD ELF
MONK OF MERCY

Merciful Mask

d6	Mask Appearance
1	Raven
2	Blank and white
3	Crying visage
4	Laughing visage
5	Skull
6	Butterfly

Hand of Healing

3rd-level Way of Mercy feature

Your mystical touch can mend wounds. As an action, you can spend 1 ki point to touch a creature and restore a number of hit points equal to a roll of your Martial Arts die + your Wisdom modifier.

When you use your Flurry of Blows, you can replace one of the unarmed strikes with a use of this feature without spending a ki point for the healing.

HAND OF HARM
3rd-level Way of Mercy feature

You use your ki to inflict wounds. When you hit a creature with an unarmed strike, you can spend 1 ki point to deal extra necrotic damage equal to one roll of your Martial Arts die + your Wisdom modifier. You can use this feature only once per turn.

PHYSICIAN'S TOUCH
6th-level Way of Mercy feature

You can administer even greater cures with a touch, and if you feel it's necessary, you can use your knowledge to cause harm.

When you use Hand of Healing on a creature, you can also end one disease or one of the following conditions affecting the creature: blinded, deafened, paralyzed, poisoned, or stunned.

When you use Hand of Harm on a creature, you can subject that creature to the poisoned condition until the end of your next turn.

FLURRY OF HEALING AND HARM
11th-level Way of Mercy feature

You can now mete out a flurry of comfort and hurt. When you use Flurry of Blows, you can now replace each of the unarmed strikes with a use of your Hand of Healing, without spending ki points for the healing.

In addition, when you make an unarmed strike with Flurry of Blows, you can use Hand of Harm with that strike without spending the ki point for Hand of Harm. You can still use Hand of Harm only once per turn.

HAND OF ULTIMATE MERCY
17th-level Way of Mercy feature

Your mastery of life energy opens the door to the ultimate mercy. As an action, you can touch the corpse of a creature that died within the past 24 hours and expend 5 ki points. The creature then returns to life, regaining a number of hit points equal to 4d10 + your Wisdom modifier. If the creature died while subject to any of the following conditions, it revives with them removed: blinded, deafened, paralyzed, poisoned, and stunned.

Once you use this feature, you can't use it again until you finish a long rest.

WAY OF THE ASTRAL SELF

> Note to self: create a spell that lets you throat-punch people with your ghost.
>
> TASHA

A monk who follows the Way of the Astral Self believes their body is an illusion. They see their ki as a representation of their true form, an astral self. This astral self has the capacity to be a force of order or disorder, with some monasteries training students to use their power to protect the weak and other instructing aspirants in how to manifest their true selves in service to the mighty.

ARMS OF THE ASTRAL SELF
3rd-level Way of the Astral Self feature

Your mastery of your ki allows you to summon a portion of your astral self. As a bonus action, you can spend 1 ki point to summon the arms of your astral self. When you do so, each creature of your choice that you can see within 10 feet of you must succeed on a Dexterity saving throw or take force damage equal to two rolls of your Martial Arts die.

For 10 minutes, these spectral arms hover near your shoulders or surround your arms (your choice). You determine the arms' appearance, and they vanish early if you are incapacitated or die.

While the spectral arms are present, you gain the following benefits:

- You can use your Wisdom modifier in place of your Strength modifier when making Strength checks and Strength saving throws.
- You can use the spectral arms to make unarmed strikes.
- When you make an unarmed strike with the arms on your turn, your reach for it is 5 feet greater than normal.
- The unarmed strikes you make with the arms can use your Wisdom modifier in place of your Strength or Dexterity modifier for the attack and damage rolls, and their damage type is force.

VISAGE OF THE ASTRAL SELF
6th-level Way of the Astral Self feature

You can summon the visage of your astral self. As a bonus action, or as part of the bonus action you take to activate Arms of the Astral Self, you can spend 1 ki point to summon this visage for 10 minutes. It vanishes early if you are incapacitated or die.

The spectral visage covers your face like a helmet or mask. You determine its appearance.

While the spectral visage is present, you gain the following benefits.

Astral Sight. You can see normally in darkness, both magical and nonmagical, to a distance of 120 feet.

Wisdom of the Spirit. You have advantage on Wisdom (Insight) and Charisma (Intimidation) checks.

Word of the Spirit. When you speak, you can direct your words to a creature of your choice that you can see within 60 feet of you, making it so only that creature can hear you. Alternatively, you can amplify your voice so that all creatures within 600 feet can hear you.

BODY OF THE ASTRAL SELF
11th-level Way of the Astral Self feature

When you have both your astral arms and visage summoned, you can cause the body of your astral self to appear (no action required). This spectral body covers your physical form like a suit of armor, connecting with the arms and visage. You determine its appearance.

While the spectral body is present, you gain the following benefits.

Deflect Energy. When you take acid, cold, fire, force, lightning, or thunder damage, you can use your reaction to deflect it. When you do so, the damage you take is reduced by 1d10 + your Wisdom modifier (minimum reduction of 1).

Empowered Arms. Once on each of your turns when you hit a target with the Arms of the Astral Self, you can deal extra damage to the target equal to your Martial Arts die.

AWAKENED ASTRAL SELF
17th-level Way of the Astral Self feature

Your connection to your astral self is complete, allowing you to unleash its full potential. As a bonus action, you can spend 5 ki points to summon the arms, visage, and body of your astral self and awaken it for 10 minutes. This awakening ends early if you are incapacitated or die.

While your astral self is awakened, you gain the following benefits.

> ### FORMS OF YOUR ASTRAL SELF
> The astral self is a translucent embodiment of the monk's soul. As a result, an astral self can reflect aspects of a monk's background, ideals, flaws, and bonds, and an astral self doesn't necessarily look anything like the monk. For example, the astral self of a lanky human might be reminiscent of a minotaur—the strength of which the monk feels within. Similarly, an orc monk might manifest gossamer arms and a delicate visage, representing the gentle beauty of the orc's soul. Each astral self is unique, and some of the monks of this monastic tradition are known more for the appearance of their astral self than for their physical appearance.
>
> When choosing this path, consider the quirks that define your monk. Are you obsessed with something? Are you driven by justice or a selfish desire? Any of these motivations could manifest in the form of your astral self.

Armor of the Spirit. You gain a +2 bonus to Armor Class.

Astral Barrage. Whenever you use the Extra Attack feature to attack twice, you can instead attack three times if all the attacks are made with your astral arms.

DRAGONBORN MONK OF
THE ASTRAL SELF

PALADIN

The paladin class receives new features and subclasses in this section.

OPTIONAL CLASS FEATURES

You gain class features in the *Player's Handbook* when you reach certain levels in your class. This section offers additional features that you can gain as a paladin. Unlike the features in the *Player's Handbook*, you don't gain the features here automatically. Consulting with your DM, you decide whether to gain a feature in this section if you meet the level requirement noted in the feature's description. These features can be selected separately from one another; you can use some, all, or none of them.

ADDITIONAL PALADIN SPELLS

2nd-level paladin feature

The spells in the following list expand the paladin spell list in the *Player's Handbook*. The list is orga- nized by spell level, not character level. Each spell is in the *Player's Handbook*, unless it has an asterisk (a spell in chapter 3). *Xanathar's Guide to Every- thing* also offers more spells.

2ND LEVEL	3RD LEVEL
Gentle repose	Spirit shroud*
Prayer of healing	
Warding bond	5TH LEVEL
	Summon celestial*

FIGHTING STYLE OPTIONS

2nd-level paladin feature

When you choose a fighting style, the following styles are added to your list of options.

BLESSED WARRIOR

You learn two cantrips of your choice from the cleric spell list. They count as paladin spells for you, and Charisma is your spellcasting ability for them. Whenever you gain a level in this class, you can replace one of these cantrips with another cantrip from the cleric spell list.

BLIND FIGHTING

You have blindsight with a range of 10 feet. Within that range, you can effectively see anything that isn't behind total cover, even if you're blinded or in dark- ness. Moreover, you can see an invisible creature within that range, unless the creature successfully hides from you.

A YOUNG PALADIN SEEKS DIVINE GUIDANCE.

INTERCEPTION

When a creature you can see hits a target, other than you, within 5 feet of you with an attack, you can use your reaction to reduce the damage the target takes by 1d10 + your proficiency bonus (to a minimum of 0 damage). You must be wielding a shield or a simple or martial weapon to use this reaction.

HARNESS DIVINE POWER

3rd-level paladin feature

You can expend a use of your Channel Divinity to fuel your spells. As a bonus action, you touch your holy symbol, utter a prayer, and regain one expended spell slot, the level of which can be no higher than half your proficiency bonus (rounded up). The number of times you can use this feature is based on the level you've reached in this class: 3rd level, once; 7th level, twice; and 15th level, thrice. You regain all expended uses when you finish a long rest.

MARTIAL VERSATILITY

4th-level paladin feature

Whenever you reach a level in this class that grants the Ability Score Improvement feature, you can replace a fighting style you know with another fighting style available to paladins. This replacement represents a shift of focus in your martial practice.

SACRED OATHS

At 3rd level, a paladin gains the Sacred Oath feature, which offers you the choice of a subclass. The following options are available to you when making that choice: Oath of Glory and Oath of the Watchers.

OATH OF GLORY

> You. You're it. You're the winner of the cosmic fortune lottery. oh, and you're going to tell absolutely everyone all about it? Just great.
>
> TASHA

Paladins who take the Oath of Glory believe they and their companions are destined to achieve glory through deeds of heroism. They train diligently and encourage their companions so they're all ready when destiny calls.

TENETS OF GLORY

The tenets of the Oath of Glory drive a paladin to attempt heroics that might one day shine in legend.

Actions over Words. Strive to be known by glorious deeds, not words.

TIEFLING
PALADIN OF GLORY

Challenges Are but Tests. Face hardships with courage, and encourage your allies to face them with you.

Hone the Body. Like raw stone, your body must be worked so its potential can be realized.

Discipline the Soul. You must marshal the discipline to overcome failings within yourself that threaten to dim the glory of you and your friends.

OATH SPELLS

3rd-level Oath of Glory feature

You gain oath spells at the paladin levels listed in the Oath of Glory Spells table. See the Sacred Oath class feature for how oath spells work.

OATH OF GLORY SPELLS

Paladin Level	Spells
3rd	guiding bolt, heroism
5th	enhance ability, magic weapon
9th	haste, protection from energy
13th	compulsion, freedom of movement
17th	commune, flame strike

CHANNEL DIVINITY
3rd-level Oath of Glory feature

You gain the following two Channel Divinity options. See the Sacred Oath class feature for how Channel Divinity works.

Peerless Athlete. As a bonus action, you can use your Channel Divinity to augment your athleticism. For the next 10 minutes, you have advantage on Strength (Athletics) and Dexterity (Acrobatics) checks; you can carry, push, drag, and lift twice as much weight as normal; and the distance of your long and high jumps increases by 10 feet (this extra distance costs movement as normal).

Inspiring Smite. Immediately after you deal damage to a creature with your Divine Smite feature, you can use your Channel Divinity as a bonus action and distribute temporary hit points to creatures of your choice within 30 feet of you, which can include you. The total number of temporary hit points equals 2d8 + your level in this class, divided among the chosen creatures however you like.

AURA OF ALACRITY
7th-level Oath of Glory feature

You emanate an aura that fills you and your companions with supernatural speed, allowing you to race across a battlefield in formation. Your walking speed increases by 10 feet. In addition, if you aren't incapacitated, the walking speed of any ally who starts their turn within 5 feet of you increases by 10 feet until the end of that turn.

When you reach 18th level in this class, the range of the aura increases to 10 feet.

GLORIOUS DEFENSE
15th-level Oath of Glory feature

You can turn defense into a sudden strike. When you or another creature you can see within 10 feet of you is hit by an attack roll, you can use your reaction to grant a bonus to the target's AC against that attack, potentially causing it to miss. The bonus equals your Charisma modifier (minimum of +1). If the attack misses, you can make one weapon attack against the attacker as part of this reaction, provided the attacker is within your weapon's range.

You can use this feature a number of times equal to your Charisma modifier (minimum of once), and you regain all expended uses when you finish a long rest.

LIVING LEGEND
20th-level Oath of Glory feature

You can empower yourself with the legends—whether true or exaggerated—of your great deeds. As a bonus action, you gain the following benefits for 1 minute:

- You are blessed with an otherworldly presence, gaining advantage on all Charisma checks.
- Once on each of your turns when you make a weapon attack and miss, you can cause that attack to hit instead.
- If you fail a saving throw, you can use your reaction to reroll it. You must use this new roll.

Once you use this bonus action, you can't use it again until you finish a long rest, unless you expend a 5th-level spell slot to use it again.

OATH OF THE WATCHERS

These paladins aren't at all up to what I expected: Worse, they send home your party's best guests.

TASHA

The Oath of the Watchers binds paladins to protect mortal realms from the predations of extraplanar creatures, many of which can lay waste to mortal soldiers. Thus, the Watchers hone their minds, spirits, and bodies to be the ultimate weapons against such threats.

Paladins who follow the Watchers' oath are ever vigilant in spotting the influence of extraplanar forces, often establishing a network of spies and informants to gather information on suspected cults. To a Watcher, keeping a healthy suspicion and awareness about one's surroundings is as natural as wearing armor in battle.

TENETS OF THE WATCHERS
A paladin who assumes the Oath of the Watchers swears to safeguard mortal realms from otherworldly threats.

Vigilance. The threats you face are cunning, powerful, and subversive. Be ever alert for their corruption.

Loyalty. Never accept gifts or favors from fiends or those who truck with them. Stay true to your order, your comrades, and your duty.

Discipline. You are the shield against the endless terrors that lie beyond the stars. Your blade must be forever sharp and your mind keen to survive what lies beyond.

Oath Spells

3rd-level Oath of the Watchers feature

You gain oath spells at the paladin levels listed in the Oath of the Watchers table. See the Sacred Oath class feature for how oath spells work.

Oath of the Watchers Spells

Paladin Level	Spells
3rd	*alarm, detect magic*
5th	*moonbeam, see invisibility*
9th	*counterspell, nondetection*
13th	*aura of purity, banishment*
17th	*hold monster, scrying*

Channel Divinity

3rd-level Oath of the Watchers feature

You gain the following Channel Divinity options. See the Sacred Oath class feature for how Channel Divinity works.

Watcher's Will. You can use your Channel Divinity to invest your presence with the warding power of your faith. As an action, you can choose a number of creatures you can see within 30 feet of you, up to a number equal to your Charisma modifier (minimum of one creature). For 1 minute, you and the chosen creatures have advantage on Intelligence, Wisdom, and Charisma saving throws.

Abjure the Extraplanar. You can use your Channel Divinity to castigate unworldly beings. As an action, you present your holy symbol and each aberration, celestial, elemental, fey, or fiend within 30 feet of you that can hear you must make a Wisdom saving throw. On a failed save, the creature is turned for 1 minute or until it takes damage.

A turned creature must spend its turns trying to move as far away from you as it can, and it can't willingly end its move in a space within 30 feet of you. For its action, it can use only the Dash action or try to escape from an effect that prevents it from moving. If there's nowhere to move, the creature can take the Dodge action.

Aura of the Sentinel

7th-level Oath of the Watchers feature

You emit an aura of alertness while you aren't incapacitated. When you and any creatures of your choice within 10 feet of you roll initiative, you all gain a bonus to initiative equal to your proficiency bonus.

At 18th level, the range of this aura increases to 30 feet.

DWARF PALADIN OF THE WATCHERS

Vigilant Rebuke

15th-level Oath of the Watchers feature

You've learned how to chastise anyone who dares wield beguilements against you and your wards. Whenever you or a creature you can see within 30 feet of you succeeds on an Intelligence, a Wisdom, or a Charisma saving throw, you can use your reaction to deal 2d8 + your Charisma modifier force damage to the creature that forced the saving throw.

Mortal Bulwark

20th-level Oath of the Watchers feature

You manifest a spark of divine power in defense of the mortal realms. As a bonus action, you gain the following benefits for 1 minute:

- You gain truesight with a range of 120 feet.
- You have advantage on attack rolls against aberrations, celestials, elementals, fey, and fiends.
- When you hit a creature with an attack roll and deal damage to it, you can also force it to make a Charisma saving throw against your spell save DC. On a failed save, the creature is magically banished to its native plane of existence if it's currently not there. On a successful save, the creature can't be banished by this feature for 24 hours.

Once you use this bonus action, you can't use it again until you finish a long rest, unless you expend a 5th-level spell slot to use it again.

RANGER

The ranger class receives new features and subclasses in this section.

OPTIONAL CLASS FEATURES

You gain class features in the *Player's Handbook* when you reach certain levels in your class. This section offers additional features that you can gain as a ranger. Unlike the features in the *Player's Handbook*, you don't gain the features here automatically. Consulting with your DM, you decide whether to gain a feature in this section if you meet the level requirement noted in the feature's description. These features can be selected separately from one another; you can use some, all, or none of them.

If you take a feature that replaces another feature, you gain no benefit from the replaced one and don't qualify for anything in the game that requires it.

DEFT EXPLORER

1st-level ranger feature, which replaces the Natural Explorer feature

You are an unsurpassed explorer and survivor, both in the wilderness and in dealing with others on your travels. You gain the Canny benefit below, and you gain an additional benefit below when you reach 6th level and 10th level in this class.

CANNY (1ST LEVEL)

Choose one of your skill proficiencies. Your proficiency bonus is doubled for any ability check you make that uses the chosen skill.

You can also speak, read, and write two additional languages of your choice.

ROVING (6TH LEVEL)

Your walking speed increases by 5, and you gain a climbing speed and a swimming speed equal to your walking speed.

TIRELESS (10TH LEVEL)

As an action, you can give yourself a number of temporary hit points equal to 1d8 + your Wisdom modifier (minimum of 1 temporary hit point). You can use this action a number of times equal to your proficiency bonus, and you regain all expended uses when you finish a long rest.

In addition, whenever you finish a short rest, your exhaustion level, if any, is decreased by 1.

FAVORED FOE

1st-level ranger feature, which replaces the Favored Enemy feature and works with the Foe Slayer feature

When you hit a creature with an attack roll, you can call on your mystical bond with nature to mark the target as your favored enemy for 1 minute or until you lose your concentration (as if you were concentrating on a spell).

The first time on each of your turns that you hit the favored enemy and deal damage to it, including when you mark it, you can increase that damage by 1d4.

You can use this feature to mark a favored enemy a number of times equal to your proficiency bonus, and you regain all expended uses when you finish a long rest.

This feature's extra damage increases when you reach certain levels in this class: to 1d6 at 6th level and to 1d8 at 14th level.

A HALFLING RANGER
EXPLORES THE WILDS.

ZUZANNA WUZYK

ADDITIONAL RANGER SPELLS

2nd-level ranger feature

The spells in the following list expand the ranger spell list in the *Player's Handbook*. The list is organized by spell level, not character level. Each spell is in the *Player's Handbook*, unless it has an asterisk (a spell in chapter 3). *Xanathar's Guide to Everything* also offers more spells.

1st Level
Entangle
Searing smite

2nd Level
Aid
Enhance ability
Gust of wind
Magic weapon
Summon beast*

3rd Level
Elemental weapon
Meld into stone
Revivify
Summon fey*

4th Level
Dominate beast
Summon elemental*

5th Level
Greater restoration

FIGHTING STYLE OPTIONS

2nd-level ranger feature

When you choose a fighting style, the following styles are added to your list of options.

BLIND FIGHTING

You have blindsight with a range of 10 feet. Within that range, you can effectively see anything that isn't behind total cover, even if you're blinded or in darkness. Moreover, you can see an invisible creature within that range, unless the creature successfully hides from you.

DRUIDIC WARRIOR

You learn two cantrips of your choice from the druid spell list. They count as ranger spells for you, and Wisdom is your spellcasting ability for them. Whenever you gain a level in this class, you can replace one of these cantrips with another cantrip from the druid spell list.

THROWN WEAPON FIGHTING

You can draw a weapon that has the thrown property as part of the attack you make with the weapon.

In addition, when you hit with a ranged attack using a thrown weapon, you gain a +2 bonus to the damage roll.

SPELLCASTING FOCUS

2nd-level ranger feature

You can use a druidic focus as a spellcasting focus for your ranger spells. A druidic focus might be a sprig of mistletoe or holly, a wand or rod made of yew or another special wood, a staff drawn whole from a living tree, or an object incorporating feathers, fur, bones, and teeth from sacred animals.

PRIMAL AWARENESS

3rd-level ranger feature, which replaces the Primeval Awareness feature

You can focus your awareness through the interconnections of nature: you learn additional spells when you reach certain levels in this class if you don't already know them, as shown in the Primal Awareness Spells table. These spells don't count against the number of ranger spells you know.

PRIMAL AWARENESS SPELLS

Ranger Level	Spell
3rd	speak with animals
5th	beast sense
9th	speak with plants
13th	locate creature
17th	commune with nature

You can cast each of these spells once without expending a spell slot. Once you cast a spell in this way, you can't do so again until you finish a long rest.

MARTIAL VERSATILITY

4th-level ranger feature

Whenever you reach a level in this class that grants the Ability Score Improvement feature, you can replace a fighting style you know with another fighting style available to rangers. This replacement represents a shift of focus in your martial practice.

NATURE'S VEIL

10th-level ranger feature, which replaces the Hide in Plain Sight feature

You draw on the powers of nature to hide yourself from view briefly. As a bonus action, you can magically become invisible, along with any equipment you are wearing or carrying, until the start of your next turn.

You can use this feature a number of times equal to your proficiency bonus, and you regain all expended uses when you finish a long rest.

Human
Fey Wanderer

represents both the mortal and the fey realms. As you wander the multiverse, your joyful laughter brightens the hearts of the downtrodden, and your martial prowess strikes terror in your foes, for great is the mirth of the fey and dreadful is their fury.

Dreadful Strikes
3rd-level Fey Wanderer feature

You can augment your weapon strikes with mind-scarring magic, drawn from the gloomy hollows of the Feywild. When you hit a creature with a weapon, you can deal an extra 1d4 psychic damage to the target, which can take this extra damage only once per turn.

The extra damage increases to 1d6 when you reach 11th level in this class.

Fey Wanderer Magic
3rd-level Fey Wanderer feature

You learn an additional spell when you reach certain levels in this class, as shown in the Fey Wanderer Spells table. Each spell counts as a ranger spell for you, but it doesn't count against the number of ranger spells you know.

FEY WANDERER SPELLS

Ranger Level	Spell
3rd	*charm person*
5th	*misty step*
9th	*dispel magic*
13th	*dimension door*
17th	*mislead*

You also possess a preternatural blessing from a fey ally or a place of fey power. Choose your blessing from the Feywild Gifts table or determine it randomly.

FEYWILD GIFTS

d6	Gift
1	Illusory butterflies flutter around you while you take a short or long rest.
2	Fresh, seasonal flowers sprout from your hair each dawn.
3	You faintly smell of cinnamon, lavender, nutmeg, or another comforting herb or spice.
4	Your shadow dances while no one is looking directly at it.
5	Horns or antlers sprout from your head.
6	Your skin and hair change color to match the season at each dawn.

RANGER ARCHETYPES

At 3rd level, a ranger gains the Ranger Archetype feature, which offers you the choice of a subclass. The following options are available to you when making that choice: the Fey Wanderer and the Swarmkeeper.

FEY WANDERER

> Do you think a kilt is a vital part of the fey wandering aesthetic? And if not, why are you so wrong?.
>
> TASHA

A fey mystique surrounds you, thanks to the boon of an archfey, the shining fruit you ate from a talking tree, the magic spring you swam in, or some other auspicious event. However you acquired your fey magic, you are now a Fey Wanderer, a ranger who

OTHERWORLDLY GLAMOUR
3rd-level Fey Wanderer feature

Your fey qualities give you a supernatural charm. As a result, whenever you make a Charisma check, you gain a bonus to the check equal to your Wisdom modifier (minimum of +1).

In addition, you gain proficiency in one of the following skills of your choice: Deception, Performance, or Persuasion.

BEGUILING TWIST
7th-level Fey Wanderer feature

The magic of the Feywild guards your mind. You have advantage on saving throws against being charmed or frightened.

In addition, whenever you or a creature you can see within 120 feet of you succeeds on a saving throw against being charmed or frightened, you can use your reaction to force a different creature you can see within 120 feet of you to make a Wisdom saving throw against your spell save DC. If the save fails, the target is charmed or frightened by you (your choice) for 1 minute. The target can repeat the saving throw at the end of each of its turns, ending the effect on itself on a successful save.

FEY REINFORCEMENTS
11th-level Fey Wanderer feature

The royal courts of the Feywild have blessed you with the assistance of fey beings: you know *summon fey* (a spell in chapter 3). It doesn't count against the number of ranger spells you know, and you can cast it without a material component. You can also cast it once without a spell slot, and you regain the ability to do so when you finish a long rest.

Whenever you start casting the spell, you can modify it so that it doesn't require concentration. If you do so, the spell's duration becomes 1 minute for that casting.

MISTY WANDERER
15th-level Fey Wanderer feature

You can slip in and out of the Feywild to move in a blink of an eye: you can cast *misty step* without expending a spell slot. You can do so a number of times equal to your Wisdom modifier (minimum of once), and you regain all expended uses when you finish a long rest.

In addition, whenever you cast *misty step*, you can bring along one willing creature you can see within 5 feet of you. That creature teleports to an unoccupied space of your choice within 5 feet of your destination space.

GNOME
SWARMKEEPER

SWARMKEEPER

> I love insects—organized, relentless, specialized little champions. And aligning their single-minded will with your own: beautiful. Just keep them out of my lab.
> TASHA

Feeling a deep connection to the environment around them, some rangers reach out through their magical connection to the world and bond with a swarm of nature spirits. The swarm becomes a potent force in battle, as well as helpful company for the ranger. Some Swarmkeepers are outcasts or hermits, keeping to themselves and their attendant swarms rather than dealing with the discomfort of others. Other Swarmkeepers enjoy building vibrant communities that work for the mutual benefit of all those they consider part of their swarm.

GATHERED SWARM
3rd-level Swarmkeeper feature

A swarm of intangible nature spirits has bonded itself to you and can assist you in battle. Until you die, the swarm remains in your space, crawling on you or flying and skittering around you within your space. You determine its appearance, or you generate its appearance by rolling on the Swarm Appearance table.

SWARM APPEARANCE

d4	Appearance
1	Swarming insects
2	Miniature twig blights
3	Fluttering birds
4	Playful pixies

Once on each of your turns, you can cause the swarm to assist you in one of the following ways, immediately after you hit a creature with an attack:

- The attack's target takes 1d6 piercing damage from the swarm.
- The attack's target must succeed on a Strength saving throw against your spell save DC or be moved by the swarm up to 15 feet horizontally in a direction of your choice.
- You are moved by the swarm 5 feet horizontally in a direction of your choice.

SWARMKEEPER MAGIC
3rd-level Swarmkeeper feature

You learn the *mage hand* cantrip if you don't already know it. When you cast it, the hand takes the form of your swarming nature spirits.

You also learn an additional spell of 1st level or higher when you reach certain levels in this class, as shown in the Swarmkeeper Spells table. Each spell counts as a ranger spell for you, but it doesn't count against the number of ranger spells you know.

SWARMKEEPER SPELLS

Ranger Level	Spell
3rd	*faerie fire, mage hand*
5th	*web*
9th	*gaseous form*
13th	*arcane eye*
17th	*insect plague*

> ### IT'S YOUR SWARM
> A Swarmkeeper's swarm and spells are reflections of the character's bond with nature spirits. Take the opportunity to describe the swarm and the ranger's magic in play. For example, when your ranger casts *gaseous form*, they might appear to melt into the swarm, instead of a cloud of mist, or the *arcane eye* spell could create an extension of your swarm that spies for you. Such descriptions don't change the effects of spells, but they are an exciting opportunity to explore your character's narrative through their class abilities. For more guidance on customizing spells, see the "Personalizing Spells" section in chapter 3.
>
> Also, remember that the swarm's appearance is yours to customize, and don't feel confined to a single appearance. Perhaps the spirits' look changes with the ranger's mood or with the seasons. You decide!

WRITHING TIDE
7th-level Swarmkeeper feature

You can condense part of your swarm into a focused mass that lifts you up. As a bonus action, you gain a flying speed of 10 feet and can hover. This effect lasts for 1 minute or until you are incapacitated.

You can use this feature a number of times equal to your proficiency bonus, and you regain all expended uses when you finish a long rest.

MIGHTY SWARM
11th-level Swarmkeeper feature

Your Gathered Swarm grows mightier in the following ways:

- The damage of Gathered Swarm increases to 1d8.
- If a creature fails its saving throw against being moved by Gathered Swarm, you can also cause the swarm to knock the creature prone.
- When you are moved by Gathered Swarm, it gives you half cover until the start of your next turn.

SWARMING DISPERSAL
15th-level Swarmkeeper feature

You can discorporate into your swarm, avoiding danger. When you take damage, you can use your reaction to give yourself resistance to that damage. You vanish into your swarm and then teleport to an unoccupied space that you can see within 30 feet of you, where you reappear with the swarm.

You can use this feature a number of times equal to your proficiency bonus, and you regain all expended uses when you finish a long rest.

BEAST MASTER COMPANIONS

The Beast Master in the *Player's Handbook* forms a mystical bond with an animal. As an alternative, a Beast Master can take the feature below to form a bond with a special primal beast instead.

PRIMAL COMPANION

3rd-level Beast Master feature, which replaces the Ranger's Companion feature

You magically summon a primal beast, which draws strength from your bond with nature. The beast is friendly to you and your companions and obeys your commands. Choose its stat block—Beast of the Land, Beast of the Sea, or Beast of the Sky—which uses your proficiency bonus (PB) in several places. You also determine the kind of animal the beast is, choosing a kind appropriate for the stat block. Whatever kind you choose, the beast bears primal markings, indicating its mystical origin.

In combat, the beast acts during your turn. It can move and use its reaction on its own, but the only action it takes is the Dodge action, unless you take a bonus action on your turn to command it to take another action. That action can be one in its stat block or some other action. You can also sacrifice one of your attacks when you take the Attack action to command the beast to take the Attack action. If you are incapacitated, the beast can take any action of its choice, not just Dodge.

If the beast has died within the last hour, you can use your action to touch it and expend a spell slot of 1st level or higher. The beast returns to life after 1 minute with all its hit points restored.

When you finish a long rest, you can summon a different primal beast. The new beast appears in an unoccupied space within 5 feet of you, and you choose its stat block and appearance. If you already have a beast from this feature, it vanishes when the new beast appears. The beast also vanishes if you die.

BEAST OF THE LAND
Medium beast

Armor Class 13 + PB (natural armor)
Hit Points 5 + five times your ranger level (the beast has a number of Hit Dice [d8s] equal to your ranger level)
Speed 40 ft., climb 40 ft.

STR	DEX	CON	INT	WIS	CHA
14 (+2)	14 (+2)	15 (+2)	8 (−1)	14 (+2)	11 (+0)

Senses darkvision 60 ft., passive Perception 12
Languages understands the languages you speak
Challenge —   **Proficiency Bonus (PB)** equals your bonus

Charge. If the beast moves at least 20 feet straight toward a target and then hits it with a maul attack on the same turn, the target takes an extra 1d6 slashing damage. If the target is a creature, it must succeed on a Strength saving throw against your spell save DC or be knocked prone.

Primal Bond. You can add your proficiency bonus to any ability check or saving throw that the beast makes.

ACTIONS

Maul. *Melee Weapon Attack:* your spell attack modifier to hit, reach 5 ft., one target. *Hit:* 1d8 + 2 + PB slashing damage.

BEAST OF THE SEA
Medium beast

Armor Class 13 + PB (natural armor)
Hit Points 5 + five times your ranger level (the beast has a number of Hit Dice [d8s] equal to your ranger level)
Speed 5 ft., swim 60 ft.

STR	DEX	CON	INT	WIS	CHA
14 (+2)	14 (+2)	15 (+2)	8 (−1)	14 (+2)	11 (+0)

Senses darkvision 60 ft., passive Perception 12
Languages understands the languages you speak
Challenge —   **Proficiency Bonus (PB)** equals your bonus

Amphibious. The beast can breathe both air and water.

Primal Bond. You can add your proficiency bonus to any ability check or saving throw that the beast makes.

ACTIONS

Binding Strike. *Melee Weapon Attack:* your spell attack modifier to hit, reach 5 ft., one target. *Hit:* 1d6 + 2 + PB piercing or bludgeoning damage (your choice), and the target is grappled (escape DC equals your spell save DC). Until this grapple ends, the beast can't use this attack on another target.

BEAST OF THE SKY
Small beast

Armor Class 13 + PB (natural armor)
Hit Points 4 + four times your ranger level (the beast has a number of Hit Dice [d6s] equal to your ranger level)
Speed 10 ft., fly 60 ft.

STR	DEX	CON	INT	WIS	CHA
6 (−2)	16 (+3)	13 (+1)	8 (−1)	14 (+2)	11 (+0)

Senses darkvision 60 ft., passive Perception 12
Languages understands the languages you speak
Challenge —   **Proficiency Bonus (PB)** equals your bonus

Flyby. The beast doesn't provoke opportunity attacks when it flies out of an enemy's reach.

Primal Bond. You can add your proficiency bonus to any ability check or saving throw that the beast makes.

ACTIONS

Shred. *Melee Weapon Attack:* your spell attack modifier to hit, reach 5 ft., one target. *Hit:* 1d4 + 3 + PB slashing damage.

ROGUE

The rogue class receives new features and subclasses in this section.

OPTIONAL CLASS FEATURE

You gain class features in the *Player's Handbook* when you reach certain levels in your class. This section offers an additional feature that you can gain as a rogue. Unlike the features in the *Player's Handbook*, you don't gain the feature here automatically. Consulting with your DM, you decide whether to gain the feature in this section if you meet the level requirement noted in the feature's description.

STEADY AIM

3rd-level rogue feature

As a bonus action, you give yourself advantage on your next attack roll on the current turn. You can use this bonus action only if you haven't moved during this turn, and after you use the bonus action, your speed is 0 until the end of the current turn.

A DROW ROGUE
TAKES AIM.

ROGUISH ARCHETYPES

At 3rd level, a rogue gains the Roguish Archetype feature, which offers you the choice of a subclass. The following options are available to you when making that choice: the Phantom and the Soulknife.

PHANTOM

> Collecting the souls of your defeated foes in everyday objects—what a good idea. Though, I'd probably need an encyclopedia to hold all my anti-admirers.
>
> TASHA

Many rogues walk a fine line between life and death, risking their own lives and taking the lives of others. While adventuring on that line, some rogues discover a mystical connection to death itself. These rogues take knowledge from the dead and become immersed in negative energy, eventually becoming like ghosts. Thieves' guilds value them as highly effective information gatherers and spies.

Many shadar-kai of the Shadowfell are masters of these macabre techniques, and some are willing to teach this path. In places like Thay in the Forgotten Realms and Karrnath in Eberron, where many necromancers practice their craft, a Phantom can become a wizard's confidant and right hand. In temples of gods of death, the Phantom might work as an agent to track down those who try to cheat death and to recover knowledge that might otherwise be lost to the grave.

How did you discover this grim power? Did you sleep in a graveyard and awaken to your new abilities? Or did you cultivate them in a temple or thieves' guild dedicated to a deity of death?

WHISPERS OF THE DEAD
3rd-level Phantom feature

Echoes of those who have died cling to you. Whenever you finish a short or long rest, you can choose one skill or tool proficiency that you lack and gain it, as a ghostly presence shares its knowledge with you. You lose this proficiency when you use this feature to choose a different proficiency that you lack.

WAILS FROM THE GRAVE
3rd-level Phantom feature

As you nudge someone closer to the grave, you can channel the power of death to harm someone else as well. Immediately after you deal your Sneak Attack damage to a creature on your turn, you can target a second creature that you can see within 30 feet of the first creature. Roll half the number of Sneak Attack dice for your level (round up), and the second creature takes necrotic damage equal to the roll's total, as wails of the dead sound around them for a moment.

You can use this feature a number of times equal to your proficiency bonus, and you regain all expended uses when you finish a long rest.

TOKENS OF THE DEPARTED
9th-level Phantom feature

When a life ends in your presence, you're able to snatch a token from the departing soul, a sliver of its life essence that takes physical form: as a reaction when a creature you can see dies within 30 feet of you, you can open your free hand and cause a Tiny trinket to appear there, a soul trinket. The DM determines the trinket's form or has you roll on the Trinkets table in the *Player's Handbook* to generate it.

You can have a maximum number of soul trinkets equal to your proficiency bonus, and you can't create one while at your maximum.

You can use soul trinkets in the following ways:

- While a soul trinket is on your person, you have advantage on death saving throws and Constitution saving throws, for your vitality is enhanced by the life essence within the object.
- When you deal Sneak Attack damage on your turn, you can destroy one of your soul trinkets that's on your person and then immediately use Wails from the Grave, without expending a use of that feature.
- As an action, you can destroy one of your soul trinkets, no matter where it's located. When you do so, you can ask the spirit associated with the trinket one question. The spirit appears to you and answers in a language it knew in life. It's under no obligation to be truthful, and it answers as concisely as possible, eager to be free. The spirit knows only what it knew in life, as determined by the DM.

GHOST WALK
13th-level Phantom feature

You can phase partially into the realm of the dead, becoming like a ghost. As a bonus action, you assume a spectral form. While in this form, you have a flying speed of 10 feet, you can hover, and attack rolls have disadvantage against you. You can also move through creatures and objects as if they were difficult terrain, but you take 1d10 force damage if you end your turn inside a creature or an object.

You stay in this form for 10 minutes or until you end it as a bonus action. To use this feature again, you must finish a long rest or destroy one of your soul trinkets as part of the bonus action you use to activate Ghost Walk.

TIEFLING
PHANTOM

DEATH'S FRIEND
17th-level Phantom feature

Your association with death has become so close that you gain the following benefits:

- When you use your Wails from the Grave, you can deal the necrotic damage to both the first and the second creature.
- At the end of a long rest, a soul trinket appears in your hand if you don't have any soul trinkets, as the spirits of the dead are drawn to you.

SOULKNIFE

> I also have the ability to manifest my thoughts in ways that cut people. I call this power ... words.
>
> TASHA

Most assassins strike with physical weapons, and many burglars and spies use thieves' tools to infiltrate secure locations. In contrast, a Soulknife strikes and infiltrates with the mind, cutting through barriers both physical and psychic. These rogues discover psionic power within themselves and channel it to do their roguish work. They find easy employment as members of thieves' guilds,

HALFLING
SOULKNIFE

though they are often mistrusted by rogues who are leery of anyone using strange mind powers to conduct their business. Most governments would also be happy to employ a Soulknife as a spy.

Amid the trees of ancient forests on the Material Plane and in the Feywild, some wood elves walk the path of the Soulknife, serving as silent, lethal guardians of their woods. In the endless war among the gith, a githzerai is encouraged to become a Soulknife when stealth is required against the githyanki foe.

As a Soulknife, your psionic abilities might have haunted you since you were a child, only revealing their full potential as you experienced the stress of adventure. Or you might have sought out a reclusive order of psychic adepts and spent years learning how to manifest your power.

Psionic Power
3rd-level Soulknife feature

You harbor a wellspring of psionic energy within yourself. This energy is represented by your Psionic Energy dice, which are each a d6. You have a number of these dice equal to twice your proficiency bonus, and they fuel various psionic powers you have, which are detailed below.

Some of your powers expend the Psionic Energy die they use, as specified in a power's description, and you can't use a power if it requires you to use a die when your dice are all expended. You regain all your expended Psionic Energy dice when you finish a long rest. In addition, as a bonus action, you can regain one expended Psionic Energy die, but you can't do so again until you finish a short or long rest.

When you reach certain levels in this class, the size of your Psionic Energy dice increases: at 5th level (d8), 11th level (d10), and 17th level (d12).

The powers below use your Psionic Energy dice.

Psi-Bolstered Knack. When your nonpsionic training fails you, your psionic power can help: if you fail an ability check using a skill or tool with which you have proficiency, you can roll one Psionic Energy die and add the number rolled to the check, potentially turning failure into success. You expend the die only if the roll succeeds.

Psychic Whispers. You can establish telepathic communication between yourself and others—perfect for quiet infiltration. As an action, choose one or more creatures you can see, up to a number of creatures equal to your proficiency bonus, and then roll one Psionic Energy die. For a number of hours equal to the number rolled, the chosen creatures can speak telepathically with you, and you can speak telepathically with them. To send or receive a message (no action required), you and the other creature must be within 1 mile of each other. A creature can't use this telepathy if it can't speak any languages, and a creature can end the telepathic connection at any time (no action required). You and the creature don't need to speak a common language to understand each other.

The first time you use this power after each long rest, you don't expend the Psionic Energy die. All other times you use the power, you expend the die.

Psychic Blades
3rd-level Soulknife feature

You can manifest your psionic power as shimmering blades of psychic energy. Whenever you take the Attack action, you can manifest a psychic blade from your free hand and make the attack with that blade. This magic blade is a simple melee weapon with the finesse and thrown properties. It has a normal range of 60 feet and no long range, and on a hit, it deals psychic damage equal to 1d6 plus the ability modifier you used for the attack roll. The blade vanishes immediately after it hits or misses its target, and it leaves no mark on its target if it deals damage.

After you attack with the blade, you can make a melee or ranged weapon attack with a second psychic blade as a bonus action on the same turn, provided your other hand is free to create it. The damage die of this bonus attack is 1d4, instead of 1d6.

Soul Blades
9th-level Soulknife feature

Your Psychic Blades are now an expression of your psi-suffused soul, giving you these powers that use your Psionic Energy dice:

Homing Strikes. If you make an attack roll with your Psychic Blades and miss the target, you can roll one Psionic Energy die and add the number rolled to the attack roll. If this causes the attack to hit, you expend the Psionic Energy die.

Psychic Teleportation. As a bonus action, you manifest one of your Psychic Blades, expend one Psionic Energy die and roll it, and throw the blade at an unoccupied space you can see, up to a number of feet away equal to 10 times the number rolled. You then teleport to that space, and the blade vanishes.

Psychic Veil
13th-level Soulknife feature

You can weave a veil of psychic static to mask yourself. As an action, you can magically become invisible, along with anything you are wearing or carrying, for 1 hour or until you dismiss this effect (no action required). This invisibility ends early immediately after you deal damage to a creature or you force a creature to make a saving throw.

Once you use this feature, you can't do so again until you finish a long rest, unless you expend a Psionic Energy die to use this feature again.

Rend Mind
17th-level Soulknife feature

You can sweep your Psychic Blades directly through a creature's mind. When you use your Psychic Blades to deal Sneak Attack damage to a creature, you can force that target to make a Wisdom saving throw (DC equal to 8 + your proficiency bonus + your Dexterity modifier). If the save fails, the target is stunned for 1 minute. The stunned target can repeat the saving throw at the end of each of its turns, ending the effect on itself on a success.

Once you use this feature, you can't do so again until you finish a long rest, unless you expend three Psionic Energy dice to use it again.

Sorcerer

The sorcerer class receives new features and subclasses in this section.

Optional Class Features

You gain class features in the *Player's Handbook* when you reach certain levels in your class. This section offers additional features that you can gain as a sorcerer. Unlike the features in the *Player's Handbook*, you don't gain the features here automatically. Consulting with your DM, you decide whether to gain a feature in this section if you meet the level requirement noted in the feature's description. These features can be selected separately from one another; you can use some, all, or none of them.

Additional Sorcerer Spells
1st-level sorcerer feature

The spells in the following list expand the sorcerer spell list in the *Player's Handbook*. The list is organized by spell level, not character level. If a spell can be cast as a ritual, the ritual tag appears after the spell's name. Each spell is in the *Player's Handbook*, unless it has an asterisk (a spell in chapter 3). *Xanathar's Guide to Everything* also offers more spells.

Cantrip (0 Level)
*Booming blade**
*Green-flame blade**
*Lightning lure**
*Mind sliver**
*Sword burst**

1st Level
Grease
*Tasha's caustic brew**

2nd Level
Flame blade
Flaming sphere
Magic weapon
*Tasha's mind whip**

3rd Level
*Intellect fortress**
Vampiric touch

4th Level
Fire shield

5th Level
Bigby's hand

6th Level
Flesh to stone
Otiluke's freezing sphere
*Tasha's otherworldly guise**

7th Level
*Dream of the blue veil**

8th Level
Demiplane

9th Level
*Blade of disaster**

Metamagic Options

3rd-level sorcerer feature

When you choose Metamagic options, you have access to the following additional options.

Seeking Spell

If you make an attack roll for a spell and miss, you can spend 2 sorcery points to reroll the d20, and you must use the new roll.

You can use Seeking Spell even if you have already used a different Metamagic option during the casting of the spell.

Transmuted Spell

When you cast a spell that deals a type of damage from the following list, you can spend 1 sorcery point to change that damage type to one of the other listed types: acid, cold, fire, lightning, poison, thunder.

Sorcerous Versatility

4th-level sorcerer feature

Whenever you reach a level in this class that grants the Ability Score Improvement feature, you can do one of the following, representing the magic within you flowing in new ways:

- Replace one of the options you chose for the Metamagic feature with a different Metamagic option available to you.
- Replace one cantrip you learned from this class's Spellcasting feature with another cantrip from the sorcerer spell list.

Magical Guidance

5th-level sorcerer feature

You can tap into your inner wellspring of magic to try to conjure success from failure. When you make an ability check that fails, you can spend 1 sorcery point to reroll the d20, and you must use the new roll, potentially turning the failure into a success.

Sorcerous Origins

At 1st level, a sorcerer gains the Sorcerous Origin feature, which offers you the choice of a subclass. The following options are available to you when making that choice: the Aberrant Mind and the Clockwork Soul.

Aberrant Mind

> Tentacles, psychic powers, beings from beyond the stars—one person's bad dream is another person's good time.
>
> TASHA

An alien influence has wrapped its tendrils around your mind, giving you psionic power. You can now touch other minds with that power and alter the world around you by using it to control the magical energy of the multiverse. Will this power shine from you as a hopeful beacon to others? Or will you be a source of terror to those who feel the stab of your mind and witness the strange manifestations of your might?

A SORCERER USES TRANSMUTED SPELL.

KIERAN YANNER

As an Aberrant Mind sorcerer, you decide how you acquired your powers. Were you born with them? Or did an event later in life leave you shining with psionic awareness? Consult the Aberrant Origins table for a possible origin of your power.

Aberrant Origins

d6	Origin
1	You were exposed to the Far Realm's warping influence. You are convinced that a tentacle is now growing on you, but no one else can see it.
2	A psychic wind from the Astral Plane carried psionic energy to you. When you use your powers, faint motes of light sparkle around you.
3	You once suffered the dominating powers of an aboleth, leaving a psychic splinter in your mind.
4	You were implanted with a mind flayer tadpole, but the ceremorphosis never completed. And now its psionic power is yours. When you use it, your flesh shines with a strange mucus.
5	As a child, you had an imaginary friend that looked like a flumph or a strange platypus-like creature. One day, it gifted you with psionic powers, which have ended up being not so imaginary.
6	Your nightmares whisper the truth to you: your psionic powers are not your own. You draw them from your parasitic twin!

Psionic Spells
1st-level Aberrant Mind feature

You learn additional spells when you reach certain levels in this class, as shown on the Psionic Spells table. Each of these spells counts as a sorcerer spell for you, but it doesn't count against the number of sorcerer spells you know.

Whenever you gain a sorcerer level, you can replace one spell you gained from this feature with another spell of the same level. The new spell must be a divination or an enchantment spell from the sorcerer, warlock, or wizard spell list.

Psionic Spells

Sorcerer Level	Spells
1st	*arms of Hadar, dissonant whispers, mind sliver*
3rd	*calm emotions, detect thoughts*
5th	*hunger of Hadar, sending*
7th	*Evard's black tentacles, summon aberration* (a spell in chapter 3)
9th	*Rary's telepathic bond, telekinesis*

TIEFLING
ABERRANT MIND

Telepathic Speech
1st-level Aberrant Mind feature

You can form a telepathic connection between your mind and the mind of another. As a bonus action, choose one creature you can see within 30 feet of you. You and the chosen creature can speak telepathically with each other while the two of you are within a number of miles of each other equal to your Charisma modifier (minimum of 1 mile). To understand each other, you each must speak mentally in a language the other knows.

The telepathic connection lasts for a number of minutes equal to your sorcerer level. It ends early if you are incapacitated or die or if you use this ability to form a connection with a different creature.

PSIONIC SORCERY
6th-level Aberrant Mind feature

When you cast any spell of 1st level or higher from your Psionic Spells feature, you can cast it by expending a spell slot as normal or by spending a number of sorcery points equal to the spell's level. If you cast the spell using sorcery points, it requires no verbal or somatic components, and it requires no material components, unless they are consumed by the spell.

PSYCHIC DEFENSES
6th-level Aberrant Mind feature

You gain resistance to psychic damage, and you have advantage on saving throws against being charmed or frightened.

REVELATION IN FLESH
14th-level Aberrant Mind feature

You can unleash the aberrant truth hidden within yourself. As a bonus action, you can spend 1 or more sorcery points to magically transform your body for 10 minutes. For each sorcery point you spend, you can gain one of the following benefits of your choice, the effects of which last until the transformation ends:

- You can see any invisible creature within 60 feet of you, provided it isn't behind total cover. Your eyes also turn black or become writhing sensory tendrils.
- You gain a flying speed equal to your walking speed, and you can hover. As you fly, your skin glistens with mucus or shines with an otherworldly light.
- You gain a swimming speed equal to twice your walking speed, and you can breathe underwater. Moreover, gills grow from your neck or fan out from behind your ears, your fingers become webbed, or you grow writhing cilia that extend through your clothing.
- Your body, along with any equipment you are wearing or carrying, becomes slimy and pliable. You can move through any space as narrow as 1 inch without squeezing, and you can spend 5 feet of movement to escape from nonmagical restraints or being grappled.

WARPING IMPLOSION
18th-level Aberrant Mind feature

You can unleash your aberrant power as a space-warping anomaly. As an action, you can teleport to an unoccupied space you can see within 120 feet of you. Immediately after you disappear, each creature within 30 feet of the space you left must make a Strength saving throw. On a failed save, a creature takes 3d10 force damage and is pulled straight toward the space you left, ending in an unoccupied space as close to your former space as possible. On a successful save, the creature takes half as much damage and isn't pulled.

Once you use this feature, you can't do so again until you finish a long rest, unless you spend 5 sorcery points to use it again.

CLOCKWORK SOUL

I rarely tell people I speak Modron because, invariably, they just want to learn how to curse, so let's get this out of the way now.

Lesson one: "beep boop" and other slams.

TASHA

The cosmic force of order has suffused you with magic. That power arises from Mechanus or a realm like it—a plane of existence shaped entirely by clockwork efficiency. You, or someone from your lineage, might have become entangled in the machinations of the modrons, the orderly beings who inhabit Mechanus. Perhaps your ancestor even took part in the Great Modron March. Whatever its origin within you, the power of order can seem strange to others, but for you, it is part of a vast and glorious system.

CLOCKWORK MAGIC
1st-level Clockwork Soul feature

You learn additional spells when you reach certain levels in this class, as shown on the Clockwork Spells table. Each of these spells counts as a sorcerer spell for you, but it doesn't count against the number of sorcerer spells you know.

Whenever you gain a sorcerer level, you can replace one spell you gained from this feature with another spell of the same level. The new spell must be an abjuration or a transmutation spell from the sorcerer, warlock, or wizard spell list.

CLOCKWORK SPELLS

Sorcerer Level	Spells
1st	*alarm, protection from evil and good*
3rd	*aid, lesser restoration*
5th	*dispel magic, protection from energy*
7th	*freedom of movement, summon construct* (a spell in chapter 3)
9th	*greater restoration, wall of force*

In addition, consult the Manifestations of Order table and choose or randomly determine a way your connection to order manifests while you are casting any of your sorcerer spells.

MANIFESTATIONS OF ORDER

d6	Manifestation
1	Spectral cogwheels hover behind you.
2	The hands of a clock spin in your eyes.
3	Your skin glows with a brassy sheen.
4	Floating equations and geometric objects overlay your body.
5	Your spellcasting focus temporarily takes the form of a Tiny clockwork mechanism.
6	The ticking of gears or ringing of a clock can be heard by you and those affected by your magic.

RESTORE BALANCE
1st-level Clockwork Soul feature

Your connection to the plane of absolute order allows you to equalize chaotic moments. When a creature you can see within 60 feet of you is about to roll a d20 with advantage or disadvantage, you can use your reaction to prevent the roll from being affected by advantage and disadvantage.

You can use this feature a number of times equal to your proficiency bonus, and you regain all expended uses when you finish a long rest.

BASTION OF LAW
6th-level Clockwork Soul feature

You can tap into the grand equation of existence to imbue a creature with a shimmering shield of order. As an action, you can expend 1 to 5 sorcery points to create a magical ward around yourself or another creature you can see within 30 feet of you. The ward lasts until you finish a long rest or until you use this feature again.

The ward is represented by a number of d8s equal to the number of sorcery points spent to create it. When the warded creature takes damage, it can expend a number of those dice, roll them, and reduce the damage taken by the total rolled on those dice.

TRANCE OF ORDER
14th-level Clockwork Soul feature

You gain the ability to align your consciousness to the endless calculations of Mechanus. As a bonus action, you can enter this state for 1 minute. For the duration, attack rolls against you can't benefit from advantage, and whenever you make an attack roll, an ability check, or a saving throw, you can treat a roll of 9 or lower on the d20 as a 10.

Once you use this bonus action, you can't use it again until you finish a long rest, unless you spend 5 sorcery points to use it again.

HUMAN CLOCKWORK SOUL

CLOCKWORK CAVALCADE
18th-level Clockwork Soul feature

You summon spirits of order to expunge disorder around you. As an action, you summon the spirits in a 30-foot cube originating from you. The spirits look like modrons or other constructs of your choice. The spirits are intangible and invulnerable, and they create the following effects within the cube before vanishing:

- The spirits restore up to 100 hit points, divided as you choose among any number of creatures of your choice in the cube.
- Any damaged objects entirely in the cube are repaired instantly.
- Every spell of 6th level or lower ends on creatures and objects of your choice in the cube.

Once you use this action, you can't use it again until you finish a long rest, unless you spend 7 sorcery points to use it again.

WARLOCK

The warlock class receives new features and subclasses in this section.

OPTIONAL CLASS FEATURES

You gain class features in the *Player's Handbook* when you reach certain levels in your class. This section offers additional features that you can gain as a warlock. Unlike the features in the *Player's Handbook*, you don't gain the features here automatically. Consulting with your DM, you decide whether to gain a feature in this section if you meet the level requirement noted in the feature's description. These features can be selected separately from one another; you can use some, all, or none of them.

ADDITIONAL WARLOCK SPELLS

1st-level warlock feature

The spells in the following list expand the warlock spell list in the *Player's Handbook*. The list is organized by spell level, not character level. Each spell is in the *Player's Handbook*, unless it has an asterisk (a spell in chapter 3). *Xanathar's Guide to Everything* also offers more spells.

CANTRIP (0 LEVEL)
Booming blade*
Green-flame blade*
Lightning lure*
Mind sliver*
Sword burst*

3RD LEVEL
Intellect fortress*
Spirit shroud*
Summon fey*
Summon shadowspawn*
Summon undead*

4TH LEVEL
Summon aberration*

5TH LEVEL
Mislead
Planar binding
Teleportation circle

6TH LEVEL
Summon fiend*
Tasha's otherworldly guise*

7TH LEVEL
Dream of the blue veil*

9TH LEVEL
Blade of disaster*
Gate
Weird

PACT BOON OPTION

3rd-level warlock feature

When you choose your Pact Boon feature, the following option is available to you.

PACT OF THE TALISMAN

Your patron gives you an amulet, a talisman that can aid the wearer when the need is great. When the wearer fails an ability check, they can add a d4 to the roll, potentially turning the roll into a success. This benefit can be used a number of times equal to your proficiency bonus, and all expended uses are restored when you finish a long rest.

If you lose the talisman, you can perform a 1-hour ceremony to receive a replacement from your patron. This ceremony can be performed during a short or long rest, and it destroys the previous amulet. The talisman turns to ash when you die.

ELDRITCH VERSATILITY

4th-level warlock feature

Whenever you reach a level in this class that grants the Ability Score Improvement feature, you can do one of the following, representing a change of focus in your occult studies:

- Replace one cantrip you learned from this class's Pact Magic feature with another cantrip from the warlock spell list.
- Replace the option you chose for the Pact Boon feature with one of that feature's other options.
- If you're 12th level or higher, replace one spell from your Mystic Arcanum feature with another warlock spell of the same level.

If this change makes you ineligible for any of your Eldritch Invocations, you must also replace them now, choosing invocations for which you qualify.

ELDRITCH INVOCATION OPTIONS

When you choose eldritch invocations, you have access to these additional options.

BOND OF THE TALISMAN
Prerequisite: 12th-level warlock, Pact of the Talisman feature

While someone else is wearing your talisman, you can use your action to teleport to the unoccupied space closest to them, provided the two of you are on the same plane of existence. The wearer of your talisman can do the same thing, using their action to teleport to you. The teleportation can be used a number of times equal to your proficiency bonus, and all expended uses are restored when you finish a long rest.

Eldritch Mind

You have advantage on Constitution saving throws that you make to maintain your concentration on a spell.

Far Scribe

Prerequisite: 5th-level warlock, Pact of the Tome feature

A new page appears in your Book of Shadows. With your permission, a creature can use its action to write its name on that page, which can contain a number of names equal to your proficiency bonus.

You can cast the *sending* spell, targeting a creature whose name is on the page, without using a spell slot and without using material components. To do so, you must write the message on the page. The target hears the message in their mind, and if the target replies, their message appears on the page, rather than in your mind. The writing disappears after 1 minute.

As an action, you can magically erase a name on the page by touching it.

Gift of the Protectors

Prerequisite: 9th-level warlock, Pact of the Tome feature

A new page appears in your Book of Shadows. With your permission, a creature can use its action to write its name on that page, which can contain a number of names equal to your proficiency bonus.

When any creature whose name is on the page is reduced to 0 hit points but not killed outright, the creature magically drops to 1 hit point instead. Once this magic is triggered, no creature can benefit from it until you finish a long rest.

As an action, you can magically erase a name on the page by touching it.

Investment of the Chain Master

Prerequisite: Pact of the Chain feature

When you cast *find familiar*, you infuse the summoned familiar with a measure of your eldritch power, granting the creature the following benefits:

- The familiar gains either a flying speed or a swimming speed (your choice) of 40 feet.
- As a bonus action, you can command the familiar to take the Attack action.
- The familiar's weapon attacks are considered magical for the purpose of overcoming immunity and resistance to nonmagical attacks.
- If the familiar forces a creature to make a saving throw, it uses your spell save DC.
- When the familiar takes damage, you can use your reaction to grant it resistance against that damage.

A TIEFLING WARLOCK CALLS ON THE POWER OF HIS TALISMAN.

Protection of the Talisman

Prerequisite: 7th-level warlock, Pact of the Talisman feature

When the wearer of your talisman fails a saving throw, they can add a d4 to the roll, potentially turning the save into a success. This benefit can be used a number of times equal to your proficiency bonus, and all expended uses are restored when you finish a long rest.

Rebuke of the Talisman

Prerequisite: Pact of the Talisman feature

When the wearer of your talisman is hit by an attacker you can see within 30 feet of you, you can use your reaction to deal psychic damage to the attacker equal to your proficiency bonus and push it up to 10 feet away from the talisman's wearer.

Undying Servitude

Prerequisite: 5th-level warlock

You can cast *animate dead* without using a spell slot. Once you do so, you can't cast it in this way again until you finish a long rest.

HUMAN WARLOCK
OF THE FATHOMLESS

OTHERWORLDLY PATRONS

At 1st level, a warlock gains the Otherworldly Patron feature, which offers you the choice of a subclass. The following options are available to you when making that choice: the Fathomless and the Genie.

THE FATHOMLESS

> I never understood why some people get so jittery about tentacles. Have you ever had octopus nigiri? One of the few pieces of evidence of a benevolent multiverse.
>
> TASHA

You have plunged into a pact with the deeps. An entity of the ocean, the Elemental Plane of Water, or another otherworldly sea now allows you to draw on its thalassic power. Is it merely using you to learn about terrestrial realms, or does it want you to open cosmic floodgates and drown the world?

Perhaps you were born into a generational cult that venerates the Fathomless and its spawn. Or you might have been shipwrecked and on the brink of drowning when your patron's grasp offered you a chance at life. Whatever the reason for your pact, the sea and its unknown depths call to you.

Entities of the deep that might empower a warlock include krakens, ancient water elementals, godlike hallucinations dreamed into being by kuo-toa, merfolk demigods, and sea hag covens.

EXPANDED SPELL LIST
1st-level Fathomless feature

The Fathomless lets you choose from an expanded list of spells when you learn a warlock spell. The following spells are added to the warlock spell list for you.

FATHOMLESS EXPANDED SPELLS

Spell Level	Spells
1st	*create or destroy water, thunderwave*
2nd	*gust of wind, silence*
3rd	*lightning bolt, sleet storm*
4th	*control water, summon elemental* (water only; a spell in chapter 3)
5th	*Bigby's hand* (appears as a tentacle), *cone of cold*

TENTACLE OF THE DEEPS
1st-level Fathomless feature

You can magically summon a spectral tentacle that strikes at your foes. As a bonus action, you create a 10-foot-long tentacle at a point you can see within 60 feet of you. The tentacle lasts for 1 minute or until you use this feature to create another tentacle.

When you create the tentacle, you can make a melee spell attack against one creature within 10 feet of it. On a hit, the target takes 1d8 cold damage, and its speed is reduced by 10 feet until the start of your next turn. When you reach 10th level in this class, the damage increases to 2d8.

As a bonus action on your turn, you can move the tentacle up to 30 feet and repeat the attack.

You can summon the tentacle a number of times equal to your proficiency bonus, and you regain all expended uses when you finish a long rest.

GIFT OF THE SEA
1st-level Fathomless feature

You gain a swimming speed of 40 feet, and you can breathe underwater.

Oceanic Soul

6th-level Fathomless feature

You are now even more at home in the depths. You gain resistance to cold damage. In addition, when you are fully submerged, any creature that is also fully submerged can understand your speech, and you can understand theirs.

Guardian Coil

6th-level Fathomless feature

Your Tentacle of the Deeps can defend you and others, interposing itself between them and harm. When you or a creature you can see takes damage while within 10 feet of the tentacle, you can use your reaction to choose one of those creatures and reduce the damage to that creature by 1d8. When you reach 10th level in this class, the damage reduced by the tentacle increases to 2d8.

Grasping Tentacles

10th-level Fathomless feature

You learn the spell *Evard's black tentacles*. It counts as a warlock spell for you, but it doesn't count against the number of spells you know. You can also cast it once without a spell slot, and you regain the ability to do so when you finish a long rest.

Whenever you cast this spell, your patron's magic bolsters you, granting you a number of temporary hit points equal to your warlock level. Moreover, damage can't break your concentration on this spell.

Fathomless Plunge

14th-level Fathomless feature

You can magically open temporary conduits to watery destinations. As an action, you can teleport yourself and up to five other willing creatures that you can see within 30 feet of you. Amid a whirl of tentacles, you all vanish and then reappear up to 1 mile away in a body of water you've seen (pond size or larger) or within 30 feet of it, each of you appearing in an unoccupied space within 30 feet of the others.

Once you use this feature, you can't use it again until you finish a short or long rest.

The Genie

> I know finding housing in Greyhawk is rough, but when genies or warlocks offer you cheap rent, run.
>
> TASHA

You have made a pact with one of the rarest kinds of genie, a noble genie. Such entities rule vast fiefs on the Elemental Planes and have great influence over lesser genies and elemental creatures. Noble genies are varied in their motivations, but most are arrogant and wield power that rivals that of lesser deities. They delight in turning the table on mortals, who often bind genies into servitude, and readily enter into pacts that expand their reach.

You choose your patron's kind or determine it randomly, using the Genie Kind table.

Genie Kind

d4	Kind	Element
1	Dao	Earth
2	Djinni	Air
3	Efreeti	Fire
4	Marid	Water

Expanded Spell List

1st-level Genie feature

The Genie lets you choose from an expanded list of spells when you learn a warlock spell. The Genie Expanded Spells table shows the genie spells that are added to the warlock spell list for you, along with the spells associated in the table with your patron's kind: dao, djinni, efreeti, or marid.

Genie's Vessel

1st-level Genie feature

Your patron gifts you a magical vessel that grants you a measure of the genie's power. The vessel is a Tiny object, and you can use it as a spellcasting focus for your warlock spells. You decide what the object is, or you can determine what it is randomly by rolling on the Genie's Vessel table.

Genie Expanded Spells

Spell Level	Genie Spells	Dao Spells	Djinni Spells	Efreeti Spells	Marid Spells
1st	*detect evil and good*	*sanctuary*	*thunderwave*	*burning hands*	*fog cloud*
2nd	*phantasmal force*	*spike growth*	*gust of wind*	*scorching ray*	*blur*
3rd	*create food and water*	*meld into stone*	*wind wall*	*fireball*	*sleet storm*
4th	*phantasmal killer*	*stone shape*	*greater invisibility*	*fire shield*	*control water*
5th	*creation*	*wall of stone*	*seeming*	*flame strike*	*cone of cold*
9th	*wish*	—	—	—	—

A WARLOCK USES A GENIE'S VESSEL TO
BATTLE A CYCLOPS.

GENIE'S VESSEL

d6	Vessel
1	Oil lamp
2	Urn
3	Ring with a compartment
4	Stoppered bottle
5	Hollow statuette
6	Ornate lantern

While you are touching the vessel, you can use it in the following ways:

Bottled Respite. As an action, you can magically vanish and enter your vessel, which remains in the space you left. The interior of the vessel is an extradimensional space in the shape of a 20-foot-radius cylinder, 20 feet high, and resembles your vessel. The interior is appointed with cushions and low tables and is a comfortable temperature. While inside, you can hear the area around your vessel as if you were in its space. You can remain inside the vessel up to a number of hours equal to twice your proficiency bonus. You exit the vessel early if you use a bonus action to leave, if you die, or if the vessel is destroyed. When you exit the vessel, you appear in the unoccupied space closest to it. Any objects left in the vessel remain there until carried out, and if the vessel is destroyed, every object stored there harmlessly appears in the unoccupied spaces closest to the vessel's former space. Once you enter the vessel, you can't enter again until you finish a long rest.

Genie's Wrath. Once during each of your turns when you hit with an attack roll, you can deal extra damage to the target equal to your proficiency bonus. The type of this damage is determined by your patron: bludgeoning (dao), thunder (djinni), fire (efreeti), or cold (marid).

The vessel's AC equals your spell save DC. Its hit points equal your warlock level plus your proficiency bonus, and it is immune to poison and psychic damage.

ZUZANNA WUZYK

If the vessel is destroyed or you lose it, you can perform a 1-hour ceremony to receive a replacement from your patron. This ceremony can be performed during a short or long rest, and the previous vessel is destroyed if it still exists. The vessel vanishes in a flare of elemental power when you die.

ELEMENTAL GIFT
6th-level Genie feature

You begin to take on characteristics of your patron's kind. You now have resistance to a damage type determined by your patron's kind: bludgeoning (dao), thunder (djinni), fire (efreeti), or cold (marid).

In addition, as a bonus action, you can give yourself a flying speed of 30 feet that lasts for 10 minutes, during which you can hover. You can use this bonus action a number of times equal to your proficiency bonus, and you regain all expended uses when you finish a long rest.

SANCTUARY VESSEL
10th-level Genie feature

When you enter your Genie's Vessel via the Bottled Respite feature, you can now choose up to five willing creatures that you can see within 30 feet of you, and the chosen creatures are drawn into the vessel with you.

As a bonus action, you can eject any number of creatures from the vessel, and everyone is ejected if you leave or die or if the vessel is destroyed.

In addition, anyone (including you) who remains within the vessel for at least 10 minutes gains the benefit of finishing a short rest, and anyone can add your proficiency bonus to the number of hit points they regain if they spend any Hit Dice as part of a short rest there.

LIMITED WISH
14th-level Genie feature

You entreat your patron to grant you a small wish. As an action, you can speak your desire to your Genie's Vessel, requesting the effect of one spell that is 6th level or lower and has a casting time of 1 action. The spell can be from any class's spell list, and you don't need to meet the requirements in that spell, including costly components; the spell simply takes effect as part of this action.

Once you use this feature, you can't use it again until you finish 1d4 long rests.

WIZARD

The wizard class receives new features and subclasses in this section.

OPTIONAL CLASS FEATURES

You gain class features in the *Player's Handbook* when you reach certain levels in your class. This section offers additional features that you can gain as a wizard. Unlike the features in the *Player's Handbook*, you don't gain the features here automatically. Consulting with your DM, you decide whether to gain a feature in this section if you meet the level requirement noted in the feature's description. These features can be selected separately from one another; you can use some, all, or none of them.

ADDITIONAL WIZARD SPELLS

1st-level wizard feature

The spells in the following list expand the wizard spell list in the *Player's Handbook*. The list is organized by spell level, not character level. A spell's school of magic is noted, and if a spell can be cast as a ritual, the ritual tag appears after the spell's name. Each spell is in the *Player's Handbook*, unless it has an asterisk (a spell in chapter 3). *Xanathar's Guide to Everything* also offers more spells.

CANTRIP (0 LEVEL)
*Booming blade** (evoc.)
*Green-flame blade** (evoc.)
*Lightning lure** (evoc.)
*Mind sliver** (ench.)
*Sword burst** (conj.)

1ST LEVEL
*Tasha's caustic brew** (evoc.)

2ND LEVEL
Augury (divin., ritual)
Enhance ability (trans.)
*Tasha's mind whip** (ench.)

3RD LEVEL
*Intellect fortress** (abjur.)
Speak with dead (necro.)
*Spirit shroud** (necro.)
*Summon fey** (conj.)

*Summon shadow-
spawn** (conj.)
*Summon undead** (conj.)

4TH LEVEL
Divination (divin., ritual)
*Summon aberration** (conj.)
*Summon construct** (conj.)
*Summon elemental** (conj.)

6TH LEVEL
*Summon fiend** (conj.)
*Tasha's otherworldly
guise** (trans.)

7TH LEVEL
*Dream of the blue
veil** (conj.)

9TH LEVEL
*Blade of disaster** (conj.)

CANTRIP FORMULAS

3rd-level wizard feature

You have scribed a set of arcane formulas in your spellbook that you can use to formulate a cantrip in your mind. Whenever you finish a long rest and consult those formulas in your spellbook, you can replace one wizard cantrip you know with another cantrip from the wizard spell list.

ARCANE TRADITIONS

At 2nd level, a wizard gains the Arcane Tradition feature, which offers you the choice of a subclass. The following options are available to you when making that choice: Bladesinging and the Order of Scribes.

BLADESINGING

> When faced with the endless onslaught of magical possibilities, many wizards suffer identity crises. Some overcome, some break, and some become sword-bards.
> TASHA

Bladesingers master a tradition of wizardry that incorporates swordplay and dance. Originally created by elves, this tradition has been adopted by non-elf practitioners, who honor and expand on the elven ways.

In combat, a bladesinger uses a series of intricate, elegant maneuvers that fend off harm and allow the bladesinger to channel magic into devastating attacks and a cunning defense. Many who have observed a bladesinger at work remember the display as one of the more beautiful experiences in their life, a glorious dance accompanied by a singing blade.

TRAINING IN WAR AND SONG

2nd-level Bladesinging feature

You gain proficiency with light armor, and you gain proficiency with one type of one-handed melee weapon of your choice.

You also gain proficiency in the Performance skill if you don't already have it.

BLADESONG

2nd-level Bladesinging feature

You can invoke an elven magic called the Bladesong, provided that you aren't wearing medium or heavy armor or using a shield. It graces you with supernatural speed, agility, and focus.

You can use a bonus action to start the Bladesong, which lasts for 1 minute. It ends early if you are incapacitated, if you don medium or heavy armor or a shield, or if you use two hands to make an attack with a weapon. You can also dismiss the Bladesong at any time (no action required).

While your Bladesong is active, you gain the following benefits:

A DROW AND A HIGH ELF BLADESINGER

CAROLINE GARIBA

- You gain a bonus to your AC equal to your Intelligence modifier (minimum of +1).
- Your walking speed increases by 10 feet.
- You have advantage on Dexterity (Acrobatics) checks.
- You gain a bonus to any Constitution saving throw you make to maintain your concentration on a spell. The bonus equals your Intelligence modifier (minimum of +1).

You can use this feature a number of times equal to your proficiency bonus, and you regain all expended uses of it when you finish a long rest.

Extra Attack
6th-level Bladesinging feature

You can attack twice, instead of once, whenever you take the Attack action on your turn. Moreover, you can cast one of your cantrips in place of one of those attacks.

Song of Defense
10th-level Bladesinging feature

You can direct your magic to absorb damage while your Bladesong is active. When you take damage, you can use your reaction to expend one spell slot and reduce that damage to you by an amount equal to five times the spell slot's level.

Song of Victory
14th-level Bladesinging feature

You can add your Intelligence modifier (minimum of +1) to the damage of your melee weapon attacks while your Bladesong is active.

Order of Scribes

> Magic is great and all, but have you smelled a book?
> TASHA

Magic of the book—that's what many folk call wizardry. The name is apt, given how much time wizards spend poring over tomes and penning theories about the nature of magic. It's rare to see wizards traveling without books and scrolls sprouting from their bags, and a wizard would go to great lengths to plumb an archive of ancient knowledge.

Among wizards, the Order of Scribes is the most bookish. It takes many forms in different worlds, but its primary mission is the same everywhere: recording magical discoveries so that wizardry can flourish. And while all wizards value spellbooks, a wizard in the Order of Scribes magically awakens their book, turning it into a trusted companion. All wizards study books, but a wizardly scribe talks to theirs!

HUMAN WIZARD,
ORDER OF SCRIBES

Wizardly Quill
2nd-level Order of Scribes feature

As a bonus action, you can magically create a Tiny quill in your free hand. The magic quill has the following properties:

- The quill doesn't require ink. When you write with it, it produces ink in a color of your choice on the writing surface.
- The time you must spend to copy a spell into your spellbook equals 2 minutes per spell level if you use the quill for the transcription.
- You can erase anything you write with the quill if you wave the feather over the text as a bonus action, provided the text is within 5 feet of you.

This quill disappears if you create another one or if you die.

Awakened Spellbook
2nd-level Order of Scribes feature

Using specially prepared inks and ancient incantations passed down by your wizardly order, you have awakened an arcane sentience within your spellbook.

While you are holding the book, it grants you the following benefits:

- You can use the book as a spellcasting focus for your wizard spells.
- When you cast a wizard spell with a spell slot, you can temporarily replace its damage type with a type that appears in another spell in your spellbook, which magically alters the spell's formula for this casting only. The latter spell must be of the same level as the spell slot you expend.
- When you cast a wizard spell as a ritual, you can use the spell's normal casting time, rather than adding 10 minutes to it. Once you use this benefit, you can't do so again until you finish a long rest.

If necessary, you can replace the book over the course of a short rest by using your Wizardly Quill to write arcane sigils in a blank book or a magic spellbook to which you're attuned. At the end of the rest, your spellbook's consciousness is summoned into the new book, which the consciousness transforms into your spellbook, along with all its spells. If the previous book still existed somewhere, all the spells vanish from its pages.

Manifest Mind
6th-level Order of Scribes feature

You can conjure forth the mind of your Awakened Spellbook. As a bonus action while the book is on your person, you can cause the mind to manifest as a Tiny spectral object, hovering in an unoccupied space of your choice within 60 feet of you. The spectral mind is intangible and doesn't occupy its space, and it sheds dim light in a 10-foot radius. It looks like a ghostly tome, a cascade of text, or a scholar from the past (your choice).

While manifested, the spectral mind can hear and see, and it has darkvision with a range of 60 feet. The mind can telepathically share with you what it sees and hears (no action required).

Whenever you cast a wizard spell on your turn, you can cast it as if you were in the spectral mind's space, instead of your own, using its senses. You can do so a number of times per day equal to your proficiency bonus, and you regain all expended uses when you finish a long rest.

As a bonus action, you can cause the spectral mind to hover up to 30 feet to an unoccupied space that you or it can see. It can pass through creatures but not objects.

The spectral mind stops manifesting if it is ever more than 300 feet away from you, if someone casts *dispel magic* on it, if the Awakened Spellbook is destroyed, if you die, or if you dismiss the spectral mind as a bonus action.

Once you conjure the mind, you can't do so again until you finish a long rest, unless you expend a spell slot of any level to conjure it again.

Master Scrivener
10th-level Order of Scribes feature

Whenever you finish a long rest, you can create one magic scroll by touching your Wizardly Quill to a blank piece of paper or parchment and causing one spell from your Awakened Spellbook to be copied onto the scroll. The spellbook must be within 5 feet of you when you make the scroll.

The chosen spell must be of 1st or 2nd level and must have a casting time of 1 action. Once in the scroll, the spell's power is enhanced, counting as one level higher than normal. You can cast the spell from the scroll by reading it as an action. The scroll is unintelligible to anyone else, and the spell vanishes from the scroll when you cast it or when you finish your next long rest.

You are also adept at crafting *spell scrolls*, which are described in the treasure chapter of the *Dungeon Master's Guide*. The gold and time you must spend to make such a scroll are halved if you use your Wizardly Quill.

One with the Word
14th-level Order of Scribes feature

Your connection to your Awakened Spellbook has become so profound that your soul has become entwined with it. While the book is on your person, you have advantage on all Intelligence (Arcana) checks, as the spellbook helps you remember magical lore.

Moreover, if you take damage while your spellbook's mind is manifested, you can prevent all of that damage to you by using your reaction to dismiss the spectral mind, using its magic to save yourself. Then roll 3d6. The spellbook temporarily loses spells of your choice that have a combined spell level equal to that roll or higher. For example, if the roll's total is 9, spells vanish from the book that have a combined level of at least 9, which could mean one 9th-level spell, three 3rd-level spells, or some other combination. If there aren't enough spells in the book to cover this cost, you drop to 0 hit points.

Until you finish 1d6 long rests, you are incapable of casting the lost spells, even if you find them on a scroll or in another spellbook. After you finish the required number of rests, the spells reappear in the spellbook.

Once you use this reaction, you can't do so again until you finish a long rest.

FEATS

New feats are presented here in alphabetical order for groups that use them.

ARTIFICER INITIATE

You've learned some of an artificer's inventiveness:

- You learn one cantrip of your choice from the artificer spell list, and you learn one 1st-level spell of your choice from that list. Intelligence is your spellcasting ability for these spells.
- You can cast this feat's 1st-level spell without a spell slot, and you must finish a long rest before you can cast it in this way again. You can also cast the spell using any spell slots you have.
- You gain proficiency with one type of artisan's tools of your choice, and you can use that type of tool as a spellcasting focus for any spell you cast that uses Intelligence as its spellcasting ability.

CHEF

Time spent mastering the culinary arts has paid off, granting you the following benefits:

- Increase your Constitution or Wisdom score by 1, to a maximum of 20.
- You gain proficiency with cook's utensils if you don't already have it.
- As part of a short rest, you can cook special food, provided you have ingredients and cook's utensils on hand. You can prepare enough of this food for a number of creatures equal to 4 + your proficiency bonus. At the end of the short rest, any creature who eats the food and spends one or more Hit Dice to regain hit points regains an extra 1d8 hit points.
- With one hour of work or when you finish a long rest, you can cook a number of treats equal to your proficiency bonus. These special treats last 8 hours after being made. A creature can use a bonus action to eat one of those treats to gain temporary hit points equal to your proficiency bonus.

CRUSHER

You are practiced in the art of crushing your enemies, granting you the following benefits:

- Increase your Strength or Constitution by 1, to a maximum of 20.
- Once per turn, when you hit a creature with an attack that deals bludgeoning damage, you can move it 5 feet to an unoccupied space, provided the target is no more than one size larger than you.
- When you score a critical hit that deals bludgeoning damage to a creature, attack rolls against that creature are made with advantage until the start of your next turn.

ELDRITCH ADEPT

ELDRITCH ADEPT

Prerequisite: Spellcasting or Pact Magic feature

Studying occult lore, you have unlocked eldritch power within yourself: you learn one Eldritch Invocation option of your choice from the warlock class. If the invocation has a prerequisite of any kind, you can choose that invocation only if you're a warlock who meets the prerequisite.

Whenever you gain a level, you can replace the invocation with another one from the warlock class.

FEY TOUCHED

Your exposure to the Feywild's magic has changed you, granting you the following benefits:

- Increase your Intelligence, Wisdom, or Charisma score by 1, to a maximum of 20.
- You learn the *misty step* spell and one 1st-level spell of your choice. The 1st-level spell must be from the divination or enchantment school of magic. You can cast each of these spells without expending a spell slot. Once you cast either of these spells in this way, you can't cast that spell in this way again until you finish a long rest. You can

also cast these spells using spell slots you have of the appropriate level. The spells' spellcasting ability is the ability increased by this feat.

FIGHTING INITIATE

Prerequisite: Proficiency with a martial weapon

Your martial training has helped you develop a particular style of fighting. As a result, you learn one Fighting Style option of your choice from the fighter class. If you already have a style, the one you choose must be different.

Whenever you reach a level that grants the Ability Score Improvement feature, you can replace this feat's fighting style with another one from the fighter class that you don't have.

GUNNER

You have a quick hand and keen eye when employing firearms, granting you the following benefits:

- Increase your Dexterity score by 1, to a maximum of 20.
- You gain proficiency with firearms (see "Firearms" in the *Dungeon Master's Guide*).
- You ignore the loading property of firearms.
- Being within 5 feet of a hostile creature doesn't impose disadvantage on your ranged attack rolls.

METAMAGIC ADEPT

Prerequisite: Spellcasting or Pact Magic feature

You've learned how to exert your will on your spells to alter how they function:

- You learn two Metamagic options of your choice from the sorcerer class. You can use only one Metamagic option on a spell when you cast it, unless the option says otherwise. Whenever you reach a level that grants the Ability Score Improvement feature, you can replace one of these Metamagic options with another one from the sorcerer class.
- You gain 2 sorcery points to spend on Metamagic (these points are added to any sorcery points you have from another source but can be used only on Metamagic). You regain all spent sorcery points when you finish a long rest.

PIERCER

You have achieved a penetrating precision in combat, granting you the following benefits:

- Increase your Strength or Dexterity by 1, to a maximum of 20.
- Once per turn, when you hit a creature with an attack that deals piercing damage, you can reroll one of the attack's damage dice, and you must use the new roll.
- When you score a critical hit that deals piercing damage to a creature, you can roll one additional damage die when determining the extra piercing damage the target takes.

POISONER

You can prepare and deliver deadly poisons, granting you the following benefits:

- When you make a damage roll that deals poison damage, it ignores resistance to poison damage.
- You can apply poison to a weapon or piece of ammunition as a bonus action, instead of an action.
- You gain proficiency with the poisoner's kit if you don't already have it. With one hour of work using a poisoner's kit and expending 50 gp worth of materials, you can create a number of doses of potent poison equal to your proficiency bonus. Once applied to a weapon or piece of ammunition, the poison retains its potency for 1 minute or until you hit with the weapon or ammunition. When a creature takes damage from the coated weapon or ammunition, that creature must succeed on a DC 14 Constitution saving throw or take 2d8 poison damage and become poisoned until the end of your next turn.

SHADOW TOUCHED

Your exposure to the Shadowfell's magic has changed you, granting you the following benefits:

- Increase your Intelligence, Wisdom, or Charisma score by 1, to a maximum of 20.
- You learn the *invisibility* spell and one 1st-level spell of your choice. The 1st-level spell must be from the illusion or necromancy school of magic. You can cast each of these spells without expending a spell slot. Once you cast either of these spells in this way, you can't cast that spell in this way again until you finish a long rest. You can also cast these spells using spell slots you have of the appropriate level. The spells' spellcasting ability is the ability increased by this feat.

SKILL EXPERT

You have honed your proficiency with particular skills, granting you the following benefits:

- Increase one ability score of your choice by 1, to a maximum of 20.
- You gain proficiency in one skill of your choice.
- Choose one skill in which you have proficiency. You gain expertise with that skill, which means your proficiency bonus is doubled for any ability check you make with it. The skill you choose must be one that isn't already benefiting from a feature, such as Expertise, that doubles your proficiency bonus.

ZOLTAN BOROS

Slasher

You've learned where to cut to have the greatest results, granting you the following benefits:

- Increase your Strength or Dexterity by 1, to a maximum of 20.
- Once per turn when you hit a creature with an attack that deals slashing damage, you can reduce the speed of the target by 10 feet until the start of your next turn.
- When you score a critical hit that deals slashing damage to a creature, you grievously wound it. Until the start of your next turn, the target has disadvantage on all attack rolls.

Telekinetic

You learn to move things with your mind, granting you the following benefits:

- Increase your Intelligence, Wisdom, or Charisma score by 1, to a maximum of 20.
- You learn the *mage hand* cantrip. You can cast it without verbal or somatic components, and you can make the spectral hand invisible. If you already know this spell, its range increases by 30 feet when you cast it. Its spellcasting ability is the ability increased by this feat.

- As a bonus action, you can try to telekinetically shove one creature you can see within 30 feet of you. When you do so, the target must succeed on a Strength saving throw (DC 8 + your proficiency bonus + the ability modifier of the score increased by this feat) or be moved 5 feet toward you or away from you. A creature can willingly fail this save.

Telepathic

You awaken the ability to mentally connect with others, granting you the following benefits:

- Increase your Intelligence, Wisdom, or Charisma score by 1, to a maximum of 20.
- You can speak telepathically to any creature you can see within 60 feet of you. Your telepathic utterances are in a language you know, and the creature understands you only if it knows that language. Your communication doesn't give the creature the ability to respond to you telepathically.
- You can cast the *detect thoughts* spell, requiring no spell slot or components, and you must finish a long rest before you can cast it this way again. Your spellcasting ability for the spell is the ability increased by this feat. If you have spell slots of 2nd level or higher, you can cast this spell with them.

ASTRIDE A UNICORN, A TELEPATHIC BARD INSPIRES HER WIZARD COMPANION.

A GROUP OF WIZARDS PLEDGES
THEMSELVES TO THEIR PATRON,
TASHA, THE WITCH QUEEN.

CHAPTER 2
GROUP PATRONS

ACH ADVENTURING GROUP IS BOUND together by the quests it embarks on and by the dangers its members face together. This chapter offers another way to bind your party together: a group patron. These patrons provide a strong binding element: an individual or an organization that unites a party as a team in service to a greater purpose. A group patron can help set the tone of your party's entire campaign. For example, a group whose patron is an academic institution is likely to have a very different story from a group that serves a military. A patron can influence characters' relationships, their backstories, and the types of dangers they face.

During character creation, every player has the opportunity to weave connections between their character and the other members of their party. Rather than (or in addition to) creating a web of established relationships, players can work with the DM to choose a group patron. And if you're interested in being your own patron, see the "Being Your Own Patron" section at the end of the chapter.

How Patrons Work

The following sections present several group patron options. The description of each patron provides an overview of the types of organizations the group patron represents, perks of membership, and quests the patron encourages adventurers to undertake.

With the input of your DM, you can customize these patrons to reflect specific establishments in your campaign world or to serve as a launchpad tailored for organizations of your design. For example, the guild group patron could represent the Harpers or the Zhentarim of the Forgotten Realms, the Clifftop Adventurers' Guild in Eberron, or a homebrew league of caravan guards. Or perhaps a criminal syndicate, military force, or other category of patron better fits the party's goals. Choose and customize the group patron that works best for your party and the types of adventures you want to explore.

Group Assistance

Having a group patron gives an adventuring group a common purpose, which inspires better coordination in the form of guidance and encouragement. As a result of this unity, each member of the party can grant advantage to an ability check, an attack roll, or a saving throw of another member of the party. To grant advantage in this way, a character and the chosen target must be able to see or hear each other, and neither can be incapacitated. Once a party member grants this advantage, that individual can't do so again until they finish a long rest.

Perks

A group patron offers your party a number of perks for your service. These range from standard business arrangements, such as a steady wage and access to staff facilities, to extraordinary boons, such as audiences with powerful figures or exceptions from certain laws. Specific perks are presented in the description of each group patron.

The DM should not feel limited to providing only the perks noted in each group patron's description. Patrons give a party access to solutions and support they wouldn't have otherwise, and a patron can use their varied resources to guide their agents or prepare them for greater adventures.

Assignments

Your group's patron occasionally offers you an assignment, a mission that provides a springboard for adventure. Of course, it's up to you how you respond to your patron's demands, and interesting stories can result if you decide to refuse an assignment.

A more hands-off patron can still significantly motivate your group. Maybe you seek adventures based on what pleases your patron, possibly earning status and rewards within your organization. An academy, for example, might not organize particular missions, so you hunt down ancient artifacts knowing that your patron will reward you for bringing them back. You have the freedom to chart your own destiny, while letting the patron shape the nature of your group and the adventures you undertake.

Example Patrons

Here are some of the most likely patrons for an adventuring group. Presented in alphabetical order, these patrons can serve as inspiration for you to create patrons of your own:

Academy	Guild
Ancient Being	Military Force
Aristocrat	Religious Order
Criminal Syndicate	Sovereign

ACADEMY

The world's mysteries are innumerable, but you pursue them with vigor. As operatives for an academy, you seek to unravel the secrets of existence and the deeper riddles beyond.

In your work, you brush shoulders with the wisest in the land, travel to places spoken of in myth, and discover truths beyond imagining. Denying ignorance, you pursue wondrous sights and endlessly unearth new facts. Undiscovered creatures, the covetous dead, and jealous rivals impede your work, but in the pursuit of knowledge, no risk is too great.

TYPES OF ACADEMIES

Any assemblage of scholars and truth-seekers can function as an academy. Generally, an academy unites a network of learned individuals, allowing them to share their knowledge, further their research, and support common goals. Passing on wisdom to the next generation is part of an academy's mandate, but members find opportunities to undertake far-flung research expeditions—only so much can be learned in libraries, after all. An academy's focus can be broad or singular, artistic or scientific, mundane or magical. For every topic with unexplored possibilities, an academy seeks to plumb its depths or elevate its study.

Roll or pick from the Academy Type table to determine the institution with which you're aligned.

ACADEMY TYPE

d6	Academy Types
1	**Boarding School.** Students and faculty enjoy a familial relationship on a self-contained campus.
2	**Arcane Enclave.** Drawn together by cutting-edge magical scholarship, the enclave's residents are hungry for secrets, reagents, and subjects.
3	**Secret Monastery.** Ageless secrets remain the focus of contemplation and rigorous training at this site.
4	**Elite Institute.** This cutthroat college of science or the arts accepts only the crème de la crème of society and talent.
5	**Vault of Secrets.** This conspiracy strives to keep or eradicate all knowledge of a specific truth.
6	**Museum of Dreams.** Magical communication or shared dreamscapes connect a network of wide-ranging specialists.

WIZARDLY BOYFRIENDS RELAX WHILE THEIR CLASSMATES PRACTICE MAGIC AT AN ARCANE ENCLAVE

Academy Perks

With an academy as your group's patron, you gain the following perks.

Compensation. The academy pays for the work you do on its behalf. The nature of your employment influences your compensation. On average, the academy pays each member of your group 1 gp per day, or enough to sustain a modest lifestyle. Alternatively, you receive a bounty (at least 250 gp) for each artifact or relevant discovery you bring back from your adventures and donate to the academy.

Documentation. Each member of your group has identification denoting your affiliation with the academy. This association carries clout in scholarly or artistic circles. The academy also secures documentation, letters of introduction, and traveling papers if your work requires them. Such documents grant you special status, such as access to forbidden regions or neutral standing in embattled areas. Such identification isn't always a boon, though. In a land frequently plundered by foreigners, your documents could mark you as nothing more than aggrandized looters to some.

Research. Research is part of your group's job, but your patron also has abundant resources to facilitate such efforts. You can call in a favor to delegate the work of researching lore (a downtime activity described in the *Player's Handbook* and *Xanathar's Guide to Everything*) to a colleague, contact, librarian, or research assistant. You're responsible for covering expenses incurred as part of this research, and the DM determines its success or failure.

Resources. Academies host libraries, museums, record repositories, and training facilities, and you can use them to further your work. You can call in a favor from faculty members to access resources not available to the public—dangerous relics or magic items, spellbooks, gear, and the like. Additionally, you can consult with the faculty of your academy as the experts in various fields.

Training. Because you're associated with the academy, you receive a discount on any education you wish to pursue. When you undergo training as a downtime activity (as described in the *Player's Handbook* or *Xanathar's Guide to Everything*), you pay half the normal cost, assuming the academy teaches that subject. Training in languages, musical instruments, and other tools is also available, at the DM's discretion. In addition, you can gain proficiency in the Arcana, History, Nature, or Religion skills by this method, as if you were learning a language. A character can learn only one of these skills in this way.

Academy Contact

How much autonomy you have in choosing your missions and how often you're expected to perform on the academy's behalf depends largely on your place in the institution's hierarchy. As students, new professors, or support staff, you aid the work of a senior professor or entire department. If you are further along in your career, you have your own goals and assistants, but still take on assignments to further the goals of esteemed experts, deans, or the academy as a whole. In any of these cases, a specific contact manages your relationship to the academy.

Roll or pick from the Academy Contact table to determine who manages the relationship between you and the academy.

Academy Contact

d6	Contact
1	**Harried Functionary.** A disinterested secretary conveys written correspondence to you from an exceptionally busy or aloof senior faculty member.
2	**Celebrated Instructor.** Despite their throngs of ambitious assistants, a celebrity researcher considers you their star pupil.
3	**Wizened Fixture.** A fantastically old, believed-to-be-deceased librarian gives you assignments from the circulation desk they never leave.
4	**Infatuated Tourist.** A flirtatious visiting scholar perceives your every report and donated discovery as a personal gift.
5	**Spectral Fragment.** A haunted piece of the academy's collection compels you to complete its secret research.
6	**Distant Observer.** A mysterious sponsor encourages your research from afar to avoid alerting nefarious forces embedded within the academy's bureaucracy.

Academy Factotums

If you have an academy as your patron, you are likely engaged in a scholarly pursuit or support someone who is. Consider being a promising student or a new member of the faculty. While you have a modest course load that you handle behind the scenes (or using any of a variety of downtime activities), your primary interests involve aiding your contact in their research. Alternatively, you might work to further the academy's efforts in another way, perhaps related to security or funding.

The Academy Factotum Roles table provides suggestions for functions you perform within an academy and the backgrounds frequently associated with each role.

Academy Factotum Roles

Role	Backgrounds
Student	Acolyte, Guild Artisan, Noble, Outlander, Sage, Urchin
Groundskeeper	Charlatan, Hermit, Outlander, Soldier, Urchin
Professor	Acolyte, Entertainer, Folk Hero, Noble, Sage
Researcher	Acolyte, Charlatan, Guild Artisan, Hermit, Sage
Financier	Charlatan, Criminal, Noble, Sailor, Urchin
Expert Speaker	Any

Academy Quests

The focus of your study and the academy's research defines the missions you undertake. Academics struggle to keep one step ahead of their scholarly rivals, making many of them suspicious of—even hostile toward—other intellectuals. Beyond rivals within their own profession, academics face challenges from their subjects (whether members of lost civilizations or magical beings) or suspicious anti-intellectuals. Not everyone wants to be the subject of scholarly scrutiny or thinks that solving the world's mysteries is important or desirable.

The Academy Quests table presents a few of the sort of endeavors your work or studies lead you to undertake.

Academy Quests

d6	Quest
1	**Aberrant Zoology.** You undertake expeditions to document, capture, and explain beings antithetical to the natural order.
2	**Arcanodynamics.** You investigate the ways magic underpins existence, exploring its flows and seeking ways to harness its nexuses.
3	**Forbidden History.** You reveal the lost truths of the world's darkest ages, pursuing the history of purposefully hidden or taboo eras.
4	**Cryptogeography.** You search for proof of a hidden land or that the world isn't structured as commonly assumed.
5	**Restorative Antiquarianism.** You track clues leading to plundered artifacts and then restore them to their rightful owners.
6	**Evolutionary Divinity.** You dare to explore what no mortal was meant to know: the origins of divinity.

Ancient Being

> Any time an unfathomably powerful entity sweeps in and offers godlike rewards in return for just a few teensy favors, it's a scam.
>
> Unless it's me. I'd never lie to you, reader dearest.
>
> TASHA

Your group is bound to the designs of an ancient being of tremendous power and influence. You might serve as the creature's eyes and ears in the world, carrying information back to it. Or perhaps you work as its direct agents, enacting its will. Whether you chose this arrangement or were tricked into it, you can count on the strange resources of your benefactor as long as you serve its purpose.

Types of Ancient Beings

From brooding dragons to unfathomable voices whispering from the dark, ancient beings guide and empower mortals for inscrutable reasons. The relationship your group has to its patron might be a clearly defined exchange, or it could be uncertain or forceful. Whatever the nature of the being, as long as your group fulfills its role, the being offers rewards.

Roll or pick from the Ancient Being table to determine the being your group serves.

Ancient Being

d6	Ancient Being
1	**Elder Dragon.** An ancient dragon seeks knowledge or power. It wishes to gather greater wealth for its hoard, its ambitions expanding in its advancing years.
2	**Lich.** An undead spellcaster of immense power employs your group. Its interests are strangely diverse and seemingly benign. Perhaps it's not as evil as conventional adventuring wisdom suggests?
3	**Bound Fiend.** This fiend is bound to a location, either in its true form or as a possessing spirit. Whether trapped in an unbreakable circle of binding sigils or sealed as a spirit within a gigantic statue, the fiend's influence drives your group.
4	**Guardian Celestial.** An angel or another powerful celestial takes an interest in a specific region of the Material Plane. It cultivates a network of mortal informants and agents to serve its agenda.

d6	Ancient Being
5	**The Endless.** This person has lived many lifetimes because they can't die—at least not permanently. No matter the cause of their demise, they return. To all appearances, they are alive and mortal, but they control the amassed resources of an immortal.
6	**Primal Manifestation.** Its existence defies mortal understanding; the being simply is. It could be a primordial force of nature awakened to self-awareness that now inhabits the landscape or an alien intellect that whispers through proxies, omens, and idols.

AZALIN, THE LICH, SPIES ON CASTLE RAVENLOFT.

ANCIENT BEING PERKS

With the ancient being as your group's patron, you gain the following perks.

Equipment. Your patron's network has access to certain magic items. You can purchase common magic items from your patron contact. The DM determines the available stock or can call for a group Intelligence (Investigation) check to ascertain if the ancient being's network can successfully locate a desired item. The DC for this check is 10 in a city, 15 in a town, and 20 in a village. If the check fails, 1d8 days must pass before the same item can be searched for again in that community.

The DM sets the price of a common magic item or determines it randomly: 2d4 × 10 gp, or half as much for a consumable item such as a potion or scroll.

Research. Relying on an ancient being's network of contacts, the being's vast collection of lore, or perhaps the being's direct teaching helps you unearth hidden secrets. If you can contact your patron or their agents, your group makes ability checks made to research lore related to your patron's interests and influence with advantage.

Sanctuary. Your patron's agents have safe houses or other secure gatherings spread across a wide region. Your group knows how to locate these friendly enclaves and can maintain a modest lifestyle in one for no cost. In return, you must defend the sanctuary or protect the secret of its existence.

Strange Gifts. Your patron grants your group a small measure of esoteric power. At 5th level, and again at 13th, you gain one supernatural gift as described in the treasure chapter of the *Dungeon Master's Guide*. The DM determines which supernatural gifts are available.

ANCIENT BEING CONTACT

The organizational contact who dispenses assignments or delivers the word of your patron runs the gamut from prosaic to otherworldly. Roll or pick from the Ancient Being Contact table to determine who or what conveys your patron's will.

ANCIENT BEING CONTACT

d6	Contact
1	**Employer.** An established member of local society acts as the interface between you and the patron and provides the cover of legitimate employment. They could be a bartender, shopkeeper, local official, or noble.
2	**Back-Room Dealers.** An exclusive area in an otherwise-ordinary establishment requires a password or token to gain entry. There you meet and communicate with shadowy agents of your patron.

d6	Contact
3	**Magical Message Drop.** Magically recorded messages from your contact or your patron appear in odd places. You know to check a predetermined location, such as a crack in an ancient monolith or a specific grave, for instructions.
4	**Visions.** Your patron doesn't use intermediaries, instead speaking to you in dreams, omens, or visions. The being appears in your mind as you sleep, taking control of your dreams to deliver instructions that become difficult to ignore.
5	**Ephemeral Echo.** Your contact never physically reveals itself to you. Perhaps it is the ghost of a dead person, an entity that appears outside the flow of time, or a projected illusion of a being that never leaves your patron's hidden sanctum.
6	**The Mouthpiece.** The ancient being's voice whispers through the lips of an ordinary person. You patron might posses the body of a stranger or a party member to converse with you.

ANCIENT BEING OPERATIVES

Consider the overarching goals of your group's ancient being patron when determining who they recruit as agents. In what arenas does that being likely hold sway? A powerful lich recruits other ambitious spellcasters, as well as skilled warriors to serve as bodyguards. A dragon values socially adept agents and those who influence society's decision-makers. Consider how your capabilities and interests align directly with those of the ancient being, or how you unwittingly fell into the patron's service.

The Ancient Being Operative Roles table suggests a variety of parts you can play within an ancient being's schemes and the backgrounds frequently associated with each role.

ANCIENT BEING OPERATIVE ROLES

Role	Backgrounds
Devotee	Acolyte, Hermit, Noble, Outlander, Sage
Infiltrator	Charlatan, Criminal, Hermit, Soldier, Urchin
Mouthpiece	Charlatan, Entertainer, Folk Hero, Hermit, Sage
Pupil	Acolyte, Entertainer, Folk Hero, Guild Artisan, Sage
Guardian	Acolyte, Folk Hero, Hermit, Outlander, Soldier
Offspring	Any

ANCIENT BEING QUESTS

Though their work remains mysterious, ancient beings send their agents to exact their will in myriad ways. Servants of other powerful beings try to stymie your patron's plans, while misguided (or entirely justified) monster hunters seek to rid the world of their ancient foe. An ancient being's lengthy history inspires unusual and potent enemies.

The Ancient Being Quests table presents a few options for the sorts of work your patron expects from you.

ANCIENT BEING QUESTS

d6	Quest
1	**Rescue.** A wayward agent went missing while gathering information or materials. You must discover their fate and recover them and their findings.
2	**Sabotage.** You must destroy an aspect of a rival's organization, either assassinating a key minion or destroying a critical object.
3	**Artifice.** Your specialized skills are instrumental to assembling components for a powerful magic ritual or object.
4	**Treachery.** A high-profile minion of another powerful figure is in a position to betray their master, to the benefit of your patron. You must convince them to defect to your organization or extract them from now-hostile territory.
5	**Culling.** A respected agent of your patron (possibly an ally or a mentor for your group) has been compromised. Perhaps they are defecting to a rival, attempting to seize the ancient being's power. Whatever the case, you must catch them to end their threat.
6	**Astral Heist.** A powerful rival of your patron stores their secrets in a mind vault on the Astral Plane. That means they can't be tricked or coerced into revealing anything, nor can their thoughts be read. You must find the vault and travel through the rival's deadly memories to find the knowledge your patron desires.

Aristocrat

Your group serves at the pleasure of a member of the nobility. Motivated by money, power, and politics, your patron uses your group to further their agenda without dirtying their hands, or perhaps they send you to the palaces of their enemies as envoys of peace. In exchange for loyalty and discretion, your patron is a powerful ally whose favor bestows far more than gold.

Types of Aristocrats

From the heads of scheming merchant families to immortal sorcerer-queens, each member of the aristocracy holds a measure of wealth and power—and they desire more. The rulers of a barony could struggle to reclaim the influence they once held, while the new head of a business dynasty might seek to catapult their fortunes to new heights. By aligning with such patrons, you stand to benefit enormously from the fruits of their ambition.

Roll or pick from the Aristocrat Types table to determine what kind of noble you serve.

Aristocrat Types

d6	Aristocrats
1	**Local Lord.** Convinced that power and prestige lie just around the corner, this minor lordling grasps for every opportunity to climb the ranks.
2	**Merchant Mastermind.** Reputation, wealth, and power are one and the same for the head of a family with world-spanning business holdings.
3	**Nomadic Princeling.** Nothing is more appealing to this princeling than treasure. Their sprawling merchant caravan trails behind their palanquin as far as the eye can see.
4	**Double Dealer.** The leader of a noble family has turned against their nation, secretly opposing their liege for personal gain or ethical reasons.
5	**Ambitious Entrepreneur.** The sole heir of a vast fortune, this entrepreneur seeks allies to expand their wealth in a new business on the international, global, or planar stage.
6	**Future Ruler.** This young noble is destined to rule, but currently their whims are fickle and dangerous.

A Wood Elf Aristocrat

Aristocrat Perks

With an aristocrat as your group's patron, you gain the following perks.

Expenses. Your patron reimburses you for extraordinary expenses incurred as part of your work. You are required to account for your expenses and must explain any extraordinary expenditures, but routine travel, ordinary equipment, and basic services don't draw a second glance.

Immunity. As long as you remain in the aristocrat's good graces, you are nearly immune to prosecution under the laws within the aristocrat's sphere of influence. When you are carrying out your orders, you have a great deal of leeway in how you choose to go about that, and the law isn't an obstacle. Committing serious crimes—especially if they are unrelated or unnecessary for the assigned work—is a sure way to fall out of your patron's good graces, however.

Luxury. Your patron deigns to host you at their home or in other luxurious accommodations for a brief period as reward for a job well done. Such a stay typically lasts for no longer than two weeks per year, during which you maintain an aristocratic lifestyle for no cost. You must defend the locale if necessary, but you're largely afforded time to relax as you please. However, poor (or outright destructive) guests rarely receive invitations to stay again.

Salary. Your employment under an aristocratic patron brings an income of 1 gp per day, or enough to maintain a modest lifestyle. At the DM's discretion, your salary increases or decreases depending on the aristocrat's nature, the type of work, and the length of your employment.

ARISTOCRAT CONTACT

Aside from a few exceptions, aristocrats prefer to have someone else handle communication with the hired help. As a result, you communicate with an intermediary who serves as a go-between in your dealings with your patron.

Roll or pick from the Aristocrat Contact table to determine who serves as your patron's proxy.

ARISTOCRAT CONTACT

d6	Contact
1	**Common Contact.** A servant with ambitions toward a title works as a go-between for your patron.
2	**Professional.** A level-headed advisor or manager of your patron's business directs you in keeping their reckless employer safe.
3	**Family Peacemaker.** A naive aristocrat appointed by your patron wants your assistance in keeping the peace between fractious family members, which isn't your patron's priority.
4	**Intimate Connection.** A common-born confidant or lover of your patron guides you in creating circumstances to bolster the noble family's best interests.
5	**Outside Insider.** An outcast noble favored by your patron works with you to uphold their family's interests despite their exile.
6	**Outsider Inside.** A mysterious entity manipulates a noble family's fortunes. Through your patron, it employs you to help guide its chosen family along a centuries-long course.

ARISTOCRAT RETAINERS

Aristocrats seek agents to pursue business, political, criminal, or personal agendas. In return, you might serve an aristocrat merely for the salary or to gain access to particular tools, information, or political clout. Or you could be a lesser family member, expected to serve the will of family leaders. Regardless of your skills or social standing, aristocratic patrons with enough foresight and imagination find a use for agents from any background.

The Aristocrat Retainer Roles table suggests a variety of parts you might play in an aristocrat's agenda and the backgrounds frequently associated with each role.

ARISTOCRAT RETAINER ROLES

Role	Backgrounds
Advisor	Acolyte, Charlatan, Folk Hero, Hermit, Sage
Bodyguard	Criminal, Folk Hero, Noble, Outlander, Soldier
Informant	Charlatan, Criminal, Entertainer, Sailor, Urchin
House Staff	Entertainer, Guild Artisan, Sailor, Soldier, Urchin
Messenger	Charlatan, Entertainer, Outlander, Sailor, Urchin
Family Scion	Any

ARISTOCRAT QUESTS

A missive from your patron proffers a different kind of mission each time. For one assignment, you act as an envoy during delicate trade negotiations; the next, you're sent trekking through mountain passes to gather a favorite flower for a party. Foes are endless, and yesterday's ally might be tomorrow's target. The only things that are certain are the variety of your patron's whims and that tomorrow there will surely be more.

The Aristocrat Quests table presents the sorts of work you might conduct at your highborn patron's request.

ARISTOCRAT QUESTS

d6	Quest
1	**Noble Union.** You work within multiple noble factions to unite rival families.
2	**Business Breakthrough.** You track down and obtain a wonder your patron believes is the key to their financial fortunes.
3	**Sabotage Rival.** You break into the business or estate of an enemy noble family and undermine their political or professional ventures.
4	**Lost Lineage.** You seek evidence of a lost branch of a noble family or proof that individuals don't possess a noble pedigree.
5	**Origin of Nobility.** You reveal the secret reason why certain individuals were elevated to noble status and how they will soon fulfill their purpose.
6	**The New Nobility.** You recreate the remarkable event that granted today's noble families their special standing, enabling the rise of new nobles.

OTT STEELTOES HOLDS ALOFT SYLGAR, THE INFAMOUS FISH OF THE CRIME LORD XANATHAR.

TYPES OF CRIMINAL SYNDICATES

Criminal syndicates range from the local thieves' guild, to a corrupt consortium of merchant princes, to a ring of otherworldly invaders infiltrating all levels of society for a nefarious purpose. Whatever form it takes, the syndicate is largely concerned with increasing wealth for its members at the expense of society at large.

Conversely, the syndicate could be an underground organization of good-hearted people fighting against a wicked power structure. Criminal syndicates with a heroic bent include the band of plucky outlaws who hijack taxes from the cruel baron and return them to the downtrodden and a hard-bitten ring of deserters who fight their homeland's invaders.

Roll or pick from the Syndicate Types table to determine what type of criminal organization you serve.

SYNDICATE TYPES

d6	Syndicate
1	**Thieves' Guild.** A disparate convocation of thieves, spies, smugglers, and other scoundrels controls criminal activity in a region of a city.
2	**Assassin Society.** The network's livelihood is death. Members of the society hone their skills as cutthroats, poisoners, body-disposal specialists, and any other profession focused on ending lives. The society is motivated by profit or labors in service to a greater cause.
3	**Magical Arms Dealer.** The syndicate has cornered the market on deadly magical devices. They offer their services and wares for a price and acquire staggering magical might for those who meet their demands.
4	**Pirate Fleet.** This alliance of pirate captains is unified under a ruling captain or admiral and adheres to a strict code of honor. They converge only in response to an outside threat.
5	**Body Snatchers.** The syndicate consists predominantly, if not entirely, of creatures that possess or impersonate other people. They seek to replace influential individuals throughout society with members of their ranks.
6	**Thought Thieves.** These psychic criminals infiltrate their target's minds to steal secrets and disguise their existence.

CRIMINAL SYNDICATE

> Crime—what's the point? Why steal from someone when you can simply outwit them or turn them into a toad?
>
> TASHA

A network of criminals employs your group. You could be full-fledged members in good standing with the syndicate or probationary inductees looking to make your mark and earn its trust. Perhaps your group works for the syndicate against your will: you owe them big for a job gone wrong, for killing the wrong person, or simply for being born into a family that's already in conflict with powerful, unscrupulous people.

CRIMINAL SYNDICATE PERKS

With the criminal syndicate as your group's patron, you gain the following perks.

Assignments. The syndicate doesn't pay you directly, but it assigns you to particular tasks on behalf of its clients or the organization. Someone hires the syndicate to perform a task (such as an assassination), and the syndicate passes 85 percent of the fee on to your group. If the aim is to enrich the syndicate (such as by pulling off a heist), you have the privilege of keeping 85 percent of what you steal. Other syndicates take more or less than a 15 percent share, at the DM's discretion.

Contraband. You have access to your syndicate's business in contraband, such as poisons or narcotics. You don't receive a discount on these goods, but you can always find someplace to purchase them.

Fences. Members or associates of your syndicate are skilled at disposing of stolen goods, and you have access to this service as well. Fences are useful for selling not just illicit goods but also expensive items such as works of art and magic items. In the case of magic items, this allows you to delegate the work of finding a buyer (a downtime activity described in the *Dungeon Master's Guide* and *Xanathar's Guide to Everything*) to the fence. When using the syndicate's fences, you run no risk of a double-cross or other mishap in finding a buyer, but the syndicate takes 20 percent of the sale price as a finder's fee.

Safe Houses. The syndicate maintains safe houses or other secret hiding spots across a wide region. Your group knows how to locate these nondescript redoubts and can maintain a poor lifestyle in one for no cost. Revealing a safe house, whether purposefully or by accident, causes you to lose favor with the syndicate and may see you banned from using them.

Syndicate-Owned Businesses. The syndicate owns several businesses, primarily as fronts for laundering money. When you buy from one of these businesses, you get a 5 percent discount. The DM decides what goods and services are available.

CRIMINAL SYNDICATE CONTACT

Each member of the syndicate has a place in the organization. You report to a contact who handles your contribution by giving you assignments, collecting the syndicate's cut of your swag, or seeing that you receive your fee for contract work from outside clients. The contact is your first point of communication if you need to reach out to highly ranked members of the syndicate's hierarchy.

Roll or pick from the Syndicate Contact table to determine your contact within a criminal organization.

SYNDICATE CONTACT

d6	Contact
1	**Personal Mentor.** This longtime member of the syndicate took you under their wing when you were young and became a parental figure.
2	**Clever Urchin.** An innocuous person, perhaps a beggar or menial laborer, knows all the right people and shares their connections with you.
3	**Former Law Enforcement.** Your contact used to be (or maybe still is) a member of local law enforcement. They have sharp insight into the law's workings in your area and a healthy dose of paranoia for that reason.
4	**Bon Vivant.** The boss of a local den of vice—whether gambling, narcotics, or other pleasures—aids you when they're not distracted by their own debauchery.
5	**Traitor.** You know your contact in the syndicate has betrayed it, but they have enough clout and leverage that you don't dare cross them—yet.
6	**Criminal Royalty.** Unknown to most, your contact is a member of local nobility or royalty. Why they maintain relations with the syndicate is a troubling mystery.

CRIMINAL SYNDICATE MEMBERS

Whether you're a lifelong scoundrel or an ambitious upstart, you seek to gain wealth, fame, and influence within a criminal syndicate. A syndicate is motivated by profit, employing agents with all manner of talents. Nimbleness and novelty prove vital not just to exploiting untapped prospects but to avoiding the law. You embody rare experience and skill, positioned at the forefront of daring new criminal ventures.

The Criminal Syndicate Member Roles suggests positions you might fill in the organization and the backgrounds frequently associated with each role.

CRIMINAL SYNDICATE MEMBER ROLES

Role	Backgrounds
Burglar	Criminal, Folk Hero, Noble, Outlander, Urchin
Muscle	Criminal, Entertainer, Outlander, Sailor, Soldier
Con Artist	Acolyte, Charlatan, Criminal, Entertainer, Noble, Urchin
Cleaner	Acolyte, Charlatan, Guild Artisan, Noble, Soldier
Mastermind	Acolyte, Criminal, Folk Hero, Noble, Sage
Mole	Any

CRIMINAL SYNDICATE QUESTS

Your work as a syndicate member involves more than simple street swindles or pickpocketing. Someone with your skills cooperates with others for greater purposes that offer both dangerous risks and splendid rewards. The law of the land is your most persistent enemy, but other criminal syndicates challenge you as well—or become your targets.

The Criminal Syndicate Quests table explores what kind of work you do for the organization.

CRIMINAL SYNDICATE QUESTS

d6	Quest
1	**Acquisition and Retrieval.** You acquire assets for the syndicate. You steal important documents or clear out locations for use as hideouts.
2	**Heists.** You plan and execute elaborate robberies that require the combined skills of your team.
3	**Gang Warfare.** You ensure that no other crime syndicate gains a significant foothold in your territory.
4	**Enforcement.** You keep the corrupt, headstrong, and avaricious members of your syndicate in line with the goals and rules of the organization.
5	**Assassination.** You dispatch prominent people—the sort who have numerous bodyguards and elaborate security systems to circumvent.
6	**Topple the Powerful.** Your syndicate is criminal and your methods illegal, but your goals are righteous. You help people who are powerless against exploitation by the powerful.

GUILD

> There's power in groups. One bee's a pest, but nobody messes with the swarm.
>
> TASHA

Your group has ties to a powerful consortium of professionals who work together for mutual benefit. You might be long-time members of such a guild, descended from a family of crafters or merchants from which you inherited membership, or perhaps you're working to earn entrance on your own merits. If you serve the guild's interests well, it promises to take care of you. Guilds hate to waste valuable assets, after all—that's just bad business.

TYPES OF GUILD

The guild structure covers a swath of business ventures, differentiated by their specialty. A conglomerate of blacksmiths, jewelers, carpenters, tailors, alchemists, scribes, and sages all could organize as a guild. Whatever their trade, these experts share contacts, exchange resources such as materials or tools, and leverage their collective influence to affect politics for their benefit. Alternatively, merchants and other business owners might also organize into guilds. Merchant barons who effectively rule a city or nation through iron-clad control of the economy or a network of innkeepers who share news and supply routes could both represent guild patrons. A guild could even embody a more sinister group, such as one that deals in terrifying wares like deadly monsters, dangerous knowledge, or souls.

Roll or pick from the Guild Types table to determine the general sort of organization you operate within.

GUILD TYPES

d6	Guild
1	**Crafters' Guild.** This conglomerate of artisans pools its resources and influence to ensure a steady exchange of gold for its crafts.
2	**Merchant Consortium.** These entrepreneurs don't create the wares they peddle, instead specializing in linking products to prospective owners. If they don't have it, they find it.
3	**Miracle Makers' Association.** The magically inclined crafters of this guild specialize in imbuing physical goods with magical effects. Rumor has it they can strip the magic from existing enchanted items and might be willing to buy or trade adventurers' spoils.
4	**Moneychangers.** These merchants deal in all forms of currency, acting as bankers, loan agents, and crucial contacts for adventurers and other individuals who deal with large sums of wealth. They exchange coin for gemstones as readily as they find buyers for historical relics and recovered art.
5	**Philosophical Faction.** These like-minded individuals follow specific teachings, spreading word of their expertise through their services and training.
6	**Identity Traders.** These enigmatic dealers buy and sell documents, memories, and the trappings of thoroughly lived lives, selling them to those in need of the ultimate fresh start.

A HERO FIGHTS THE BULLYWUG WHO GUARDS THE VILLAINOUS MASTER OF THE BAKERS' GUILD.

Guild Perks

With a guild as your group's patron, you gain the following perks. These perks require an annual contribution of 15 gp paid to the guild (replacing the 5 gp per month cost for characters with the Guild Artisan background). These dues fund the guild's services and activities.

Accommodations. You can stay at your organization's guildhall. The rooms are comparable to those in a comfortable inn, but at a modest price (5 sp per day).

Equipment. You can requisition the use of specialized tools, laboratories, libraries, or other crafting space and equipment to use within the guildhall. When you make an ability check with a set of artisan's tools using the guild's equipment, add double your normal proficiency bonus to the check.

Resources. You can leverage the guild's extensive contacts to locate exotic materials for crafting, spell components, or magic items, or buyers for them (a downtime activity in the *Dungeon Master's Guide* and *Xanathar's Guide to Everything*). You

can locate or sell legal commodities using the guild's resources, and any prices tip in your favor by 10 percent.

Training. The guild retains knowledgeable tutors in subjects pertinent to its interests. When you undertake the training downtime activity (as described in the *Player's Handbook* and *Xanathar's Guide to Everything*), the training takes half as long if you are studying a subject the guild specializes in. The DM decides if the guild has tutors available for a given subject.

Guild Contact

Even as a member in good standing of the guild, you can't simply stroll up to the guild master and demand their attention. Your superiors within the guild manage work contracts, request the use of guild resources, and facilitate getting your group in contact with the right people to assist their interests.

Roll or pick from the Guild Contact table to determine your immediate contact within the guild.

GUILD CONTACT

d6	Contact
1	**The Perfectionist.** Your contact is a skilled but obsessive creator consumed with the quest to create something perfect that will define their life's work and secure their legacy. They lose sight of right and wrong in pursuit of the finest materials and exciting opportunities.
2	**Attentive Overseer.** A guild representative takes personal interest in your group's tasks. They follow your exploits and know of your adventures before you return to report. Despite the unsettling depth of their knowledge, they seem genuinely eager to shepherd your work.
3	**Hidden Benefactor.** Whoever your contact is, they don't communicate directly. They send messages via couriers or letters. No one in the guild knows who the contact is, or if they do, they aren't telling you. Regardless, the contact's information is good, and they pay on time.
4	**Discerning Mentor.** No matter how well you perform, or how perfect your creations, nothing is ever good enough for this contact. They point out every flaw and missed opportunity. Are they bitter, lashing out at anyone around them, or do they recognize your potential and try to push you to greatness?
5	**Golem Guide.** Your guild contact is the soul of a long-dead artisan preserved in a construct body. This golem is wise and knowledgeable, but it has difficulty grasping the passage of time and the state of the world compared to its original era.
6	**Fallen Muse.** Your contact is a fallen celestial. Whether they regret their transgressions or hunger for vengeance, they provide divine inspiration and guidance to you and to the guild. Somehow your group and the guild inspire their hope for ascension.

GUILD REPRESENTATIVES

As a guild member, you might be a professional who works directly toward the guild's specialty or whose fortunes align with the guild's interests. Alternatively, you could provide the guild with services to which their members aren't suited. For example, guards, explorers, negotiators, and spies can be useful to a guild, whether its interests lie in trade goods, entertainment, or more questionable ventures. Whether a guild operates entirely within the law and how public its interests are also influences which of your skills it deems most valuable.

The Guild Representative Roles table suggests positions you might fill in a guild and the backgrounds frequently associated with each role.

GUILD REPRESENTATIVE ROLES

Role	Backgrounds
Researcher	Acolyte, Entertainer, Guild Artisan, Sage
Negotiator	Charlatan, Entertainer, Guild Artisan, Noble, Sailor
Saboteur	Charlatan, Criminal, Guild Artisan, Soldier, Urchin
Guard	Criminal, Folk Hero, Outlander, Sailor, Soldier
Explorer	Acolyte, Folk Hero, Guild Artisan, Outlander, Sailor
Expert	Any

GUILD QUESTS

As a member of the guild, you're called on to ply your skills in the organization's service. You are required to undertake various tasks, either for the guild's benefit or on behalf of an influential client. Competition is fierce in the business world, and the challenges presented by rivals or circumstances can pressure you into dealings you find distasteful.

The Guild Quests table presents a few options for the sorts of work the guild requires of you.

GUILD QUESTS

d6	Quest
1	**Deliver Goods.** You need to deliver an order to an important customer or partner of the guild. The delivery must arrive by a critical deadline—regardless of who or what tries to stop you.
2	**Acquire Materials.** Your guild requires materials that are rare and difficult to procure, either for a guild project or for a paying client. Your group must gather the missing components from a dangerous location or a recalcitrant owner while outpacing a rival to the prize.
3	**Eliminate a Rival.** A competitor has humiliated the guild one too many times, and it's time for that to stop. Your group is charged with assuring the rival never darkens the guild's reputation again. Can you trick them into permanent disgrace, or must you resort to more direct methods?
4	**The Masterpiece.** An exquisite work of art for an influential client, either created by your guild or acquired through agents, has gone missing. You must track down its whereabouts and secure it before time runs out and the guild suffers a penalty.

d6	Quest
5	**The Collector.** Your guild is tasked to create or acquire something wondrous for a wealthy but secretive client's collection. Guild members who previously failed to fulfill this assignment ended up missing. The collector promises to return your comrades if you provide what the collector seeks, but if you fail, you'll become part of the collection.
6	**The Bill Comes Due.** Your guild master achieved their vaunted position by means of an otherworldly bargain. That price has come due, and they are desperate to avoid paying. You must defeat whatever's coming to collect the master's debt or find another acceptable payment.

MILITARY FORCE

> The whole machine of war is barbaric.
>   In a sane world, conflicts would be resolved by contests of apocalyptic magics or by continent-reshaping brawls between titanic, soul-fueled reptiles. You know, reasonable options.
>
>   TASHA

Your group serves as a team of soldiers in a larger military force, one dedicated to combat missions or other dangerous tasks. You could be a band of mercenaries, a special forces unit, or a squad of regular infantry. Perhaps you protect a nation's people from monsters, or you fight secret battles in the wake of a war that has supposedly ended. Or the nation requires military forces at the edges of civilization to protect the frontier and to lead advancement into new territory.

TYPES OF MILITARY FORCES

Military forces represent a variety of organized bands of warriors. They can be the disciplined regiments of a nation's standing army, a fleet of ships comprising a kingdom's armada, or a devastating horde of warriors and magical beasts. A given kingdom's military could be a rigidly ordered force or a blood-soaked throng.

Roll or pick from the Military Force Types table to determine the general type of military patron you serve.

MILITARY FORCE TYPES

d6	Military Organization
1	**Standing Army.** A standing army serves as the highly disciplined and structured guardian of a province or an entire nation. Strict tiers of command ensure coordination between branches of the force.
2	**Mercenary Company.** Hard-bitten veterans of numerous conflicts, mercenaries serve an employer for coin rather than out of loyalty.
3	**Expeditionary Force.** This military force is far from home, fighting behind enemy lines or striking into wild, unsettled lands. The force must be fast, self-sufficient, and either diplomatic or decisive to assure their survival.
4	**Horde.** The horde is almost a force of nature, and what it lacks in discipline it makes up in ferocity. It doesn't have a rigid command structure, instead functioning like a pyramid of smaller armies. Horde commanders owe fealty to stronger leaders above them, all the way up to the warlord.
5	**Planar Conscripts.** This military force battles for cosmic stakes on far-flung planes of the multiverse or fights against extraplanar invasion on the Material Plane. Warriors include conscripts pressed into service in the Blood War, fodder in the thrall of ruthless yugoloth mercenaries, or members of a glorious celestial host defending against fiendish incursion.
6	**Sky Warriors.** This military force consists of winged creatures, employs magical flight, or sails airships as a sky navy. Traditional defenses are ineffective against attacks from the air, positioning the sky warriors as a fearsome nation or expensive and coveted mercenaries.

MILITARY FORCE PERKS

With a military force as your group's patron, you gain the following perks.

Armory. You can purchase nonmagical weapons and armor at a 20 percent discount at a facility associated with your military force. You can buy magic items at the DM's discretion, but you receive no discount.

Chain of Command. You are part of a hierarchy that provides you with orders. If you cause trouble in your own nation, you answer to your officers, not local law enforcement.

Official Access. Your rank in the military force grants you access to places that are off limits to civilians. With your commander's permission, you can enter dangerous training grounds or military installations, like an army's regional headquarters or a repository of top-secret intelligence. You can also request that your commander grant you authority to act in their name or provide access to experts or leaders higher in the chain of command.

Orders. You undertake your missions at the direction of a commanding officer, who expects your absolute obedience. These missions have clear and precise goals, leading you on the path of adventure. In rare cases, you're trusted with open-ended tasks that afford you leeway in interpreting orders.

Salary. Each member of your group earns a regular salary or share of the military force's spoils. The amount varies depending on your organization and your position within it, but at minimum you enjoy a modest lifestyle. You receive a small salary (as little as 1 sp per day) and food and housing on a military base. Or you receive 1 gp per day but rely on that money for room and board. With higher rank comes higher pay. As an officer, you maintain a comfortable lifestyle.

Military Force Contact

Your primary contact within your hierarchy is your superior officer, the person who gives you orders and is responsible for your success or failure.

Roll or pick from the Military Force Contact table to determine who assigns you missions.

Commanding Officer

d6	Officer
1	**Tested Veteran.** Your commander is a battle-scarred officer who experienced horrors in combat. They rely on something to dull the pain of their memories or wounds, from a favorite writer's prose to a distracting vice.
2	**Taskmaster.** This angry officer yells every order, reprimands you for the smallest mistake, and fully expects you to fail at every mission you undertake. This might be tough love or simple brutishness.
3	**Protective Officer.** A kindly officer is hesitant to send you into danger and constantly reminds you to be careful.
4	**Bitter Soldier.** Your commander carries deep grudges against your force's enemies. They leap at any chance to do those foes harm, even if it puts your group in terrible risk.
5	**Hopeful Commander.** This optimistic officer knows that a new era of peace is just over the horizon. You just need to complete these last few missions, then it should all finally be over.
6	**Devout Leader.** Your commander is a person of deep faith. They believe that your success or failure lies entirely in divine hands and you are the instruments of that will.

A Dragonborn
Messenger of the
Purple Dragon Knights

Military Force Envoys

You might join a military force for a wide range of reasons, or the military has reasons for seeking you out. Those with specialized skills contribute to a range of missions, from infiltration and mystical operations to diplomacy and strategy. Perhaps your past deeds or the will of your family pushes you toward military service, regardless of whether you believe you're suited to such a life.

The Military Force Envoy Roles table suggests a variety of military roles you could fill and the backgrounds frequently associated with each role.

Military Force Envoy Roles

Role	Backgrounds
Combatant	Criminal, Folk Hero, Outlander, Sailor, Soldier
Tactician	Acolyte, Folk Hero, Noble, Outlander, Sage, Soldier
Medic	Acolyte, Folk Hero, Hermit, Sage, Soldier
Scout	Hermit, Outlander, Sailor, Soldier, Urchin
Provocateur	Acolyte, Charlatan, Criminal, Entertainer, Noble
Spy	Any

MILITARY QUESTS

The wide-ranging work of a military unit calls for both power and subtlety. Your missions could run the risk of shattering a fragile peace recently established with a rival nation and plunging multiple nations back into war. Or perhaps your group's missions pit you against rival combatants during an active engagement, as you influence the war effort. Rival mercenary companies, armed resistance fighters, and monsters drawn to the presence of bloodshed also present familiar threats.

The Military Quests table provides possible missions you're tasked to accomplish.

MILITARY QUESTS

d6	Quest
1	**Strike Force.** You undertake a quick, strategic, and devastating attack against an enemy force.
2	**Defensive Operations.** You must preserve the safety of an important location such as a civilian population center, a supply depot, or strategically critical bridge or seaport.
3	**Special Forces.** You are assigned to a covert operation behind enemy lines. This is similar to the work of a spy or an assassin but with a broader scope. You engage in equipment sabotage or execute targeted strikes against high-value targets.
4	**Reconnaissance.** You gather information on enemy troop numbers, placements, movement, or supply caches and routes.
5	**Seek and Destroy.** You are responsible for hunting down specific high-value and dangerous targets, which include deserters, suspected enemy special forces, or magical war machines run amok.
6	**Siege.** You are assigned to initiate a siege on an enemy stronghold or help break a siege in progress on an allied fortress.

RELIGIOUS ORDER

> Sure, serve that religious order, and soon you'll be doing a thousand loads of your high priest's laundry, because—conveniently—it's divine will.
>
> TASHA

Your group acts in the service of a religious institution. The patronage of a religious order isn't simply a matter of each member of your party belonging to the same faith, though. The faith's administration—with its own resources, goals, and leaders—directly sponsors and guides your adventures.

TYPES OF RELIGIOUS ORDERS

Not every religious order represents an alliance of worshipers devoted to godly ideals. Perhaps your group is a team of devotees pursuing a cause for your faith, or maybe you're a bunch of cynics taking advantage of a wealthy congregation. Your collective faith could compel you to hunt evil monsters or stave off otherworldly invasions, to protect the powerless from oppression, or to spread the teachings of your religion in a hostile land. Or perhaps you serve a corrupt hierarchy by making its enemies quietly disappear—though even cynical mercenaries can become true believers when confronted with the miraculous.

Roll or pick from the Religious Order Types table to determine the type of religious patron you serve.

RELIGIOUS ORDER TYPES

d6	Religious Order
1	**Undead Hunters.** This community of scholars and monster hunters laboriously researches the unquiet dead, tracking them to their lairs and permanently laying them to rest.
2	**Devout Scholars.** This federation prizes knowledge and texts pertaining to their god. They collect rare holy books and record the life stories of miracle-working prophets.
3	**Relic Collectors.** This order of archaeologist-monks seeks to fill their museum-like temple with storied holy relics.
4	**Charitable Missionaries.** Adhering to the belief that religion empowers civilization, this order travels far to help the downtrodden, seeking to draw new believers by their virtuous example.
5	**Militant Inquisitors.** This dogmatically rigid hierarchy seeks to stamp out all threats to their beliefs.
6	**Doomsaying Evangelists.** This order believes the world is about to end. They're convinced that if they persuade everyone else of this fact they might stave off the impending doom.

RELIGIOUS ORDER PERKS

With a religious order as your group's patron, you gain the following perks.

Divine Service. In times of need, your group can appeal to the priests of your faith for magical aid. An NPC cleric or druid of your faith who is of sufficiently high level casts any spell of up to 5th level on your group's behalf, without charge. The caster provides any costly material components needed for the spell, as long as you demonstrate your need and are in good standing with the faith.

ACOLYTES PREPARE FOR A COUATL FESTIVAL.

Equipment. Each member of your party has a holy symbol or druidic focus, even if it isn't needed for spellcasting. Each of you also has a book containing prayers, rites, and scriptures of your faith.

Proficiencies. Each member of your party gains proficiency in the Religion skill, if the character doesn't already have it.

RELIGIOUS ORDER CONTACT

Your established order enjoys a robust following. It might be a cloister of priestly scholars who use your group as the adventuring arm of the organization, or perhaps a legion of paladins who call on your group's finesse where swords and shields fail. You might receive orders directly from the immortal entity you worship or through an earthly agent, such as a high priest or an archdruid.

Roll or pick from the Religious Order Contact table to determine who relays messages to and from your order's deity.

RELIGIOUS ORDER CONTACT

d6	Contact
1	**Shadow Tongue.** A mysterious speaker for your order advises your next steps but fears being discovered by a powerful rival faith.
2	**Inspired Creator.** A gifted artisan conveys the will of the divine through prophetic song or artwork.
3	**Mysterious Text.** The gradual translation of a secret holy text points you toward the next step of a divine destiny.
4	**Fierce Inquisitor.** A severe hierarch directs you to cleanse wickedness from a region, from the order, or from within yourself.
5	**Beloved Healer.** A famed healer guides you to where you'll be needed most, even if their reasons are unclear until you arrive.
6	**Divinity's Voice.** Otherworldly messages direct you to undertake divine quests.

ZUZANNA WUZYK

Religious Order Member

Your primary duty to a religious order is to further your god's reach. That obligation ranges from proselytizing or performing religious services to meting out divine punishments or recovering lost relics. Beyond that, the needs of your order vary widely. Your patron relies on your group due to your particular skills or, perhaps, because it's divine whim.

The Religious Order Member Roles table suggests positions you might fill in an order and the backgrounds frequently associated with each role.

Religious Order Member Roles

Role	Backgrounds
Councilor	Acolyte, Folk Hero, Hermit, Sage, Urchin
Defender	Acolyte, Criminal, Folk Hero, Outlander, Soldier
Ascetic	Acolyte, Entertainer, Hermit, Sage, Soldier
Inquisitor	Acolyte, Criminal, Noble, Sailor, Soldier
Emissary	Acolyte, Charlatan, Entertainer, Noble, Sailor
Chosen One	Any

Religious Order Quests

The services you provide your religious order vary depending on the deity you serve and your party's aptitudes. Regardless, religious orders are opposed by antagonistic faiths, foes whose rivalry with your order emulates the conflict between your respective gods. Some religious orders also hunt and destroy fiends, undead, or other beings they consider abominations, seeking to rid the word of their influence. Others root out heretics, real or imagined, to demonstrate the primacy of their deity.

The Religious Order Quests table presents a few examples of how you can honor and serve your deity.

Religious Order Quests

d6	Quest
1	**Safe Escape.** A band of the faithful wandered into territory hostile to your order. You must find them and escort them to safety.
2	**Relic Recovery.** You seek a lost symbol of the order discovered in a dangerous place or in the hands of an enemy.
3	**Cult Hunt.** You hunt a cell of zealots dangerous to your order or mortals at large.
4	**Desperate Pilgrimage.** You protect members of the order as they participate in a pilgrimage that takes them through dangerous lands.
5	**Expunge Heresy.** You seek out the source of blasphemy that's taken root within the order.
6	**Prevent Prophecy.** A rival order stands on the cusp of fulfilling a prophecy with deadly ramifications. You strive to undermine their blasphemous agenda.

Sovereign

> I never had much interest in ruling, partly because the titles all sound so stuffy. But "witch queen" has a lovely ring to it, don't you think?
>
> TASHA

A leader without allies is not long a leader. You serve a sovereign—a national figure or otherwise—and work to achieve their goals no matter the cost.

As agents of a sovereign, you serve as diplomats or enforcers, spies or fixers, bringers of aid or executors of justice. You work within the system to uphold the status quo or step beyond the law to prevent war and worse. Politics, espionage, and mystery are facts of your world, as is hope and the fragile promise of peace.

Types of Sovereigns

Broadly defined, a sovereign ranges from the head of a government to the leader of a powerful, private institution. Queens, chieftains, sultans, and rajahs are ready choices for powerful individuals who patronize a party of adventurers. Those on track to become such individuals—such as cunning senators, royal heirs, or influential celebrities—also fill a sovereign's role. When choosing or creating a sovereign to serve, consider whether that leader commands a government organization or another faction. While this section assumes your patron is the head of a country or other national body, they could oversee a powerful private division, a cult of personality, or an elaborate expedition. Also, consider the scale of your patron's organization. While serving as spies engaging in international intrigues could lead to world-changing escapades, being fixers for the mayor of a struggling town offers a personal connection to a place and its people.

Roll or pick from the Sovereign Types table to determine what sort of liege you serve.

SOVEREIGN TYPES

d6	Sovereign
1	**Village Elder.** The wizened leader of a community offers both civic and moral leadership.
2	**Young Noble.** An ambitious noble eagerly seeks to reform society to align with a personal vision.
3	**Shipwrecked Governor.** A desperate leader struggles to keep people alive in a wilderness they're not prepared to endure.
4	**Ruler Returned.** A tribe's revered leader has returned from the dead and seeks to resurrect their past glories.
5	**Hidden Power.** A mysterious figure manipulates the nation's puppet leader and guides the government's true agenda.
6	**True Regent.** The rightful heir to the throne struggles to reclaim power from a perfect impostor.

A MERFOLK SOVEREIGN

SOVEREIGN PERKS

With the sovereign as your group's patron, you gain the following perks.

Elite Access. While in service to the sovereign, you have access to the highest echelons of society. With your patron's permission, you can gain access to the halls of power, from national capitols and military headquarters to noble estates and troves of state secrets. You can also request that the sovereign grant you access to perks of their position, like access to diplomatic receptions or use of the royal guards.

Expenses. Your patron reimburses you for extraordinary expenses incurred as part of your work. You are required to account for your expenses and must explain any extraordinary expenditures, but routine travel, ordinary equipment, and basic services don't draw a second glance.

Immunity. As long as you remain in the sovereign's good graces, you are nearly immune to prosecution under the laws within their sphere of influence. When you are carrying out your orders, you have a great deal of leeway in how you choose to go about that, and the law isn't an obstacle. Committing serious crimes—especially if they are unrelated or unnecessary for the assigned work—is a sure way to fall out of your patron's good graces, however.

Salary. Your employment under a sovereign patron brings an income of 1 gp per day, or enough to maintain a modest lifestyle. At the DM's discretion, your salary increases or decreases depending on the sovereign's nature, the type of work you perform, and the length of your employment.

Sovereign Contact

You might benefit from direct contact with your group patron. This includes audiences or secret meetings with the sovereign, depending on the nature of your work. Alternatively, the sovereign might purposefully want to keep their distance from you, either due to their busy schedules or to maintain plausible deniability regarding your work. In such cases, an advisor or functionary oversees your assignments, serving as the primary contact between you and the sovereign.

Roll or pick from the Sovereign Contact table to determine who manages the relationship between you and the throne, if not the sovereign directly.

Sovereign Contact

d6	Contact
1	**Intimate Confidant.** The sovereign's friend or lover seeks to aid their companion in any way possible.
2	**Spymaster.** An intelligence operative attends to the nation's dirty work so the sovereign keeps their hands clean.
3	**Administrator.** This severe bureaucrat disagrees with many of the sovereign's policies but takes loyal service seriously.
4	**Executive Assistant.** The responsibilities of an exacting butler or other servant at the royal household far exceed their title.
5	**Envoy.** A semi-retired, leisure-loving ambassador speaks in suggestion and innuendo.
6	**Spectral Assembly.** A ghostly council of the nation's previous regents manifests to avert disasters.

Sovereign Proxies

You serve a sovereign out of national pride, out of tradition, or for your own practical reasons. The needs of a leader potentially embroil you directly in political intrigues, court maneuverings, or threats from national foes. It's up to you and the sovereign to determine whether your work is publicly acknowledged or top secret—and if the latter, what happens if your work is exposed.

The Sovereign Proxy Roles table suggests ways you might serve a sovereign and the backgrounds frequently associated with each role.

Sovereign Proxy Roles

Role	Backgrounds
Advisor	Acolyte, Folk Hero, Noble, Sage, Soldier
Ambassador	Charlatan, Folk Hero, Guild Artisan, Noble, Sailor
Secret Agent	Charlatan, Criminal, Entertainer, Soldier, Urchin
Champion	Criminal, Noble, Outlander, Soldier, Urchin
Jester	Charlatan, Criminal, Entertainer, Outlander, Urchin
Confidant	Any

Sovereign Quests

The services you provide a sovereign largely depend on the nature of your group patron and their nation. While some of your missions involve official tasks—missions undertaken in the sovereign's name—others might be covert, making your patron's identity a highly guarded secret. Political rivals, enemy countries, and natural disasters all pose dangers to the sovereign's nation. Yet a sovereign who sows chaos, enacts tyrannical decrees, or jeopardizes a population's way of life is likely to inspire rebellions. In such cases, a sovereign's agents must decide where their loyalties lie.

The Sovereign Quests table presents a few of the sorts of missions you undertake for your liege.

Sovereign Quests

d6	Quest
1	**International Espionage.** You attempt to steal intelligence, national symbols, or super weapons from an enemy power.
2	**Undermine Rival.** You seek to weaken or remove a rival to the regent's rule—perhaps a general, an archdruid, or a noble with a claim to the throne.
3	**Expel Corruption.** You help the sovereign reform their government, rooting out institutional vices.
4	**Subvert Blame.** The sovereign is caught in an embarrassing affair. Make it disappear.
5	**Test Heir.** You prepare the sovereign's heir for the challenge of taking the throne.
6	**Desperate Diplomacy.** You seek to make peace with a force or entity that could wipe out your nation.

IN THE CITY OF SIGIL, GUILDMASTER RHYS REALIZES THAT FINDING CAPABLE RECRUITS IS ONE OF THE MAIN CHALLENGES OF BEING A PATRON.

BEING YOUR OWN PATRON

For some players, the idea of running a crime syndicate, mercenary company, arcane scholars' collective, or other organization is far more exciting than working for someone else. Founding your own organization offers a greater degree of autonomy, though potentially at the cost of support and reliable work.

When you're the boss, the perks of belonging to an organization become expenses you have to worry about; when you run your own mercenary company, for example, you need to stock your own armory, rather than drawing on an existing organization's stockpile. The organization brings in income, but you'll have to spend it to keep the organization running.

When you run your own organization, use the Running a Business downtime activity (described in the *Dungeon Master's Guide*) to reflect your organization's ongoing activities. More than one character can take part in this activity at a time. When rolling to determine the business's performance, add the total days spent by the characters to the roll to determine the business's success (still observing the maximum of 30). If the business earns a profit, multiply that profit by 4 + the number of characters who took part in this downtime activity.

Don't discount the value of adopting an NPC to serve as your contact within your own organization. A secretary, majordomo, or apprentice keeps up with your group's bureaucracy while you're conducting missions and passes along information that could lead to your next adventure!

HARNESSING
ABYSSAL POWER

IN HER LAB, TASHA
CONFERS WITH THE
DEMON LORD GRAZ'ZT
THROUGH A MAGIC MIRROR.

CHAPTER 3
MAGICAL MISCELLANY

MAGIC IS EVERYWHERE IN D&D. MANY creatures in the D&D multiverse exist solely because of the influence of magic, spellcasters harness magical energy every day in the form of spells, and supernatural power thrums at the heart of the magic items sought by adventurers. This chapter is all about those last two things—spells and magic items.

The chapter first presents new spells for player characters and monsters to use. Those spells are followed by suggestions on customizing the look of your spells. The chapter then offers a selection of new magic items, including artifacts of mythic power and magic items that can be printed on one's body in the form of tattoos.

The DM decides how the options in this chapter appear in a campaign and may choose to use some, all, or none of them, so make sure to let your DM know which options you'd most like to use in play.

SPELLS

> Well, darn. Whatever could have happened to the spells Mordenkainen's Bountiful Back-Patting, Heward's Hot Air, and all the rest? I'm sure I submitted the spells they insisted I include herein. Seems they got lost in the shuffle. Shame.
>
> TASHA

This section contains new spells that the DM may add to a campaign, making them available to player character and monster spellcasters alike. The Spells table lists the new spells, ordering them by level. The table also notes the school of magic of a spell, whether it requires concentration, whether it bears the ritual tag, and which classes have access to it.

If you'd like to use any of these spells, talk to your DM, who may allow some, all, or none of them.

SPELLS

Level	Spell	School	Conc.	Ritual	Class
0	Booming Blade	Evocation	No	No	Artificer, Sorcerer, Warlock, Wizard
0	Green-Flame Blade	Evocation	No	No	Artificer, Sorcerer, Warlock, Wizard
0	Lightning Lure	Evocation	No	No	Artificer, Sorcerer, Warlock, Wizard
0	Mind Sliver	Enchantment	No	No	Sorcerer, Warlock, Wizard
0	Sword Burst	Conjuration	No	No	Artificer, Sorcerer, Warlock, Wizard
1st	Tasha's Caustic Brew	Evocation	Yes	No	Artificer, Sorcerer, Wizard
2nd	Summon Beast	Conjuration	Yes	No	Druid, Ranger
2nd	Tasha's Mind Whip	Enchantment	No	No	Sorcerer, Wizard
3rd	Intellect Fortress	Abjuration	Yes	No	Artificer, Bard, Sorcerer, Warlock, Wizard
3rd	Spirit Shroud	Necromancy	Yes	No	Cleric, Paladin, Warlock, Wizard
3rd	Summon Fey	Conjuration	Yes	No	Druid, Ranger, Warlock, Wizard
3rd	Summon Shadowspawn	Conjuration	Yes	No	Warlock, Wizard
3rd	Summon Undead	Necromancy	Yes	No	Warlock, Wizard
4th	Summon Aberration	Conjuration	Yes	No	Warlock, Wizard
4th	Summon Construct	Conjuration	Yes	No	Artificer, Wizard
4th	Summon Elemental	Conjuration	Yes	No	Druid, Ranger, Wizard
5th	Summon Celestial	Conjuration	Yes	No	Cleric, Paladin
6th	Summon Fiend	Conjuration	Yes	No	Warlock, Wizard
6th	Tasha's Otherworldly Guise	Transmutation	Yes	No	Sorcerer, Warlock, Wizard
7th	Dream of the Blue Veil	Conjuration	No	No	Bard, Sorcerer, Warlock, Wizard
9th	Blade of Disaster	Conjuration	Yes	No	Sorcerer, Warlock, Wizard

LIVIA PRIMA

SPELL DESCRIPTIONS

The spells are presented in alphabetical order.

BLADE OF DISASTER

9th-level conjuration

Casting Time: 1 bonus action
Range: 60 feet
Components: V, S
Duration: Concentration, up to 1 minute

You create a blade-shaped planar rift about 3 feet long in an unoccupied space you can see within range. The blade lasts for the duration. When you cast this spell, you can make up to two melee spell attacks with the blade, each one against a creature, loose object, or structure within 5 feet of the blade. On a hit, the target takes 4d12 force damage. This attack scores a critical hit if the number on the d20 is 18 or higher. On a critical hit, the blade deals an extra 8d12 force damage (for a total of 12d12 force damage).

As a bonus action on your turn, you can move the blade up to 30 feet to an unoccupied space you can see and then make up to two melee spell attacks with it again.

The blade can harmlessly pass through any barrier, including a wall of force.

BOOMING BLADE

Evocation cantrip

Casting Time: 1 action
Range: Self (5-foot radius)
Components: S, M (a melee weapon worth at least 1 sp)
Duration: 1 round

You brandish the weapon used in the spell's casting and make a melee attack with it against one creature within 5 feet of you. On a hit, the target suffers the weapon attack's normal effects and then becomes sheathed in booming energy until the start of your next turn. If the target willingly moves 5 feet or more before then, the target takes 1d8 thunder damage, and the spell ends.

This spell's damage increases when you reach certain levels. At 5th level, the melee attack deals an extra 1d8 thunder damage to the target on a hit, and the damage the target takes for moving increases to 2d8. Both damage rolls increase by 1d8 at 11th level (2d8 and 3d8) and again at 17th level (3d8 and 4d8).

DREAM OF THE BLUE VEIL

7th-level conjuration

Casting Time: 10 minutes
Range: 20 feet
Components: V, S, M (a magic item or a willing creature from the destination world)
Duration: 6 hours

> ### TRAVELING TO OTHER WORLDS
>
> The Material Plane holds an infinite number of worlds. Some—like Oerth, Toril, Krynn, and Eberron—are well documented, but there are countless others. You and your friends may even have created some homemade D&D worlds yourselves!
>
> It was not always so. Various scholars speak of a primordial state, a single reality they call the First World, which preceded the multiverse as we know it. Many of the peoples and monsters that inhabit the worlds in the Material Plane originated there. After the First World was shattered by a great cataclysm—giving birth to the worlds that came in its wake—the progeny of the first elves, dwarves, beholders, and other iconic creatures took root on world after world, like seeds scattered by a cosmic wind. If the musings of these great sages are true, every world is a reflection—and in some cases, a distortion—of the First World.
>
> Transit between these worlds is rare but not impossible and can be accomplished in various ways. One such method is called the Great Journey, an epic voyage fraught with peril and littered with obstacles to be overcome. This journey most often occurs aboard a vessel powered by magic.
>
> Another method is the Dream of Other Worlds; travelers fall into a deep slumber and dream themselves into a new realm. The spell *dream of the blue veil* employs this method of transit.
>
> The most direct method is the Leap to Another Realm; a spellcaster casts *teleportation circle* or *teleport*, aiming to appear in a known teleportation circle or some other location in another world.
>
> Whatever method you use to reach a world, the DM determines whether you succeed and where exactly you appear if you do arrive in that realm.

You and up to eight willing creatures within range fall unconscious for the spell's duration and experience visions of another world on the Material Plane, such as Oerth, Toril, Krynn, or Eberron. If the spell reaches its full duration, the visions conclude with each of you encountering and pulling back a mysterious blue curtain. The spell then ends with you mentally and physically transported to the world that was in the visions.

To cast this spell, you must have a magic item that originated on the world you wish to reach, and you must be aware of the world's existence, even if you don't know the world's name. Your destination in the other world is a safe location within 1 mile of where the magic item was created. Alternatively, you can cast the spell if one of the affected creatures was born on the other world, which causes your destination to be a safe location within 1 mile of where that creature was born.

The spell ends early on a creature if that creature takes any damage, and the creature isn't transported. If you take any damage, the spell ends for you and all the other creatures, with none of you being transported.

IRINA NORDSOL

GREEN-FLAME BLADE
Evocation cantrip

Casting Time: 1 action
Range: Self (5-foot radius)
Components: S, M (a melee weapon worth at
  least 1 sp)
Duration: Instantaneous

You brandish the weapon used in the spell's casting
and make a melee attack with it against one creature within 5 feet of you. On a hit, the target suffers
the weapon attack's normal effects, and you can
cause green fire to leap from the target to a different
creature of your choice that you can see within 5
feet of it. The second creature takes fire damage
equal to your spellcasting ability modifier.

This spell's damage increases when you reach
certain levels. At 5th level, the melee attack deals an
extra 1d8 fire damage to the target on a hit, and the
fire damage to the second creature increases to 1d8
+ your spellcasting ability modifier. Both damage
rolls increase by 1d8 at 11th level (2d8 and 2d8) and
17th level (3d8 and 3d8).

INTELLECT FORTRESS
3rd-level abjuration

Casting Time: 1 action
Range: 30 feet

Components: V
Duration: Concentration, up to 1 hour

For the duration, you or one willing creature you
can see within range has resistance to psychic damage, as well as advantage on Intelligence, Wisdom,
and Charisma saving throws.

At Higher Levels. When you cast this spell using
a spell slot of 4th level or higher, you can target one
additional creature for each slot level above 3rd. The
creatures must be within 30 feet of each other when
you target them.

LIGHTNING LURE
Evocation cantrip

Casting Time: 1 action
Range: Self (15-foot radius)
Components: V
Duration: Instantaneous

You create a lash of lightning energy that strikes
at one creature of your choice that you can see
within 15 feet of you. The target must succeed on a
Strength saving throw or be pulled up to 10 feet in a
straight line toward you and then take 1d8 lightning
damage if it is within 5 feet of you.

This spell's damage increases by 1d8 when you
reach 5th level (2d8), 11th level (3d8), and 17th
level (4d8).

INTELLECT FORTRESS

MIND SLIVER

Enchantment cantrip

Casting Time: 1 action
Range: 60 feet
Components: V
Duration: 1 round

You drive a disorienting spike of psychic energy into the mind of one creature you can see within range. The target must succeed on an Intelligence saving throw or take 1d6 psychic damage and subtract 1d4 from the next saving throw it makes before the end of your next turn.

This spell's damage increases by 1d6 when you reach certain levels: 5th level (2d6), 11th level (3d6), and 17th level (4d6).

SPIRIT SHROUD

3rd-level necromancy

Casting Time: 1 bonus action
Range: Self
Components: V, S
Duration: Concentration, up to 1 minute

You call forth spirits of the dead, which flit around you for the spell's duration. The spirits are intangible and invulnerable.

Until the spell ends, any attack you make deals 1d8 extra damage when you hit a creature within 10 feet of you. This damage is radiant, necrotic, or cold (your choice when you cast the spell). Any creature that takes this damage can't regain hit points until the start of your next turn.

In addition, any creature of your choice that you can see that starts its turn within 10 feet of you has its speed reduced by 10 feet until the start of your next turn.

At Higher Levels. When you cast this spell using a spell slot of 4th level or higher, the damage increases by 1d8 for every two slot levels above 3rd.

ANDREW MAR

SUMMON ABERRATION
4th-level conjuration

Casting Time: 1 action
Range: 90 feet
Components: V, S, M (a pickled tentacle and an eyeball in a platinum-inlaid vial worth at least 400 gp)
Duration: Concentration, up to 1 hour

You call forth an aberrant spirit. It manifests in an unoccupied space that you can see within range. This corporeal form uses the Aberrant Spirit stat block. When you cast the spell, choose Beholderkin, Slaad, or Star Spawn. The creature resembles an aberration of that kind, which determines certain traits in its stat block. The creature disappears when it drops to 0 hit points or when the spell ends.

The creature is an ally to you and your companions. In combat, the creature shares your initiative count, but it takes its turn immediately after yours. It obeys your verbal commands (no action required by you). If you don't issue any, it takes the Dodge action and uses its move to avoid danger.

ABERRANT SPIRIT
Medium aberration

Armor Class 11 + the level of the spell (natural armor)
Hit Points 40 + 10 for each spell level above 4th
Speed 30 ft.; fly 30 ft. (hover) (Beholderkin only)

STR	DEX	CON	INT	WIS	CHA
16 (+3)	10 (+0)	15 (+2)	16 (+3)	10 (+0)	6 (−2)

Damage Immunities psychic
Senses darkvision 60 ft., passive Perception 10
Languages Deep Speech, understands the languages you speak
Challenge —   **Proficiency Bonus** equals your bonus

Regeneration (Slaad Only). The aberration regains 5 hit points at the start of its turn if it has at least 1 hit point.

Whispering Aura (Star Spawn Only). At the start of each of the aberration's turns, each creature within 5 feet of the aberration must succeed on a Wisdom saving throw against your spell save DC or take 2d6 psychic damage, provided that the aberration isn't incapacitated.

ACTIONS

Multiattack. The aberration makes a number of attacks equal to half this spell's level (rounded down).

Claws (Slaad Only). *Melee Weapon Attack:* your spell attack modifier to hit, reach 5 ft., one target. *Hit:* 1d10 + 3 + the spell's level slashing damage. If the target is a creature, it can't regain hit points until the start of the aberration's next turn.

Eye Ray (Beholderkin Only). *Ranged Spell Attack:* your spell attack modifier to hit, range 150 ft., one creature. *Hit:* 1d8 + 3 + the spell's level psychic damage.

Psychic Slam (Star Spawn Only). *Melee Spell Attack:* your spell attack modifier to hit, reach 5 ft., one creature. *Hit:* 1d8 + 3 + the spell's level psychic damage.

At Higher Levels. When you cast this spell using a spell slot of 5th level or higher, use the higher level wherever the spell's level appears in the stat block.

SUMMON BEAST
2nd-level conjuration

Casting Time: 1 action
Range: 90 feet
Components: V, S, M (a feather, tuft of fur, and fish tail inside a gilded acorn worth at least 200 gp)
Duration: Concentration, up to 1 hour

You call forth a bestial spirit. It manifests in an unoccupied space that you can see within range. This corporeal form uses the Bestial Spirit stat block. When you cast the spell, choose an environment: Air, Land, or Water. The creature resembles an animal of your choice that is native to the chosen environment, which determines certain traits in its stat block. The creature disappears when it drops to 0 hit points or when the spell ends.

The creature is an ally to you and your companions. In combat, the creature shares your initiative count, but it takes its turn immediately after yours. It obeys your verbal commands (no action required by you). If you don't issue any, it takes the Dodge action and uses its move to avoid danger.

BESTIAL SPIRIT
Small beast

Armor Class 11 + the level of the spell (natural armor)
Hit Points 20 (Air only) or 30 (Land and Water only) + 5 for each spell level above 2nd
Speed 30 ft.; climb 30 ft. (Land only); fly 60 ft. (Air only); swim 30 ft. (Water only)

STR	DEX	CON	INT	WIS	CHA
18 (+4)	11 (+0)	16 (+3)	4 (−3)	14 (+2)	5 (−3)

Senses darkvision 60 ft., passive Perception 12
Languages understands the languages you speak
Challenge —   **Proficiency Bonus** equals your bonus

Flyby (Air Only). The beast doesn't provoke opportunity attacks when it flies out of an enemy's reach.

Pack Tactics (Land and Water Only). The beast has advantage on an attack roll against a creature if at least one of the beast's allies is within 5 feet of the creature and the ally isn't incapacitated.

Water Breathing (Water Only). The beast can breathe only underwater.

ACTIONS

Multiattack. The beast makes a number of attacks equal to half this spell's level (rounded down).

Maul. *Melee Weapon Attack:* your spell attack modifier to hit, reach 5 ft., one target. *Hit:* 1d8 + 4 + the spell's level piercing damage.

SUMMON CELESTIAL

At Higher Levels. When you cast this spell using a spell slot of 3rd level or higher, use the higher level wherever the spell's level appears in the stat block.

SUMMON CELESTIAL

5th-level conjuration

Casting Time: 1 action
Range: 90 feet
Components: V, S, M (a golden reliquary worth at least 500 gp)
Duration: Concentration, up to 1 hour

You call forth a celestial spirit. It manifests in an angelic form in an unoccupied space that you can see within range. This corporeal form uses the Celestial Spirit stat block. When you cast the spell, choose Avenger or Defender. Your choice determines the creature's attack in its stat block. The creature disappears when it drops to 0 hit points or when the spell ends.

The creature is an ally to you and your companions. In combat, the creature shares your initiative count, but it takes its turn immediately after yours. It obeys your verbal commands (no action required by you). If you don't issue any, it takes the Dodge action and uses its move to avoid danger.

At Higher Levels. When you cast this spell using a spell slot of 6th level or higher, use the higher level wherever the spell's level appears in the stat block.

CELESTIAL SPIRIT
Large celestial

Armor Class 11 + the level of the spell (natural armor) + 2 (Defender only)
Hit Points 40 + 10 for each spell level above 5th
Speed 30 ft., fly 40 ft.

STR	DEX	CON	INT	WIS	CHA
16 (+3)	14 (+2)	16 (+3)	10 (+0)	14 (+2)	16 (+3)

Damage Resistances radiant
Condition Immunities charmed, frightened
Senses darkvision 60 ft., passive Perception 12
Languages Celestial, understands the languages you speak
Challenge —   **Proficiency Bonus** equals your bonus

ACTIONS

Multiattack. The celestial makes a number of attacks equal to half this spell's level (rounded down).

Radiant Bow (Avenger Only). Ranged Weapon Attack: your spell attack modifier to hit, range 150/600 ft., one target. *Hit:* 2d6 + 2 + the spell's level radiant damage.

Radiant Mace (Defender Only). Melee Weapon Attack: your spell attack modifier to hit, reach 5 ft., one target. *Hit:* 1d10 + 3 + the spell's level radiant damage, and the celestial can choose itself or another creature it can see within 10 feet of the target. The chosen creature gains 1d10 temporary hit points.

Healing Touch (1/Day). The celestial touches another creature. The target magically regains hit points equal to 2d8 + the spell's level.

BRIAN VALEZA

Summon Construct
4th-level conjuration

Casting Time: 1 action
Range: 90 feet
Components: V, S, M (an ornate stone and metal lockbox worth at least 400 gp)
Duration: Concentration, up to 1 hour

You call forth the spirit of a construct. It manifests in an unoccupied space that you can see within range. This corporeal form uses the Construct Spirit stat block. When you cast the spell, choose a material: Clay, Metal, or Stone. The creature resembles a golem or a modron (your choice) made of the chosen material, which determines certain traits in its stat block. The creature disappears when it drops to 0 hit points or when the spell ends.

The creature is an ally to you and your companions. In combat, the creature shares your initiative count, but it takes its turn immediately after yours.

CONSTRUCT SPIRIT
Medium construct

Armor Class 13 + the level of the spell (natural armor)
Hit Points 40 + 15 for each spell level above 3rd
Speed 30 ft.

STR	DEX	CON	INT	WIS	CHA
18 (+4)	10 (+0)	18 (+4)	14 (+2)	11 (+0)	5 (–3)

Damage Resistances poison
Condition Immunities charmed, exhaustion, frightened, incapacitated, paralyzed, petrified, poisoned
Senses darkvision 60 ft., passive Perception 10
Languages understands the languages you speak
Challenge —   **Proficiency Bonus** equals your bonus

Heated Body (Metal Only). A creature that touches the construct or hits it with a melee attack while within 5 feet of it takes 1d10 fire damage.

Stony Lethargy (Stone Only). When a creature the construct can see starts its turn within 10 feet of the construct, the construct can force it to make a Wisdom saving throw against your spell save DC. On a failed save, the target can't use reactions and its speed is halved until the start of its next turn.

ACTIONS

Multiattack. The construct makes a number of attacks equal to half this spell's level (rounded down).

Slam. *Melee Weapon Attack:* your spell attack modifier to hit, reach 5 ft., one target. *Hit:* 1d8 + 4 + the spell's level bludgeoning damage.

REACTIONS

Berserk Lashing (Clay Only). When the construct takes damage, it makes a slam attack against a random creature within 5 feet of it. If no creature is within reach, the construct moves up to half its speed toward an enemy it can see, without provoking opportunity attacks.

It obeys your verbal commands (no action required by you). If you don't issue any, it takes the Dodge action and uses its move to avoid danger.

At Higher Levels. When you cast this spell using a spell slot of 4th level or higher, use the higher level wherever the spell's level appears in the stat block.

SUMMON ELEMENTAL
4th-level conjuration

Casting Time: 1 action
Range: 90 feet
Components: V, S, M (air, a pebble, ash, and water inside a gold-inlaid vial worth at least 400 gp)
Duration: Concentration, up to 1 hour

You call forth an elemental spirit. It manifests in an unoccupied space that you can see within range. This corporeal form uses the Elemental Spirit stat block. When you cast the spell, choose an element: Air, Earth, Fire, or Water. The creature resembles a bipedal form wreathed in the chosen element, which determines certain traits in its stat block. The creature disappears when it drops to 0 hit points or when the spell ends.

The creature is an ally to you and your companions. In combat, the creature shares your initiative count, but it takes its turn immediately after yours. It obeys your verbal commands (no action required

ELEMENTAL SPIRIT
Medium elemental

Armor Class 11 + the level of the spell (natural armor)
Hit Points 50 + 10 for each spell level above 4th
Speed 40 ft.; burrow 40 ft. (Earth only); fly 40 ft. (hover) (Air only); swim 40 ft. (Water only)

STR	DEX	CON	INT	WIS	CHA
18 (+4)	15 (+2)	17 (+3)	4 (–3)	10 (+0)	16 (+3)

Damage Resistances acid (Water only); lightning and thunder (Air only); piercing and slashing (Earth only)
Damage Immunities poison; fire (Fire only)
Condition Immunities exhaustion, paralyzed, petrified, poisoned, unconscious
Senses darkvision 60 ft., passive Perception 10
Languages Primordial, understands the languages you speak
Challenge —   **Proficiency Bonus** equals your bonus

Amorphous Form (Air, Fire, and Water Only). The elemental can move through a space as narrow as 1 inch wide without squeezing.

ACTIONS

Multiattack. The elemental makes a number of attacks equal to half this spell's level (rounded down).

Slam. *Melee Weapon Attack:* your spell attack modifier to hit, reach 5 ft., one target. *Hit:* 1d10 + 4 + the spell's level bludgeoning damage (Air, Earth, and Water only) or fire damage (Fire only).

by you). If you don't issue any, it takes the Dodge action and uses its move to avoid danger.

At Higher Levels. When you cast this spell using a spell slot of 5th level or higher, use the higher level wherever the spell's level appears in the stat block.

SUMMON FEY
3rd-level conjuration

Casting Time: 1 action
Range: 90 feet
Components: V, S, M (a gilded flower worth at least 300 gp)
Duration: Concentration, up to 1 hour

You call forth a fey spirit. It manifests in an unoccupied space that you can see within range. This corporeal form uses the Fey Spirit stat block. When you cast the spell, choose a mood: Fuming, Mirthful, or Tricksy. The creature resembles a fey creature of your choice marked by the chosen mood, which determines one of the traits in its stat block. The creature disappears when it drops to 0 hit points or when the spell ends.

The creature is an ally to you and your companions. In combat, the creature shares your initiative

---

FEY SPIRIT
Small fey

Armor Class 12 + the level of the spell (natural armor)
Hit Points 30 + 10 for each spell level above 3rd
Speed 40 ft.

STR	DEX	CON	INT	WIS	CHA
13 (+1)	16 (+3)	14 (+2)	14 (+2)	11 (+0)	16 (+3)

Condition Immunities charmed
Senses darkvision 60 ft., passive Perception 10
Languages Sylvan, understands the languages you speak
Challenge —   **Proficiency Bonus** equals your bonus

ACTIONS

Multiattack. The fey makes a number of attacks equal to half this spell's level (rounded down).

Shortsword. *Melee Weapon Attack:* your spell attack modifier to hit, reach 5 ft., one target. *Hit:* 1d6 + 3 + the spell's level piercing damage + 1d6 force damage.

BONUS ACTIONS

Fey Step. The fey magically teleports up to 30 feet to an unoccupied space it can see. Then one of the following effects occurs, based on the fey's chosen mood:

Fuming. The fey has advantage on the next attack roll it makes before the end of this turn.
Mirthful. The fey can force one creature it can see within 10 feet of it to make a Wisdom saving throw against your spell save DC. Unless the save succeeds, the target is charmed by you and the fey for 1 minute or until the target takes any damage.
Tricksy. The fey can fill a 5-foot cube within 5 feet of it with magical darkness, which lasts until the end of its next turn.

---

count, but it takes its turn immediately after yours. It obeys your verbal commands (no action required by you). If you don't issue any, it takes the Dodge action and uses its move to avoid danger.

At Higher Levels. When you cast this spell using a spell slot of 4th level or higher, use the higher level wherever the spell's level appears in the stat block.

SUMMON FIEND
6th-level conjuration

Casting Time: 1 action
Range: 90 feet
Components: V, S, M (humanoid blood inside a ruby vial worth at least 600 gp)
Duration: Concentration, up to 1 hour

FIENDISH SPIRIT
Large fiend

Armor Class 12 + the level of the spell (natural armor)
Hit Points 50 (Demon only) or 40 (Devil only) or 60 (Yugoloth only) + 15 for each spell level above 6th
Speed 40 ft.; climb 40 ft. (Demon only); fly 60 ft. (Devil only)

STR	DEX	CON	INT	WIS	CHA
13 (+1)	16 (+3)	15 (+2)	10 (+0)	10 (+0)	16 (+3)

Damage Resistances fire
Damage Immunities poison
Condition Immunities poisoned
Senses darkvision 60 ft., passive Perception 10
Languages Abyssal, Infernal, telepathy 60 ft.
Challenge —   **Proficiency Bonus** equals your bonus

Death Throes (Demon Only). When the fiend drops to 0 hit points or the spell ends, the fiend explodes, and each creature within 10 feet of it must make a Dexterity saving throw against your spell save DC. A creature takes 2d10 + this spell's level fire damage on a failed save, or half as much damage on a successful one.

Devil's Sight (Devil Only). Magical darkness doesn't impede the fiend's darkvision.

Magic Resistance. The fiend has advantage on saving throws against spells and other magical effects.

ACTIONS

Multiattack. The fiend makes a number of attacks equal to half this spell's level (rounded down).

Bite (Demon Only). *Melee Weapon Attack:* your spell attack modifier to hit, reach 5 ft., one target. *Hit:* 1d12 + 3 + the spell's level necrotic damage.

Claws (Yugoloth Only). *Melee Weapon Attack:* your spell attack modifier to hit, reach 5 ft., one target. *Hit:* 1d8 + 3 + the spell's level slashing damage. Immediately after the attack hits or misses, the fiend can magically teleport up to 30 feet to an unoccupied space it can see.

Hurl Flame (Devil Only). *Ranged Spell Attack:* your spell attack modifier to hit, range 150 ft., one target. *Hit:* 2d6 + 3 + the spell's level fire damage. If the target is a flammable object that isn't being worn or carried, it also catches fire.

SUMMON SHADOWSPAWN

You call forth a fiendish spirit. It manifests in an un-occupied space that you can see within range. This corporeal form uses the Fiendish Spirit stat block. When you cast the spell, choose Demon, Devil, or Yugoloth. The creature resembles a fiend of the cho-sen type, which determines certain traits in its stat block. The creature disappears when it drops to 0 hit points or when the spell ends.

The creature is an ally to you and your compan-ions. In combat, the creature shares your initiative count, but it takes its turn immediately after yours. It obeys your verbal commands (no action required by you). If you don't issue any, it takes the Dodge ac-tion and uses its move to avoid danger.

At Higher Levels. When you cast this spell using a spell slot of 7th level or higher, use the higher level wherever the spell's level appears in the stat block.

SUMMON SHADOWSPAWN
3rd-level conjuration

Casting Time: 1 action
Range: 90 feet
Components: V, S, M (tears inside a gem worth at least 300 gp)
Duration: Concentration, up to 1 hour

You call forth a shadowy spirit. It manifests in an unoccupied space that you can see within range. This corporeal form uses the Shadow Spirit stat block. When you cast the spell, choose an emotion: Fury, Despair, or Fear. The creature resembles a misshapen biped marked by the chosen emotion, which determines certain traits in its stat block. The creature disappears when it drops to 0 hit points or when the spell ends.

The creature is an ally to you and your compan-ions. In combat, the creature shares your initiative

SHADOW SPIRIT
Medium monstrosity

Armor Class 11 + the level of the spell (natural armor)
Hit Points 35 + 15 for each spell level above 3rd
Speed 40 ft.

STR	DEX	CON	INT	WIS	CHA
13 (+1)	16 (+3)	15 (+2)	4 (−3)	10 (+0)	16 (+3)

Damage Resistances necrotic
Condition Immunities frightened
Senses darkvision 120 ft., passive Perception 10
Languages understands the languages you speak
Challenge —   **Proficiency Bonus** equals your bonus

Terror Frenzy (Fury Only). The spirit has advantage on attack rolls against frightened creatures.

Weight of Sorrow (Despair Only). Any creature, other than you, that starts its turn within 5 feet of the spirit has its speed reduced by 20 feet until the start of that creature's next turn.

ACTIONS

Multiattack. The spirit makes a number of attacks equal to half this spell's level (rounded down).

Chilling Rend. *Melee Weapon Attack:* your spell attack modifier to hit, reach 5 ft., one target. *Hit:* 1d12 + 3 + the spell's level cold damage.

Dreadful Scream (1/Day). The spirit screams. Each creature within 30 feet of it must succeed on a Wisdom saving throw against your spell save DC or be frightened of the spirit for 1 minute. The frightened creature can repeat the saving throw at the end of each of its turns, ending the effect on itself on a success.

BONUS ACTIONS

Shadow Stealth (Fear Only). While in dim light or darkness, the spirit takes the Hide action.

count, but it takes its turn immediately after yours. It obeys your verbal commands (no action required by you). If you don't issue any, it takes the Dodge action and uses its move to avoid danger.

At Higher Levels. When you cast this spell using a spell slot of 4th level or higher, use the higher level wherever the spell's level appears in the stat block.

SUMMON UNDEAD
3rd-level necromancy

Casting Time: 1 action
Range: 90 feet
Components: V, S, M (a gilded skull worth at least 300 gp)
Duration: Concentration, up to 1 hour

You call forth an undead spirit. It manifests in an unoccupied space that you can see within range. This corporeal form uses the Undead Spirit stat block. When you cast the spell, choose the crea-

UNDEAD SPIRIT
Medium undead

Armor Class 11 + the level of the spell (natural armor)
Hit Points 30 (Ghostly and Putrid only) or 20 (Skeletal only) + 10 for each spell level above 3rd
Speed 30 ft.; fly 40 ft. (hover) (Ghostly only)

STR	DEX	CON	INT	WIS	CHA
12 (+1)	16 (+3)	15 (+2)	4 (−3)	10 (+0)	9 (−1)

Damage Immunities necrotic, poison
Condition Immunities exhaustion, frightened, paralyzed, poisoned
Senses darkvision 60 ft., passive Perception 10
Languages understands the languages you speak
Challenge —   **Proficiency Bonus** equals your bonus

Festering Aura (Putrid Only). Any creature, other than you, that starts its turn within 5 feet of the spirit must succeed on a Constitution saving throw against your spell save DC or be poisoned until the start of its next turn.

Incorporeal Passage (Ghostly Only). The spirit can move through other creatures and objects as if they were difficult terrain. If it ends its turn inside an object, it is shunted to the nearest unoccupied space and takes 1d10 force damage for every 5 feet traveled.

ACTIONS

Multiattack. The spirit makes a number of attacks equal to half this spell's level (rounded down).

Deathly Touch (Ghostly Only). *Melee Weapon Attack:* your spell attack modifier to hit, reach 5 ft., one creature. *Hit:* 1d8 + 3 + the spell's level necrotic damage, and the creature must succeed on a Wisdom saving throw against your spell save DC or be frightened of the undead until the end of the target's next turn.

Grave Bolt (Skeletal Only). *Ranged Spell Attack:* your spell attack modifier to hit, range 150 ft., one target. *Hit:* 2d4 + 3 + the spell's level necrotic damage.

Rotting Claw (Putrid Only). *Melee Weapon Attack:* your spell attack modifier to hit, reach 5 ft., one target. *Hit:* 1d6 + 3 + the spell's level slashing damage. If the target is poisoned, it must succeed on a Constitution saving throw against your spell save DC or be paralyzed until the end of its next turn.

ture's form: Ghostly, Putrid, or Skeletal. The spirit resembles an undead creature with the chosen form, which determines certain traits in its stat block. The creature disappears when it drops to 0 hit points or when the spell ends.

The creature is an ally to you and your companions. In combat, the creature shares your initiative count, but it takes its turn immediately after yours. It obeys your verbal commands (no action required by you). If you don't issue any, it takes the Dodge action and uses its move to avoid danger.

At Higher Levels. When you cast this spell using a spell slot of 4th level or higher, use the higher level wherever the spell's level appears in the stat block.

Tasha's Mind Whip

SWORD BURST
Conjuration cantrip

Casting Time: 1 action
Range: Self (5-foot radius)
Components: V
Duration: Instantaneous

You create a momentary circle of spectral blades that sweep around you. All other creatures within 5 feet of you must each succeed on a Dexterity saving throw or take 1d6 force damage.

This spell's damage increases by 1d6 when you reach 5th level (2d6), 11th level (3d6), and 17th level (4d6).

TASHA'S CAUSTIC BREW
1st-level evocation

Casting Time: 1 action
Range: Self (30-foot line)
Components: V, S, M (a bit of rotten food)
Duration: Concentration, up to 1 minute

A stream of acid emanates from you in a line 30 feet long and 5 feet wide in a direction you choose. Each creature in the line must succeed on a Dexterity saving throw or be covered in acid for the spell's duration or until a creature uses its action to scrape or wash the acid off itself or another creature. A creature covered in the acid takes 2d4 acid damage at start of each of its turns.

At Higher Levels. When you cast this spell using a spell slot of 2nd level or higher, the damage increases by 2d4 for each slot level above 1st.

TASHA'S MIND WHIP
2nd-level enchantment

Casting Time: 1 action
Range: 90 feet
Components: V
Duration: 1 round

You psychically lash out at one creature you can see within range. The target must make an Intelligence saving throw. On a failed save, the target takes 3d6 psychic damage, and it can't take a reaction until the end of its next turn. Moreover, on its next turn, it must choose whether it gets a move, an action, or a bonus action; it gets only one of the three. On a successful save, the target takes half as much damage and suffers none of the spell's other effects.

At Higher Levels. When you cast this spell using a spell slot of 3rd level or higher, you can target one additional creature for each slot level above 2nd. The creatures must be within 30 feet of each other when you target them.

Tasha's Otherworldly Guise
6th-level transmutation

Casting Time: 1 bonus action
Range: Self
Components: V, S, M (an object engraved with a symbol of the Outer Planes, worth at least 500 gp)
Duration: Concentration, up to 1 minute

Uttering an incantation, you draw on the magic of the Lower Planes or Upper Planes (your choice) to transform yourself. You gain the following benefits until the spell ends:

- You are immune to fire and poison damage (Lower Planes) or radiant and necrotic damage (Upper Planes).
- You are immune to the poisoned condition (Lower Planes) or the charmed condition (Upper Planes).
- Spectral wings appear on your back, giving you a flying speed of 40 feet.
- You have a +2 bonus to AC.
- All your weapon attacks are magical, and when you make a weapon attack, you can use your spellcasting ability modifier, instead of Strength or Dexterity, for the attack and damage rolls.
- You can attack twice, instead of once, when you take the Attack action on your turn. You ignore this benefit if you already have a feature, like Extra Attack, that lets you attack more than once when you take the Attack action on your turn.

PERSONALIZING SPELLS

Just as every performer lends their art a personal flair and every warrior asserts their fighting styles through the lens of their own training, so too can a spellcaster use magic to express their individuality. Regardless of what type of spellcaster you're playing, you can customize the cosmetic effects of your character's spells. Perhaps you wish the effects of your caster's spells to appear in their favorite color, to suggest the training they received from a celestial mentor, or to exhibit their connection to a season of the year. The possibilities for how you might cosmetically customize your character's spells are endless. However, such alterations can't change the effects of a spell. They also can't make one spell seem like another—you can't, for example, make a *magic missile* look like a *fireball*.

A FARMER SORCERER HURLS MAGIC MISSILES THAT LOOK LIKE CHICKENS.

When customizing your spellcaster's magic, consider developing a theme—often, the broader and more versatile the better. You may describe your caster's magic whenever you wish, particularly when it makes an interesting addition to a story. You may also use it to reinforce other choices you've made for your character, like making a bard's spells tied more closely to their favored art form or a cleric's spells themed around their deity.

For example, the *fireball* of a wizard with a fondness for storms might erupt to look like burning clouds or a burst of red lightning (without affecting the spell's damage type), while the same wizard's *haste* spell might limn the target in faint thunderheads.

Alternatively, a cleric who serves a moon god might radiate faint moonlight around their hands when they cast *cure wounds*, or their *shield of faith* might surround the target with glimmering crescent moons.

Further still, a druid could choose a cherry blossom theme for their magic, causing delicate branches and pink leaves to grow when they cast *entangle* or *shillelagh*, and their *faerie fire* spell could appear more like wind-tossed petals than flames.

The Magic Themes table offers just a few suggestions that might inspire you while personalizing your character's spells.

MAGIC THEMES

d10	Theme
1	Book pages, origami, quills, and ink, all accompanied by rustling sounds and library scents
2	Brine-scented shapes of sharks, jellyfish, octopi, and other sea creatures
3	Food or utensils that carry the scent of cuisine from the spellcaster's homeland
4	Rich, copper scents accompanied by what appears to be the caster's own imbalanced humors
5	Bursts and strokes of watercolor painted by an invisible brush
6	Transparent weapons, armor, miniature war machines, and phantom soldiers
7	Golden rays that carry faint warmth and the hint of windblown sand
8	Rowdy barnyard animals accompanied by the warm scents of coops and stables
9	Manifestations of deep emotions, like the faint shackles of melancholy, sepia shades of nostalgia, or heart-shaped bursts of affection
10	Tiny whimsical or fearsome beings from the spellcaster's inescapable, recurring dreams

MAGIC ITEMS

Who doesn't love magic items? The desire for them is one of the few things Mordenkainen and I have in common. And magic tattoos—they're especially fun. I think tattoos are a reason robes are so popular with wizards. Robes cover the ankle and lower-back tattoos so many of us got as apprentices. Don't even ask.

TASHA

This section presents magic items that can be introduced into any campaign. Here you'll find items of all rarities, including artifacts. Magic spellcasting focuses for every spellcasting class are also available here. And some of the items in this section represent a new type of wondrous item: magic tattoos.

The Magic Items table lists all the magic items in this chapter and notes the rarity of each one. The table also indicates whether an item requires attunement. All the items use the magic items rules in the *Dungeon Master's Guide*.

MAGIC ITEMS

Rarity	Item	Attunement
Common	Illuminator's Tattoo	Yes
Common	Masquerade Tattoo	Yes
Common	Prosthetic Limb	No
Common+	Spellwrought Tattoo	No
Uncommon+	All-Purpose Tool	Yes
Uncommon+	Amulet of the Devout	Yes
Uncommon+	Arcane Grimoire	Yes
Uncommon+	Barrier Tattoo	Yes
Uncommon+	Bloodwell Vial	Yes
Uncommon	Coiling Grasp Tattoo	Yes
Uncommon	Eldritch Claw Tattoo	Yes
Uncommon	Feywild Shard	Yes
Uncommon	Guardian Emblem	Yes
Uncommon+	Moon Sickle	Yes
Uncommon	Nature's Mantle	Yes
Uncommon+	Rhythm-Maker's Drum	Yes
Rare	Alchemical Compendium	Yes
Rare	Astral Shard	Yes
Rare	Astromancy Archive	Yes
Rare	Atlas of Endless Horizons	Yes
Rare	Bell Branch	Yes
Rare	Devotee's Censer	Yes
Rare	Duplicitous Manuscript	Yes
Rare	Elemental Essence Shard	Yes
Rare	Far Realm Shard	Yes
Rare	Fulminating Treatise	Yes

SIDHARTH CHATURVEDI

An orc artist creates a tattoo on his elf friend.

Rarity	Item	Attunement
Rare	Heart Weaver's Primer	Yes
Rare	Libram of Souls and Flesh	Yes
Rare	Lyre of Building	Yes
Rare	Outer Essence Shard	Yes
Rare	Planecaller's Codex	Yes
Rare	Protective Verses	Yes
Rare	Reveler's Concertina	Yes
Rare	Shadowfell Brand Tattoo	Yes
Rare	Shadowfell Shard	Yes
Very Rare	Absorbing Tattoo	Yes
Very Rare	Cauldron of Rebirth	Yes
Very Rare	Crystalline Chronicle	Yes
Very Rare	Ghost Step Tattoo	Yes
Very Rare	Lifewell Tattoo	Yes
Legendary	Blood Fury Tattoo	Yes
Artifact	Baba Yaga's Mortar and Pestle	Yes
Artifact	Crook of Rao	Yes
Artifact	Demonomicon of Iggwilv	Yes
Artifact	Luba's Tarokka of Souls	Yes
Artifact	Mighty Servant of Leuk-o	Yes
Artifact	Teeth of Dahlver-Nar	Yes

Magic Tattoos

Blending magic and artistry with ink and needles, magic tattoos imbue their bearers with wondrous abilities. Magic tattoos are initially bound to magic needles, which transfer their magic to a creature.

Once inscribed on a creature's body, damage or injury doesn't impair the tattoo's function, even if the tattoo is defaced. When applying a magic tattoo, a creature can customize the tattoo's appearance. A magic tattoo can look like a brand, scarification, a birthmark, patterns of scale, or any other cosmetic alteration.

The rarer a magic tattoo is, the more space it typically occupies on a creature's skin. The Magic Tattoo Coverage table offers guidelines for how large a given tattoo is.

Magic Tattoo Coverage

Tattoo Rarity	Area Covered
Common	One hand or foot or a quarter of a limb
Uncommon	Half a limb or the scalp
Rare	One limb
Very Rare	Two limbs or the chest or upper back
Legendary	Two limbs and the torso

MAGIC ITEM DESCRIPTIONS

The following magic items are presented in alphabetical order.

ABSORBING TATTOO

Wondrous item (tattoo), very rare (requires attunement)

Produced by a special needle, this magic tattoo features designs that emphasize one color.

Tattoo Attunement. To attune to this item, you hold the needle to your skin where you want the tattoo to appear, pressing the needle there throughout the attunement process. When the attunement is complete, the needle turns into the ink that becomes the tattoo, which appears on the skin.

If your attunement to the tattoo ends, the tattoo vanishes, and the needle reappears in your space.

Damage Resistance. While the tattoo is on your skin, you have resistance to a type of damage associated with that color, as shown on the table below. The DM chooses the color or determines it randomly.

d10	Damage Type	Color
1	Acid	Green
2	Cold	Blue
3	Fire	Red
4	Force	White
5	Lightning	Yellow
6	Necrotic	Black
7	Poison	Violet
8	Psychic	Silver
9	Radiant	Gold
10	Thunder	Orange

Damage Absorption. When you take damage of the chosen type, you can use your reaction to gain immunity against that instance of the damage, and you regain a number of hit points equal to half the damage you would have taken. Once this reaction is used, it can't be used again until the next dawn.

ALCHEMICAL COMPENDIUM

Wondrous item, rare (requires attunement by a wizard)

Acrid odors cling to this stained, heavy volume. The book's metal fittings are copper, iron, lead, silver, and gold, some frozen mid-transition from one metal to another. When found, the book contains the following spells: *enlarge/reduce*, *feather fall*, *flesh to stone*, *gaseous form*, *magic weapon*, and *polymorph*. It functions as a spellbook for you.

While you are holding the book, you can use it as a spellcasting focus for your wizard spells.

The book has 3 charges, and it regains 1d3 expended charges daily at dawn. You can use the charges in the following ways while holding it:

- If you spend 1 minute studying the book, you can expend 1 charge to replace one of your prepared wizard spells with a different spell in the book. The new spell must be of the transmutation school.
- As an action, you can touch a nonmagical object that isn't being worn or carried and spend a number of charges to transform the target into another object. For 1 charge, the object can be no larger than 1 foot on a side. You can spend additional charges to increase the maximum dimensions by 2 feet per charge. The new object must have a gold value equal to or less than the original.

ALL-PURPOSE TOOL

Wondrous item, uncommon (+1), rare (+2), very rare (+3) (requires attunement by an artificer)

This simple screwdriver can transform into a variety of tools; as an action, you can touch the item and transform it into any type of artisan's tool of your choice (see the "Equipment" chapter in the *Player's Handbook* for a list of artisan's tools). Whatever form the tool takes, you are proficient with it.

While holding this tool, you gain a bonus to the spell attack rolls and the saving throw DCs of your artificer spells. The bonus is determined by the tool's rarity.

As an action, you can focus on the tool to channel your creative forces. Choose a cantrip that you don't know from any class list. For 8 hours, you can cast that cantrip, and it counts as an artificer cantrip for you. Once this property is used, it can't be used again until the next dawn.

AMULET OF THE DEVOUT

Wondrous item, uncommon (+1), rare (+2), very rare (+3) (requires attunement by a cleric or paladin)

This amulet bears the symbol of a deity inlaid with precious stones or metals. While you wear the holy symbol, you gain a bonus to spell attack rolls and the saving throw DCs of your spells. The bonus is determined by the amulet's rarity.

While you wear this amulet, you can use your Channel Divinity feature without expending one of the feature's uses. Once this property is used, it can't be used again until the next dawn.

Arcane Grimoire

Wondrous item, uncommon (+1), rare (+2), very rare (+3) (requires attunement by a wizard)

While you are holding this leather-bound book, you can use it as a spellcasting focus for your wizard spells, and you gain a bonus to spell attack rolls and to the saving throw DCs of your wizard spells. The bonus is determined by the book's rarity.

You can use this book as a spellbook. In addition, when you use your Arcane Recovery feature, you can increase the number of spell slot levels you regain by 1.

Astral Shard

Wondrous item, rare (requires attunement by a sorcerer)

This crystal is a solidified shard of the Astral Plane, swirling with silver mist. As an action, you can attach the shard to a Tiny object (such as a weapon or a piece of jewelry) or detach it. It falls off if your attunement to it ends. You can use the shard as a spellcasting focus for your sorcerer spells while you hold or wear it.

When you use a Metamagic option on a spell while you are holding or wearing the shard, immediately after casting the spell you can teleport to an unoccupied space you can see within 30 feet of you.

Astromancy Archive

Wondrous item, rare (requires attunement by a wizard)

This brass disc of articulated, concentric rings unfolds into an armillary sphere. As a bonus action, you can unfold it into the sphere or back into a disc. When found, it contains the following spells, which are wizard spells for you while you are attuned to it: *augury, divination, find the path, foresight, locate creature,* and *locate object.* It functions as a spellbook for you, with spells encoded on the rings.

While you are holding the archive, you can use it as a spellcasting focus for your wizard spells.

The archive has 3 charges, and it regains 1d3 expended charges daily at dawn. You can use the charges in the following ways while holding it:

- If you spend 1 minute studying the archive, you can expend 1 charge to replace one of your prepared wizard spells with a different spell in the archive. The new spell must be of the divination school.
- When a creature you can see within 30 feet of you makes an attack roll, an ability check, or a saving throw, you can use your reaction to expend 1 charge and force the creature to roll a d4 and apply the number rolled as a bonus or penalty (your choice) to the original roll. You can do this after you see the roll but before its effects are applied.

ATLAS OF
ENDLESS HORIZONS

Atlas of Endless Horizons

Wondrous item, rare (requires attunement by a wizard)

This thick book is bound in dark leather, crisscrossed with inlaid silver lines suggesting a map or chart. When found, the book contains the following spells, which are wizard spells for you while you are attuned to the book: *arcane gate, dimension door, gate, misty step, plane shift, teleportation circle,* and *word of recall.* It functions as a spellbook for you.

While you are holding the book, you can use it as a spellcasting focus for your wizard spells.

The book has 3 charges, and it regains 1d3 expended charges daily at dawn. You can use the charges in the following ways while holding it:

- If you spend 1 minute studying the book, you can expend 1 charge to replace one of your prepared wizard spells with a different spell in the book. The new spell must be of the conjuration school.
- When you are hit by an attack, you can use your reaction to expend 1 charge to teleport up to 10 feet to an unoccupied space you can see. If your new position is out of range of the attack, it misses you.

BABA YAGA'S MORTAR AND PESTLE
Wondrous item, artifact (requires attunement)

The creations of the immortal hag Baba Yaga defy the laws of mortal magic. Among the notorious implements that cement her legend on countless worlds are the artifacts that propel her through the planes: *Baba Yaga's Mortar and Pestle*. These signature tools of Baba Yaga are a single artifact for purposes of attunement. Should the two objects become separated, the pestle appears next to the mortar at the next dawn.

Random Properties. This artifact has the following random properties, which you can determine by rolling on the tables in the "Artifacts" section of the *Dungeon Master's Guide*:

- 2 minor beneficial properties
- 1 major beneficial property
- 1 minor detrimental property

Properties of the Mortar. The mortar is a Tiny wooden bowl. However, the mortar increases in size to accommodate anything you place inside, expanding—if there's enough space—up to Large size, meaning it can hold even a Large creature.

Properties of the Pestle. The pestle is a 6-inch-long, worn wooden tool. Once during your turn while you are holding the pestle, you can extend it into a quarterstaff or shrink it back into a pestle (no action required). As a quarterstaff, the pestle is a magic weapon that grants a +3 bonus to attack and damage rolls made with it.

The pestle has 12 charges. When you hit with a melee attack using the pestle, you can expend up to 3 of its charges to deal an extra 1d8 force damage for each charge expended. The pestle regains all expended charges daily at dawn.

Perfect Tools. While holding the mortar and pestle, you can use your action to say the name of any nonmagical plant, mineral, or fluid and an amount of the material worth 10 gp or less. The mortar instantly fills with the desired amount of that material. Once you use this action, you can't do so again until you finish a short or long rest.

You can also use the artifact as alchemist's supplies, brewer's supplies, cook's utensils, an herbalism kit, and a poisoner's kit. You have advantage on any check you make using the artifact as one of these tools.

Primal Parts. As an action while the pestle and the mortar is within 5 feet of you, you can command the pestle to grind. For the next minute, or until you use your action to verbally command it to stop, the pestle moves on its own, grinding the contents of the mortar into a mush or fine powder that's equally useful for cooking or alchemy. At the start of each of your turns, whatever is in the mortar takes 4d10 force damage. If this reduces the target's hit points

A NIGHT HAG TAKES BABA YAGA'S MORTAR AND PESTLE FOR A SPIN.

to 0, the target is reduced to powder, pulp, or paste, as appropriate. Only magic items are unaffected. If you wish, when the pestle stops, you can have the mortar separate its contents—like powdered bone, crushed herbs, pulped organs—into separate piles.

Traverse the Night. If you are holding the pestle while you are inside the mortar, you can use your action to verbally command the mortar to travel to a specific place or creature. You don't need to know where your destination is, but it must be a specific destination—not just the nearest river or a red dragon's lair. If the stated destination is within 1,000 miles of you, the mortar lifts into the air and vanishes. You and any creatures in the mortar travel through a dreamlike sky, with hazy reflections of the world passing by below. Creatures might see images of you streaking through the sky between your point of origin and the destination. You arrive at the location 1 hour later or, if it is night, 1 minute later.

Bones Know Their Home. When you command the mortar to travel, you can instead throw out the dust or paste of something ground by the mortar and name a location on a different plane of existence or a different world on the Material Plane. If that material came from a creature native to the named plane or world, the mortar travels through an empty night sky to an unoccupied space at that destination, arriving in 1 minute.

Destroying the Mortar and Pestle. The mortar and pestle are destroyed if they are crushed underfoot by the *Dancing Hut of Baba Yaga* or by Baba Yaga herself.

BARRIER TATTOO

Wondrous item (tattoo), rarity varies (requires attunement)

Produced by a special needle, this magic tattoo depicts protective imagery and uses ink that resembles liquid metal.

Tattoo Attunement. To attune to this item, you hold the needle to your skin where you want the tattoo to appear, pressing the needle there throughout the attunement process. When the attunement is complete, the needle turns into the ink that becomes the tattoo, which appears on the skin.

If your attunement to the tattoo ends, the tattoo vanishes, and the needle reappears in your space.

Protection. While you aren't wearing armor, the tattoo grants you an Armor Class depending on the tattoo's rarity, as shown below. You can use a shield and still gain this benefit.

Rarity	AC
Uncommon	12 + your Dexterity modifier
Rare	15 + your Dexterity modifier (maximum of +2)
Very Rare	18

BELL BRANCH

Wondrous item, rare (requires attunement by a druid or warlock)

This silver implement is shaped like a tree branch and is strung with small golden bells. The branch is a spellcasting focus for your spells while you hold it.

The branch has 3 charges, and it regains 1d3 expended charges daily at dawn. You can use the charges in the following ways while holding it:

- As a bonus action, you can expend 1 charge to detect the presence of aberrations, celestials, constructs, elementals, fey, fiends, or undead within 60 feet of you. If such creatures are present and don't have total cover from you, the bells ring softly, their tone indicating the creature types present.
- As an action, you can expend 1 charge to cast *protection from evil and good*.

BLOOD FURY TATTOO

Wondrous item (tattoo), legendary (requires attunement)

Produced by a special needle, this magic tattoo evokes fury in its form and colors.

Tattoo Attunement. To attune to this item, you hold the needle to your skin where you want the tattoo to appear, pressing the needle there throughout the attunement process. When the attunement is complete, the needle turns into the ink that becomes the tattoo, which appears on the skin.

If your attunement to the tattoo ends, the tattoo vanishes, and the needle reappears in your space.

Bloodthirsty Strikes. The tattoo has 10 charges, and it regains all expended charges daily at dawn. While this tattoo is on your skin, you gain the following benefits:

- When you hit a creature with a weapon attack, you can expend a charge to deal an extra 4d6 necrotic damage to the target, and you regain a number of hit points equal to the necrotic damage dealt.
- When a creature you can see damages you, you can expend a charge and use your reaction to make a melee attack against that creature, with advantage on your attack roll.

BLOODWELL VIAL

Wondrous item, uncommon (+1), rare (+2), very rare (+3) (requires attunement by a sorcerer)

To attune to this vial, you must place a few drops of your blood into it. The vial can't be opened while your attunement to it lasts. If your attunement to the vial ends, the contained blood turns to ash. You can use the vial as a spellcasting focus for your spells while wearing or holding it, and you gain a bonus to spell attack rolls and to the saving throw DCs of your sorcerer spells. The bonus is determined by the vial's rarity.

In addition, when you roll any Hit Dice to recover hit points while you are carrying the vial, you can regain 5 sorcery points. This property of the vial can't be used again until the next dawn.

CAULDRON OF REBIRTH

Wondrous item, very rare (requires attunement by a druid or warlock)

This Tiny pot bears relief scenes of heroes on its cast iron sides. You can use the cauldron as a spellcasting focus for your druid spells, and it functions as a suitable component for the *scrying* spell. When you finish a long rest, you can use the cauldron to create a *potion of greater healing*. The potion lasts for 24 hours, then loses its magic if not consumed.

As an action, you can cause the cauldron to grow large enough for a Medium creature to crouch within. You can revert the cauldron to its normal size as an action, harmlessly shunting anything that can't fit inside to the nearest unoccupied space.

If you place the corpse of a humanoid into the cauldron and cover the corpse with 200 pounds of

CAULDRON OF REBIRTH

salt (which costs 10 gp) for at least 8 hours, the salt is consumed and the creature returns to life as if by *raise dead* at the next dawn. Once used, this property can't be used again for 7 days.

COILING GRASP TATTOO

Wondrous item (tattoo), uncommon (requires attunement)

Produced by a special needle, this magic tattoo has long intertwining designs.

Tattoo Attunement. To attune to this item, you hold the needle to your skin where you want the tattoo to appear, pressing the needle there throughout the attunement process. When the attunement is complete, the needle turns into the ink that becomes the tattoo, which appears on the skin.

If your attunement to the tattoo ends, the tattoo vanishes, and the needle reappears in your space.

Grasping Tendrils. While the tattoo is on your skin, you can, as an action, cause the tattoo to extrude into inky tendrils, which reach for a creature you can see within 15 feet of you. The creature must succeed on a DC 14 Strength saving throw or take 3d6 force damage and be grappled by you. As an action, the creature can escape the grapple by succeeding on a DC 14 Strength (Athletics) or Dexterity

(Acrobatics) check. The grapple also ends if you halt it (no action required), if the creature is ever more than 15 feet away from you, or if you use this tattoo on a different creature.

CROOK OF RAO

Wondrous item, artifact (requires attunement)

Ages ago, the serene god Rao created a tool to shield his fledgling faithful against the evils of the Lower Planes. Yet, as eons passed, mortals developed their own methods of dealing with existential threats, and the crook was largely forgotten. In recent ages, though, the *Crook of Rao* was rediscovered and leveraged against the rising power of the Witch Queen Iggwilv (one of the names of the wizard Tasha). Although she was defeated, Iggwilv managed to damage the crook during the battle, infecting it with an insidious curse—and the potential for future victory. In the aftermath, the crook was again lost. Occasionally it reappears, but the famed artifact is not what it was. Whether or not the artifact's bearers realize its full threat, few risk using the *Crook of Rao*—potentially for the final time.

Random Properties. The artifact has the following random properties, which you can determine by rolling on the tables in the "Artifacts" section of the *Dungeon Master's Guide*:

- 2 minor beneficial properties
- 1 major beneficial property
- 1 minor detrimental property

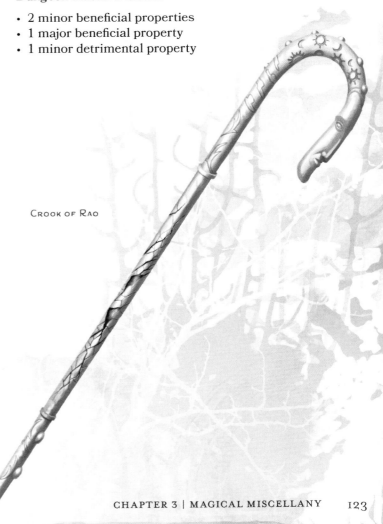

CROOK OF RAO

ZUZANNA WUZYK, ROBSON MICHEL

Spells. The crook has 6 charges. While holding it, you can use an action to expend 1 or more of its charges to cast one of the following spells (save DC 18) from it: *aura of life* (2 charges), *aura of purity* (2 charges), *banishment* (1 charge), *beacon of hope* (1 charge), *mass cure wounds* (3 charges). The crook regains 1d6 expended charges daily at dawn.

Absolute Banishment. While you are attuned to the crook and holding it, you can spend 10 minutes to banish all but the mightiest fiends within 1 mile of you. Any fiend with a challenge rating of 19 or higher is unaffected. Each banished fiend is sent back to its home plane and can't return to the plane the *Crook of Rao* banished it from for 100 years.

Failing Matrix. Whenever the *Crook of Rao*'s Absolute Banishment property is used, or when its last charge is expended, roll on the Extraplanar Reversal table. Any creatures conjured as a result of this effect appear in random unoccupied spaces within 60 feet of you and are not under your control.

Extraplanar Reversal

d100	Effect
1–25	A portal to a random plane opens. The portal closes after 5 minutes.
26–45	2d4 **imps** and 2d4 **quasits** appear.
46–60	1d8 **succubi/incubi** appear.
61–70	1d10 **barbed devils** and 1d10 **vrocks** appear.
71–80	1 **arcanaloth**, 1 **night hag**, and 1 **rakshasa** appear.
81–85	1 **ice devil** and 1 **marilith** appear.
86–90	1 **balor** and 1 **pit fiend** appear. At the DM's discretion, a portal opens into the presence of an archdevil or demon lord instead, then closes after 5 minutes.
91–00	Iggwilv's Curse (see the Iggwilv's Curse property).

Iggwilv's Curse. When the Crook was last used against Iggwilv, the Witch Queen lashed out at the artifact, infecting its magical matrix. Over the years, this curse has spread within the crook, threatening to violently pervert its ancient magic. If this occurs, the *Crook of Rao*, as it is currently known, is destroyed, its magical matrix inverting and exploding into a 50-foot-diameter portal. This portal functions as a permanent *gate* spell cast by Iggwilv. The gate then, once per round on initiative count 20, audibly speaks a fiend's name in Iggwilv's voice, doing so until the gate calls on every fiend ever banished by the *Crook of Rao*. If the fiend still exists, it is drawn through the gate. This process takes eighteen years to complete, at the end of which the gate becomes a permanent portal to Pazunia, the first layer of the Abyss.

Destroying or Repairing the Crook. The *Crook of Rao* can either be destroyed or repaired by journeying to Mount Celestia and obtaining a tear from the eternally serene god Rao. One way to make the emotionless god cry would be to reunite Rao with the spirit of his first worshiper who sought revelations beyond the multiverse long ago. The Crook dissolves if immersed in the god's tear for a year and a day. If washed in the tear daily for 30 days, the Crook loses its Failing Matrix property.

CRYSTALLINE CHRONICLE
Wondrous item, very rare (requires attunement by a wizard)

An etched crystal sphere the size of a grapefruit hums faintly and pulses with irregular flares of inner light. While you are touching the crystal, you can retrieve and store information and spells within the crystal at the same rate as reading and writing. When found, the crystal contains the following spells: *detect thoughts, intellect fortress,* Rary's telepathic bond, sending, telekinesis, Tasha's mind whip,** and *Tenser's floating disk* (spells with an asterisk appear in this book). It functions as a

CRYSTALLINE
CHRONICLE

IRINA NORDSOL

spellbook for you, with its spells and other writing psychically encoded within it.

While you are holding the crystal, you can use it as a spellcasting focus for your wizard spells, and you know the *mage hand*, *mind sliver* (appears in this book), and *message* cantrips if you don't already know them.

The crystal has 3 charges, and it regains 1d3 expended charges daily at dawn. You can use the charges in the following ways while holding it:

- If you spend 1 minute studying the information within the crystal, you can expend 1 charge to replace one of your prepared wizard spells with a different spell in the book.
- When you cast a wizard spell, you can expend 1 charge to cast the spell without verbal, somatic, or material components of up to 100 gp value.

Demonomicon of Iggwilv
Wondrous item, artifact (requires attunement)

An expansive treatise documenting the Abyss's infinite layers and inhabitants, the *Demonomicon of Iggwilv* is the most thorough and blasphemous tome of demonology in the multiverse. The tome recounts both the oldest and most current profanities of the Abyss and demons. Demons have attempted to censor the text, and while sections have been ripped from the book's spine, the general chapters remain, ever revealing demonic secrets. And the book holds more than blasphemies. Caged behind lines of script roils a secret piece of the Abyss itself, which keeps the book up-to-date, no matter how many pages are removed, and it longs to be more than mere reference material.

Random Properties. The artifact has the follow random properties, which you can determine by rolling on the tables in the "Artifacts" section of the *Dungeon Master's Guide*:

- 2 minor beneficial properties
- 1 minor detrimental property
- 1 major detrimental property

Spells. The book has 8 charges. It regains 1d8 expended charges daily at dawn. While holding it, you can use an action to cast *Tasha's hideous laughter* from it or to expend 1 or more of its charges to cast one of the following spells (save DC 20) from it: *magic circle* (1 charge), *magic jar* (3 charges), *planar ally* (3 charges), *planar binding* (2 charges), *plane shift* (to layers of the Abyss only; 3 charges), *summon fiend* (3 charges; appears in this book).

Abyssal Reference. You can reference the *Demonomicon* whenever you make an Intelligence check to discern information about demons or a Wisdom (Survival) check related to the Abyss. When you do so, you can add double your proficiency bonus to the check.

DEMONOMICON
OF IGGWILV

Fiendish Scourging. Your magic causes pain to fiends. While carrying the book, when you make a damage roll for a spell you cast against a fiend, you use the maximum possible result instead of rolling.

Ensnarement. While carrying the book, whenever you cast the *magic circle* spell naming only fiends, or the *planar binding* spell targeting a fiend, the spell is cast at 9th level, regardless of what level spell slot you used, if any. Additionally, the fiend has disadvantage on its saving throw against the spell.

Containment. The first 10 pages of the *Demonomicon* are blank. As an action while holding the book, you can target a fiend that you can see that is trapped within a *magic circle*. The fiend must succeed on a DC 20 Charisma saving throw with disadvantage or become trapped within one of the *Demonomicon*'s empty blank pages, which fills with writing detailing the trapped creature's widely known name and depravities. Once used, this action can't be used again until the next dawn.

When you finish a long rest, if you and the *Demonomicon* are on the same plane of existence, the trapped creature of the highest challenge rating within the book can attempt to possess you. You must make a DC 20 Charisma saving throw. On a failure, you are possessed by the creature, which controls you like a puppet. The possessing creature can release you as an action, appearing in the closest unoccupied space. On a successful save, the fiend can't try to possess you again for 7 days.

When the tome is discovered, it has 1d4 fiends occupying its pages, typically an assortment of demons.

Destroying the Demonomicon. To destroy the book, six different demon lords must each tear out a sixth of the book's pages. If this occurs, the pages reappear after 24 hours. Before all those hours pass, anyone who opens the book's remaining binding is transported to a nascent layer of the Abyss that lies hidden within the book. At the heart of this deadly, semi-sentient domain lies a long-lost artifact, *Fraz-Urb'luu's Staff*. If the staff is dragged from the pocket plane, the tome is reduced to a mundane and quite out-of-date copy of the *Tome of Zyx*, the work that served as the foundation for the *Demonomicon*. Once the staff emerges, the demon lord Fraz-Urb'luu instantly knows.

DEVOTEE'S CENSER

Weapon (flail), rare (requires attunement by a cleric or paladin)

The rounded head of this flail is perforated with tiny holes, arranged in symbols and patterns. The flail counts as a holy symbol for you. When you hit with an attack using this magic flail, the target takes an extra 1d8 radiant damage.

DEVOTEE'S CENSER

As a bonus action, you can speak the command word to cause the flail to emanate a thin cloud of incense out to 10 feet for 1 minute. At the start of each of your turns, you and any other creatures in the incense each regain 1d4 hit points. This property can't be used again until the next dawn.

DUPLICITOUS MANUSCRIPT

Wondrous item, rare (requires attunement by a wizard)

To you, this book is a magical spellbook. To anyone else, the book appears to be a volume of verbose romance fiction. As an action, you can change the book's appearance and alter the plot of the romance.

When found, the book contains the following spells: *hallucinatory terrain*, *major image*, *mirror image*, *mislead*, *Nystul's magic aura*, *phantasmal force*, and *silent image*. It functions as a spellbook for you.

While you are holding the book, you can use it as a spellcasting focus for your wizard spells.

The book has 3 charges, and it regains 1d3 expended charges daily at dawn. You can use the charges in the following ways while holding it:

- If you spend 1 minute studying the book, you can expend 1 charge to replace one of your prepared wizard spells with a different spell in the book. The new spell must be of the illusion school.
- When a creature you can see makes an Intelligence (Investigation) check to discern the true nature of an illusion spell you cast, or makes a saving throw against an illusion spell you cast, you can use your reaction and expend 1 charge to impose disadvantage on the roll.

ELDRITCH CLAW TATTOO

Wondrous item (tattoo), uncommon (requires attunement)

Produced by a special needle, this magic tattoo depicts clawlike forms and other jagged shapes.

Tattoo Attunement. To attune to this item, you hold the needle to your skin where you want the tattoo to appear, pressing the needle there throughout the attunement process. When the attunement is complete, the needle turns into the ink that becomes the tattoo, which appears on the skin.

If your attunement to the tattoo ends, the tattoo vanishes, and the needle reappears in your space.

Magical Strikes. While the tattoo is on your skin, your unarmed strikes are considered magical for the purpose of overcoming immunity and resistance to nonmagical attacks, and you gain a +1 bonus to attack and damage rolls with unarmed strikes.

Eldritch Maul. As a bonus action, you can empower the tattoo for 1 minute. For the duration, each of your melee attacks with a weapon or an unarmed strike can reach a target up to 15 feet away from you, as inky tendrils launch toward the target. In addition, your melee attacks deal an extra 1d6 force damage on a hit. Once used, this bonus action can't be used again until the next dawn.

ELEMENTAL ESSENCE SHARD

Wondrous item, rare (requires attunement by a sorcerer)

This crackling crystal contains the essence of an elemental plane. As an action, you can attach the shard to a Tiny object (such as a weapon or a piece of jewelry) or detach it. It falls off if your attunement to it ends. You can use the shard as a spellcasting focus while you hold or wear it.

Roll a d4 and consult the Elemental Essence Shards table to determine the shard's essence and property. When you use a Metamagic option on a spell while you are holding or wearing the shard, you can use that property.

ELEMENTAL ESSENCE SHARDS

d4	Property
1	**Air.** You can immediately fly up to 60 feet without provoking opportunity attacks.
2	**Earth.** You gain resistance to a damage type of your choice until the start of your next turn.
3	**Fire.** One target of the spell that you can see catches fire. The burning target takes 2d10 fire damage at the start of its next turn, and then the flames go out.
4	**Water.** You create a wave of water that bursts out from you in a 10-foot radius. Each creature of your choice that you can see in that area takes 2d6 cold damage and must succeed on a Strength saving throw against your spell save DC or be pushed 10 feet away from you and fall prone.

FAR REALM SHARD

Wondrous item, rare (requires attunement by a sorcerer)

This writhing crystal is steeped in the warped essence of the Far Realm. As an action, you can attach the shard to a Tiny object (such as a weapon or a piece of jewelry) or detach it. It falls off if your attunement to it ends. You can use the shard as a spellcasting focus while you hold or wear it.

When you use a Metamagic option on a spell while you are holding or wearing the shard, you can

LEFT TO RIGHT: FAR REALM, FEYWILD, AND SHADOWFELL SHARDS

cause a slimy tentacle to rip through the fabric of reality and strike one creature you can see within 30 feet of you. The creature must succeed on a Charisma saving throw against your spell save DC or take 3d6 psychic damage and become frightened of you until the start of your next turn.

FEYWILD SHARD

Wondrous item, uncommon (requires attunement by a sorcerer)

This warm crystal glints with the sunset colors of the Feywild sky and evokes whispers of emotional memory. As an action, you can attach the shard to a Tiny object (such as a weapon or a piece of jewelry) or detach it. It falls off if your attunement to it ends. You can use the shard as a spellcasting focus while you hold or wear it.

When you use a Metamagic option on a spell while you are holding or wearing the shard, you can roll on the Wild Magic Surge table in the *Player's Handbook*. If the result is a spell, it is too wild to be affected by your Metamagic, and if it normally requires concentration, it doesn't require concentration in this case; the spell lasts for its full duration.

If you don't have the Wild Magic Sorcerous Origin, once this property is used to roll on the Wild Magic Surge table, it can't be used again until the next dawn.

FULMINATING TREATISE

GHOST STEP TATTOO

Wondrous item (tattoo), very rare (requires attunement)

Produced by a special needle, this tattoo shifts and wavers on the skin, parts of it appearing blurred.

Tattoo Attunement. To attune to this item, you hold the needle to your skin where you want the tattoo to appear, pressing the needle there throughout the attunement process. When the attunement is complete, the needle turns into the ink that becomes the tattoo, which appears on the skin.

If your attunement to the tattoo ends, the tattoo vanishes, and the needle reappears in your space.

Ghostly Form. The tattoo has 3 charges, and it regains all expended charges daily at dawn. As a bonus action while the tattoo is on your skin, you can expend 1 of the tattoo's charges to become incorporeal until the end of your next turn. For the duration, you gain the following benefits:

- You have resistance to bludgeoning, piercing, and slashing damage from nonmagical attacks.
- You can't be grappled or restrained.
- You can move through creatures and solid objects as if they were difficult terrain. If you end your turn in a solid object, you take 1d10 force damage. If the effect ends while you are inside a solid object, you instead are shunted to the nearest unoccupied space, and you take 1d10 force damage for every 5 feet traveled.

GUARDIAN EMBLEM

Wondrous item (holy symbol), uncommon (requires attunement by a cleric or paladin)

This emblem is the symbol of a deity or a spiritual tradition. As an action, you can attach the emblem to a suit of armor or a shield or remove it.

The emblem has 3 charges. When you or a creature you can see within 30 feet of you suffers a critical hit while you're wearing the armor or wielding the shield that bears the emblem, you can use your reaction to expend 1 charge to turn the critical hit into a normal hit instead.

The emblem regains all expended charges daily at dawn.

HEART WEAVER'S PRIMER

Wondrous item, rare (requires attunement by a wizard)

This pristine book smells faintly of a random scent you find pleasing. When found, the book contains the following spells: *antipathy/sympathy, charm person, dominate person, enthrall, hypnotic pattern, modify memory,* and *suggestion.* It functions as a spellbook for you.

FULMINATING TREATISE

Wondrous item, rare (requires attunement by a wizard)

This thick, scorched spellbook reeks of smoke and ozone, and sparks of energy crackles along the edges of its pages. When found, the book contains the following spells: *contingency, fireball, gust of wind, Leomund's tiny hut, magic missile, thunderwave,* and *wall of force.* It functions as a spellbook for you.

While you are holding the book, you can use it as a spellcasting focus for your wizard spells.

The book has 3 charges, and it regains 1d3 expended charges daily at dawn. You can use the charges in the following ways while holding it:

- If you spend 1 minute studying the book, you can expend 1 charge to replace one of your prepared wizard spells with a different spell in the book. The new spell must be of the evocation school.
- When one creature you can see takes damage from an evocation spell you cast, you can use your reaction and expend 1 charge to deal an extra 2d6 force damage to the creature and knock the creature prone if it is Large or smaller.

While you are holding the book, you can use it as a spellcasting focus for your wizard spells.

The book has 3 charges, and it regains 1d3 expended charges daily at dawn. You can use the charges in the following ways while holding it:

- If you spend 1 minute studying the book, you can expend 1 charge to replace one of your prepared wizard spells with a different spell in the book. The new spell must be of the enchantment school.
- When you cast an enchantment spell, you can expend 1 charge to impose disadvantage on the first saving throw one target makes against the spell.

Illuminator's Tattoo

Wondrous item (tattoo), common (requires attunement)

Produced by a special needle, this magic tattoo features beautiful calligraphy, images of writing implements, and the like.

Tattoo Attunement. To attune to this item, you hold the needle to your skin where you want the tattoo to appear, pressing the needle there throughout the attunement process. When the attunement is complete, the needle turns into the ink that becomes the tattoo, which appears on the skin.

If your attunement to the tattoo ends, the tattoo vanishes, and the needle reappears in your space.

Magical Scribing. While this tattoo is on your skin, you can write with your fingertip as if it were an ink pen that never runs out of ink.

As an action, you can touch a piece of writing up to one page in length and speak a creature's name. The writing becomes invisible to everyone other than you and the named creature for the next 24 hours. Either of you can dismiss the invisibility by touching the script (no action required). Once used, this action can't be used again until the next dawn.

Libram of Souls and Flesh

Wondrous item, rare (requires attunement by a wizard)

With covers made of skin and fittings of bone, this tome is cold to the touch, and it whispers faintly. When found, the book contains the following spells, which are wizard spells for you while you are attuned to the book: *animate dead, circle of death, false life, finger of death, speak with dead, summon undead* (appears in this book), *vampiric touch.* It functions as a spellbook for you.

While you are holding the book, you can use it as a spellcasting focus for your wizard spells.

The book has 3 charges, and it regains 1d3 expended charges daily at dawn. You can use the charges in the following ways while holding it:

- If you spend 1 minute studying the book, you can expend 1 charge to replace one of your prepared wizard spells with a different spell in the book. The new spell must be of the necromancy school.
- As an action, you can expend 1 charge to take on a semblance of undeath for 10 minutes. For the duration, you take on a deathly appearance, and undead creatures are indifferent to you, unless you have damaged them. You also appear undead to all outward inspection and to spells used to determine the target's status. The effect ends if you deal damage or force a creature to make a saving throw.

Lifewell Tattoo

Wondrous item (tattoo), very rare (requires attunement)

Produced by a special needle, this magic tattoo features symbols of life and rebirth.

Tattoo Attunement. To attune to this item, you hold the needle to your skin where you want the tattoo to appear, pressing the needle there throughout the attunement process. When the attunement is complete, the needle turns into the ink that becomes the tattoo, which appears on the skin.

If your attunement to the tattoo ends, the tattoo vanishes, and the needle reappears in your space.

Necrotic Resistance. You have resistance to necrotic damage.

Life Ward. When you would be reduced to 0 hit points, you drop to 1 hit point instead. Once used, this property can't be used again until the next dawn.

Luba's Tarokka of Souls

Wondrous item, artifact (requires attunement)

Not all lingering spirits are tragic souls, lost on their way to the hereafter. Some languish as prisoners, souls so wicked mortals dare not free them upon an unsuspecting afterlife.

Created by a figure of Vistani legend, *Luba's Tarokka of Souls* shaped the destiny of countless heroes. The prophecies of this deck of cards also revealed great evils and guided its creator into the path of nefarious forces. Untold times the deck's creator, Mother Luba, narrowly escaped doom, spared only by her keen insights. But even for her, not all wickedness could be escaped. In the most dire cases, Mother Luba managed to ensnare beings of pure evil amid the strands of fate, imprisoning them within her tarroka deck. There these foul spirits dwell still, trapped within a nether-realm hidden amid shuffling cards, waiting for fate to turn foul—as it inevitably will.

LUBA'S TAROKKA OF SOULS

Like all tarokka decks, the *Tarokka of Souls* is a lavishly illustrated collection of fifty-four cards, comprising the fourteen cards of the high deck and forty other cards divided into four suits: coins, glyphs, stars, and swords.

Random Properties. The artifact has the following random properties, which you can determine by rolling on the tables in the "Artifacts" section of the *Dungeon Master's Guide*:

- 2 minor detrimental properties
- 2 minor beneficial properties

Spells. While holding the deck, you can use an action to cast one of the following spells (save DC 18) from it: *comprehend languages*, *detect evil and good*, *detect magic*, *detect poison and disease*, *locate object*, or *scrying*. Once you use the deck to cast a spell, you can't cast that spell again from it until the next dawn.

Enduring Vision. While holding the deck, you automatically succeed on Constitution saving throws made to maintain your concentration on divination spells.

Twist of Fate. As an action, you can draw a card from the deck and twist the fortune of another creature you can see within 15 feet of you. Choose one of the following effects:

Weal. The creature has advantage on attack rolls, ability checks, and saving throws for the next hour.

Woe. The creature has disadvantage on attack rolls, ability checks, and saving throws for the next hour.

The deck can be used in this way twice, and you regain all expended uses at the next dawn.

Prisoners of Fate. Whenever you use the Twist of Fate property, there is a chance that one of the souls trapped in the deck escapes. Roll d100 and consult the Souls of the Tarokka table. If you roll one of the high cards, the soul associated with it escapes. You can find its statistics in the *Monster Manual*. If you roll a soul that has already escaped, roll again.

SOULS OF THE TAROKKA

d100	Card	Soul
1	Artifact	Flameskull
2	Beast	Wraith
3	Broken One	Banshee
4	Darklord	Vampire
5	Donjon	Mummy
6	Executioner	Death knight
7	Ghost	Ghost
8	Horseman	Mummy lord
9	Innocent	Ghost
10	Marionette	Mummy
11	Mists	Wraith
12	Raven	Vampire spawn
13	Seer	Vampire
14	Tempter	Vampire spawn
15–00	—	—

The released soul appears at a random location within 10d10 miles of you and terrorizes the living. Until the released soul is destroyed, it gains the benefit of a weal from the deck's Twist of Fate property, and both you and the original target of Twist of Fate suffer the effect of woe.

Shuffling Fate. If you go 7 days without using the Twist of Fate property, your attunement to *Luba's Taroka of Souls* ends, and you can't attune to it again until after another creature uses Twist of Fate on you.

Destroying the Deck. *Luba's Tarokka of Souls* can be destroyed only if all fourteen souls within are released and destroyed. This reveals a fifteenth soul, a **lich**, that inhabits the Nether card, which appears only when the fourteen souls are defeated. If this ancient entity is destroyed, the Nether card vanishes and the deck becomes a normal tarokka deck, with no special properties, but it includes a new card of the DM's design.

LYRE OF BUILDING

Wondrous item, rare (requires attunement by a bard)

While holding this lyre, you can cast *mending* as an action. You can also play the lyre as a reaction when an object or a structure you can see within 300 feet of you takes damage, causing it to be immune to that damage and any further damage of the same type until the start of your next turn.

In addition, you can play the lyre as an action to cast *fabricate*, *move earth*, *passwall*, or *summon construct* (appears in this book), and that spell can't be cast from it again until the next dawn.

MASQUERADE TATTOO

Wondrous item (tattoo), common (requires attunement)

Produced by a special needle, this magic tattoo appears on your body as whatever you desire.

Tattoo Attunement. To attune to this item, you hold the needle to your skin where you want the tattoo to appear, pressing the needle there throughout the attunement process. When the attunement is complete, the needle turns into the ink that becomes the tattoo, which appears on the skin.

If your attunement to the tattoo ends, the tattoo vanishes, and the needle reappears in your space.

Fluid Ink. As a bonus action, you can shape the tattoo into any color or pattern and move it to any area of your skin. Whatever form it takes, it is always obviously a tattoo. It can range in size from no smaller than a copper piece to an intricate work of art that covers all your skin.

Disguise Self. As an action, you can use the tattoo to cast the *disguise self* spell (DC 13 to discern the disguise). Once the spell is cast from the tattoo, it can't be cast from the tattoo again until the next dawn.

MIGHTY SERVANT OF LEUK-O

Wondrous item, artifact (requires attunement)

Named for the warlord who infamously employed it, the *Mighty Servant of Leuk-o* is a fantastically powerful, 10-foot-tall machine that turns into an animate construct when piloted. Crafted of a gleaming black alloy of unknown origin, the servant is often described as a combination of a disproportioned dwarf and an oversized beetle. The servant contains enough space for 1 ton of cargo and a crew compartment within, from which up to two Medium creatures can control it—and potentially execute a spree of unstoppable destruction.

Tales of the servant's origins involve more conjecture than fact, often referring to otherworldly beings, the mysterious Barrier Peaks in Oerth, and the supposedly related device known as the *Machine of Lum the Mad*. The best details on the device's origins and operation can be found in the *Mind of Metal*, a tome of artificer's secrets that connects the device to the traditions of the lost Olman people, and which was written by Lum the Mad's several times over granddaughter, Lum the Maestro, while she reconstructed the long disassembled *Mighty Servant of Leuk-o*.

Dangerous Attunement. Two creatures can be attuned to the servant at a time. If a third creature tries to attune to it, nothing happens.

The servant's controls are accessed by a hatch in its upper back, which is easily opened while there are no creatures attuned to the artifact.

Attuning to the artifact requires two hours, which can be undertaken as part of a long rest, during which time you must be inside the servant, interacting with its controls. While crew members are attuning themselves, any creature or structure outside and within 50 feet of the servant has a 25 percent chance of being accidentally targeted by one of its Destructive Fist attacks once during the attunement. This process must be undergone every time a creature attunes itself to the artifact.

MIGHTY SERVANT OF LEUK-O

While there are no attuned creatures inside the servant, it is an inert object.

Ghost in the Machine. Upon his death, the soul of the mighty warlord Leuk-o was drawn into the artifact and has become its animating force. The servant has been known to attack or move of its own accord, particularly if doing so will cause destruction. Once every 24 hours, the servant, at the DM's discretion, takes one action while uncrewed.

If the servant loses half of its hit points or more, each creature attuned to it must succeed on a DC 20

Controlling the Servant. While any creatures are attuned to the artifact, attuned creatures can open the hatch as easily as any other door. Other creatures can open the hatch as an action with a successful DC 25 Dexterity check using thieves' tools. A *knock* spell cast on the hatch also opens it until the start of the caster's next turn.

A creature can enter or exit through the hatch by spending 10 feet of movement. Those inside the servant have total cover from effects originating outside it. The controls within it allow creatures to see outside without obstruction.

While you are inside the servant, you can command it by using the controls. During your turn (for either attuned creature), you can command it in the following ways:

- Open or close the hatch (no action required, once per turn)
- Move the servant up to its speed (no action required)
- As an action, you can command the servant to take one of the actions in its stat block or some other action.
- When a creature provokes an opportunity attack from the servant, you can use your reaction to command the servant to make one Destructive Fist attack against that creature.

MIGHTY SERVANT OF LEUK-O
Huge construct

Armor Class 22 (natural armor)
Hit Points 310 (27d12 + 135)
Speed 60 ft.

STR	DEX	CON	INT	WIS	CHA
30 (+10)	14 (+2)	20 (+5)	1 (−5)	14 (+2)	10 (+0)

Saving Throws Wis +9, Cha +7
Skills Perception +9
Damage Resistances piercing, slashing
Damage Immunities acid, bludgeoning, cold, fire, lightning, necrotic, poison, psychic, radiant
Condition Immunities all conditions but invisible and prone
Senses blindsight 120 ft., passive Perception 19
Languages understands the languages of creatures attuned to it but can't speak
Challenge —   **Proficiency Bonus** +7

Immutable Existence. The servant is immune to any spell or effect that would alter its form or send it to another plane of existence.

Magic Resistant Construction. The servant has advantage on saving throws against spells and other magical effects, and spell attacks made against it have disadvantage.

Regeneration. The servant regains 10 hit points at the start of its turn. If it is reduced to 0 hit points, this trait doesn't function until an attuned creature spends 24 hours repairing the artifact or until the artifact is subjected to lightning damage.

Standing Leap. The servant's long jump is up to 50 feet and its high jump is up to 25 feet, with or without a running start.

Unusual Nature. The servant doesn't require air, food, drink, or sleep.

ACTIONS

Destructive Fist. *Melee or Ranged Weapon Attack:* +17 to hit, reach 10 ft. or range 120 ft., one target. *Hit:* 36 (4d12 + 10) force damage. If the target is an object, it takes triple damage.

Crushing Leap. If the servant jumps at least 25 feet as part of its movement, it can then use this action to land on its feet in a space that contains one or more other creatures. Each of those creatures is pushed to an unoccupied space within 5 feet of the servant and must make a DC 25 Dexterity saving throw. On a failed save, a creature takes 26 (4d12) bludgeoning damage and is knocked prone. On a successful save, a creature takes half as much damage and isn't knocked prone.

Wisdom saving throw or be charmed for 24 hours. While charmed in this way, the creature goes on a destructive spree, seeking to destroy structures and attack any unattuned creatures within sight of the servant, starting with those threatening the artifact—preferably using the servant, if possible.

Self-Destruct. By inputting a specific series of lever pulls and button presses, the servant's two crew members can cause it to explode. The self-destruct code is not revealed to crew members when they attune to the artifact. If the code is discovered (the DM determines how), it requires two attuned crew members to be inside the servant and spend their actions on 3 consecutive rounds performing the command. Should the crew members begin the process of entering the code, though, the servant uses its Ghost in the Machine property and turns the crew members against each other.

If the crew members successfully implement the code, at the end of the third round, the servant explodes. Every creature in a 100-foot-radius sphere centered on the servant must make a DC 25 Dexterity saving throw. On a failed save, a creature takes 87 (25d6) force damage, 87 (25d6) lightning damage, and 87 (25d6) thunder damage. On a successful save, a creature takes half as much damage. Objects and structures in the area take triple damage. Creatures inside the servant are slain instantly and leave behind no remains.

This does not destroy the servant permanently. Rather, 2d6 days later, its parts—left arm, left leg, right arm, right leg, lower torso, and upper torso—drop from the sky in random places within 1,000 miles of the explosion. If brought within 5 feet of one another, the pieces reconnect and reform the servant.

Destroying the Servant. The servant can be destroyed in two ways. After it has self-destructed, its disconnected pieces can be melted down in one of the forge-temples of its ancient Olman creators. Alternatively, if the servant strikes the *Machine of Lum the Mad*, both artifacts explode in an eruption that is three times the size and three times the damage as the servant's self-destruct property.

MOON SICKLE

Weapon (sickle), uncommon (+1), rare (+2), very rare (+3) (requires attunement by a druid or ranger)

This silver-bladed sickle glimmers softly with moonlight. While holding this magic weapon, you gain a bonus to attack and damage rolls made with it, and you gain a bonus to spell attack rolls and the saving throw DCs of your druid and ranger spells. The bonus is determined by the weapon's rarity. In addition, you can use the sickle as a spellcasting focus for your druid and ranger spells.

When you cast a spell that restores hit points, you can roll a d4 and add the number rolled to the amount of hit points restored, provided you are holding the sickle.

NATURE'S MANTLE

Wondrous item, uncommon (requires attunement by a druid or ranger)

This cloak shifts color and texture to blend with the terrain surrounding you. While wearing the cloak, you can use it as a spellcasting focus for your druid and ranger spells.

While you are in an area that is lightly obscured, you can Hide as a bonus action even if you are being directly observed.

OUTER ESSENCE SHARD

Wondrous item, rare (requires attunement by a sorcerer)

This flickering crystal holds the essence of an Outer Plane. As an action, you can attach the shard to a Tiny object (such as a weapon or a piece of jewelry) or detach it. It falls off if your attunement to it ends. You can use the shard as a spellcasting focus while you hold or wear it.

Roll a d4 and consult the Outer Essence Shards table to determine the shard's essence and property.

NATURE'S MANTLE

When you use a Metamagic option on a spell while you are holding or wearing the shard, you can use that property.

Outer Essence Shards

d4	Property
1	**Lawful.** You can end one of the following conditions affecting yourself or one creature you can see within 30 feet of you: charmed, blinded, deafened, frightened, poisoned, or stunned.
2	**Chaotic.** Choose one creature who takes damage from the spell. That target has disadvantage on attack rolls and ability checks made before the start of your next turn.
3	**Good.** You or one creature of your choice that you can see within 30 feet of you gains 3d6 temporary hit points.
4	**Evil.** Choose one creature who takes damage from the spell. That target takes an extra 3d6 necrotic damage.

Planecaller's Codex
Wondrous item, rare (requires attunement by a wizard)

The pages of this book are bound in fiend hide, and its cover is embossed with a diagram of the Great Wheel of the multiverse. When found, the book contains the following spells: *banishment*, *find familiar*, *gate*, *magic circle*, *planar binding*, and *summon elemental* (appears in this book). It functions as a spellbook for you.

While you are holding the book, you can use it as a spellcasting focus for your wizard spells.

The book has 3 charges, and it regains 1d3 expended charges daily at dawn. You can use the charges in the following ways while holding it:

- If you spend 1 minute studying the book, you can expend 1 charge to replace one of your prepared wizard spells with a different spell in the book. The new spell must be of the conjuration school.
- When you cast a conjuration spell that summons or creates one creature, you can expend 1 charge to grant that creature advantage on attack rolls for 1 minute.

Prosthetic Limb
Wondrous item, common

This item replaces a lost limb—a hand, an arm, a foot, a leg, or a similar body part. While the prosthetic is attached, it functions identically to the part it replaces. You can detach or reattach it as an action, and it can't be removed against your will. It detaches if you die.

Protective Verses
Wondrous item, rare (requires attunement by a wizard)

This leather-bound spellbook is reinforced with iron and silver fittings and an iron lock (DC 20 to open). As an action, you can touch the book's cover and cause it to lock as if you cast *arcane lock* on it. When found, the book contains the following spells: *arcane lock*, *dispel magic*, *globe of invulnerability*, *glyph of warding*, *Mordenkainen's private sanctum*, *protection from evil*, and *symbol*. It functions as a spellbook for you.

While you are holding the book, you can use it as a spellcasting focus for your wizard spells.

The book has 3 charges, and it regains 1d3 expended charges daily at dawn. You can use the charges in the following ways while holding it:

- If you spend 1 minute studying the book, you can expend 1 charge to replace one of your prepared wizard spells with a different spell in the book. The new spell must be of the abjuration school.
- When you cast an abjuration spell, you can expend 1 charge to grant a creature you can see within 30 feet of you 2d10 temporary hit points.

Reveler's Concertina
Wondrous item, rare (requires attunement by a bard)

While holding this concertina, you gain a +2 bonus to the saving throw DC of your bard spells.

As an action, you can use the concertina to cast *Otto's irresistible dance* from the item. This property of the concertina can't be used again until the next dawn.

Rhythm-Maker's Drum
Wondrous item, uncommon (+1), rare (+2), very rare (+3) (requires attunement by a bard)

While holding this drum, you gain a bonus to spell attack rolls and to the saving throw DCs of your bard spells. The bonus is determined by the drum's rarity.

As an action, you can play the drum to regain one use of your Bardic Inspiration feature. This property of the drum can't be used again until the next dawn.

Shadowfell Brand Tattoo
Wondrous item (tattoo), rare (requires attunement)

Produced by a special needle, this magic tattoo is dark in color and abstract.

Tattoo Attunement. To attune to this item, you hold the needle to your skin where you want the tattoo to appear, pressing the needle there throughout the attunement process. When the attunement is complete, the needle turns into the ink that becomes the tattoo, which appears on the skin.

If your attunement to the tattoo ends, the tattoo vanishes, and the needle reappears in your space.

Shadow Essence. You gain darkvision with a range of 60 feet, and you have advantage on Dexterity (Stealth) checks.

Shadowy Defense. When you take damage, you can use your reaction to become insubstantial for a moment, halving the damage you take. Then the reaction can't be used again until the next sunset.

SHADOWFELL SHARD

Wondrous item, rare (requires attunement by a sorcerer)

This dull, cold crystal sits heavy and leaden, saturated by the Shadowfell's despair. As an action, you can attach the shard to a Tiny object (such as a weapon or a piece of jewelry) or detach it. It falls off if your attunement to it ends. You can use the shard as a spellcasting focus while you hold or wear it.

When you use a Metamagic option on a spell while you are holding or wearing the shard, you can momentarily curse one creature targeted by the spell; choose one ability score, and until the end of your next turn, the creature has disadvantage on ability checks and saving throws that use that ability.

SPELLWROUGHT TATTOO

Wondrous item (tattoo), rarity varies

Produced by a special needle, this magic tattoo contains a single spell of up to 5th level, wrought on your skin by a magic needle. To use the tattoo, you must hold the needle against your skin and speak the command word. The needle turns into ink that becomes the tattoo, which appears on the skin in whatever design you like. Once the tattoo is there, you can cast its spell, requiring no material components. The tattoo glows faintly while you cast the spell and for the spell's duration. Once the spell ends, the tattoo vanishes from your skin.

The level of the spell in the tattoo determines the spell's saving throw DC, attack bonus, spellcasting ability modifier, and the tattoo's rarity, as shown in the Spellwrought Tattoo table.

SPELLWROUGHT TATTOO

Spell Level	Rarity	Spellcasting Ability Mod.	Save DC	Attack Bonus
Cantrip	Common	+3	13	+5
1st	Common	+3	13	+5
2nd	Uncommon	+3	13	+5
3rd	Uncommon	+4	15	+7
4th	Rare	+4	15	+7
5th	Rare	+5	17	+9

A TOOTH OF DAHLVER-NAR

TEETH OF DAHLVER-NAR

Wondrous item, artifact (requires attunement)

The *Teeth of Dahlver-Nar* are stories given form. They are a collection of teeth, each suggestive of wildly different origins and made from various materials. The collection rests within a leather pouch, stitched with images of heroes and whimsical creatures. Where the teeth fall, they bring legends to life.

Using the Teeth. While you are holding the pouch, you can use an action to draw one tooth. Roll on the Teeth of Dahlver-Nar table to determine which tooth you draw, and you can either sow the tooth or implant it (both of which are described later).

If you don't sow or implant the tooth, roll a die at the end of your turn. On an even number, the tooth vanishes, and creatures appear as if you sowed the tooth, but they are hostile to you and your allies. On an odd number, the tooth replaces one of your teeth as if you implanted it (potentially replacing another implanted tooth, see below).

Each tooth can only be used once. Track which teeth have been used. If a tooth's result is rolled after it's been used, you draw the next lowest unused tooth on the table.

Sowing Teeth. To sow the tooth, you place it on the ground in an unoccupied space within your reach, or you throw it into an unoccupied space within 10 feet of you in a body of water that is at least 50 feet wide and 50 feet long. Upon doing so, the tooth burrows into the ground and vanishes, leaving no hole behind, or it vanishes into the water. The creatures noted in the Creatures Summoned column appear in an unoccupied space as close to where the tooth was sown as possible. The creatures are allies to you, speak all languages you speak, and linger for 10 minutes before disappearing, unless otherwise noted.

Implanting Teeth. To implant the tooth, you place it in your mouth, whereupon one of your own teeth falls out, and the drawn tooth takes its place, resizing to fit in your mouth. Once the tooth is implanted, you gain the effect noted in the Implanted Effect column. The tooth can't be removed while you are attuned to the teeth, and you can't voluntarily end your attunement to them. If removed after your death, the tooth vanishes. You can have a maximum number of the teeth implanted at one time equal to 1 + your Constitution modifier (minimum of 2 teeth total). If you try to implant more teeth, the newly implanted tooth replaces one of the previous teeth, determined randomly. The replaced tooth vanishes, and you lose the implanted effect.

Recovering Teeth. Once all the teeth have vanished, their pouch also vanishes. The pouch with all the teeth then appears in a random destination, which could be on a different world of the Material Plane.

Destroying the Teeth. Each tooth must be destroyed individually by sowing it in the area where the tooth's story originated, with the intention to destroy it. When planted in this way, creatures summoned are not friendly to you and do not vanish. Some of the creatures summoned merely head off in search of home, while others act as their tales dictate. In either case, the tooth is gone forever.

Teeth of Dahlver-Nar

1d20	Tale and Tooth	Creatures Summoned	Implanted Effect
1	The Staring Cats of Uldun-dar (ivory cat molar)	9 **cats**	The tooth has 8 charges. As an action, you can expend 1 charge to cast the *revivify* spell from the tooth. If you are dead at the start of your turn, the tooth expends 1 charge and casts *revivify* on you.
2	Duggle's Surprising Day (human molar)	1 **commoner**	When you finish a long rest, the tooth casts *sanctuary* (DC 18) on you, and the spell lasts for 24 hours or until you break it.
3	The Golden Age of Dhakaan (golden goblin bicuspid)	10 **goblins**, 1 **goblin boss**	When you are hit by an attack and an ally is within 5 feet of you, you can use your reaction to cause them to be hit instead. You can't use this reaction again until you finish a short or long rest.
4	The Mill Road Murders (halfling canine)	3 **green hags** in a coven	When you damage a target that hasn't taken a turn in this combat, the target takes an extra 3d10 slashing damage from ghostly blades.
5	Dooms of the Malpheggi (emerald lizardfolk fang)	1 **lizardfolk queen** and 4 **lizardfolk**	You gain reptilian scales, granting you a +2 bonus to your AC. Additionally, when you finish a long rest, you must succeed on a DC 15 Constitution saving throw or gain 1 level of exhaustion.
6	The Stable Hand's Secret (sweet-tasting human canine)	2 **incubi**	When you make a Charisma check against a humanoid, you can roll a d10 and add the number rolled as a bonus to the result. The creature then becomes hostile to you at the next dawn.
7	The Donkey's Dream (rainbow-colored donkey molar)	1 **unicorn**	The tooth has 3 charges. As an action, you can expend 1 charge to touch a creature. The target regains 2d8 + 2 hit points, and all diseases and poisons affecting it are removed. When you use this action, a shimmering image of a unicorn's horn appears until the end of your turn, sprouting from your forehead. The tooth regains all expended charges daily at dawn. You gain the following flaw: "When I see wickedness in action, I must oppose it."
8	Beyond the Rock of Bral (silver mind flayer tooth)	2 **mind flayers**	You gain telepathy out to 120 feet as described in the *Monster Manual*, and you can cast the *detect thoughts* spell at will, requiring no components. You also have disadvantage on Wisdom (Insight) and Wisdom (Perception) checks from constant whispers of memories and nearby minds.

1d20	Tale and Tooth	Creatures Summoned	Implanted Effect
9	The Disappearances of Half Hollow (vomerine tooth of a Large toad)	4 giant toads	Your long jump is up to 30 feet and your high jump is up to 15 feet, with or without a running start.
10	Legendry of Phantoms and Ghosts (obsidian human molar)	1 giant octopus, 1 mage, 1 specter	As an action, you can use the tooth to cast the *Evard's black tentacles* spell (DC 18). Once this property is used, it can't be used again until the next dawn.
11	The Thousand Deaths of Jander Sunstar (yellowed vampire fang)	1 vampire	You can make a bite attack as an unarmed strike. On a hit, it deals 1d6 piercing damage plus 3d6 necrotic damage. You regain a number of hit points equal to the necrotic damage dealt. While you are in sunlight, you can't regain hit points.
12	Nightmares of Kaggash (twisted beholder tooth)	1 beholder	As an action, you can cast the *eyebite* spell from the tooth. Once you use this action, it can't be used again until the next dawn. Whenever you finish a long rest, roll a d20. On a 20, an aberration chosen by the DM appears within 30 feet of you and attacks.
13	Three Bridges to the Sky (lapis lazuli oni fang)	3 oni	You gain a flying speed of 30 feet, and you can use the tooth to cast the *detect magic* spell at will. While you are attuned to fewer than 3 magic items, you gain 1 level of exhaustion that can't be removed until you are attuned to three or more magic items.
14	The Claws of Dragotha (broken translucent fang)	1 adult red dracolich	You can use the tooth to cast the *create undead* spell. Once this property is used, it can't be used again until the next dawn. Each time you create an undead creature using the tooth, a skeleton, zombie, or ghoul also appears at a random location within 5 miles of you, searching for the living to kill. A humanoid killed by these undead rises as the same type of undead at the next midnight.
15	Ashes of the Ages and Eternal Fire (jade humanoid bicuspid)	1 dao, 1 djinni, 1 efreeti, 1 marid	You can use the tooth to cast *counterspell* at 9th level. Once you use this property, it can't be used again until the next dawn. Whenever you finish a long rest, if you haven't used the tooth to counter a spell since your last long rest, your hit point maximum is reduced by 2d10. If this reduces your hit point maximum to 0, you die.
16	Daughters of Bel (green steel pit fiend fang)	1 pit fiend	You can use the tooth to cast *dominate monster* (DC 18). Once you use this property, it can't be used again until the next dawn. You smell strongly of burning sulfur.
17	Why the Sky Screams (blue dragon fang)	1 ancient blue dragon	You gain immunity to lightning damage and vulnerability to thunder damage.
18	The Last Tarrasque (jagged sliver of tarrasque tooth)	1 tarrasque (ignores you and your commands; appears for 1d4 rounds then vanishes)	You deal double damage to objects and structures. If you take 20 or more damage in one turn, you must succeed on a DC 18 Wisdom saving throw or spend your next turn in a murderous fury. During this rage, you must use your action to make an unarmed strike against a creature that damaged you, or a random creature you can see if you weren't damaged by a creature, moving as close as you can to the target if necessary.
19	Incendax's Tooth (ruby-veined red dragon fang)	1 ancient red dragon	You gain immunity to fire damage, and as an action, you can exhale fire in a 90-foot cone. Each creature in that area must make a DC 24 Dexterity saving throw, taking 26d6 fire damage on a failed save, or half as much damage on a successful one. After using the breath weapon, you gain 2 levels of exhaustion.
20	Dahlver-Nar's Tooth (dusty human molar)	1 priest	As an action you can call on a divine force to come to your aid. Describe the assistance you seek, and the DM decides the nature of the intervention; the effect of any cleric spell would be appropriate. Once this property is used, it can't be used again for 7 days.

TASHA PREPARES TO WIN
ANOTHER GAME OF WIZARDLY
CHESS AGAINST HER RIVAL
MORDENKAINEN.

CHAPTER 4
DUNGEON MASTER'S TOOLS

THE DUNGEON MASTER EMPLOYS MANY tools when preparing and running a D&D campaign. As a DM, your tools include your imagination, your ability to discern what entertains your players, your storytelling acumen, your sense of humor, your ability to listen well, your facility with the game's rules, and more. This chapter adds to your toolbox with guidance and optional rules for a variety of situations. The chapter also includes a selection of ready-to-use puzzles, which you can drop into any campaign.

The tools herein build on the material in the *Dungeon Master's Guide* and the *Monster Manual*. You may use some, all, or none of these tools, and feel free to customize how they work. Your group's enjoyment is paramount, so make these rules your own, aiming to match your group's tastes.

SESSION ZERO

> Establish boundaries. And if anyone crosses them, speak up. If they don't listen, there's always cloudkill ...
> **TASHA**

Before making characters or playing the game, the DM and players can run a special session—colloquially called session zero—to establish expectations, outline the terms of a social contract, and share house rules. Making and sticking to these rules can help ensure that the game is a fun experience for everyone involved.

Often a session zero includes building characters together. As the DM, you can help players during the character creation process by advising them to select options that will serve the adventure or campaign that awaits.

CHARACTER AND PARTY CREATION

Each player has options when it comes to choosing a character race, class, and background, though you may restrict certain options that are deemed unsuitable for the campaign. If there are multiple players in the group, you should encourage them to choose different classes so that the adventuring party has a range of abilities. It's less important that the party include multiple backgrounds, as sometimes it's fun to play an all-soldier party or a troupe of adventuring entertainers. The backgrounds they choose define who their characters were before becoming adventurers and also include roleplaying hooks in the form of ideals, bonds, and flaws—things you ought to know. For example, if a player chooses the criminal background, one of the options for the character's bond is, "I'm trying to pay off an old debt I owe to a generous benefactor." If that's the character's bond, you should work with the player to decide who that generous benefactor is and build relevant storylines into the larger campaign.

PARTY FORMATION

During session zero, your role is to let the players build the characters they want and to help them come up with explanations for how their characters came together to form an adventuring party. It can be helpful to assume that the characters know each other and have some sort of history together, however brief that history might be. Here are some questions you can ask the players as they create characters to get a sense of the party's relationships:

- Are any of the characters related to each other?
- What keeps the characters together as a party?
- What does each character like most about every other member of the adventuring party?
- Does the group have a patron? See chapter 2, "Group Patrons," for patron examples.

If the players are having trouble coming up with a story for how their characters met, they may choose an option from the Party Origin table or let a d6 roll choose it for them. You should spend part of session zero helping the players flesh out the details. For example, if the characters came together to overcome a common foe, the identity of this enemy needs to be determined. If a funeral gathered the group, the identity of the deceased and each character's relationship to them will need to be fleshed out.

PARTY ORIGIN

d6	Origin Story
1	The characters grew up in the same place and have known each other for years.
2	The characters have united to overcome a foe.
3	The characters were brought together by a common benefactor who wishes to sponsor their adventures.
4	A funeral brings the characters together.
5	A festival brings the characters together.
6	The characters find themselves trapped together.

During a festival below one of the walking statues of Waterdeep, young friends dream of embarking on adventures together.

Running a Game for One Player

A DM running a game for one player should spend part of session zero working with that player to come up with their character's backstory, then let the player decide if they want the character to have a sidekick (see the "Sidekicks" section in this chapter).

You might need to help the player run the sidekick for the first few sessions and should make sure the player understands the functions and limitations of sidekicks:

- Sidekicks are stalwart companions who can perform tasks both in and out of combat, including things such as setting up camp and carrying gear.
- Ideally, a sidekick's abilities should complement those of the main character. For example, a spellcaster makes a good sidekick for a fighter or rogue.

Social Contract

D&D is first and foremost meant to be a fun-for-all experience. If one or more participants aren't having fun, the game won't last long. Session zero is the perfect time for you and the players to discuss the experience they're hoping for, as well as topics, themes, and behavior they deem inappropriate. Out of this discussion, a social contract begins to form.

Sometimes a social contract takes shape organically, but it's good practice to have a direct conversation during session zero to establish boundaries and expectations. A typical social contract in a D&D group includes implicit or explicit commitments to the following points:

- You will respect the players by running a game that is fun, fair, and tailored for them. You will allow every player to contribute to the ongoing story and give every character moments to shine. When a player is talking, you are listening.
- The players will respect you and the effort it takes to create a fun game for everyone. The players will allow you to direct the campaign, arbitrate the rules, and settle arguments. When you are talking, the players are listening.

- The players will respect one another, listen to one another, support one another, and do their utmost to preserve the cohesion of the adventuring party.
- Should you or a player disrespect each other or violate the social contract in some other way, the group may dismiss that person from the table.

This social contract covers the basics, but individual groups might require additional agreed-upon terms to guarantee a fun play experience for all. And a social contract typically evolves as a group's members learn more about one another.

Hard and Soft Limits

Once you and the players have acknowledged the terms of the game's social contract and agreed to uphold them, the conversation can segue into a discussion about soft and hard limits. There are many ways to mediate this discussion, and you might want to do some research to find an approach that might work well for your group. For purposes of this explanation, these terms are described as follows:

A **soft limit** is a threshold that one should think twice about crossing, as it is likely to create genuine anxiety, fear, and discomfort.

A **hard limit** is a threshold that should never be crossed.

Every member of the group has soft and hard limits, and it behooves everyone in the group to know what they are. Make sure everyone at the table is comfortable with how this discussion takes place. Players might not want to discuss their limits aloud around the table, especially if they're new to roleplaying games or haven't spent a lot of time with certain other members of the group. One way to alleviate such discomfort is to encourage the players to share their limits privately with you and allow you to present them without attribution to the whole group. For example, the players could write their limits on index cards for you to read aloud. However these limits are presented, it would be useful for you or one of the players to compile the limits into one list that can be shared with the whole group. Keep in mind that any discussion about limits should be treated with care—even sharing a person's limits can be a very painful experience, and this conversation should be handled with respect.

Common in-game limits include—but are not limited to—themes or scenes of sex, exploitation, racial profiling, slavery, violence toward children and animals, gratuitous swearing, and intra-party romance. Common out-of-game limits include unwanted physical contact, dice-sharing, dice-throwing, shouting, vulgarity, rules lawyering, distracting use of cell phones, and generally disrespectful behavior.

The discussion of limits is important because DMs and players can have phobias or triggers that others might not be aware of. Any in-game topic or theme that makes a member of the gaming group feel unsafe or uncomfortable should be avoided. If a topic or theme makes one or more players nervous but they give you consent to include it in-game, incorporating it should be handled with care, and you must be ready to veer away from such topics and themes quickly.

While session zero is the perfect place to start this discussion, it might not be the only time limits are addressed. Someone might cross a line and need to be reminded of a limit, or someone might not think to include some of their limits in the initial discussion. Players can also discover new limits as the campaign unfolds. Make a plan to check in with the group to make sure the list of hard and soft limits is up to date, and remind everyone to revisit this list often in case it changes.

Game Customization

In addition to shaping the game around the characters in the adventuring party, you should be prepared to customize the game to suit the players' tastes. The "Know Your Players" section in the introduction of the *Dungeon Master's Guide* provides some guidance for doing so, based on known player archetypes. To help identify what types of players are in the group, you can ask each player any or all of the following questions:

- Which of the three pillars of adventuring (combat, exploration, roleplaying) interest you the most?
- How much humor do you like in the game?
- What level of technology do you prefer?
- Do you enjoy solving in-game puzzles and riddles?
- Do you like to track experience points, or would you rather have your character advance in level when I tell you to?

House Rules

House rules include optional rules, such as those presented in chapter 9 of the *Dungeon Master's Guide*, and rules you create. If you plan to use any house rules, session zero is a good time to discuss those rules with the players and solicit their input.

House rules are best presented as experiments, and time will tell if they're good for your game. If you introduce a house rule in session zero that turns out to have an adverse effect on people's enjoyment of the game, you may jettison or revise the house rule to create a better gaming experience for everyone. Don't feel bad if a house rule doesn't end up working as well as you expected it to. Remember: the goal is to ensure everyone is having fun.

SIDEKICKS

This section provides a straightforward way to add a special NPC—called a sidekick—to the group of adventurers. These rules take a creature with a low challenge rating and give it levels in one of three simple classes: Expert, Spellcaster, or Warrior.

A sidekick can be incorporated into a group at the party's inception, or a sidekick might join them during the campaign. For example, the characters might meet a villager, an animal, or another creature, forge a friendship, and invite the creature to join them on their adventures.

You can also use these rules to customize a monster for your own use as DM.

CREATING A SIDEKICK

A sidekick can be any type of creature with a stat block in the *Monster Manual* or another D&D book, but the challenge rating in its stat block must be 1/2 or lower. You take that stat block and add to it, as explained in the "Gaining a Sidekick Class" section.

To join the adventurers, the sidekick must be the friend of at least one of them. This friendship might be connected to a character's backstory or to events that have transpired in play. For example, a sidekick could be a childhood friend or pet, or it might be a creature the adventurers saved. As DM, you determine whether there is sufficient trust established for the creature to join the group.

You decide who plays the sidekick. Here are some options:

- A player plays the sidekick as their second character—ideal when you have only one or two players.
- A player plays the sidekick as their only character—ideal for a player who wants a character who's simpler than a typical player character.
- The players jointly play the sidekick.
- You play the sidekick.

There's no limit on the number of sidekicks in a group, but having more than one per player character can noticeably slow down the game. And when estimating the difficulty of an upcoming encounter, count each sidekick as a character.

GAINING A SIDEKICK CLASS

When you create a sidekick, you choose the class it will have for the rest of its career: Expert, Spellcaster, or Warrior, each of which is detailed below. If a sidekick class contains a choice, you may make the choice or let the players make it.

STARTING LEVEL

The starting level of a sidekick is the same as the average level of the group. For example, if a 1st-level group starts out with a sidekick, that sidekick is also 1st level, but if a 10th-level group invites a sidekick to join them, that sidekick starts at 10th level.

LEVELING UP A SIDEKICK

Whenever a group's average level goes up, the sidekick gains a level. It doesn't matter how much of the group's recent adventures the sidekick experienced; the sidekick levels up because of a combination of the adventures it shared with the group and its own training.

HIT POINTS

Whenever the sidekick gains a level, it gains one Hit Die, and its hit point maximum increases. To determine the amount of the increase, roll the Hit Die (the type of die appears in the sidekick's stat block), and add its Constitution modifier. It gains a minimum of 1 hit point per level.

If the sidekick drops to 0 hit points and isn't killed outright, it falls unconscious and subsequently makes death saving throws, just like a player character.

PROFICIENCY BONUS

The sidekick's proficiency bonus is determined by its level in its class, as shown in the class's table.

Whenever the sidekick's proficiency bonus increases by 1, add 1 to the to-hit modifier of all the attacks in its stat block, and increase the DCs in its stat block by 1.

ABILITY SCORE INCREASES

Whenever the sidekick gains the Ability Score Improvement feature, adjust anything in its stat block that relies on an ability modifier that you increase. For example, if the sidekick has an attack that uses its Strength modifier, increase the attack's modifiers to hit and damage if the Strength modifier increases.

If it's unclear whether a melee attack in the stat block uses Strength or Dexterity, the attack can use either.

EXPERT

The Expert is a master of certain tasks or knowledge, favoring cunning over brawn. It might be a scout, a musician, a librarian, a clever street kid, a wily merchant, or a burglar.

To gain the Expert class, a creature must have at least one language in its stat block that it can speak.

A sidekick gains the following class features as it gains levels, as summarized on the Expert table.

EXPERTS, LEFT TO RIGHT: A TORTLE, A WINGED KOBOLD, AND A KENKU

BONUS PROFICIENCIES

1st-level Expert feature

The sidekick gains proficiency in one saving throw of your choice: Dexterity, Intelligence, or Charisma.

In addition, the sidekick gains proficiency in five skills of your choice, and it gains proficiency with light armor. If it is a humanoid or has a simple or martial weapon in its stat block, it also gains proficiency with all simple weapons and with two tools of your choice.

HELPFUL

1st-level Expert feature

The sidekick is adept at giving well-timed assistance; the sidekick can take the Help action as a bonus action.

CUNNING ACTION

2nd-level Expert feature

The sidekick's agility or quick thinking allows it to act speedily. On its turn in combat, it can take the Dash, Disengage, or Hide action as a bonus action.

EXPERTISE

3rd-level Expert feature

Choose two of the sidekick's skill proficiencies. The sidekick's proficiency bonus is doubled for any ability check it makes that uses any of the chosen proficiencies.

THE EXPERT

Level	Proficiency Bonus	Features
1st	+2	Bonus Proficiencies, Helpful
2nd	+2	Cunning Action
3rd	+2	Expertise
4th	+2	Ability Score Improvement
5th	+3	—
6th	+3	Coordinated Strike
7th	+3	Evasion
8th	+3	Ability Score Improvement
9th	+4	—
10th	+4	Ability Score Improvement
11th	+4	Inspiring Help (1d6)
12th	+4	Ability Score Improvement
13th	+5	—
14th	+5	Reliable Talent
15th	+5	Expertise
16th	+5	Ability Score Improvement
17th	+6	—
18th	+6	Sharp Mind
19th	+6	Ability Score Improvement
20th	+6	Inspiring Help (2d6)

At 15th level, choose two more of the sidekick's skill proficiencies to gain this benefit.

ABILITY SCORE IMPROVEMENT
4th-level Expert feature

At 4th level and again at 8th, 10th, 12th, 16th, and 19th level, the sidekick increases one ability score of your choice by 2, or the sidekick increases two ability scores of your choice by 1. The sidekick can't increase an ability score above 20 using this feature.

COORDINATED STRIKE
6th-level Expert feature

The sidekick is adept at fighting in concert with a companion. When the sidekick uses its Helpful feature to aid an ally in attacking a creature, that target can be up to 30 feet away from the sidekick, and the sidekick can deal an extra 2d6 damage to it the next time the sidekick hits it with an attack roll before the end of the current turn. The extra damage is the same type of damage dealt by the attack.

EVASION
7th-level Expert feature

Because of extraordinary good luck, the sidekick is skilled at avoiding danger. When the sidekick is subjected to an effect that allows it to make a Dexterity saving throw to take only half damage, it instead takes no damage if it succeeds on the saving throw, and only half damage if it failed. The sidekick doesn't benefit from this feature while incapacitated.

INSPIRING HELP
11th-level Expert feature

When the sidekick takes the Help action, the creature who receives the help also gains a 1d6 bonus to the d20 roll. If that roll is an attack roll, the creature can forgo adding the bonus to it, and then if the attack hits, the creature can add the bonus to the attack's damage roll against one target.

At 20th level, the bonus increases to 2d6.

RELIABLE TALENT
14th-level Expert feature

The sidekick has refined its skills to an exceptional degree. Whenever the sidekick makes an ability check that includes its whole proficiency bonus, it can treat a d20 roll of 9 or lower as a 10.

SHARP MIND
18th-level Expert feature

The sidekick gains proficiency in one of the following saving throws of your choice: Intelligence, Wisdom, or Charisma.

SPELLCASTER

A sidekick who becomes a Spellcaster walks the paths of magic. The sidekick might be a hedge wizard, a priest, a soothsayer, a magical performer, or a person with magic in their veins.

To gain the Spellcaster class, a creature must have at least one language in its stat block that it can speak.

A sidekick gains the following class features as it gains levels in this class, as summarized on the Spellcaster table.

BONUS PROFICIENCIES
1st-level Spellcaster feature

The sidekick gains proficiency in one saving throw of your choice: Wisdom, Intelligence, or Charisma.

In addition, the sidekick gains proficiency in two skills of your choice from the following list: Arcana, History, Insight, Investigation, Medicine, Performance, Persuasion, and Religion.

The sidekick gains proficiency with light armor, and if it is a humanoid or has a simple or martial weapon in its stat block, it also gains proficiency with all simple weapons.

SPELLCASTING
1st-level Spellcaster feature

The sidekick gains the ability to cast spells. (If the creature already has the Spellcasting trait, this feature replaces that trait.) Choose the Spellcaster's role: Mage, Healer, or Prodigy. This choice determines the spell list and spellcasting ability used by the sidekick, as shown on the Spellcasting table.

SPELLCASTING

Role	Spell List	Ability
Mage	Wizard	Intelligence
Healer	Cleric and Druid	Wisdom
Prodigy	Bard and Warlock	Charisma

Spell Slots. The Spellcaster table shows how many spell slots the sidekick has to cast its Spellcaster spells of 1st level and higher. To cast one of these spells, the sidekick must expend a slot of the spell's level or higher. The sidekick regains all expended spell slots when it finishes a long rest.

Spells Known. The sidekick knows two cantrips and one 1st-level spell of your choice from its spell list. Here are recommendations for a 1st-level spellcaster of each role:

Mage: *mage hand, ray of frost, thunderwave*
Healer: *cure wounds, guidance, sacred flame*
Prodigy: *eldritch blast, healing word, light*

The Cantrips Known and Spells Known columns of the Spellcaster table shows when the sidekick

SPELLCASTERS, LEFT TO RIGHT: A
BULLYWUG, A GOBLIN, AND A TABAXI

THE SPELLCASTER

Level	Proficiency Bonus	Features	Cantrips Known	Spells Known	1st	2nd	3rd	4th	5th
1st	+2	Bonus Proficiencies, Spellcasting	2	1	2	—	—	—	—
2nd	+2	—	2	2	2	—	—	—	—
3rd	+2	—	2	3	3	—	—	—	—
4th	+2	Ability Score Improvement	3	3	3	—	—	—	—
5th	+3	—	3	4	4	2	—	—	—
6th	+3	Potent Cantrips	3	4	4	2	—	—	—
7th	+3	—	3	5	4	3	—	—	—
8th	+3	Ability Score Improvement	3	5	4	3	—	—	—
9th	+4	—	3	6	4	3	2	—	—
10th	+4	—	4	6	4	3	2	—	—
11th	+4	—	4	7	4	3	3	—	—
12th	+4	Ability Score Improvement	4	7	4	3	3	—	—
13th	+5	—	4	8	4	3	3	1	—
14th	+5	Empowered Spells	4	8	4	3	3	1	—
15th	+5	—	4	9	4	3	3	2	—
16th	+5	Ability Score Improvement	4	9	4	3	3	2	—
17th	+6	—	4	10	4	3	3	3	1
18th	+6	Ability Score Improvement	4	10	4	3	3	3	1
19th	+6	—	4	11	4	3	3	3	2
20th	+6	Focused Casting	4	11	4	3	3	3	2

learns more spells of your choice. Each of the spells in the Spells Known column must be of a level for which the sidekick has spell slots, as shown on the table. For instance, when the sidekick reaches 5th level in this class, it can learn one new spell of 1st or 2nd level.

Additionally, when the sidekick gains a level in this class, you can choose one of the spells it knows from this class and replace it with another spell from its spell list. The new spell must be a cantrip or of a level for which the sidekick has spell slots.

Spellcasting Ability. The sidekick's spellcasting ability for these spells depends on the choice you made on the Spellcasting table.

The sidekick uses its spellcasting ability whenever a spell refers to that ability. In addition, it uses its spellcasting ability modifier when setting the saving throw DC for a spell it casts and when making an attack roll with one.

> Spell save DC = 8 + sidekick's proficiency bonus + spellcasting ability modifier
>
> Spell attack modifier = sidekick's proficiency bonus + spellcasting ability modifier

Spellcasting Focus. The sidekick can use a focus for its spells depending on the choice you made on the Spellcasting table. A Mage can use an arcane focus, a Priest can use a holy symbol, and a Prodigy can use an arcane focus or a musical instrument.

ABILITY SCORE IMPROVEMENT
4th-level Spellcaster feature

At 4th level and again at 8th, 12th, 16th, and 18th level, the sidekick increases one ability score of your choice by 2, or the sidekick increases two ability scores of your choice by 1. The sidekick can't increase an ability score above 20 using this feature.

POTENT CANTRIPS
6th-level Spellcaster feature

The sidekick can add its spellcasting ability modifier to the damage it deals with any cantrip.

EMPOWERED SPELLS
14th-level Spellcaster feature

Choose one school of magic. Whenever the sidekick casts a spell of that school by expending a spell slot, the sidekick can add its spellcasting ability modifier to the spell's damage roll or healing roll, if any.

FOCUSED CASTING
20th-level Spellcaster feature

Taking damage can't break the sidekick's concentration on a spell.

WARRIOR

A Warrior sidekick grows in martial prowess as it fights by your side. It might be a soldier, a town guard, a battle-trained beast, or any other creature honed for combat.

A sidekick gains the following class features as it gains levels in this class, as summarized on the Warrior table.

BONUS PROFICIENCIES
1st-level Warrior feature

The sidekick gains proficiency in one saving throw of your choice: Strength, Dexterity, or Constitution.

In addition, the sidekick gains proficiency in two skills of your choice from the following list: Acrobatics, Animal Handling, Athletics, Intimidation, Nature, Perception, and Survival.

The sidekick gains proficiency with all armor, and if it is a humanoid or has a simple or martial weapon in its stat block, it gains proficiency with shields and all simple and martial weapons.

MARTIAL ROLE
1st-level Warrior feature

Each warrior focuses on offense or defense in their training. Choose one of the following options:

Attacker. The sidekick gains a +2 bonus to all attack rolls.
Defender. The sidekick can use its reaction to impose disadvantage on the attack roll of a creature within 5 feet of it whose target isn't the sidekick, provided the sidekick can see the attacker.

SECOND WIND
2nd-level Warrior feature

The sidekick can use a bonus action on its turn to regain hit points equal to 1d10 + its level in this class. Once it uses this feature, it must finish a short or long rest before it can use it again.

The sidekick can use this feature twice between rests starting at 20th level.

IMPROVED CRITICAL
3rd-level Warrior feature

The sidekick's attack rolls score a critical hit on a roll of 19 or 20 on the d20.

ABILITY SCORE IMPROVEMENT
4th-level Warrior feature

At 4th level and again at 8th, 12th, 14th, 16th, and 19th level, the sidekick increases one ability score of your choice by 2, or the sidekick increases two ability scores of your choice by 1. The sidekick can't increase an ability score above 20 using this feature.

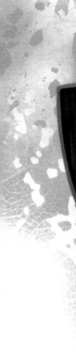

EXTRA ATTACK

6th-level Warrior feature

The sidekick can attack twice, instead of once, whenever it takes the Attack action on its turn.

The number of attacks increases to three when the sidekick reaches 15th level.

If the sidekick has the Multiattack action, it can use Extra Attack or Multiattack on a turn, not both.

BATTLE READINESS

7th-level Warrior feature

The sidekick has advantage on initiative rolls.

IMPROVED DEFENSE

10th-level Warrior feature

The sidekick's Armor Class increases by 1.

INDOMITABLE

11th-level Warrior feature

The sidekick can reroll a saving throw that it fails, but it must use the new roll. When it uses this feature, it can't use the feature again until it finishes a long rest.

The sidekick can use this feature twice between long rests starting at 18th level.

THE WARRIOR

Level	Proficiency Bonus	Features
1st	+2	Bonus Proficiencies, Martial Role
2nd	+2	Second Wind (1 use)
3rd	+2	Improved Critical
4th	+2	Ability Score Improvement
5th	+3	—
6th	+3	Extra Attack (1 extra)
7th	+3	Battle Readiness
8th	+3	Ability Score Improvement
9th	+4	—
10th	+4	Improved Defense
11th	+4	Indomitable (1 use)
12th	+4	Ability Score Improvement
13th	+5	—
14th	+5	Ability Score Improvement
15th	+5	Extra Attack (2 extra)
16th	+5	Ability Score Improvement
17th	+6	—
18th	+6	Indomitable (2 uses)
19th	+6	Ability Score Improvement
20th	+6	Second Wind (2 uses)

Parleying with Monsters

> Why fight if a lively chat is possible? If things get out of hand, just show yourself out with a dimension door.
> TASHA

Meeting a monster doesn't have to spark a fight. An offering, like food, can calm some hostile monsters, and sapient creatures often prefer to talk than to draw weapons. If the adventurers try to parley with a monster, you may improvise the encounter or use the social interaction rules in the *Dungeon Master's Guide*. Consider granting the characters advantage on any ability check they make to communicate with a creature if they offer something it wants. The "Monsters' Desires" section below suggest things that a creature might like, depending on its type.

Monster Research

Adventurers can research what a creature is likely to desire. The Monster Research table suggests which skills can be used to learn about a creature of a particular type. The DC for a relevant ability check equals 10 + the creature's challenge rating.

Monster Research

Type	Suggested Skills
Aberration	Arcana
Beast	Animal Handling, Nature, or Survival
Celestial	Arcana or Religion
Construct	Arcana
Dragon	Arcana, History, or Nature
Elemental	Arcana or Nature
Fey	Arcana or Nature
Fiend	Arcana or Religion
Giant	History
Humanoid	History
Monstrosity	Nature or Survival
Ooze	Arcana or Survival
Plant	Nature or Survival
Undead	Arcana or Religion

Monsters' Desires

Aberrations

d4	Desired Offering
1	The brain or other organs of a rare creature
2	Flattery and obsequiousness
3	Secrets or lore it doesn't already know
4	Accepting a strange, organic graft onto your body

Beasts

d4	Desired Offering
1	Fresh meat
2	A soothing melody
3	Brightly colored beads, cloth, feathers, or string
4	An old stuffed animal or other soft trinket

Celestials

d4	Desired Offering
1	The tale of a heroic figure
2	An oath to do three charitable deeds before dawn
3	The crown of a defeated tyrant
4	A holy relic or treasured family heirloom

Constructs

d4	Desired Offering
1	Oil to apply to the construct's joints
2	A magic item with charges, to be used as fuel
3	A vessel infused with elemental power
4	Adamantine or mithral components

Dragons

d4	Desired Offering
1	Gold or gems
2	Anything from a draconic rival's hoard
3	An antique passed down at least three generations
4	A flattering artistic depiction of the dragon

Elementals

d4	Desired Offering
1	A gem worth at least 50 gp, which the creature eats
2	An exceedingly pure sample of a favored element
3	A way to return the elemental to its home plane
4	Performing a dance from the elemental's home plane

Fey

d4	Desired Offering
1	The memory of your first kiss
2	The color of your eyes
3	An object of deep sentimental value to you
4	Reciting a sublime poem

Fiends

d4	Desired Offering
1	Your soul
2	A desecrated holy object
3	Blood from a living or recently slain loved one
4	Breaking a sacred promise in the fiend's presence

ADVENTURERS OFFER MEAT TO AN OWLBEAR.

GIANTS

d4	Desired Offering
1	A dwarf admitting giant-craft to be superior to dwarf-craft
2	A strong working animal
3	Multiple barrels of ale
4	Treasure stolen from a rival giant

HUMANOIDS

d4	Desired Offering
1	Promising to find a lost item of great importance to their culture
2	Challenging them to a type of friendly contest, such as dancing, singing, or drinking
3	Recovering something they've lost
4	Information on a foe's secrets or weaknesses

MONSTROSITIES

d4	Desired Offering
1	Dislodging the stuck scraps of the creature's last meal
2	The creature's favorite food
3	Driving off the creature's rival
4	Making movements that mimic the monster's mating dance

OOZES

d4	Desired Offering
1	A vial of putrid liquids
2	A cloth bearing a noxious odor
3	Bones or metal, which the ooze promptly absorbs
4	A gallon of any effervescent fluid

PLANTS

d4	Desired Offering
1	A pound of mulch
2	Water from a spring infused with Feywild energy
3	Clearing invasive vegetation from the creature's territory
4	Destroying all axes and fire-making implements the party carries

UNDEAD

d4	Desired Offering
1	A vial of blood
2	A personal memento from the creature's past
3	Materials, tools, or the skills to sun-proof a crumbling mausoleum
4	Completing a task the creature was unable to finish in life

ROBIN OLAUSSON

Environmental Hazards

> When your earliest memories are of growing up in the Feywild, things like time-warping mushrooms, mind-bending fruit, and giant tabby cats seem far less whimsical and way more, "Could we please just move to the Material Plane so I can have some scrap of a normal childhood?!"
>
> TASHA

This section explores how to add fantastical challenges to any locale and ways to further bring an adventure's setting to life.

When a creature's name appears in bold in a table herein, that indicates that you can find the creature's stat block in the *Monster Manual*.

Supernatural Regions

Not all lands thrive as nature intended. Magical forces, strange interlopers, or tragic events can alter an area's destiny, fundamentally changing the land. While the flora, fauna, structures, and inhabitants might remain unaffected, the land's innate character takes on new qualities.

A supernatural region is permeated by a preternatural force in an area as large or small as you wish. In the affected area, certain effects and brief encounters reinforce an underlying theme. These effects occur as characters traverse an influenced region or add interest to a specific affected location.

The descriptions of the following supernatural regions summarize the region, present a table of potential effects within the affected area, and note triggers for a random effect. Feel free to customize the effects of each region to suit any adventure.

The effects of a region occur whenever you please, at the time each description suggests, or under one or more of the following circumstances:

- Soon after the party first enters the region
- When a creature loses more than half its hit points
- When a creature casts a spell of 1st level or higher
- When a creature activates a magic item
- When a creature makes an exceptionally loud noise or otherwise attracts attention
- When the party spends at least 30 minutes in the same region

Blessed Radiance

The grace of the Upper Planes touches this region. Consider rolling on the Blessed Radiance Effects table when the following circumstances occur in the region:

- A creature succeeds on a saving throw compelled by the abilities of a fiend or an undead
- A creature is the target of a cleric or paladin spell of 3rd level or higher
- A creature scores a critical hit against a fiend or an undead
- A creature experiences an epiphany or inspiring triumph in the service of righteousness or in defiance of wickedness

Blessed Radiance Effects

d100	Effect
01–06	Golden light fills a 20-foot-radius, 40-foot-high cylinder centered on one character in the region and then fades. That character and their friends in the cylinder gain the benefits of the *divine favor* spell for 1 hour.
07–12	Radiant energy erupts in a 10-foot-radius sphere centered on one random creature in the region. Each creature in the sphere that isn't undead regains 3d6 hit points. Each undead creature in the sphere takes 3d6 radiant damage.
13–18	Aberrations, fiends, and undead in the region have disadvantage on attack rolls and ability checks for the next 24 hours.
19–24	Each creature carrying the holy symbol of a deity from a non-evil plane while in the region gains advantage on saving throws for the next 24 hours.
25–30	One character in the region is suffused with celestial power. For 1 minute, the character's melee attacks deal an extra 2d6 radiant damage on a hit.
31–36	One simple or martial weapon that is nonmagical and carried by one character in the region gains the properties of a *mace of disruption* for 24 hours.
37–42	A flying, gleaming sword (use the **flying sword** stat block in the *Monster Manual*) appears within 60 feet of an aberration, a fiend, or an undead, which becomes the sword's target. The sword deals radiant damage instead of slashing damage and knows the exact location of its target while the target is within the region. The sword vanishes when it or its target is reduced to 0 hit points.
43–48	One character in the region hears whispers from celestial beings or refrains of celestial choirs. The character can ask those voices one question as if using the *commune* spell.

A BLESSED KI-RIN SHRINE

d100	Effect
49–54	Aberrations, fiends, and undead in the region give off a crimson glow for 1 minute. The creatures shed dim light in a 10-foot radius, attacks against them have advantage if the attacker can see them, and the creatures can't benefit from being invisible.
55–60	Celestial power explodes in a 30-foot-radius sphere of divine light centered on an aberration, a fiend, or an undead creature within the region. Each creature in the sphere must make a DC 15 Constitution saving throw. On a failure, the creature takes 4d6 radiant damage and is blinded. On a success, it takes half damage and isn't blinded.
61–66	One character in the region feels a profound sense of purpose and gains the benefit of the *bless* spell for 1 minute. They can choose two other creatures they can see to gain the spell's benefits as well.
67–72	A booming voice thunders in Celestial and can be heard throughout the region. Each creature in the region must make a DC 15 Constitution saving throw. On a success, the creature gains 2d10 temporary hit points. On a failure, the creature is deafened for 1 minute.

d100	Effect
73–78	One character in the region gains the ability to cure afflictions for 1 hour. As an action, they can cast *lesser restoration* or *greater restoration* without expending a spell slot and requiring no material components.
79–84	The effects of a *hallow* spell (save DC 17), with one of its extra effects (DM's choice), settle over the region for 24 hours.
85–90	An angelic voice rings throughout the region. Each creature there must succeed on a DC 15 Wisdom saving throw or perform the grovel option of the *command* spell.
91–95	One character in the region permanently gains resistance to necrotic damage. Reroll if you've already rolled this effect.
96–00	One character in the region gains the ability to use the Divine Intervention cleric feature, which succeeds automatically. The character can use the feature granted in this way only once and must use it within 7 days. Reroll if you've already rolled this effect.

Far Realm

As souls travel away from the Material Plane after death, they either dwell in the Astral Plane as spirits or are pulled toward one of the Outer Planes to continue their journey. But some entities find ways to travel beyond the Outer Planes to dwell in the Far Realm. There they transform over eons into abominations or elder evils, seething in a reality with its own laws. All who stay in the Far Realm are eventually twisted into alien shapes by the realm's eldritch forces.

The Far Realm's pernicious influence is often subtle, leaking into the Material Plane through thin places in reality or as invasive thoughts that inspire life to propagate along alien paths.

Consider rolling on the Far Realm Effects table when the following circumstances occur in a region touched by the Far Realm:

- A warlock whose Otherworldly Patron is a Great Old One rolls a 1 or 20 on the d20 for an ability check, an attack roll, or a saving throw.
- The characters take a short or long rest in the region.
- A creature spends more than an hour reading an eldritch tome written by those who have seen or otherwise interacted with the Far Realm.

Far Realm Effects

d100	Effect
01–09	A structure in the region whispers faintly. Any creature within 60 feet of the structure that can hear it must succeed on a DC 12 Wisdom saving throw or be charmed. While charmed in this way, the creature must move toward the source of the whispering, avoiding obvious hazards. When it reaches the source, it is incapacitated. The creature can repeat the saving throw when it takes damage and at the end of every hour, ending the effect on itself on a success.
10–18	An elder evil turns its attention to the region, imposing the pressure of its unfathomable presence upon the place. Any creature that finishes a rest in the region must succeed on a DC 12 Charisma saving throw, or it gains no benefit from finishing the rest. It instead finds strange scrawls, stacked stones, or its belongings arranged in intricate, abstruse patterns nearby.
19–27	Local plants and animals share a malevolent intelligence. Roll a d6. On a 1–2, an *insect plague* spell is centered on one random creature in the region. On a 3–4, 1d4 **swarms of ravens** and 1d4 **swarms of rats** gather and attack any other creatures in the region. On a 5–6, a **treant** (in forested terrain) or a **galeb duhr** (in rockier terrain) attacks.
28–36	Distance no longer functions in a comprehensible manner within the region. Creatures make ranged attack rolls with disadvantage, and the range of those attacks is halved.
37–45	The landscape melts into a mass of writhing flesh, eyes, and fanged mouths. From an unoccupied space in the fleshy ground arise 1d4 + 5 **gibbering mouthers** that attack anyone in sight.
46–54	Unintelligible murmurings threaten to overcome the mind of one random creature within the region. At the start of the creature's turn, it must succeed on a DC 13 Intelligence saving throw or use its action to make one melee attack against the nearest creature it can see. If there are no other creatures within reach, the target spends its action babbling.
55–63	Bizarre appendages squirm beneath the ground and around trees or other structures within this region. Dozens of limbs burst forth, entangling anyone within a 30-foot sphere surrounding one random creature. Each creature in the sphere must succeed on a DC 14 Dexterity saving throw or take 3d6 bludgeoning damage and be restrained. Any creature that ends its turn in the area takes 3d6 bludgeoning damage. A creature can free itself or someone else within reach from being restrained in this way by using an action to make a successful DC 14 Strength or Dexterity check (its choice).
64–72	Creatures in the region can't leave it and find themselves covering the same ground over and over. By the time they realize this, 2d10 hours have passed, during which they have made no progress in their effort to leave. The effect then ends, and each creature must succeed on a DC 10 Constitution saving throw or gain 1 level of exhaustion.

A Far Realm Incursion with Mind Flayer Nautiloids

TITUS LUNTER

d100	Effect
73–79	One random creature in the region hears strange whispers and must succeed on a DC 14 Wisdom saving throw or become charmed. While charmed in this way, the creature focuses on copying the blasphemous designs that appear in its mind using whatever medium it has available (ink, charcoal, mud, or its own blood). Unless restrained, the creature completes the designs in 1 hour of work. When the creature finishes its work, it is no longer charmed, and a **death slaad** appears within 30 feet of it and attacks anyone in sight.
80–85	Natural features and structures in this region writhe to spell out words and form strange symbols. Any creature that tries to read the messages must make a DC 20 Intelligence (Arcana) check. On a success, the creature gains insight as if it had cast the *contact other plane* spell. On a failure, the creature is affected as if it failed a saving throw against the *confusion* spell. This effect ends at the end of the creature's next turn.

d100	Effect
86–90	In this region, circular things (such as buttons, crystal balls, the sun, and so on) seem appallingly wrong. One random creature that starts its turn in this region must succeed on a DC 14 Intelligence saving throw or spend their turn loudly trying to destroy these objects.
91–95	Glaring eyes, which weep viscid tears, appear on inanimate objects throughout the region. These eyes watch the characters, and creatures within the region can't be surprised by the characters for as long as the eyes exist. An eye closes and disappears if it takes any damage. Reroll if you've already rolled this effect.
96–00	A tear in reality creates a rift in the region, similar to the spell *gate*, that passes through the Far Realm and connects with a random plane. Any creature that enters the rift takes 10d10 psychic damage from the horrors of the Far Realm and appears in an empty space closest to the rift's opening on another random plane. The rift vanishes after 2d10 + 2 hours.

HAUNTED

Haunted environs include homes burdened by dark deeds, the sites of mass killings, and locations where individuals died while experiencing powerful fear, sorrow, or hatred. Haunted places bear echoes of the past and, like ghosts, harass visitors even as they seek respite from age-old traumas. Few places are meaninglessly haunted, and you can easily customize the general results on the following table to suit all manner of macabre tales.

Consider rolling on the Haunted Effects table when the following circumstances occur in the region:

- A creature gains the frightened condition.
- Multiple creatures are unable to see.
- A creature is alone.
- Midnight or another ominous hour arrives.
- A ghost or other creature tied to the region's grim history menaces the party.

HAUNTED EFFECTS

d100	Effect
01–05	A violent thunderstorm begins, centered over the region. It doesn't end until the party leaves the region.
06–10	A random building in the region gains the benefits of the *guards and wards* spell (save DC 13) for the next 24 hours.
11–15	A mundane part of one random character's surroundings—perhaps a tree bole or a taxidermied animal head—animates for 1 minute and whispers a warning or threatens to reveal one of the character's secrets.
16–20	All bright light weakens to dim light for 24 hours. Sources that provide dim light, such as candles, do not shed any light.
21–25	The temperature in the region drops by 10 degrees Fahrenheit every hour for the next 1d6 hours, after which the temperature returns to normal. If cold enough, ice crystals form in sinister patterns.
26–30	One random creature's shadow acts independently for the next 24 hours. The shadow acts out of sync with its owner, perhaps dramatically choking or trying to murder another shadow.

d100	Effect
31–35	After the next sunset, the sun doesn't rise again for 36 hours. During this time, the sky over the region might hold a crimson moon, be obscured by roiling fog, or display blinking, alien stars.
36–40	During the next night, one random sleeping creature vanishes and reappears approximately a foot beneath where they were sleeping—typically buried in undisturbed dirt or in a space beneath floorboards. The creature or someone else can free it with a successful DC 13 Strength (Athletics) check.
41–45	One random creature in the region is targeted by the *levitate* spell (save DC 15) for 1 minute.
46–50	A nonviolent but unsettling **ghost**—perhaps a pet, an accident-prone child, or a dismembered big toe—appears and follows one random creature for 24 hours before vanishing. The ghost vanishes if reduced to 0 hit points.
51–55	One player character's appearance changes for the next 24 hours to reflect the region's haunted history. For example, they might manifest the distinctive facial scar associated with a notorious tyrant who died in the region.
56–60	For the next 24 hours, any humanoid killed in the region rapidly decomposes and rises as a **skeleton** 1d10 minutes after dying.
61–65	Over the next 24 hours, whenever any creature is wounded, its blood (or similar fluid) spreads to form a short message or grisly tableau.
66–70	A spirit inhabits one character's simple or martial weapon, making it a sentient magic item until the character leaves the region. Randomly generate the item's properties as described in the "Sentient Magic Items" section of the *Dungeon Master's Guide*.
71–75	A spectral force manifests to one character in the region, allowing them to ask one question and receive a short answer as through the *augury* spell. The force manifests as a planchette moving on a talking board, writing on foggy glass, or insects swarming to create messages.
76–80	During the next night, one sleeping character in the region receives a vision as if the target of the *dream* spell. The dream is brief and unsettling, revealing some element of the environment's history and putting the character in the place of someone who suffered a grim fate there.

A HAUNTED MANOR

d100	Effect
81–85	A coffin or small enclosed space in the region—perhaps an antique box, stone cairn, or tree stump sealed with rocks—radiates palpable malice. The first time a creature opens it, roll a die. If you roll an even number, the creature receives a terrible vision and is frightened of all creatures for the next 24 hours. If you roll an odd number, an avatar of death appears and attacks as though summoned by the Skull card from a *deck of many things*.
86–90	Over the next 24 hours, whenever any creature in the region regains hit points from a spell, the healing magic leaves scars. This might be accompanied by a purging of black bile or a spectral force tearing free from the creature. These scars can be removed only by *greater restoration* or *wish*.

d100	Effect
91–95	For 24 hours, a luminous wisp of vapor floats above a corpse or grave in the region. If the wisp is put in a container, a creature holding the receptacle can cast the *resurrection* spell once, requiring no components and causing the wisp to vanish. Any creature returned to life in this way experiences strange dreams.
96–00	A mysterious mist rises from the shadows. This dense fog heavily obscures everything in a 50-foot-radius sphere around one random creature in the region. Any creature that starts its turn in the mist must succeed on a DC 10 Constitution saving throw or gain 1 level of exhaustion. This exhaustion can't be removed while the creature is in the mist. Additionally, creatures notice unsettling sights through the fog, such as ominous ruins or soundless silhouettes fleeing pursuit. The mists can't be dispersed by any wind, but clear after 1 minute.

INFESTED

On many worlds, the biomass of insects radically outweighs that of higher organisms. Mass migrations and deadly insect species can imperil larger creatures, but most insects remain nothing more than an annoyance. However, through wild population booms, magical manipulation, supernatural growth, interbreeding with otherworldly species, or stranger circumstances, insects can overrun an entire region. Swarms of insects become the dominant species in an area, consuming plants and animals, creating elaborate hives or tunnels, and infesting structures and the earth.

The following effects represent a region overrun by insects or hives of similar creatures, likely manipulated by magic, otherworldly intelligence, or environmental factors to infest an area in countless numbers and drive out all competing life.

Consider rolling on the Infested Effects table when the following circumstances occur in the region:

- Webs, cocoons, hives, anthills, or other insect dwellings are disturbed.
- A creature attacks an insect swarm or a Small or larger insect, such as a giant centipede or giant spider, in the region.
- A creature begins a short or long rest.

INFESTED EFFECTS

d100	Infested Effects
01–05	Intense buzzing or grinding noises fill the region for the next 24 hours. With the exception of truly cacophonous sounds, creatures can only hear speech and noises that originate within 10 feet of them.
06–10	A mass migration of insects begins, with waves of Tiny bugs crawling over everything in the region. Creatures cannot take a short or long rest in the region for the next 24 hours.
11–15	A swarm of bioluminescent flies converges on one random creature in the region. For the next minute, the creature sheds dim light in a 10-foot radius, any attack against it has advantage if the attacker can see it, and the creature can't benefit from being invisible.
16–20	A boil of termites bursts from the ground, along with dozens of bones and a treasure of the DM's choice (see "Random Treasure" in the *Dungeon Master's Guide*).

d100	Infested Effects
21–25	A cricket-shaped creature with the statistics of a **cat** bounds up to one random creature and follows it like an affectionate pet for 24 hours before scampering off.
26–30	A cluster of 1d4 + 2 faintly glowing grubs appears in an unoccupied space within 30 feet of the party. Any creature that consumes one of these succulent grubs receives the benefits of a *potion of healing*.
31–35	A large, psychedelically colored moth flies over the party, dusting the characters with strange powder. Creatures the moth flies over must succeed on a DC 16 Constitution saving throw or be charmed by all creatures for 1 hour.
36–45	The region is choked with wispy webbing, which acts as difficult terrain.
46–50	Nearly every surface is covered with discarded cicadae-like shells that crunch loudly when trod upon, imposing disadvantage on Dexterity (Stealth) checks made while moving across them. The shells vanish after 1 hour.
51–55	A massive, bloated maggot emerges from the ground within 10 feet of the party and bursts, covering the ground with ichor in a 10-foot square centered on it. This region is affected by the *grease* spell (save DC 13) for 1 minute.
56–60	The ground opens up beneath one random creature, creating a quicksand pit (see the *Dungeon Master's Guide*).
61–65	One random creature in the region must succeed on a DC 16 Constitution saving throw or contract the sight rot disease (see the *Dungeon Master's Guide*) from minute parasites.
66–70	Dung-colored bugs cover the ground. Creatures that move at half their normal walking speed can ignore the bugs. Those that move faster must succeed on a DC 16 Constitution saving throw or become poisoned until the start of their next turn. A creature poisoned in this way has its speed reduced to 0, as it is overcome by the squashed insects' foul smell. Creatures that don't need to breathe automatically succeed on this saving throw.
71–75	One of the characters in the region must succeed on a DC 15 Wisdom saving throw or be transformed into a giant spider, as if by the *polymorph* spell. The spell lasts for 1 hour or until dispelled.

AN INFESTED CITY

d100	Infested Effects
76–80	One random creature in the region must succeed on a DC 16 Constitution saving throw, or it acquires a ravenous silverfish infestation among its gear. The infestation is discovered the next time the creature finishes a short or long rest. If the creature has any paper material, the silverfish destroy one random book or other paper item that isn't magical.
81–85	One random creature in the region must succeed on a DC 16 Constitution saving throw or become host to a particularly aggressive tapeworm. The affected creature gains no benefit from eating until it receives treatment that removes a disease. A creature immune to disease automatically succeeds on this saving throw.

d100	Infested Effects
86–90	Biting mites infest creatures' clothing in the region. Any creature wearing medium or heavy armor has disadvantage on attack rolls, ability checks, and saving throws for the next 24 hours.
91–95	Tiny arachnids invade unattended spaces. The next time one random creature in the region dons its clothing or armor after finishing a long rest, it must succeed on a DC 16 Constitution saving throw or take 11 (2d10) poison damage.
96–00	Countless tiny, bloodsucking insects infest the region for the next 1d6 hours. Every hour, each creature in the region must succeed on a DC 10 Constitution saving throw or gain 1 level of exhaustion. The insects don't affect creatures that are immune to disease.

Mirror Zone

A mirror zone occurs where planar and magical energies converge and create a place of reflections. Creatures, objects, and energy reflect, refract, duplicate, or are transported elsewhere. Such locations arise from the intrusion of a theorized Plane of Mirrors upon the Material Plane, or where powerful magic governing transition, protection, or divination had unexpected results.

Consider rolling on the Mirror Zone Effects table when the following circumstances occur in the region:

- A creature shatters a mirror.
- A creature uses any teleportation magic.
- An illusion appears.
- A creature impersonates another creature.

Mirror Zone Effects

d100	Effect
01–06	Creatures in the region begin to display features other than their own for the next 24 hours. During that time, affected creatures have advantage on Charisma (Deception) checks and ability checks made to disguise themselves.
07–12	The *hallucinatory terrain* spell (save DC 15) affects the natural terrain of the region, changing it into a different kind of terrain (DM's choice).
13–18	One random creature in the region gains the benefits of the *blink* spell for 1 minute, shimmering with overlapping shattered reflections.
19–24	Creatures in the region don't cast reflections. Wisdom (Insight) checks made against those creatures have disadvantage, and the creatures have disadvantage on Charisma (Persuasion) checks made against anyone who notices their lack of reflection. When they leave the region, creatures regain their reflections, and the effect ends.
25–34	Reflections of 1d4 creatures in the region emerge from mirrors and attack. The reflections are two-dimensional, shimmering versions of the creatures that cast them. Treat the reflections as **shadows** that are fey instead of undead and vulnerable to bludgeoning damage instead of radiant.
35–40	One character in the region gains the benefit of the *mirror image* spell. The images created sometimes move or speak of their own volition.

d100	Effect
41–46	For the next 24 hours, certain wounds caused in the region attract spectral slivers of glass that cause extra damage. Any creature, other than a construct or an undead, hit by an attack that deals piercing or slashing damage begins to bleed, losing 1d4 hit points at the start of each of its turns. If the bleeding creature is hit by another such attack, the bleeding increases by 1d4. Any creature can take an action to stanch the wound with a successful DC 10 Wisdom (Medicine) check. The bleeding also stops if the target receives magical healing.
47–52	Mirrors and other highly reflective surfaces allow magical transport while in the region. Any creature that touches its reflection in an object that it isn't wearing or carrying can immediately cast the *misty step* spell, requiring no components.
53–58	One character can cast the *scrying* spell (save DC 17) once within the next 24 hours, requiring no components but using a mirror or other reflective surface.
59–64	The skin of one random creature in the region becomes silvery and reflective for the next 24 hours. For the duration, that creature has advantage on saving throws against spells, and spell attacks have disadvantage against that creature.
65–70	A longsword or shortsword with a blade made of a jagged mirror appears in an unoccupied space within 60 feet of a random creature in the region. The weapon is a *sword of wounding* (see the *Dungeon Master's Guide*). If the weapon's wielder rolls a 1 or 20 on an attack roll using the weapon, the weapon shatters and is destroyed after that attack.
71–76	For the next 24 hours, when anyone in the region hits a creature with an attack roll and deals damage to it, the attacker must succeed on a DC 13 Charisma saving throw or take force damage equal to half the damage dealt.

A Tailor Shop in a Mirror Zone

d100	Effect
77–82	Two shimmering, vertical, reflective disks of energy appear in unoccupied spaces in the region for 1 minute. Each is 6 feet in diameter and floats 1 foot above the ground. One appears in an unoccupied space within 30 feet of the party. Any creature that moves through the disk instantly appears within 5 feet of the other disk or the nearest unoccupied space.
83–88	The next time one character in the party sees their reflection in the region, that reflection of comes to life and engages its counterpart in conversation. It offers to answer one question posed to it as if the creature cast the *divination* spell. After answering the question, the reflection returns to normal.

d100	Effect
89–94	Floating shards of broken mirrors swirl through the region, showing reflections of creatures and places that aren't present, for the next minute before vanishing. On initiative count 20 (losing all ties), the shards make a ranged weapon attack (+6 to hit) against one random creature in the region. On a hit, the target takes 10 (3d6) slashing damage.
95–00	A duplicate of one random creature in the region appears in an unoccupied space within 30 feet of that creature. The duplicate's appearance, game statistics, and equipment are identical to the creature's. The duplicate immediately attacks the creature, seeking to slay it. If the duplicate dies, it and all its equipment shatter into mirror shards. If the duplicate fails to slay the creature within 1 hour, the duplicate vanishes.

ZOLTAN BOROS

ANIMALS CONVERSE AFTER GAINING SAPIENCE
FROM AMBIENT PSYCHIC ENERGY.

PSYCHIC RESONANCE

In an area of psychic resonance, magic imposes strange effects on creatures and objects. These manifestations stem from strong emotions combined with magic use or from the presence of psionic creatures.

Consider rolling on the Psychic Resonance Effects table when the following circumstances occur in the region:

- A creature endures a powerful emotional experience.
- A creature takes an amount of psychic damage greater than its Constitution score.
- A creature becomes charmed or frightened.
- A creature experiences telepathic communication.

PSYCHIC RESONANCE EFFECTS

d100	Effect
01–06	One random creature in the region gains the ability to cast the *detect thoughts* spell (save DC 13) once over the next 24 hours, requiring no components. Intelligence is the spellcasting ability for this spell.
07–12	One random creature in the region is affected by the *mind blank* spell for the next 24 hours.
13–18	For 1 minute on initiative count 20 (losing all ties), Tiny and Small objects in the region that aren't being worn or carried are flung by an unseen force. One random creature in the region must succeed on a DC 15 Dexterity saving throw or take 2d4 bludgeoning damage from the flung objects.
19–24	Memories become sharp and clear for 1 hour. During this time, each creature in the region adds double its proficiency bonus to Intelligence checks made to recall information.
25–34	Headaches and nosebleeds plague humanoids in the region, imposing disadvantage on Wisdom (Perception) checks for 1 hour.
35–40	Psychic power builds in the mind of one random creature in the region. Once within the next minute, the creature can use a bonus action to magically assault the mind of another creature it can see. The target must succeed on a DC 14 Intelligence saving throw or take 4d10 psychic damage.

BRYNN METHENEY

d100	Effect
41–46	Lurking fears become nightmares. Any creature that finishes a short or long rest in the region must succeed on a DC 10 Wisdom saving throw or gain no benefit for finishing the rest.
47–52	For 1 hour, each creature in the region gains the ability to communicate telepathically with any creature it can see within 60 feet. If the target understands any languages, it can respond telepathically.
53–58	One random creature in the region can sense the presence of nearby minds for 1 hour. For the duration, the creature gains advantage on Wisdom (Perception) checks made to locate other creatures within 120 feet of it, even creatures behind total cover.
59–64	Creatures in the region suffer from disjointed thoughts and difficulty concentrating for 1 hour. For the duration, creatures have disadvantage on Intelligence checks and Constitution saving throws to maintain concentration on spells.
65–70	One random creature in the region hears strange whispers in its mind. The whispers are fragments of thoughts from other creatures nearby. The creature has advantage on Wisdom (Insight) checks for 1 hour.
71–76	One random creature in the region gains the ability to cast the *telekinesis* spell (save DC 15) once over the next 24 hours, requiring no components. Intelligence is the spellcasting ability for this spell.
77–82	Thoughts in the region attract ambient psychic energy, forming protective fields around creatures' minds. Creatures in the region gain resistance to psychic damage for the next hour.
83–88	For 1 minute on initiative count 20 (losing all ties), one random creature in the region must succeed on a DC 15 Intelligence saving throw or take 2d6 psychic damage.
89–94	Compassion and joy fill the mind of one random creature in the region for 1 minute. For the duration, the creature has advantage on Intelligence, Wisdom, and Charisma saving throws, and disadvantage on attack rolls.
95–00	The mind of every beast in the region is flooded with psychic energy. This energy causes each beast's Intelligence score to become 10, if it wasn't already higher, and the beast gains the ability to speak Common and Sylvan fluently. These changes are permanent.

UNRAVELING MAGIC

The source of magic is damaged or corrupted in this region. Magic is unpredictable, and strange results occur when a creature casts a spell. Such regions come into being when potent rituals go awry (or if they succeed, in the case of dangerous and destructive undertakings), in the aftermath of cataclysmic magical battles, or where an artifact was destroyed.

Consider rolling on the Unraveling Magic Effects table when the following circumstances occur in the region:

- Any charges are expended in a magic item.
- A spell slot of 1st level or higher is expended.
- A dragon, a fey, or an elemental of challenge rating 5 or higher dies.

UNRAVELING MAGIC EFFECTS

d100	Effect
01–05	All magic items in the region temporarily lose their magical properties, becoming nonmagical for 1 hour. Artifacts are unaffected. When the items regain their magic, a creature's attunement to any of them is restored.
06–10	The region becomes a dead-magic zone for 1 hour. For the duration, the entire region is affected by the *antimagic field* spell.
11–15	One random creature in the region must succeed on a DC 15 Dexterity saving throw or be enclosed in *Otiluke's resilient sphere* for 1 minute.
16–20	One random creature in the region that has expended spell slots regains one expended spell slot of a random level.

d100	Effect
21–25	Flares of magical energy flash through the region for 1 minute. For the duration, each round on initiative count 20 (losing all ties) one random creature in the region takes 2d4 damage of a type determined by a d6: 1, acid; 2, cold; 3, fire; 4, force; 5, lightning; or 6, thunder.
26–30	One of the characters in the region must succeed on a DC 15 Wisdom saving throw or be transformed into a blink dog, as if by the *polymorph* spell. The spell lasts for 1 hour or until dispelled.
31–35	One random creature in the region that has spell slots expends one spell slot of a random level in a harmless shower of sparks and sounds.
36–40	All fire in the region freezes into ice that gives off a blue light equal to the illumination it normally provides. In addition, the region radiates extreme cold (see the *Dungeon Master's Guide*) for 1 day.

d100	Effect
41–45	One random creature in the region with spell slots becomes a focal point for ambient magic for 1 hour. At the end of each of the creature's turns, other creatures within 10 feet of it must succeed on a Dexterity saving throw against the spellcaster's spell save DC or take 1d6 force damage.
46–50	The *flaming sphere* spell (save DC 15) spontaneously activates in an unoccupied space within 5 feet of the party. On initiative count 20 (losing all ties), the sphere moves 30 feet toward the nearest creature. The sphere vanishes after 1 minute.
51–55	Simple or martial weapons in the region that are nonmagical crackle with power. For 1 hour, they become magic weapons that grant a +1 bonus to attack and damage rolls made with them.
56–60	Swirling energy surrounds one random creature in the region for 24 hours. For the duration, the creature gains resistance to force damage and its speed is reduced by 10 feet.

JULIAN KOK

d100	Effect
61–65	Each character in the region suddenly learns some magic. A character learns one wizard cantrip of the character's choice and knows the cantrip for 1d8 days.
66–70	One random creature in the region crackles with sparks of light for 1 hour. For the duration, the creature magically sheds bright light in a 10-foot radius and dim light for an additional 10 feet. In addition, any creature it touches (requiring an unarmed strike if the target is unwilling) takes 1d6 force damage.
71–75	Lightning arcs in a 5-foot wide line between two creatures in the region that are within 30 feet of each other and not behind total cover. Each creature in the line (including the two) must make a DC 13 Dexterity saving throw, taking 4d6 lightning damage on a failed save or half as much damage on a successful one.
76–80	The *reverse gravity* spell (save DC 18) activates for 1 minute, centered on the ground beneath one random creature in the region.
81–85	On initiative count 20 (losing all ties), two random creatures in the region must each make a DC 15 Charisma saving throw. If either save fails, the creatures magically teleport, switching places. If both saves succeed, they don't teleport.
86–90	One random creature in the region breaks spells for 1 hour. Whenever anyone within 20 feet of the creature casts a spell, the spellcaster must succeed on a DC 15 saving throw using its spellcasting ability, or the spell drains away without effect. The spell slot, charge, or feature use that powered the spell is wasted.
91–95	During the next 24 hours, the first time a creature in the region targets another creature with a spell, the caster must make a DC 11 saving throw using its spellcasting ability. On a failed save, the spell targets the caster instead. On a successful save, the spell functions normally. This effect then ends.
96–00	One random creature in the region can suddenly cast the *wish* spell once, within the next minute. Reroll if you've rolled this effect in the past 24 hours.

MAGICAL PHENOMENA

Magic has the ability to make even the most serene natural settings unpredictable. Whether the result of magical calamities, otherworldly influences, or nexuses of inexplicable forces, the subsequent effects range from whimsical to deadly.

ELDRITCH STORMS

When magical currents become trapped amid winds and clouds, eldritch storms can result.

Flaywind. Supernaturally powerful winds—like those from planes such as Pandemonium or Minethys, the third layer of Carceri—can spawn flaywinds. A flaywind is an intense sandstorm, gathering large rocks and other debris in addition to sand or grit. The area within the storm is heavily obscured, and a creature exposed to the storm takes 1d4 slashing damage at the start of each of its turns. Only substantial cover or shelter offers protection against the flensing grit.

A flaywind leaves 4d6 feet of sand or debris in its wake. A successful DC 15 Intelligence (Arcana) or (Nature) check or Wisdom (Survival) check allows a character to recognize a flaywind 1 minute before it strikes, allowing time to seek shelter. A flaywind typically lasts 1d4 × 10 hours.

Flame Storm. Sooty thunderclouds shot through with red and orange lightning release a deluge of fiery droplets. Any creature caught in the burning rain takes 2d6 fire damage at the start of each of its turns. The droplets ignite any flammable objects that aren't being worn or carried; otherwise, the droplets burn out immediately. The smoke, soot, crackle, and low roar of the storm impose disadvantage on Wisdom (Perception) checks and ranged attack rolls.

A flame storm usually lasts 2d4 minutes, though the originating storm clouds can persist for days, creating multiple flame storms.

Necrotic Tempest. Storms infused with the essence of death roil with dark clouds that manifest leering skulls and bone-white lightning. Any creature exposed to the storm that isn't a construct or an undead must succeed on a DC 13 Constitution saving throw at the end of each minute or take 3d6 necrotic damage.

A creature that dies in a necrotic tempest rises as a **skeleton** or **zombie** (your choice) 1d10 minutes later.

A necrotic tempest lasts for 1d4 hours and leaves crops withered and wells undrinkable for 1d4 days after its passing.

Thrym's Howl. These bone-chilling blizzards drive a wall of wind and snow like a living glacier. The storm projects extreme cold (see the *Dungeon Master's Guide*). Due to the howling wind and dense blue-white ice particles, the area in the storm

ELDRITCH STORM

is heavily obscured, and ranged attack rolls and Wisdom (Perception) checks made within it have disadvantage.

Any creature exposed to the storm at the start of its turn takes 2d6 cold damage and can't regain hit points until it spends at least 1 hour in a warm environment. A creature that dies in the storm freezes solid. Creatures that are immune to cold damage are immune to the effects of the storm and can see normally within it.

Thrym's howl typically lasts 2d10 hours.

EMOTIONAL ECHOES

Occasionally a place becomes infused with the powerful emotions of those who once dwelt, worked, celebrated, or suffered there. Areas with emotional echoes are typically associated with one common emotion, such as joy or sorrow. Such an area might be as small as a room in a house or as large as a forest. Once per day, if a creature within the area expresses even the faintest hint of the prevailing emotion, the land seeks to hold onto that creature and inspire it to produce more of the feeling tied to the emotional echo. The creature is targeted by a *suggestion* spell (DC 16), with the intent of making it linger in the area and perform an act related to its associated emotion. The effect lasts 24 hours.

The following list notes some of the most common emotional echoes, where they tend to appear, and how they typically influence creatures:

Boldness: Appears in battlefields and echoing canyons, encouraging creatures to shout hidden truths and act out their greatest victories

Doubt: Appears around cliffs or deserts and makes creatures hesitate, mistrusting their ability to climb or escape their current difficulties

Fear: Appears in caves and ruins, overwhelming creatures with dread and urging them to give voice to their deepest fears

Hatred: Appears in volcanic regions and provokes creatures to scream and destroy things

Inspiration: Appears around memorials or natural wonders, causing creatures to create works of art on the spot and obsess over them

Joy: Appears in glens or flowering fields, inspiring creatures to dance, relax, and sing

Love: Appears along beaches or orchards and encourages creatures to confess their love to others and endlessly list their favorite things

Sorrow: Appears in ruins and swamps, particularly around quicksand, and overwhelms creatures with sobbing and confessions of regret

Enchanted Springs

Enchanted springs brim with miraculous waters, whether they tap into magical sources hidden beneath the earth or they're blessed by eldritch beings. Those who find these mystical sites might bathe or drink from the pools and temporarily gain a measure of the waters' magic. All manner of protectors or covetous guardians might lurk around these springs, driving off strangers or demanding a worthy price for access to the mystical waters.

While many enchanted springs bear the blessings of wild gods or fey beings, some are tainted. These might be waters that were long ago polluted by the ichor of an evil entity. As with pristine enchanted springs, folk seek out such defiled places, whether to purify them or claim their foul powers.

Regardless of whether a spring is pure or tainted, creatures might need to drink the water to experience the spring's effects, simply touch the water, or bathe in it for a minute to trigger an effect.

Bottling an enchanted spring's water removes its magical properties, unless the bottle is a specially prepared vial blessed by whatever being enchanted the spring in the first place.

Enchanted Spring Effects

d12	Effect
1	Any creature that touches or drinks the water of this spring feels blessed. The creature gains the benefits of a *bless* spell for 1 hour.
2	Bathing in the spring covers a creature with a glowing coat of golden feathers. While the creature isn't wearing armor, the feathers grant a +1 bonus to AC. The feathers vanish after 1d4 days.
3	A creature that touches or drinks the water of this spring develops an overwhelming desire to sing. Every sentence the creature speaks for the next 24 hours rings with lyrical splendor, which grants it advantage on all Charisma checks.
4	Bathing in the spring grants a creature the benefits of the *greater restoration* spell. As a side effect, the creature's skin, hair, and eyes become a shimmering golden color for 1d4 days.
5	Bathing in the spring grants a creature the benefits of the *spider climb* spell for 24 hours.
6	A creature that touches or drinks the water of this spring grows the tail of its favorite animal. The tail is not under the creature's control; it moves or reacts to emotions. The tail vanishes after 24 hours.

Enchanted Spring

d12	Effect
7	Any creature with an Intelligence score of 6 or higher that touches or drinks the water of this spring gains advantage on Wisdom (Insight) checks and can cast the *detect thoughts* spell once, requiring no components. The effects of the spring fade when either the spell is used or 24 hours pass, whichever happens first.
8	Bathing in the spring causes 1d10 flowers to grow from a creature's head. The flowers smell lovely, and they renew their vitality and scent every day. The flowers vanish after 7 days.
9	A creature that touches or drinks the water of this spring grows 1d4 eyestalks. These eyestalks let the creature see in all directions and grant it advantage on Wisdom (Perception) checks that rely on sight. The eyestalks vanish after 1d4 days.
10	Bathing in the spring causes a creature's voice to sound sinister. For the next 24 hours, the creature's voice grants it advantage on Charisma (Intimidation) checks and disadvantage on Charisma (Deception) and Charisma (Persuasion) checks.
11	A creature that touches or drinks the water of this spring grows a set of donkey ears. The ears grant the creature advantage on Wisdom (Perception) checks that rely on hearing. The ears vanish after 1d4 days.
12	Bathing in the spring causes a creature to develop a third eye on its forehead. The eye grants the creature truesight out to a range of 60 feet. The eye vanishes after 24 hours.

MAGIC MUSHROOMS

Magic Mushrooms

Mushrooms can be deadly, delicious, or both. Some have magical properties, especially those that grow in areas suffused by mystical energy, such as the Underdark and the Feywild.

Creatures proficient in the Medicine, Nature, or Survival skills might be versed on the subject of fungi, especially the magical kind, since the beneficial effects can save lives or bestow unusual powers. But when an unknown variety of fungus is encountered, only an expert can identify it and determine its properties.

To determine the effects of eating such fungus, roll on the Magic Mushroom Effects table.

Magic Mushroom Effects

d10	Effects
1	The creature's skin turns an unusual color. Roll a d4: 1, purple with yellow splotches; 2, bright orange with tiger stripes; 3, tree-frog green with red squiggles; 4, hot pink with yellow spots. This change is permanent unless removed by a *greater restoration* spell or similar magic.
2	The creature gains the enlarge or reduce effect (50 percent chance of either) of the *enlarge/reduce* spell for 1 hour.
3	The creature regains 5d8 + 20 hit points.
4	Vocally, the creature can only cluck and croon like a chicken. The creature can also understand and speak to chickens. This curse lasts for 1 hour unless ended by a *remove curse* spell or similar magic.
5	The creature can understand and speak all languages for 1d4 days.
6	The creature gains the benefits of the *telepathy* spell for the next 24 hours.
7	The creature gains the benefits of the *speak with plants* spell for 8 hours.
8	The creature immediately casts the *time stop* spell, requiring no components. Constitution is the spellcasting ability for this spell.
9	The creature immediately casts the *detect thoughts* spell, requiring no components. Constitution is the spellcasting ability for this spell.
10	Magical mists pour out of the creature's eyes and ears, acting as a *fog cloud* spell for 1 hour that is centered on the creature and moves with it.

Mimic Colony

Mimic Colonies

Mimics imitate terrain and dungeon dressing to hunt for food. Rare specimens develop a deeper understanding of the world and can communicate with other creatures. In extremely rare cases, groups of these creatures band together, creating colonies. These bonded mimics cooperate to create larger objects than any lone mimic could approximate. A mimic colony can work together to form buildings, bridges, crystal formations, cliff faces, statues, and nearly anything it desires. Entire villages appearing out of nowhere might be composed of mimics!

Mimic Communication. Members of the colony develop telepathy and the ability to speak. While within 10 miles of the colony, any mimic can communicate telepathically with other creatures within 120 feet of it and can speak Common and Undercommon fluently (or two other languages of the DM's choice). The colony's offspring gain these abilities innately and can use them even away from the colony, as shown in the Juvenile Mimic stat block.

Confronting a Colony. A mimic colony's primary goal is survival. If threatened by a force the mimics can't overcome, they are willing to bargain. Mimic colonies have learned that adventurers they can't defeat can be bought off with information about nearby creatures or locations, hidden treasure (which the colony obtained from prior "food"), or even one of their own young.

Juvenile Mimic

Tiny monstrosity (shapechanger)

Armor Class 11
Hit Points 7 (2d4 + 2)
Speed 10 ft., climb 10 ft.

STR	DEX	CON	INT	WIS	CHA
1 (−5)	12 (+1)	13 (+1)	10 (+0)	13 (+1)	10 (+0)

Skills Stealth +3
Damage Immunities acid
Condition Immunities prone
Senses darkvision 60 ft., Passive Perception 11
Languages Common, Undercommon, telepathy 120 ft.
Challenge 0 (10 XP) **Proficiency Bonus** +2

False Appearance (Object Form Only). While the mimic remains motionless, it is indistinguishable from an ordinary object.

Spider Climb. The mimic can climb difficult surfaces, including upside down on ceilings, without needing to make an ability check.

Actions

Bite. *Melee Weapon Attack:* +3 to hit, reach 5 ft., one target. *Hit:* 1 piercing damage plus 2 (1d4) acid damage.

Shape-Shift. The mimic polymorphs into an object or back into its true, amorphous form. Its statistics are the same in each form. Any equipment it is wearing or carrying isn't transformed. It reverts to its true form if it dies.

If the colony's survival is threatened and it thinks it has a chance of surviving a fight, it can leverage its combined might using special lair actions. On initiative count 20 (losing all ties), the mimic colony takes a lair action, causing one of the following effects; it can't use the same effect two rounds in a row:

- The mimic colony chooses up to three creatures within 300 feet of it. Each target must succeed on a DC 15 Strength saving throw or have its speed reduced to 0 until initiative count 20 on the following round, as pieces of the environment grasp the target. If a target fails the save by 5 or more, it is restrained instead for that duration.
- The mimic colony uses the Help action, aiding a creature of its choice within 300 feet of it.
- The mimic colony chooses up to three creatures within 300 feet of it. Each target must succeed on a DC 15 Dexterity saving throw or take 13 (3d8) acid damage, as orifices appear on surfaces in the environment and launch caustic spittle.
- The mimic colony chooses a cube of nonmagical, inanimate material in physical contact with it. The cube can be up to 15 feet on a side. The colony reshapes that material however it likes. This transformation lasts for 1 hour.

When determining the difficulty of an encounter with a hostile mimic colony, consider the colony to be one additional creature of challenge rating 2.

PRIMAL FRUIT

In wild places brimming with nature's power, gardens meticulously tended by eccentric wizards, and blessed groves touched by divine providence, plants can sometimes produce fruit bursting with primal magic. Not every fruit-bearing plant holds this stored magic, but those that do bear obvious signs: their colors are more vibrant or shift randomly, their skin sparkles in the light or glows in the dark, soft hums emanate from them, or they feel peculiar to the touch.

A fruit-bearing plant that is suffused with magic might produce 1d6 pieces of primal fruit every week. Primal fruit remains potent for 1 week, after which it loses its magical properties but remains edible.

As an action, a creature can eat a piece of primal fruit to gain its effects. This fruit can be squeezed into juice or cooked into a dish and retains its magic. Choose an effect or roll on the Primal Fruit Effects table to determine what happens when a piece of the fruit is consumed. An *identify* spell or similar magic reveals the beneficial effect of a piece of fruit before it is eaten, but it doesn't reveal a curse or side effect.

Primal Fruit Effects

d8	Effect
1	The creature regains 3d8 + 4 hit points, and its skin sheds bright light in a 5-foot radius and dim light for an additional 5 feet for 1 hour
2	The creature feels a surge of might. For 1 hour, the creature has advantage on attack rolls using Strength, Strength checks, and Strength saving throws. When the effect ends, the creature gains 1 level of exhaustion.
3	Waves of vitality crash over the creature. The creature's hit point maximum increases by 2d10, and it gains the same number of hit points. The increase lasts until the creature finishes a long rest, at which time the creature must succeed on a DC 15 Charisma saving throw or be cursed with a random form of lycanthropy (see "Lycanthropes" in the *Monster Manual*).
4	The creature's skin prickles faintly. For 1 hour, it gains resistance to one damage type (chosen by the DM).
5	Euphoric visions of bright light swim through the creature's mind. The creature gains the benefits of the *death ward* spell for 8 hours and must succeed on a DC 13 Constitution saving throw or be poisoned for the duration.
6	A faint humming drones in the background of everything the creature hears for 1 hour, during which the creature has advantage on saving throws against spells.
7	The creature doesn't require food, drink, or sleep for 1d4 days. For the duration, the creature can't be put to sleep by magic, and its dreams intrude upon its waking thoughts, imposing disadvantage on its Wisdom (Perception) checks.
8	Whispers intrude on the creature's mind for 24 hours. For the duration, the creature can telepathically communicate with any creature it can see within 120 feet of it. If the other creature understands at least one language, it can respond telepathically.

Unearthly Roads

Currents of magic run through the world—invisible, artery-like networks that exert subtle influence and connect disparate lands. The greatest of these magical streams are persistent paths, often known by colloquial names or simply as unearthly roads. An unearthly road acts like a sort of planar portal that stretches from one place to another, be they sites on the same world or on different planes of existence. Unearthly roads allow creatures to cross great distances rapidly, moving from an entrance gate to an exit gate or visa versa. These paths operate like long tunnels, and a creature that travels on an unearthly road progresses 21 miles of distance in the time it would normally take it to travel 1 mile. While on the road, glimpses of the world beyond might be visible in blurred or distorted visions of scenery or especially prominent landmarks. Creatures or specific details are not visible beyond an unearthly road.

Some unearthly roads serve as trade routes or secret connections between distant lands. Others shift locations at noteworthy times or in response to external phenomena, like on specific anniversaries or in response to the phases of the moon. Some might also require a particular item, ritual, or action to open their gates. The Unearthly Road Keys table offers suggestions on how to enter an unearthly road.

Unearthly Road Keys

d6	Key
1	Throwing a silver orb through an ancient arch
2	Spilling a pint of humanoid blood
3	Calling the name of a specific archfey three times
4	Wearing the regalia of a lost royal dynasty
5	Permanently sacrificing a memory of joy
6	Being the descendant of a legendary hero

Natural Hazards

Even without the threats of supernatural environments, the world is a dangerous place. The following natural hazards expand on those presented in the *Dungeon Masters Guide*.

Avalanches

A typical avalanche (or rockslide) is 300 feet wide, 150 feet long, and 30 feet thick. Creatures in the path of an avalanche can avoid it or escape it if they're close to its edge, but outrunning one is almost impossible.

When an avalanche occurs, all nearby creatures must roll initiative. Twice each round, on initiative counts 10 and 0, the avalanche travels 300 feet until it can travel no more. When an avalanche moves, any creature in its space moves along with it and falls prone, and the creature must make a DC 15 Strength saving throw, taking 1d10 bludgeoning damage on a failed save, or half as much damage on a successful one.

When an avalanche stops, the snow and other debris settle and bury creatures. A creature buried in this way is blinded and restrained, and it has total cover. The creature gains 1 level of exhaustion for every 5 minutes it spends buried. It can try to dig itself free as an action, breaking the surface and ending the blinded and restrained conditions on itself

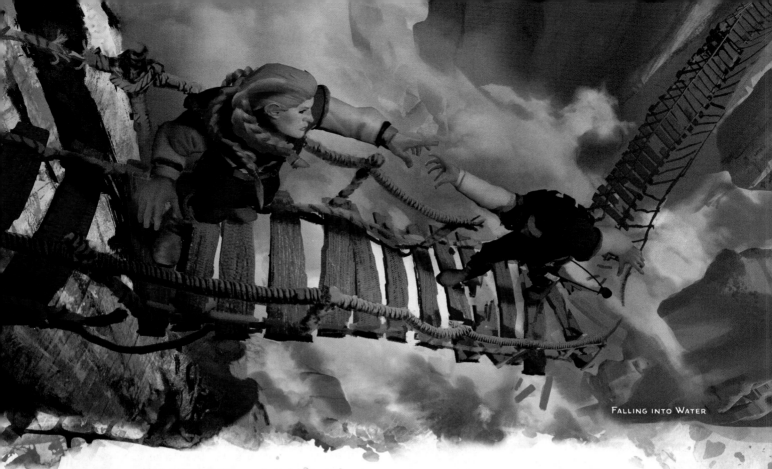

FALLING INTO WATER

with a successful DC 15 Strength (Athletics) check. A creature that fails this check three times can't attempt to dig itself out again.

A creature that is not restrained or incapacitated can spend 1 minute freeing a buried creature. Once free, that creature is no longer blinded or restrained by the avalanche.

FALLING INTO WATER

A creature that falls into water or another liquid can use its reaction to make a DC 15 Strength (Athletics) or Dexterity (Acrobatics) check to hit the surface head or feet first. On a successful check, any damage resulting from the fall is halved.

FALLING ONTO A CREATURE

If a creature falls into the space of a second creature and neither of them is Tiny, the second creature must succeed on a DC 15 Dexterity saving throw or be impacted by the falling creature, and any damage resulting from the fall is divided evenly between them. The impacted creature is also knocked prone, unless it is two or more sizes larger than the falling creature.

SPELL EQUIVALENTS OF NATURAL HAZARDS

Numerous spells emulate the wrath of nature, and you can use spell effects to represent a variety of natural hazards. The Spells as Natural Hazards table presents some common environmental dangers and the spells you may use to approximate them.

SPELLS AS NATURAL HAZARDS

Natural Hazard	Approximate Spell
Ball lightning	Chromatic orb
Blizzard	Cone of cold, ice storm, sleet storm
Earthquake	Earthquake
Falling debris	Conjure barrage, conjure volley
Flood	Control water, tsunami
Fog	Fog cloud
Lava bomb	Fireball, produce flame
Lightning	Call lightning, lightning bolt
Meteor	Fireball, meteor swarm
Mirage	Hallucinatory terrain
Pyroclastic flow	Incendiary cloud
Radiation	Blight, circle of death
Smoke	Fog cloud
St. Elmo's fire	Faerie fire
Swamp gas	Dancing lights
Tidal wave	Tsunami
Toxic eruption	Acid splash
Toxic gas	Cloudkill, stinking cloud
Thunder	Thunderwave
Volcanic lightning	Storm of vengeance
Whirlpool	Control water
Wildfire	Fire storm, wall of fire
Windstorm	Gust of wind

PUZZLES

> Why create a solvable puzzle? Just pose an enigmatic question without an answer and watch your trespassers squirm!
>
> TASHA

Devious traps and multifaceted mysteries might be staples of fantasy adventures, but they're not the easiest challenges for a DM to present on the fly. This section presents a selection of puzzles designed to invite group participation and challenge adventurers of any stripe—from genius scholars to martial masters. Each puzzle is flexible enough to be included in your campaign as presented or customized to fit the needs of a specific adventure.

WHY USE PUZZLES?

Puzzles provide exciting opportunities to use wit to overcome obstacles and allow characters to collaborate to make discoveries. You might add a puzzle to an adventure for any of the following reasons:

- To encourage a party to discover information through teamwork
- To provide an opportunity for characters to use their skills in uncommon ways
- To make a setting feel more whimsical, mysterious, or otherworldly
- To explain why no one has ever discovered something hidden close at hand
- To reveal a secret no one knows and magic can't reveal

Some puzzles can take considerable time to solve, so be mindful of how often you use them in your adventures. Remember, most puzzles don't need to be solved immediately, and they might be all the more satisfying if their riddles linger unresolved for multiple sessions.

PUZZLE ELEMENTS

Text that appears in a box like this is meant to be read aloud or paraphrased for the players when their characters first arrive in a location with a puzzle or when otherwise noted.

Additionally, the following sections appear in each puzzle:

Difficulty. Each puzzle is classified as easy, medium, or hard. The harder the puzzle, the more likely the players will need hints to solve it.

Puzzle Features. This section presents an overview of the puzzle's features and how they can be interacted with.

Solution. This section explains how the puzzle is solved.

Hint Checks. This section suggests hints that characters might use their skills to reveal. Provide one or more of the hints if the characters get stuck. If a character has proficiency in a hint's associated skill, give them that hint if they ask you for help.

Customizing the Puzzle. This section explores how to integrate the puzzle into your adventures, alter its difficulty, or make other adjustments.

HINTS

If players request a hint while attempting to solve a puzzle, consult that puzzle's "Hint Checks" section. Each hint is associated with a skill and a DC. If a character in the party has proficiency in a skill related to a hint, share that hint with them. If the same skill is listed multiple times with the same or higher DCs, reveal hints with the lowest DCs first then hints with higher DCs if the group requests additional help.

If no character has proficiency in any of the listed skills, characters can make ability checks using the listed skills and DCs. Those who succeed on a check learn the associated hint.

Don't hesitate to reveal hints to the party. Hints provide characters with relevant skills the opportunity to shine, even if they're not usually particularly cunning. Additionally, if party members have backgrounds or campaign experiences that might tie into a puzzle, those make great reasons to provide characters with additional hints.

RUNNING PUZZLES

Once you've presented a puzzle to a group, feel free to add and clarify details as you would in any other type of encounter. Try not to give away details of the puzzle's solution in your descriptions, but there's nothing wrong with letting a hint slip here or there.

Don't worry whether it's a player or a character who's solving a puzzle. While hint checks provide a way for character experience to contribute to a puzzle's solution, ultimately the boundaries between a player's and a character's ability to solve a puzzle isn't as important as the group enjoying the challenge. However, if a player knows the answer to a puzzle in advance, urge them to share only hints their character learns.

After presenting a puzzle, encourage the party to solve it together, to pool hints, and to share their insights. Work with the group to share any puzzle handouts and to take turns talking through their thoughts. Ultimately, solving a puzzle will be a victory for the whole group, not one individual.

Creature Paintings

Difficulty: Easy

This short puzzle works anywhere that makes sense for characters to peruse several paintings, such as in a museum or manor. These paintings could even appear in a sketchbook found in a dusty old drawer. This counting puzzle leads to a name of a creature.

Fit this into your campaign by making the name of the creature the first item on a scavenger hunt or the first clue in a larger mystery.

> This gallery is decorated with seven framed paintings of creatures. A few chairs and benches have been placed in front of the art for viewing.
>
> A plaque mounted on one of the walls bears the following dedication: "In order to gain all knowledge, one must know where to start. Count on your enemies to reveal the source of the secret. This room is dedicated to the defeat of all monsters within."

Characters should be free to explore the gallery and inspect the paintings and dedication to discover the parts of the puzzle.

Puzzle Features

There are seven paintings on the walls. The paintings feature a gruesome werewolf under a full moon, a trio of gnolls fighting over a spear, a grinning beholder, two trolls sitting under a tree, five kobolds around a bonfire, two gelatinous cubes patrolling a dungeon corridor, and three dragons in flight.

Solution

Each painting features a number of creatures of a particular kind, as summarized in the Creature Paintings table. Counting into each creature's name by the number of creatures in the painting reveals a letter. When unscrambled, the letters spell out "owlbear." Characters are likely to reveal these letters in random order. Arranging them in the correct order is part of the puzzle.

Creature Paintings

Painting	Number	Letter
Gnolls	3	O
Werewolf	1	W
Kobolds	5	L
Beholder	1	B
Gelatinous Cubes	2	E
Dragons	3	A
Trolls	2	R

Significance of "Owlbear"

This puzzle's solution, "owlbear," might be the passphrase to bypass a future trap or unlock a magically sealed door. It might also be a clue that points to a hidden treasure. For example, there might be a stuffed owlbear in another room that has treasure hidden inside it.

Hint Checks

Any character has the option of making these ability checks to receive a hint:

Intelligence (Investigation) DC 10. The character deduces that the number of creatures in a painting is important and uses that number to determine which letter of the creature's name they should review.

Wisdom (Perception) DC 10. When looking at the dedication, the words "count on" alert the character that they should count the creatures.

Customizing the Puzzle

You can replace the monsters in the artwork with distinctive objects, members of obvious professions, and anything else that might logically be in a group. Then, follow the letter-counting method detailed in this puzzle to determine how many subjects should feature in each piece of art.

RECKLESS STEPS

Difficulty: Easy

This puzzle features a word search on floor tiles, which might present a barrier to exploration in myriad scenarios. To cross safely, characters must first uncover what words they're searching for and then find them in the tiles.

> You enter a cobweb-filled room lit by torches on opposite walls. Dust on the floor has collected in grooves that cover rows of five-foot-square tiles. On the opposite wall, a solitary arch leads from the room. One wall bears the following inscription:
>
> *Eight appear before your eyes,*
> *   And eight remain in schooled disguise.*
> *Avoid all magic in this room,*
> *   Lest reckless steps ensure your doom.*

The tiles covering the floor of this room each bear a single letter written in the Common alphabet, making the room a giant word search. Traps beneath many of the tiles threaten those who move through the room heedless of the hidden words.

PUZZLE FEATURES

The floor of this 60-foot-by-70-foot room is made of 5-foot-square stone tiles laid out in a grid. Each tile has a letter chiseled into it, as shown in puzzle handout 1 at the end of this chapter. Place a copy of the handout for this puzzle on the table, and allow players to use miniatures to show how their characters navigate the room.

To safely walk across the room, a character must step on the correct tiles. Stepping on an incorrect tile sets off a trap.

TRAPS

Certain tiles (as indicated in this trap's "Solution" section) are trapped. A trapped tile is triggered when more than 20 pounds of weight are placed on it, activating the pressure plate underneath and causing jets of poisonous gas to spout from the cracks between the tiles. Any creature above the trapped floor tile or one of its adjacent tiles must make a DC 15 Constitution saving throw, taking 11 (2d10) poison damage on a failed save, or half as much damage on a successful one.

As an action, a character can disable a trap with a successful DC 15 Dexterity check using thieves' tools. If a character fails to disable the trap, the tile's trap can no longer be disabled.

Characters can attempt to jump over trapped tiles, using the jump rules in the *Player's Handbook*.

Solution

The only safe tiles for characters to step on are the ones with the faded black letters in diagram 4.1. Red letters spell out either "magic" or one of the schools of magic: abjuration, conjuration, divination, enchantment, evocation, illusion, necromancy, and transmutation. Stepping on one of these tiles triggers a poison trap, as described earlier.

Hint Checks

Any character has the option of making these ability checks to receive a hint:

Intelligence (Arcana) DC 10. The character sees one instance of a school of magic on the floor.

Intelligence (Investigation) DC 10. The character interprets the clue in the wall verse: there are eight schools of magic.

Wisdom (Perception) DC 10. Each character who succeeds on this check sees an instance of the word "magic" in the floor.

Customizing the Puzzle

Consider using this puzzle's structure to create any number of thematic word searches hiding deadly traps. Once you've created a hint suggesting what types of words to look for, it's a simple matter to create your own grid of hidden words.

Raising the Difficulty

You can increase this puzzle's difficulty by changing the word search's letters to use another alphabet, such as those presented in the *Player's Handbook*. Alternatively, you can create an entirely new code to replace the letters, requiring the characters to find a cipher to reveal the tiles' meanings before they can undertake the puzzle and cross the room safely.

You can also increase the difficulty by introducing trap variants, as described below.

Trap Variants

Rather than have the same poison gas trap on every trapped tile, each word can have a distinct trap associated with it, as described below:

Magic. The trap triggers normally, as described in this puzzle's "Traps" section.

Abjuration. The trap casts *dispel magic* on each creature in the room, using a 9th-level spell slot.

Conjuration. The trap teleports the creature that triggered it back to the entrance of the room. That creature must also make a DC 15 Constitution saving throw, taking 11 (2d10) force damage on a failed save, or half as much damage on a successful one.

Divination. The creature that triggered the trap must succeed on a DC 15 Intelligence saving throw or be unable to perceive any of the letters

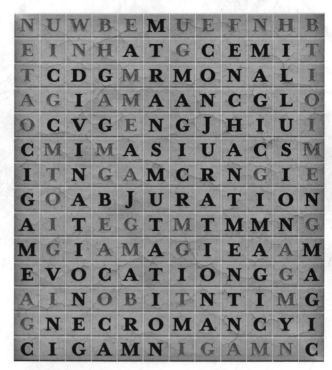

DIAGRAM 4.1: RECKLESS STEPS PUZZLE SOLUTION

on the tiles by sight or touch. Any magic that ends a curse ends this effect on the character. A player whose character is affected by this trap should not be allowed to reference the accompanying player handout until the effect on that character ends.

Enchantment. The trap casts *suggestion* (save DC 15) on the creature that triggered it. On a failed save, a gentle voice only the creature can hear tells it to move 5 feet in a random direction. This movement might cause it to trigger another trap.

Evocation. Magical fire erupts from the trapped tile. The creature that triggered this trap must succeed on a DC 15 Dexterity saving throw, taking 11 (2d10) fire damage on a failed save, or half as much damage on a successful one.

Illusion. A suit of **animated armor** appears in an unoccupied space within 5 feet of the creature that set off this trap. The armor attacks only the creature that summoned it and can't leave the room. It doesn't set off any of the room's traps and disappears if it takes any damage. Otherwise, it lasts for 1 minute.

Necromancy. Any creature that triggers this trap hears a banshee's wail in its mind. Unless the creature is a construct or undead, it must succeed on a DC 13 Constitution saving throw. On a failure, the creature drops to 0 hit points. On a success, it takes 10 (3d6) psychic damage.

Transmutation. The trap casts *polymorph* (save DC 15) on the creature that triggered it. On a failed save, the creature turns into a giant frog.

Skeleton Keys

Difficulty: Easy

This puzzle presents a quick encounter useful for providing treasure or information. It features a box with four locks.

> You come upon a sinister metal box with an iron lock built into each of its four sides. Each lock sports a keyhole with a sculpted image above it. Four iron keys hang from hooks on a nearby wall, and each key has a different number of teeth. Above the keys, the following verse has been etched into the wall:
>
> *The spells on these locks are all the same.*
> *Though each possesses a unique name.*
> *Count on your answer to unlock the way,*
> *But use the wrong key to your dismay.*

All four locks must be opened before the box's contents (whatever they might be) can be accessed.

Puzzle Features

Show the players puzzle handout 2 (see the end of this chapter) when their characters examine the keys. Each key has a different number of teeth: six, five, four, and three, respectively.

Each lock has a creature molded in iron above it: a bat, snake, spider, or wolf, respectively. These locks can't be picked. If anything other than the correct key is placed inside a lock, creatures corresponding to the image above the lock (1d4 **giant bats**, 1d4 **giant poisonous snakes**, 1d4 **giant wolf spiders**, or 1d4 **wolves**) are summoned into the room. Each summoned creature is hostile and disappears after 10 minutes or when reduced to 0 hit points. These beasts can't be charmed or frightened.

Solution

Once the characters identify the creature depicted above each lock, they should count the letters in each creature's name. The number of letters in a creature's name corresponds to the number of teeth on the correct key, as shown in the Skeleton Keys Solution table.

Skeleton Keys Solution

Lock	Key
Bat	Three teeth
Snake	Five teeth
Spider	Six teeth
Wolf	Four teeth

Hint Checks

Any character has the option of making these ability checks to receive a hint:

Intelligence (Nature) DC 10. The character knows that "natural" knowledge about bats, snakes, spiders, and wolves in general won't help here.

Wisdom (Perception) DC 10. The character realizes that the keys' skull-shaped heads are all the same and probably have no bearing on the puzzle's solution.

Customizing the Puzzle

The focal parts of this puzzle are the locks and keys, not the chest. You could easily convert this puzzle to feature any types of locks, be they on doors, cells, books, or some more esoteric barrier.

Beyond the form the locks and keys take, you might also consider adjusting the creatures depicted with each lock to suit your adventures. Just keep in mind that the number of teeth on each key must match the number of letters in your substitutions, and those substitutions should be things the characters can identify.

Raising the Difficulty

Rather than associating each lock with a particular image of a creature, consider presenting a riddle alongside each lock. The answer to each riddle should be the related creature's name, allowing characters to match the riddles' answers to the proper keys.

ALL THAT GLITTERS

Difficulty: Medium

This gem-filled room can be placed in any dungeon, estate, or building with multiple rooms and might serve as both a trap and a place to obtain a reward.

> Dozens of gems lie strewn upon the floor. Amid the treasure stands a marble statue with its hands clasped in front of it. A placard at the statue's base reads, "Only one treasure may leave this room. Cross with another and find your tomb."

PUZZLE FEATURES

The statue, which is impervious to damage, depicts Ioun or some other god of knowledge or order. Any character who succeeds on a DC 10 Intelligence (Religion) check can identify the figure being depicted.

DIAMOND

Between the palms of the statue's clasped hands is a diamond, which can only be found and retrieved once the puzzle is solved. Once the characters solve the puzzle, the statue's hands open, allowing the diamond to be taken. Upon breaching the threshold of the room with the diamond, a trapped soul in the form of a friendly, thankful spirit is released. The spirit leaves to pursue its own goals, and the diamond is left behind as a reward. The diamond is worth 5,000 gp.

GEMSTONES

An inventory of the room reveals the following gemstones scattered across the floor: eighteen pieces of jade, sixteen onyxes, fourteen amethysts, thirteen sapphires, twelve rubies, nine pieces of amber, eight citrines, five garnets, and one piece of quartz.

If a creature attempts to leave the room with any of these stones, the gem disappears and an angry spirit trapped inside it is released. The spirit manifests as a hostile undead creature of your choice, such as a **ghost**, **specter**, or **skeleton**. When this creature is reduced to 0 hit points, its form dissipates, leaving no trace of itself behind.

NAMED SPIRITS

Characters hear each spirit whisper its name before it dissipates. The names themselves are not important, other than they must start with the appropriate letter of the alphabet.

The following list provides names for all the imprisoned spirits, each name starting with the letter associated with the spirit's gemstone prison:

A SPIRIT ESCAPES A GEMSTONE.

Quartz. Antonio
Garnet. Ella, Ethan, Ember, Edwina, Ernest
Citrine. Hobert, Holden, Hilda, Haddon, Hugo, Hera, Hessy, Hemma
Amber. Ivy, Iris, Ian, Idris, Iggy, Imelda, Ice, Innis, Isabella
Ruby. Lou, Leela, Lowan, Lannis, Lake, Luke, Leila, Leean, Luna, Luvia, Lee, Leira
Sapphire. Mona, Maethius, Merry, Moon, Medea, Martha, Marni, Moen, Mava, Moloth, Mo, Mia, Miranda
Amethyst. Nox, Neville, Norman, Ned, Nadia, Nian, Nero, Nick, Narice, Nava, Nia, Nicol, Nestor, Nera
Onyx. Paul, Pam, Pluck, Petra, Pax, Pia, Paden, Po, Pacey, Pima, Peck, Pablo, Piers, Pom, Peleg, Peet
Jade. Ren, Ryannis, Rue, Romag, Redd, Remy, Ria, River, Rhonda, Resta, Rhys, Ron, Ricker, Rey, Ro, Rowan, Regan, Rhiannon

SOLUTION

An inventory of the room reveals gemstones in the amounts shown in the Gem Inventory table. The table lists the gems in alphabetical order, but you should list them in any other order when describing them to players so not to accidentally give away a hint.

Each type of gem is associated with a letter of the alphabet, and each gem's letter is revealed by counting into the alphabet by a number of letters equal to the number of gems of its type. For example, there is one piece of quartz, so "quartz" corresponds to the first letter of the alphabet (A), while there are fourteen amethysts, so "amethyst" corresponds to the fourteenth letter of the alphabet (N).

GEM INVENTORY

Gem	Amount	Letter
Amber	9	I
Amethyst	14	N
Citrine	8	H
Garnet	5	E
Jade	18	R
Onyx	16	P
Quartz	1	A
Ruby	12	L
Sapphire	13	M

Once the gems are sorted by type and alphabetized, characters can count into the alphabet by how many of each are in the room to reveal the words "in her palm." When a character speaks this phrase aloud, the statue's folded hands open, revealing the previously hidden diamond.

HINT CHECKS

Any character has the option of making these ability checks to receive a hint:

Intelligence (Arcana) DC 15. The character can determine that there are spirits imprisoned in the gemstones scattered on the floor.

Intelligence (Religion) DC 10. The character knows that the statue represents a god of knowledge and order, and the character has a strong feeling that the order of the gems in the room is important.

Wisdom (Insight) DC 10. The character senses that the number of each type of gem isn't arbitrary.

CUSTOMIZING THE PUZZLE

This puzzle explores how to use groups of objects to disguise a message. So long as your groups can be arranged in a logical order (like the gems being arranged alphabetically in this puzzle), all you must do is adjust the number of items to correspond to a particular letter of the alphabet. Alternatively, perhaps another organizing principle orders your groups. For example, tombstones that feature varying numbers of skulls might be arranged by dates, while stacks of books might be ordered by shared page-counts. These details can be easy to miss, though, so make sure you present a riddle or other signpost to make sure your players notice there's a puzzle at hand.

LOWERING THE DIFFICULTY

To make the puzzle easier to solve, a spirit can provide a hint in addition to giving its name. Coaxing a hint from a spirit requires a successful DC 15 Charisma (Persuasion or Intimidation) check. Consider hints like "A is the first letter in the alphabet" and "The gemstones, in order, will help for a spell."

RELEASING THE SPIRITS

If the characters don't attempt to remove gems from the room, or if they spend too long deliberating, create a new trigger to release the spirits. For example, perhaps a spirit is released if a character places a gem near the statue or if it's held for too long.

EYE OF THE BEHOLDER

Difficulty: Medium

This map puzzle is designed to lead a party through a dungeon where a roaming beholder doesn't wish to be disturbed. A series of clues tie to the word "eye," and the characters must determine how to get through the area safely.

> A disorienting wave sweeps over you. Suddenly, your surroundings are unfamiliar and shrouded in shadows.
>
> Out of the gloom appears a hooded goblin carrying a lantern.
>
> "Hello, friends!" the goblin says. "I can help you through these parts—if you can figure out my riddles. You don't want to make a wrong turn in here, as there are eyes everywhere. Solve the riddles and follow my directions to the letter."

The **goblin** is friendly, and its offer is genuine. It's name is Igor (pronounced *eye*-gor), which it reveals only if asked. The characters find themselves in a maze that emits magical darkness that can't be dispelled. No vision can penetrate this darkness, and only the goblin's lantern can illuminate it. Igor's lantern emits light in a 5-foot radius, but only so long as the goblin holds it. The lantern goes dark if any other creature takes custody of it.

PUZZLE FEATURES

The magical maze the characters find themselves in is comprised of an endless series of identical chambers. Each chamber has four passages, one at each cardinal direction. The goblin guide poses riddles that can lead the party along the path that ultimately

Once the goblin has the characters' attention, it provides the first riddle, then waits for the party to venture down a passage of its choice. The goblin stops at each intersection and either provides the next riddle (if the party chose the correct path) or avoids the monster the group encounters (if the party chose the incorrect path), leading the characters back to the last correct chamber along the path after any battle.

The goblin's riddles (and their answers) are as follows:

- What beast has the sharpest eye? (Eagle)
- Threads get pulled through the eye of what? (Needle)
- What is the eye to the soul? (Window)
- Whose eye matters to a witch's brew? (Newt)
- This eye curses you with misfortune. (Evil)
- This eye brings a temporary calm. (Storm)
- Roll a one on a six-sided die. Roll another and get the same. Take both together, and what's their name? (Snake eyes)

SOLUTION

The answer to each riddle begins with a letter indicating the direction of the path the characters should follow next. The path provided by the riddles' answers takes the following route: east, north, west, north, east, south, south. This path leads the characters through some chambers more than once, which is a necessary part of the magic that will allow them to escape.

HINT CHECKS

Any character has the option of making these ability checks to receive a hint:

Charisma (Persuasion) DC 15. The goblin provides a hint in the form of a synonym of the riddle's answer (for example, "lizard" for "newt").

Intelligence (Investigation) DC 10. After a few riddles are answered correctly, a character notices that all the answers relate to eyes.

Wisdom (Insight) DC 15. After one or more correct answers are given, the character realizes that each answer corresponds to a cardinal direction.

CUSTOMIZING THE PUZZLE

The characters can easily persuade the goblin to join their party. What other secrets does the goblin know? Does he have an agenda for helping the characters find their freedom? And why has he lingered in the maze if he knows the way out? There might be more to this guide than meets the eye.

exits the maze. Each time the party moves through the correct passage and enters a new room, the goblin provides them with a new riddle that hints which direction to travel in next. If they make an error, the characters encounter a monster of your choice and then must backtrack from their last correct turn. After three wrong turns, the party encounters the **beholder**.

HALLWAYS

The halls of this maze are 60 feet long and 10 feet wide. If the characters move away from the guide during combat or for any other reason, the goblin encourages them to follow him back to the last correct turn.

THE GOBLIN'S RIDDLES

Upon meeting the characters (and to discourage them from attacking), the goblin makes it clear there is no way out of the maze without his help. Characters can determine that the goblin is sincere in wanting to help with a successful DC 10 Wisdom (Insight) check.

Four by Four

Difficulty: Medium

This puzzle is easily situated in a dungeon, a dusty mausoleum, or an abandoned shrine.

> You enter a dimly lit chamber. Nine dwarf skulls rest near a four-foot-square set of tiles in the floor, and carved into a nearby stone altar is the following inscription:
>
> *Brave warriors met their demise foretold.*
> *Their secret kept shall yet unfold.*
> *If crowns placed correctly on the shrine,*
> *Celestial beds for four of nine.*

Solving this puzzle causes a secret compartment in the altar to open, revealing treasure hidden within. The compartment can't be opened in any other way.

Puzzle Features

Nine dwarf skulls rest near a grid of 1-foot-square tiles, as shown in puzzle handout 3 (see the end of this chapter). Columns and rows in the grid are labeled with the markings I, II, or III.

Solution

The numbers labeling each row and column denote how many skulls belong within. Characters must place the skulls so that the correct number of skulls appear both in the rows and columns, while still covering four of the stars. This puzzle has multiple possible solutions, with one shown in diagram 4.2.

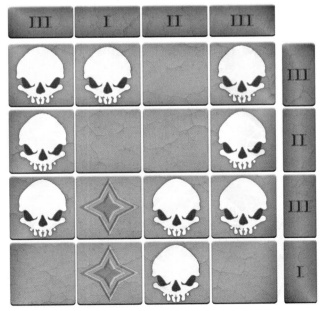

DIAGRAM 4.2: FOUR BY FOUR PUZZLE SOLUTION

Hint Checks

Dwarf characters have advantage on ability checks to gain hints in this room. Any character has the option of making these ability checks to receive a hint:

Intelligence (Investigation) DC 15. The verse indicates to the character that four of the skulls need to rest on tiles engraved with stars.

Wisdom (Insight) DC 15. The I, II, and III markings around the edge of the grid likely denote how many skulls must be placed in those rows and columns.

Customizing the Puzzle

If one of the characters is a dwarf, this might be the perfect time to bring in a familial storyline. Are these the skulls of their long-lost clan? Does one of the skulls belong to a relative that they have been seeking? And what do they think the puzzle is implying with only four of the nine skulls receiving "celestial beds"?

Illusive Island

Difficulty: Medium

Three numerical dials seal a box, door, or other locked object. Figuring out the correct combination is the goal of this puzzle, as there are no visible locks to pick.

Puzzle Features

The numbers the dials are originally set to don't matter. If the players ask, choose any three digits you please.

A corked wooden tube contains two clues: a map of an island and a set of directions.

Map

Give the players a copy of puzzle handout 4 (see the end of this chapter). This map depicts an unfamiliar island with various landmarks but no key.

Directions

The directions are written on a single sheet of parchment and recount the route a group took in their search for treasure:

> **Day 1.** Our search for the lost treasure began at the northwest inlet, Windstaff Cove. After unloading our necessities, we traveled east to Lone Pine, then south-west past Northridge to the Palms Oasis. As evening approached, we continued southeast to Anchor Point, then camped in the Great Dunes.
>
> **Day 2.** In the morning, we arose at the Dunes and headed to Deadman's Cave. After finding it empty, our party continued to the Golden Ziggurat. Heading due east, we made camp at the Swirling Sands.
>
> **Day 3.** After a strange night's sleep, we awoke on the third day back at Anchor Point with no memory or trace of traveling there. The Swirling Sands must have taken us in the night! We skirted the Swirling Sands to reach the Red Tower but still couldn't find the treasure. Thinking that we may have overlooked something in the cave, we headed back. From there, we headed to the southern coast to see if the treasure was at Kraken Point. Finding nothing, we returned to Anchor Point. What awaited us there was unlike any treasure we'd imagined.

Solution

Characters who follow the directions and trace their paths on the map reveal three numbers: 3, 4, and 8 (see diagram 4.3). Turning the dials to these numbers in the same order opens the locked object.

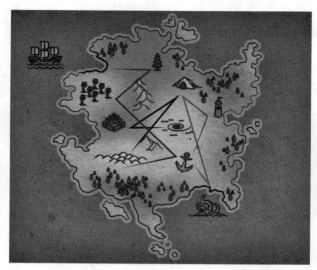

Diagram 4.3: Illusive Island Puzzle Solution

Hint Checks

Any character has the option of making these ability checks to receive a hint:

Intelligence (Investigation) DC 10. The word "trace" from the Day 3 entry strikes the character as important, suggesting that the map is meant to be drawn on.

Wisdom (Insight) DC 15. The map doesn't have labels, which means the names of the landmarks aren't significant. What's important are their positions relative to one another.

Wisdom (Perception) DC 10. The fact that the expedition lasted three days is significant, as there are three dials.

Wisdom (Survival) DC 15. The character knows the directions don't represent an efficient way to search an area and deduces the directions must be presenting some sort of message.

Customizing the Puzzle

Consider creating your own map and series of directions to customize this puzzle. By crafting directions that suit locations in your campaign's' setting, you can create a puzzle that's integrated into your adventure's plot, using a map the characters might already possess. Your version of the puzzle can add as many digits and directions as you see fit, or it might reveal letters, symbols, or short words, depending on the complexity of your design.

Raising the Difficulty

You can increase this puzzle's challenge by dividing the map into pieces that need to be separately discovered, or the characters might need to learn the directions from someone who personally explored the island. As long as the order of locations doesn't change, the code remains correct.

MATERIAL COMPONENTS

Difficulty: Medium

This puzzle might appear in a wizard's workshop, study, or spellbook. The solution leads to a password that reveals new or rare spells (such as those in chapter 3). Alternatively, the password can be used for any other function that fits with your story.

> You find an old piece of paper bearing a list of spells and components. Random letters are also scratched quickly on the paper between the two lists. A message at the top of the page says, "read untouched to gain new spells."

Give the players a copy of puzzle handout 5 (see the end of this chapter).

PUZZLE FEATURES

The wizard's study is filled with spell components, books, potions, and various odds and ends. While the various supplies might help characters solve

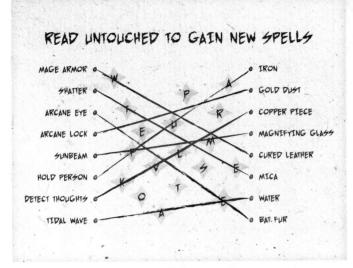

DIAGRAM 4.4: MATERIAL COMPONENTS PUZZLE SOLUTION

the puzzle, the only item the characters need is the parchment. If the puzzle is giving them grief, they can take the parchment with them and find others who can help them solve it.

BOOKCASES

All around the wizard's study are shelves and cases filled with books, scrolls, and other supplies. A character who makes a successful DC 12 Intelligence (Arcana) check notices a spell component with no gp value from the list (such as a chip of mica or a bit of bat fur).

LISTS

The parchment has a list of spells and a list of material components. However, the components to the right don't match with the adjacent spells to the left. The parchment itself doesn't have any magical qualities, but the word it reveals potentially does.

Wizards and other spellcasters can identify the correct spell components for any spell they know, but they must succeed on the Intelligence (Arcana) checks noted in the "Hint Checks" section below to recall the correct material components for any less familiar spells.

SOLUTION

Drawing a line from a spell to its material component crosses out letters that fall between the columns, as shown in diagram 4.4. Once all spells are connected to components, the untouched letters spell out "presto," which, when said aloud with the paper in hand, causes one or more *spell scrolls* (or some other treasure of your choice) to magically appear.

HINT CHECKS

Any character has the option of making these ability checks to receive a hint:

Intelligence (Arcana) DC 10. The character recalls up to three of the material components for spells on the list they don't currently know.

Wisdom (Insight) DC 15. The character suspects that the jumbled letters in the middle—or some number of them—probably spell out a command word, pass-phrase, or important clue.

Wisdom (Perception) DC 10. The character notices that straight lines drawn between spells and material components cross through some of the letters in the center.

CUSTOMIZING THE PUZZLE

While spells and components make easy to associate lists, you might also consider creating your own version of this puzzle using paired sets of monsters and creature types, planes of existence and their native inhabitants, famous figures in a setting and their homelands, and so forth.

LOWERING THE DIFFICULTY

If your party doesn't include characters with considerable magical expertise, consider adding art to the room's walls or on decorative book covers that reveal connections between the listed spells and components. These images might give away a few connections between the lists or lower the DCs of the puzzle's hint checks.

RAISING THE DIFFICULTY

Rather than using common spells the characters might be familiar with, a more challenging version of this puzzle might feature lost spells or other lore the party has no way of knowing. Only by consulting experts, undertaking research, or further adventuring might the party reveal the connections between the two lists.

MEMBERS ONLY

Difficulty: Medium

A secret club, cultist meeting, or thieves' guild requires a password to enter. In this puzzle, those who guard a certain door are so secretive that they change the password constantly, fearing someone might have infiltrated their members' ranks.

> You watch a figure approach an oak door with a slide window. The figure knocks, and a guard opens the window and says, "Six." The figure replies, "Three." The guard then opens the door, allowing the figure to enter.

This building seems to have only one entrance: the oak door with a small slide window. A guard opens the window and speaks a seemingly random number to anyone who knocks on the door.

PUZZLE FEATURES

Even after observing the building from all angles, characters only see members entering through the one door after speaking to the guard.

DOOR

The door is made of oak reinforced with 3-inch-wide iron bars. Three deadbolts secure the door, which is also barred from the inside, so there are no locks that can be picked from the outside.

GUARD

A guard stands on the other side of the door around the clock, and the only way to speak with the guard is through the door's slide window. The guard can be any sort of talking creature, such as an **assassin**, a **cult fanatic**, or a **thug**. More monstrous options include a **bugbear**, **wereboar**, or **nycaloth**.

If a character knocks on the door, the guard slides open the window and gruffly gives a number, expecting the proper response. The guard gives a different number each time someone knocks. Any proper response grants a single character entry, and the guard only allows one member to enter at a time.

Characters who provide incorrect answers and attempt to enter again must disguise themselves in some way or be refused entry. The guard only willingly opens the door for someone who speaks the correct password. The guard raises the alarm if unauthorized people try to open or bypass the door, calling six more guards to help defend the entrance.

MEMBERS

If the characters continue watching the door, they see up to four more visitors approach it. To eavesdrop on each exchange, the characters must succeed on a DC 12 group Dexterity (Stealth) check to remain hidden; if the group check fails, the visitor notices they're being observed and speaks quietly enough that their answer can't be overheard.

Second Visitor. The guard opens the window and says, "Twelve." The visitor responds with "Six" and is allowed inside.

Third Visitor. The guard opens the window and says, "Ten." The visitor responds with "Five" and is turned away.

Fourth Visitor. The guard opens the window and says, "Seven." The visitor responds with "Five" and is allowed inside.

Fifth Visitor. The guard opens the window and says, "Zero." The visitor responds with "One" and is turned away.

SOLUTION

Each member that approaches the door is given a number by the guard. There is no mathematical equation here; the only valid response to a number given by the guard is the number of letters in the guard's number.

For example, one member was given the number "six." There are three letters in the word "six," so the password for that member is "three." More potential answers are provided in the Potential Passwords table.

POTENTIAL PASSWORDS

Number Provided	Response Required
One	Three
Two	Three
Three	Five
Four	Four
Five	Four
Six	Three
Eight	Five
Nine	Four
Eleven	Six
Thirteen	Eight

HINT CHECKS

Any character has the option of making these ability checks to receive a hint:

Intelligence (Investigation) DC 15. The character deduces there is no mathematical equation that connects the numbers exchanged between the guard and visitors.

Wisdom (Insight) DC 15. The character suspects that the answer has to do with the word, not the number.

CUSTOMIZING THE PUZZLE

Part of what makes this puzzle challenging is that it misleads players into thinking they're overhearing a mathematical equation. To figure out the solution, they have to first overcome their own assumptions. An easier version of this puzzle might involve counting the letters in any type of word the guard provides and responding with that number. Alternatively, the response to the guard's number might be any word with the same number of letters as that number—for example, "five" has four letters, making "duck" or "smog" suitable responses. The more your puzzle plays with numbers as words rather than digits, the more challenging it's likely to be.

EXACT CHANGE

Difficulty: Hard

This puzzle provides an elaborate, coin-based lock to any sort of door, vault, or other barrier.

> The door here is locked and has no handle. Instead, there is a slot in the door with an engraving above it that reads, "Insert exact change here." Nearby, a wooden bowl of coins rests atop a wooden table.
>
> The tabletop is engraved with nine squares in a three-by-three grid. Nailed to the table's leg is a piece of parchment with the following instructions:
>
> *Fifteen per column, fifteen per row;*
> *Diagonally, the same is so.*
> *A plea of warning to carefully count;*
> *No two places may hold the same amount.*
> *What coins in the center be fed through the door;*
> *Exact change for passage or trouble galore.*

PUZZLE FEATURES

The bowl on the table contains forty-five gold coins. The puzzle requires that an exact number of coins be fed into the slot into the door. If the wrong amount is deposited, it triggers either an alarm or a trap of your choice.

SOLUTION

Diagram 4.5 shows how to divide the forty-five coins so that every square has a different amount and each row and column adds up to fifteen.

DIAGRAM 4.5: EXACT CHANGE PUZZLE SOLUTION

The verse explains that the door requires the amount of coins shown in the center square. Upon inserting exactly five coins, the locked door opens.

HINT CHECKS

Any character has the option of making these ability checks to receive a hint:

Intelligence (Investigation) DC 15. The character realizes that if diagonal corners add up to ten, it makes filling out the rest of the grid much easier.

Wisdom (Insight) DC 15. The character figures out the placement of two numbers other than the center number.

FOUR ELEMENTS

Difficulty: Hard

This puzzle might appear anywhere elementals of earth, air, fire, and water serve as guardians. If the puzzle isn't solved correctly, one or more of these guardian elementals magically transform from statues and attack the characters.

The door slams behind you as you enter this hexagonal room. Four of the walls are covered in mosaics, each depicting the destructive force of one of the four elements. Four nine-foot-tall, stone statues of elementals line the far wall across from the closed door. Above the statues is a row of square tiles with triangular symbols painted on them. Four of these tiles have fallen off and lie strewn upon the floor, which bears the following inscription:

Four elementals trapped in stone,
Their elements ordered to lock their home.
Even patterns against all odd,
A tile misplaced awakens its god.
In proper order safely seal these four,
Or best one of each to open the door.

Once the characters enter this room, the door behind them slams shut. It can be opened only by completing this puzzle, and there are no other exits.

PUZZLE FEATURES

The mosaics, statues, and tiles are described below in greater detail.

MOSAICS

The four wall mosaics depict the following:

- A water elemental crashes through a city wall in a huge wave. In the center of the image is a triangle pointing downward.
- An earth elemental looms over a group of warriors. A triangle pointing downward with a horizontal line through it is carved into its chest.
- A fire elemental burns through a forest town. In the center of the flames is a triangle pointing upward.
- An air elemental gusts through a stormy sky. Within the clouds is a triangle pointing upward with a line running horizontally through it.

STATUES

The statues are actual elementals magically bound in stone. The magic that turned these elementals into statues is slowly coming undone, as the tile pattern that binds them has fallen apart.

TILES

If the characters don't replace the four fallen tiles in their proper sequence, all four statues revert to their true forms at the same time and attack the characters. The exact timing of this event is left to you, but the characters should be given enough time to take a crack at solving the puzzle. The characters can also release the elementals individually by putting titles in the wrong order or orientation.

Puzzle handout 6 (see the end of this chapter) illustrates the row of tiles set into the wall above the statues. Without a check, the characters realize that four of the tiles fell down when the door slammed shut behind them. With a successful DC 15 Intelligence (Arcana) check, a character can determine that these tiles are what keeps the elementals bound.

If a tile is placed in the wrong place in the row, the corresponding elemental is freed from its stone prison and attacks. Only one of each elemental appears:

- If the improperly placed tile has an open triangle pointing downward, the **water elemental** is freed.
- If the improperly placed tile has an open triangle pointing upward, the **fire elemental** is freed.
- If the improperly placed tile has a triangle pointing upward with a horizontal line running through it, the **air elemental** is freed.
- If the improperly placed tile has a triangle pointing downward with a horizontal line running through it, the **earth elemental** is freed.

SOLUTION

The correct, complete pattern is shown here:

The odd-numbered tiles form a recurring pattern of open triangles that alternate between pointing up and down. Tiles 1, 5, 9, and 13 are upward-pointing triangles, while tiles 3, 7, and 11 are downward-pointing triangles.

The even-numbered tiles display a different pattern. Tiles 2 and 4 point downward, but the first of them has a line through the triangle. Tiles 6 and 8 follow the same pattern, but the triangles point up. The pattern then repeats, with tiles 10 and 12 being the same as tiles 2 and 4 and tile 14 being the same as tile 6.

Solving the puzzle or defeating all four elementals causes the door to the room to swing open.

HINT CHECKS

Any character has the option of making these ability checks to receive a hint:

Intelligence (Investigation) DC 15. The character notes the words "even" and "odd" in the verse on the room's floor and believes they have some significance to the missing tiles.

Wisdom (Perception) DC 10. The character can deduce which tiles correspond to which elementals.

CUSTOMIZING THE PUZZLE

Interweaving multiple patterns makes it easy to disguise them. With this in mind, you might use any group of symbols to create as elaborate a series of patterns as you please, then challenge players to fill in a missing segment. While the symbols in this puzzle refer to the four elements, you might use holy symbols, colors, dolls on a shelf, or any other repeating design to convey your puzzle.

When an elemental is defeated, it might leave behind a valuable gemstone, a map fragment, a clue to some other puzzle, or something similar.

RAISING THE DIFFICULTY

To increase the difficulty of this puzzle, enforce a time factor: perhaps one elemental breaks free at the end of every five minutes of real time that pass until the puzzle is solved.

You can also raise the difficulty by having statues depict genies instead of elementals. In this case, replace the four elementals with a **dao**, a **djinni**, an **efreeti**, and a **marid**. These genies are compelled to attack the characters and can't be reasoned with.

HAUNTED HALLWAY

Difficulty: Hard

Many unquiet spirits linger in the world because they can't bare to leave something behind. In this puzzle, finding the solution also means helping a lost soul find peace.

> Six alcoves line this hall, each one numbered from one to six. On the floor of each alcove, a lit candle gently flickers.
>
> From the hall's far end drifts a low moan. There, barely visible, sobs the apparition of a small girl hovering over a discarded rag doll. "Names, names," she cries. "I can remember them all except the one I need."

The spirit, Dolora, is a harmless apparition who won't engage the party in combat. If threatened, she vanishes and reappears at the opposite end of the hall, sobbing anew.

If approached with compassion, Dolora bemoans the fact that she can't pick up her doll until she speaks its name, which she has forgotten. She refuses to leave this place without the doll.

Dolora, who only recalls fragmented memories of her life, can't answer many questions. This is particularly true about the messages associated with the alcoves in the hall (see "Alcoves" later in this section). While Dolora can't answer vague questions about the candles' clues (such as "Who is this talking about?"), she can provide the names of specific people when prompted. For example, if a character asks directly, "What was your mother's name?" Dolora provides the correct response. She also spells out the name, which is a clue that the spelling is important.

PUZZLE FEATURES

Dolora can't leave the hall and avoids the alcoves.

ALCOVES

The hall is lined with six alcoves, each one with a unique numeral between 1 and 6 carved above it. A verse scratched into the back wall of each alcove is made visible by the candlelight. Each verse is presented below, accompanied by a parenthetical explanation that shouldn't be shared with the players or their characters:

Verse 1. "Not his keeper, nor he mine; loved and hated at the same time." (This refers to Dolora's brother, whose name was Sam.)

Verse 2. "My first vision: her hazel eyes. My first sound: her lullabies." (This refers to Dolora's mother, whose name was Delia.)

Verse 3. "Her lives she lost, all three by three, and through the dark this hunter sees." (This refers to Dolora's cat, whose name was Fifi.)

Verse 4. "Lines in his face of life lived long; stories were his paternal song." (This refers to Dolora's grandfather, whose name was Tobias.)

Verse 5. "Mentor and guide, her lessons learned. Knowledge measured by letters I earned." (This refers to Dolora's teacher, whose name was Johana.)

Verse 6. "Loved to eat hay, just as her friends did; lived in one room with a shoat and a kid." (This refers to Dolora's horse, whose name was Alexia.)

Each verse describes someone who was close to Dolora. Once the characters determine who a verse is talking about, they may ask Dolora to provide the correct name. For example, "What is your cat's name?" is a valid question for verse 3. The spirit then answers, "Fifi," and she spells it aloud.

CANDLES

Each candle is a simple, 6-inch-tall wax taper. While in this hall, the candles never melt down and can't be extinguished.

RAG DOLL

If the characters examine the rag doll or ask Dolora about it, she imparts the following information:

> "My doll knows all six—the first for the first, the second for the second, the third for the third, the fourth for the fourth, the fifth for the fifth, and the sixth for the sixth."

Solution

Once the characters learn all six names, they must extract one letter from each name, as noted in the Remembered Names table. An alcove's number determines which letter to extract; for example, "Alexia" is the name connected to the verse in alcove 6, and the sixth letter in that name is A.

Remembered Names

Alcove	Name	Letter
1	Sam	S
2	Delia	E
3	Fifi	F
4	Tobias	I
5	Johana	N
6	Alexia	A

The doll's name is Sefina. Once Dolora is told this, she picks up the doll, speaks its name, and disappears with it, her spirit having been laid to rest. If there's some piece of information you wish to have the spirit reveal to the party, such as the location of a nearby treasure or the secret of a more dangerous spirit, Dolora whispers this as she fades away.

Hint Checks

Any character has the option of making these ability checks to receive a hint:

Charisma (Persuasion) DC 10. Dolora thinks of the character as her friend. When this character figures out the answer to a riddle, Dolora calls out the name of the person it's about unprompted (for example, as soon as the character says "mother" aloud, Dolora calls out "Delia").

Charisma (Intimidation) DC 15. The character frightens Dolora into divulging information. She tells the character that she remembers the names of people she knew. Dolora also reveals that it's important that their names be spelled correctly, though she doesn't say why.

Intelligence (Investigation) DC 15. The character interprets Dolora's cryptic clue about the doll as follows: "all six" refers to the six letters of the doll's name, which can be determined by gathering information from the verses in the six alcoves.

What's on the Menu

Difficulty: Hard

The characters discover that a popular local tavern is a front for a secret organization that they seek to join or infiltrate. The name of the tavern can be whatever you want it to be. One suggestion is the Cloak & Dagger.

To get their foot in the proverbial door, the characters must speak the correct password to the tavern-keeper, Holda Heidrun. They can discover this password by solving a puzzle hidden in the tavern's menu.

> The tavern is crowded with happy people enjoying their food and drinks. Behind the bar, a stocky woman is wiping down the wooden bar top. She looks up as you enter and nods toward an empty table before her attention is drawn elsewhere. You see a copy of the tavern's menu on the table.

Customize the tavern and flesh out its occupants as you see fit.

In addition to being the tavern-keeper, Holda Heidrun is the keeper of many secrets. If the characters prod her for information, she asks for the password, and if the characters don't know it, she divulges nothing of consequence. "If you're worth your weight in copper," she says, "you'd speak the password to earn my trust."

Puzzle Features

A sign at the bar declares that a meal costs 1 sp, a mug of ale costs 4 cp, a glass of fine wine costs 1 sp, and a bottle of fine wine costs 3 sp. The menu on the table contains a list of specialties the tavern serves, and how much each item costs. Only the menu is needed to solve the puzzle.

Menu

Characters who peruse the menu see the items listed in the Menu Items table, in the order given.

Menu Items

Item	Price
Corn and lentil soup	12 cp
Rabbit stew	1 cp
Ale and cheese pastry	7 cp
Brandied ham and carrots	9 cp
Grilled fish and carrots	6 cp
Seared boar and potatoes	9 cp
Dragonfire mead	11 cp

MEALS	1 SILVER
ALE	4 COPPE
WINE, GLASS	1 SILVER
, BOTTLE	3 SILVER

HINT CHECKS

Any character has the option of making these ability checks to receive a hint:

Charisma (Intimidation or Persuasion) DC 15. The character convinces Holda to whisper the following hint: "Count your lucky coppers that we have seven choices on the menu for you."

Dexterity (Stealth) DC 15. The character blends in with the crowd to eavesdrop on another table, overhearing the patrons discussing how they must have gotten a misprinted menu because the prices don't seem right, or bemoaning the fact that the menu doesn't list items in alphabetical order.

Intelligence (History) DC 15. The character recalls stories of how secret messages used to be sent through taverns using common items anyone could access, such as menus.

Wisdom (Perception) DC 15. The character notices the prices on the menu don't make much sense. For example, why is rabbit stew so much cheaper than corn and lentil stew?

CUSTOMIZING THE PUZZLE

"Chimera" might not be the password but rather a reference to something or someone else in the tavern. Characters who solve the puzzle and succeed on a DC 15 Wisdom (Perception) check might notice another patron wearing a cloak pin shaped like a chimera, or spot a shield emblazoned with a chimera hanging on a wall that conceals a secret door. Only after speaking to the patron or seeing what's on the other side of the secret door do the characters obtain the actual password, which can be anything you want.

You can easily change "chimera" to something else by swapping out menu items, choosing different letters within the replacement items, and adjusting the prices accordingly.

LOWERING THE DIFFICULTY

Other tavern patrons can provide additional hints by talking among themselves in places where the characters can overhear them. A patron might say something like, "This inn keeps getting more expensive. With these fancy new meals, I'm surprised they aren't charging a copper per letter!"

A too-helpful barmaid might take pity on the struggling characters and walk them through the various menu items in the order that would allow them to skip the anagram (ale and cheese pastry, brandied ham and carrots, corn and lentil soup, dragonfire mead, grilled fish and carrots, rabbit stew, and seared boar and potatoes). She might even recommend that the characters "start with the ale and cheese pastry, and continue on from there."

SOLUTION

Arrange the menu items in alphabetical order, then count into each item by the number of letters indicated in its price, as shown in the What's On the Menu Solution table. Stringing the seven letters together forms the password: chimera.

WHAT'S ON THE MENU SOLUTION

Item (Price)	Letter
Ale and cheese pastry (7 cp)	C (7th letter)
Brandied ham and carrots (9 cp)	H (9th letter)
Corn and lentil soup (12 cp)	I (12th letter)
Dragonfire mead (11 cp)	M (11th letter)
Grilled fish and carrots (6 cp)	E (6th letter)
Rabbit stew (1 cp)	R (1st letter)
Seared boar and potatoes (3 cp)	A (3rd letter)

The characters can figure out the password without putting the menu items in alphabetical order. Once they get all seven letters, they must solve the anagram to get the password.

Speaking the correct password to Holda grants access to whatever secrets she's keeping—fuel for the characters' next adventure.

CLAUDIO POZAS

Puzzle Handouts

PUZZLE HANDOUT 1: RECKLESS STEPS

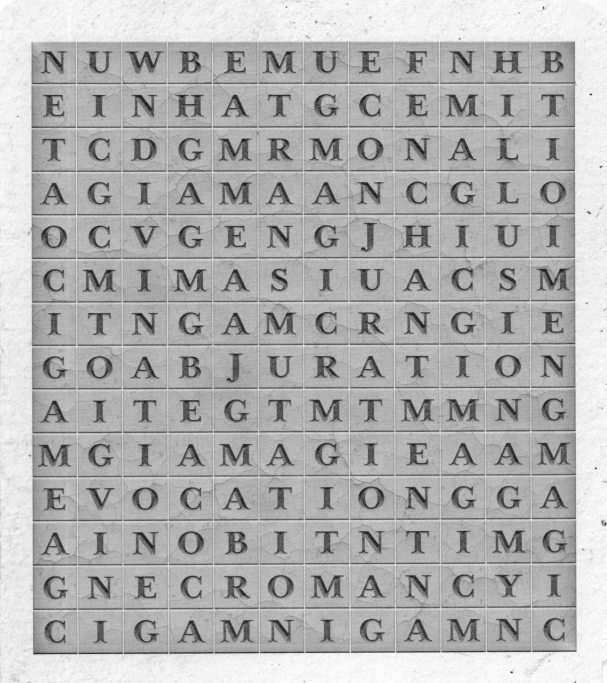

N U W B E M U E F N H B
E I N H A T G C E M I T
T C D G M R M O N A L I
A G I A M A A N C G L O
O C V G E N G J H I U I
C M I M A S I U A C S M
I T N G A M C R N G I E
G O A B J U R A T I O N
A I T E G T M T M M N G
M G I A M A G I E A A M
E V O C A T I O N G G A
A I N O B I T N T I M G
G N E C R O M A N C Y I
C I G A M N I G A M N C

PUZZLE HANDOUT 2: SKELETON KEYS

PUZZLE HANDOUT 3: FOUR BY FOUR

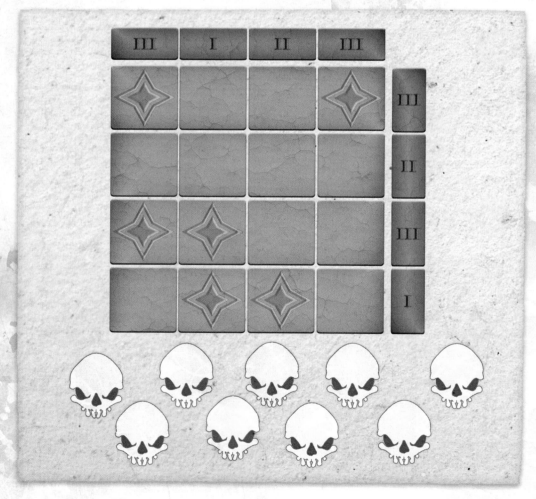

PUZZLE HANDOUT 5: MATERIAL COMPONENTS

READ UNTOUCHED TO GAIN NEW SPELLS

MAGE ARMOR •   • IRON

SHATTER •   • GOLD DUST

ARCANE EYE •   • COPPER PIECE

ARCANE LOCK •   • MAGNIFYING GLASS

SUNBEAM •   • CURED LEATHER

HOLD PERSON •   • MICA

DETECT THOUGHTS •   • WATER

TIDAL WAVE •   • BAT FUR

W   A
T   P   R
E   U   E
F   L   M
K   V   S
O   T   E
A

PUZZLE HANDOUT 6: FOUR ELEMENTS

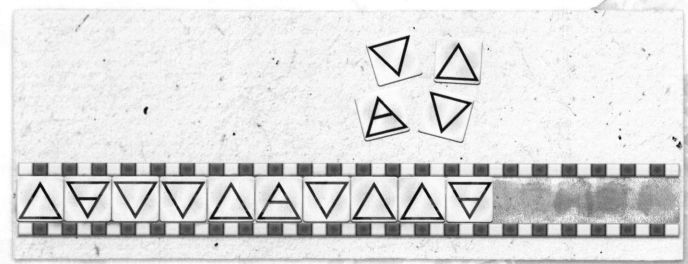